· SAFE IN HIS ARMS

It was nearly midnight before the last of the police and fire personnel left and Aubrey and Jesse were alone again.

"What if the whole house has been booby-trapped?" she asked. "Am I going to pull a book from the shelves tomorrow and set off explosives?"

Jesse stepped close and rested his hands on her shoulders. "Stop it. I wanted you to be aware of danger, but I don't want you to make yourself sick imagining exploding books or poisoned salt shakers."

Aubrey sent an anxious glance toward the saltcellar on the breakfast table. "I don't salt my food," she said.

"That's probably real healthy," Jesse commented, putting his arms around her. She reached up to meet his kiss. His mouth was warm, and the pressure of his lips so tender she clung to him, needing to be with him. Her fear banished, she began to unsnap his shirt, and when he laughed, way back in his throat, she knew she wasn't the first woman to undress him.

"I bet you're real popular in Arizona," she whispered.

"Honey, I'm popular everywhere I go." Jesse laughed, then lifted her clear off her feet. "That doesn't mean I'm easy, though."

Aubrey slid her arms around his neck. "Liar, but you're a long way from the rodeo. I expect more than eight seconds from you."

Jesse silenced her with a very convincing kiss . . .

A TOUCH OF LOVE

Phoebe Conn

Zebra Books
Kensington Publishing Corp.

http://www.zebrabooks.com

ZEBRA BOOKS are published by

Kensington Publishing Corp.
850 Third Avenue
New York, NY 10022

Zebra and the Z logo Reg. U.S. Pat. & TM Off.

First Printing: June, 1997
10 9 8 7 6 5 4 3 2 1

Printed in the United States of America

Life begets life.
Energy creates energy.
It is by spending oneself
that one becomes rich.

Sarah Bernhardt

Chapter I

"His eyes are as blue as the Montana sky," Trisha Lynch whispered in a syrupy drawl.

"That sounds like a line from a Country/Western song," Aubrey responded with a laugh. "And if it isn't, it certainly should be." While she had also noticed the good-looking man seated in the last row, he had failed to inspire any such poetic descriptions in her mind.

He was dressed in Western attire, complete with ostrich-hide boots and a straw Stetson he seemed in no hurry to remove, but she could not imagine what a real cowboy would be doing in her creative imagery seminar. He had to be a dentist, or an executive who enjoyed going Country on the weekends. He was definitely a hunk, all right, and well groomed with a neatly trimmed mustache, but just one of the audience as far as she was concerned.

"Try to contain yourself," Aubrey teased her irrepressible assistant. "In case you've forgotten, this isn't a workshop for singles."

Startled by that reminder, Trisha inquired softly, "Do you suppose he's in the wrong room?"

"It's a distinct possibility, but didn't he turn in a registation form when he paid his fee?"

Trisha checked through the stack of papers on the desk, certain she would recognize his scrawl. "Yes, his is here. His name's Jesse, Jesse James."

"Oh wonderful, a cowboy with a sense of humor. Sounds like he's just your type." Aubrey turned away as Trisha's grin widened. She scanned the room hurriedly to make certain they had set up enough chairs. The Pasadena Civic was a gloriously ornate auditorium from which the Emmy and Grammy Award shows were televised but the stark meeting rooms in the east wing possessed the hollow charm of an aircraft hangar.

Aubrey made a mental note never to book another seminar in a location so lacking in ambience. Then, after clearing her throat, she began an enthusiastic greeting. With the poise of an accomplished actress and a honey-smooth voice, she made an instant impression on her audience. Her compelling warmth radiated clear to the attractive cowboy in the last row.

"Good morning. I'm Aubrey Glenn, and most of you have already met my assistants, Trisha Lynch and Shelley Sandler." She paused while the two young women nodded to acknowledge her introduction. She then turned toward the young man who handled their sound and recording equipment. "Gardner Evans is our engineer. If you would like a tape of today's session, please speak to him during the break."

Aubrey waited until Gardner had waved to the crowd, then continued speaking without referring to notes. "I want to welcome you to the first in a series of seminars which will provide an opportunity for you to acquire techniques which have the potential to improve every aspect of your life. Over six Saturdays, we'll be presenting proven ways to use creative imagery to banish stress, enhance your intuition, and achieve your personal and professional goals.''

''Bullshit,'' Jesse whispered under his breath. He crossed his arms over his chest and slumped down another couple of inches in his chair. He had deliberately chosen a seat on the aisle so he could stretch out his legs, but he was still far from comfortable. He was one of perhaps a dozen men in a room of nearly one hundred women. Everyone else sat perched on the edge of the chair, many clasping copies of Aubrey Glenn's bestselling book on creative imagery, *The Mind's Eye*.

He had assumed she would be dressed like a hippie in a long, flowing tie-dye outfit and dripping with crystal-encrusted jewelry. Not that he could recall hippies all that clearly. Born in 1958, he had spent the sixties in a grade school in a dusty Arizona town where fashion hadn't been a big priority. Regardless of his expectations, however, Aubrey's stylish, powder-blue knit dress was no disappointment. Its fluid lines showed off her slim figure to perfection. Even if he failed to agree with anything she said, she was no strain on the eyes.

She was wearing sterling silver jewelry, but only a few pieces that appeared to be handcrafted. Her strawberry-blonde hair was a mass of curls that extended past her shoulders, and from the generous sprinkling of freckles dusting her pale golden skin, he thought her curls had to be natural. It was easy to imagine she had been an adorable little girl, for she projected a childlike innocence still. She was pretty with the natural, fresh-scrubbed look he had always admired, but he doubted he was her type, and that put the brakes on his interest real fast.

Jesse's attention strayed briefly to the petite brunette on Aubrey's right. She was dressed in a red plaid shirt and short black skirt. Her glossy hair curved under in a sleek pageboy, but although she glanced at him frequently with an unmistakable invitation glistening in her dark eyes, he offered no equally encouraging smile.

Nor did he find Aubrey's other assistant, a blonde with a shy glance, appealing. She was also in pale blue, but unlike Aubrey's, her gauze floral dress hid rather than enhanced her slender figure. He dismissed her as too reserved to provide the excitement he craved in bed, then reminded himself that he had come here with only one purpose in mind: to hear Aubrey Glenn. As he again focused his attention on her, his insolent expression mirrored his skepticism. He was clearly daring her to teach him something he was firmly convinced he damn well didn't want to know.

People generally attended Aubrey's seminars to strengthen the skills she had covered in *The Mind's Eye*, but occasionally she encountered a disgruntled soul who either asked challenging questions or continually regarded her with a threatening stare. That the cowboy was apparently the latter type was a relief, and she simply ignored him.

"My topic today is: following your heart. It's the path to your authentic self, and often revealed through intuition. Shakespeare said it best. 'This above all: to thine own self be true, And it must follow as the night the day, Thou canst not then be false to any man.' " Aubrey paused while appreciative murmurs passed through the crowd.

"We'll begin with an exercise to relax your muscles, and then move into guided imagery to free your mind. After the break, we'll give each of you a journal and some time to compose your initial goals. Then in the coming weeks, we'll work together, and in small groups, to give imagery to your dreams, and provide the tools to bring those images into reality."

Aubrey concluded her introduction with a phrase many in the audience repeated with her. "Whatever we can imagine, we can achieve." She cued Gardner, who began the soft musical selection which would accompany the first gentle exercises. As she encouraged everyone to draw in a deep breath, she saw the cowboy's head nod toward his chest. He certainly deserved high marks for relaxation. He was sound asleep.

At the close of the seminar, more than half the participants came forward to ask Aubrey to autograph copies of *The Mind's Eye*. She complied, graciously writing a personal note in each. After she took time to evaluate the session with her assistants, it was past four o'clock by the time she began the four-mile drive home. As she pulled into her driveway she didn't notice the Chevy pick-up truck parked across the street until Jesse got out and started walking toward her. She slammed on her brakes and took the precaution of leaving her car parked in the driveway rather than putting it in the garage.

There were half a dozen children playing baseball in a neighbor's front yard, but she didn't feel altogether safe as she quickly slid out of her Volvo and greeted him. "I no longer do private consultations, Mr. James. I thought I made that clear before we adjourned this afternoon." After the way he had bolted from the room when she drew the seminar to a close, she was astonished to find him there.

That she knew his name, or at least the name he had given, brought a rakish grin to Jesse's lips. He had waited nearly two hours for her to arrive home and he was not in the best of moods. At least he hadn't been until she called him Mr. James.

"That was a feeble attempt at humor. I'm Jesse Barrett," he said as he extended his hand.

Aubrey had to juggle her notebook and purse to shake hands with him, but managed it without mishap. Up close she could see Jesse's tan was too deep to have come from a tanning salon and as she felt the calluses on his palm she realized he was exactly what he seemed at first glance: a cowboy.

While his eyes were shaded by the brim of his hat, they were as vivid a blue as Trisha had reported. His features were even but seemed to be permanently settled in a cynical frown that lifted only momentarily when he smiled. He was handsome, but his expression was so forbidding that she broke their contact as quickly as politely possible.

"Mr. Barrett then," she began again.

"I'm Edith Pursely's nephew. She was certain you'd remember her."

Although caught by surprise, Aubrey was greatly relieved by that announcement. She had the fondest memories of Edith Pursely, a charming woman who had always possessed immense enthusiasm and energy equal to that of her teenaged students. Relaxing visibly, she leaned back against her station wagon. "Mrs. Pursely was my favorite teacher, of course I remember her. How is she?"

As Jesse debated how much to reveal, he glanced toward Aubrey's Spanish-style home. The two-story, tiled-roof house was painted a warm apricot shade with deep blue trim. He doubted the paint was more than six months old and the petunia-filled flower beds clearly displayed the owner's pride in the stately residence. The whole street was lined with an impressive array of distinctive homes built before tract housing became popular in Southern California.

From what his aunt had told him, it was not simply this street, but the whole suburb of San Marino that conveyed the impression of long-established wealth and comfort. He was insulted Aubrey hadn't invited him to come inside her home after he had identified himself, and struggled not to let it show. He yanked off his hat and raked his fingers through sun-bleached curls that were several shades paler than his light brown brows and mustache.

"I'm sorry to tell you that she's had a real rough time of it lately. She lost her husband five years ago, and she has arthritis that gives her quite a bit of pain. She wanted very much to attend your seminar, but she just didn't feel up to it. I was hoping you'd get home in time to visit her this afternoon. I hope it's not too late now."

Aubrey found herself listening to the concern in Jesse's voice as well as his words. He had an accent, not a deep Southern drawl, but a very attractive accent all the same. Had she misread his preoccupied mood during the seminar as hostility, when in reality he had been worried about his aunt? Her first impression of people rarely proved to be wrong, but this appeared to be one of those times. Because she took great pride in her intuition, she was always embarrassed when it failed her.

"I would love to see Edith. Is that why you came to the seminar, just to invite me to visit her?"

The lie rolled easily off Jesse's lips. "Yes. She'd like very much to talk with you if you have the time. If now isn't convenient, then what about tomorrow?"

Aubrey saw no reason to keep Jesse and his aunt waiting another day. She turned around, tossed her notebook into her car's backseat, and pulled her keys from her purse. "Why don't I follow you? Does she still live on Fletcher?"

"I'll drive you over."

Aubrey glanced across the street at Jesse's truck. It looked brand new but she shook her head. "Then you'd have to go to the trouble of bringing me back home later. I'll just follow you."

Jesse's eyes narrowed slightly, but he nodded and crossed the jacaranda-lined street to his truck. Conscious of her gaze following him, he tried not to limp, but his long stride was never completely smooth by the end of the day.

It took only a few minutes to cross into the city of South Pasadena. When they turned down Fletcher Avenue Aubrey recognized Edith's house immediately. She had been there often during high school when the drama department was preparing for a play. They had painted sets in the backyard and held cast parties there. It was a marvelous old house, built at the turn of the century, with a chimney made of stones dug out of the yard and a wide porch that extended across the front. The gray house looked forlorn in the late afternoon sun, and Aubrey feared both it and its owner had seen far better days. She parked behind Jesse's truck, and he immediately jumped out to come back and open her door for her.

"Thank you, Mr. Barrett."

"Jesse."

Aubrey smiled. She had never thought of cowboys as having an abundance of manners, but she chided herself silently that she was thinking only of Western movies that portrayed a fanciful view of life on the frontier rather than the present day.

"You're a real cowboy, aren't you?" she asked rather shyly as they approached his aunt's front door. The walk was bordered by rose bushes in full bloom. The soil surrounding the gnarled old plants had been recently turned and rid of weeds. She thought it a good bet Jesse had been the gardener.

"As real as they get," he replied. "I own a ranch in Arizona, but I try to visit my aunt at least once a year."

"Arizona? Trisha will be disappointed to hear that. She was certain you were from Montana."

Shocked by the accuracy of that guess, Jesse hesitated

as he reached for the doorknob. "She's right. I was born there."

"You see, intuition is an innate ability that can be fine-tuned."

"So you say." Thinking it a poor time to pick an argument, Jesse pulled open the screen door and stood aside to allow Aubrey to enter his aunt's home.

Visiting Edith Pursely was like stepping back in time. A quick glance around the front room revealed it to be unchanged since Aubrey had last been there more than a dozen years ago. Edith was seated in an overstuffed chair watching the early broadcast of the evening news, but she immediately turned off the television when she saw her guest.

"Jesse told me he'd bring you home with him, but I didn't dare hope that he really would."

Aubrey hurried to the smiling woman's side. Other than the fact her hair had gone from gray to white, Edith appeared as untouched by time as her home. Her fair complexion was still unlined and her figure was as trim as the day she had attended Aubrey's graduation.

"All he had to do was mention your name." Without waiting for an invitation, Aubrey took the chair at Edith's left and leaned forward. "I was sorry to learn you've not been well. I wish I'd known. I would have come to see you much sooner."

"He talks too much," Edith scolded, and with an embarrassed flutter of her hands she sent him away. "Go make us some tea, Jesse. Now that Aubrey is here we want to make her feel welcome."

"Yes, ma'am."

Aubrey turned to watch as he left the room. "He seems like a very nice young man," she remarked in too low a voice for him to overhear.

Edith beamed with pride. "Yes he is, and he's single, too.

I know you're married, but perhaps you have an attractive friend who'd like to meet him. I'm sure he gets lonesome for women when he comes to visit me. He has lots of girlfriends at home.''

"Yes, I'm sure he must," Aubrey readily agreed. She glanced around the room again, and her eyes came to rest on the oil painting hanging above the fireplace. Roger Pursely had been an amateur artist, but unfortunately not a talented one. Obviously that didn't matter to Edith who continued to display his work. "I was sorry to hear about your husband. I'm divorced now, so I know how much you must miss him."

Startled by that odd combination of comments, Edith adjusted her glasses to get a better look at her guest. Aubrey was as strikingly pretty as she had been in high school, but if Edith was not mistaken, there was a hint of sorrow in her manner, too. "Yes, I do miss him terribly. But what happened? You were popular and wonderfully easy to get along with. You are the very last person I would ever have expected to get a divorce."

Edith hesitated, obviously expecting Aubrey to provide some details on the breakup of her marriage, but she was not even tempted. "No, I didn't expect it either." She was relieved when Jesse reentered the room and provided the perfect excuse to drop such a personal topic.

Jesse placed the tray holding a ceramic teapot and three cups on the table beside his aunt. "Would one of you ladies like to pour the tea while I get the cookies?"

"Ladies," Edith whispered when they were again alone. "He's four years older than you are. Had I known you were divorced, I would have—"

"Edith, please!" Aubrey couldn't help but laugh, for she and Jesse Barrett were an extremely unlikely couple. "I came here to see you, not to look for an eligible male."

Edith's blue eyes sparkled with the mischief that had

made her a popular drama teacher. "Serendipity exists, you know that it does."

"Yes, that's certainly true, but—"

Jesse returned then with a plate of chocolate chip cookies his aunt had baked that morning. He could tell from the color in Aubrey's cheeks that they had been talking about him, and that didn't please him at all. In his aunt's view, it was high time he was married and had a kid or two. He didn't agree. Realizing he had forgotten the sugar bowl and lemon slices, he went back to the kitchen and this time also remembered the spoons and napkins.

"I've not kept track of anyone from high school," Aubrey admitted, "other than to scan the *San Marino Tribune* each week for news of old friends."

"I hear from quite a few each Christmas."

"That's good. Is anyone doing anything particularly interesting?" Aubrey hoped to include Jesse in their conversation, but he seemed content to sit on the couch, sip his tea, and munch cookies.

"Nothing to compare with your achievements," Edith revealed with a nervous smile.

Aubrey was aware of a subtle change in Edith's manner. She glanced frequently at her nephew as if expecting him to contribute some significant remark, but he remained silent until they had all finished their tea. Once they had finished exchanging pleasantries the conversation grew increasingly strained. Aubrey was looking for a graceful way to excuse herself when Edith suddenly set her cup aside and reached out to touch her hand.

"I need your help."

"Of course. I'll be happy to help you in any way I can," Aubrey said.

"Roger was my second husband," Edith revealed with another anxious glance toward Jesse. "We had no children, but I had a son from my first marriage. I'm sure you never met him. Peter was grown before I ever started to teach."

Aubrey tried not to let apprehension show in her expression, but she could not help but feel she had been lured to Edith Pursley's home under false pretenses. Edith was a teacher she had recalled fondly, but she could not work miracles for anyone, no matter how deep their faith in her might be. When she looked over at Jesse, he was regarding her with the same skeptical glance she had observed at the seminar. Clearly he thought her visit a waste of time, and she felt all the more offended.

Edith opened the drawer in the table beside her chair and withdrew a manila folder filled with faded clippings. "His name was Peter Ferrell. He, his wife, and their twin sons disappeared from their home more than two years ago. Maybe you read about it in the *Times.*"

Aubrey's heart sank as Edith handed her the folder. She glanced through the clippings but the *Los Angeles Times* printed accounts of so many heartbreaking tragedies she didn't recall the mysterious disappearance of the Ferrell family. "Perhaps I did at the time, but I don't remember it now."

"Take the folder with you and look it over. I'm sure it will help you to know everything before you try to contact them."

So that was it. Aubrey closed the folder and passed it back to Edith. "Many people misunderstand what I do, but training others in the art of following their hearts and trusting their intuition is in fact the opposite of psychic ability. I encourage people to turn their focus inward, to know themselves. A psychic is a person who sees into another's heart. I'm not a psychic, Edith. I can't locate missing persons."

Edith appeared distressed for a moment, but quickly grew more insistent. "The police are certain my son and his family were murdered. Their only suspect was a man named Harlan Caine, a developer in whose company Peter had invested. They had a bitter argument a couple of days before the disappearance, but there are no witnesses, and no evidence has been found to link Caine to the crime. If you have heightened intuition, couldn't you sense the murderer's guilt if you met him?''

"I sincerely doubt it, but even if I could, my impressions wouldn't be admissible in court." Aubrey sounded truly regretful. "I'm sorry, but what you ask is impossible. I've enjoyed seeing you again, but I must leave now. I really must." Aubrey rose, bent down to give Edith's cheek a light kiss, and then hurried toward the door.

Undaunted, the elderly woman nodded to her nephew, and Jesse went after Aubrey. He didn't speak until they reached her car. He was impressed by the fact she had refused his aunt's request. He had fully expected her to ask for money and to make an elaborate show, then an undoubtedly unsuccessful attempt to locate his cousin.

"Let me take you to dinner," he offered.

Ignoring his invitation, Aubrey faced him squarely. "I know you dozed off during the relaxation exercises, but didn't you hear a word I said today?"

Jesse jammed his hands in his hip pockets and debated the wisdom of revealing the truth. He had heard her clearly enough. He just didn't believe any of it. "I didn't doze off. I was just more relaxed to start with is all. Let's just say meditation and self-actualization aren't as interesting to me as they are to you. The police are stymied on Pete's case. My aunt can't afford detectives on her pension. Maybe she was wrong to believe you had psychic abilities, but hell, I thought it was worth our time to ask.

"My aunt never has more than a can of soup in the evenings and I'm starving for a steak. Let me take you to dinner. I don't think a couple of cookies is sufficient payment for the time you took to come over here."

Aubrey sighed impatiently. She hadn't meant to be rude, but she found it extremely difficult to be gracious when presented with requests she couldn't fulfill. "Dinner really isn't necessary. Besides, I prefer vegetarian fare."

Jesse glanced toward the rapidly darkening heavens. *I should have known,* he moaned inwardly. "I'll take you to a place that has seafood, too. Do you eat that?"

"Occasionally, but—"

Jesse had noted she didn't wear a wedding ring and knew she was definitely the type who would if she were married. "Do you already have a date?"

"Well, no, but—"

"We'll take my truck this time," Jesse insisted, and before Aubrey could argue with him she found herself seated in a comfortable leather booth in a dimly lit restaurant three blocks away.

"Are you certain they serve food here? I thought the Barkley was only a bar."

"Best food in town," Jesse bragged with a sly grin. He still thought Aubrey had a peculiar way of making a living, but the troubled look in her blue-green eyes as she spoke with his aunt had been too sincere for him to distrust her any longer. "Look, I know I didn't add anything to your class today, and I hope you won't be insulted when I don't show up again next Saturday."

"I'll send you a refund."

"No, you needn't bother."

"It's no bother. You only enrolled in the seminar to have the opportunity to invite me to your aunt's home. Keeping your money would be unethical."

"Well, if you consider it a question of ethics, then go right ahead and mail me the refund."

"First thing Monday morning." Aubrey found it difficult

to see the Barkley's other patrons in the dim light, but she hoped the place wasn't a hangout for the Hell's Angels or some other raucous group she would sooner avoid.

Jesse saw her apprehensive glance and gave her hand a comforting pat. "Don't go out much, do you?"

"Not to places like this," Aubrey replied. The truth was she hadn't dated anyone since her divorce had become final the previous October, but she wasn't about to admit that. Of course, this couldn't be considered a real date.

Their waitress appeared then in a scanty black satin outfit that Aubrey thought was either two sizes two small, or intentionally cut low in the bodice and high on the thigh to titillate the male patrons. Either way, the young woman's outfit made her feel even more out of place.

"Do you have Perrier?" she asked softly.

"Of course, hon. Want that with lime?"

"Please."

"I'll have the same," Jesse responded when the provocatively dressed woman turned toward him.

"My Volvo has a stick shift, so I'm certain I could drive your truck home if you'd like to have something to drink."

Jesse shook his head and the waitress left their table, but not before giving him her most alluring smile.

"I quit drinking a couple of years ago," Jesse explained. "It was after I got so drunk at a party that I fell out of a kid's tree house and damn near broke my neck. I thought if I had no more sense than that when I got a few beers in me, I ought to stay off the stuff."

"I know what you mean," Aubrey admitted with an embarrassed smile. "I have no tolerance for alcohol. I've never fallen out of a tree house, but whenever I drink I get the giggles and can't stop."

"I'll bet that's something to see."

"No, it isn't." With his gentle teasing, Aubrey felt her natural reserve melting in spite of her best intentions to maintain a professional attitude. "I'm sorry you didn't get anything out of our seminar. Most people really enjoy them. Everyone has too much stress in their lives, and creative imagery is an effective way to dissolve it."

Jesse's glance swept over her face, knowing the freckles were there even if they didn't show in the dim light. "I'd say I got something out of it," he remarked with a sly grin. "You're here with me now, aren't you?"

"Well, yes, but—" The waitress returned and Aubrey took a hasty gulp of Perrier rather than return Jesse's stare when it was now so blatantly appreciative. Trisha usually asked her if she had had a nice weekend. She could imagine her assistant's shock if she admitted she had let the cowboy who had come to their seminar pick her up and take her to dinner.

Jesse was sure Aubrey was blushing. She had run her seminar with a professional polish, but now she seemed so ill at ease that she reminded him of a teenager out on her first date. "How long have you been divorced?"

"What makes you think I'm divorced?"

"All the pretty women in California have been divorced at least once. Come on, tell me your story. I'll bet it's far more interesting than the deep breathing exercises we did today."

Unconsciously Aubrey squared her shoulders. She didn't confide in anyone the personal details of her life, least of all friendly cowboys. "Tell me something about yourself instead. What do you raise on your ranch?"

"Cattle, but my specialty is producing Brahma bulls for the professional rodeo circuit."

Aubrey's eyes widened. "I've always considered rodeo the most brutal of sports. In fact, I'm not sure it even qualifies as a sport anymore. I can understand ranchhands competing against each other for fun, but to ride bulls for money—"

"Hell, nobody's going to ride bulls for free!" Just the thought made Jesse chuckle. "Rodeo's a sport all right, and an intensely competitive one. If a cowboy isn't in the prize money fairly often, he has to quit and find steady work. That's the most brutal thing about it."

"Do you ride bulls, or merely raise them?" Aubrey held her breath, suddenly certain she was dining with a mild-mannered maniac.

"I used to ride until I was forced into retirement by a particularly obnoxious brute who shattered my right knee. Most people think it's the bull's horns that will get you, but it's the hind feet that are the worst. They pack a real wallop, and human knees just aren't designed to take that kind of punishment."

"Doesn't that tell you something?"

"Yeah, I know. It's a damn fool way to make a living, but I loved it. I'm sure you wouldn't quit what you're doing just because people called you a fool."

"Oh, I've been called far worse things, Mr. Barrett."

"Jesse."

"Jesse." Aubrey managed a faint smile. "Perhaps we ought to find something less controversial to discuss."

"All right. I raise a few llamas, too. They're real lovable even if the bulls aren't." He pronounced the Spanish word correctly, making a y of the double l.

"Llamas?" she repeated.

"Yes, they have a lot of personality and they're becoming very popular for pets. Some cities have had to change the zoning laws to allow them, but they're no more trouble than a large dog, and they're a lot more fun."

"I've seen them at the zoo, but I didn't realize anyone else owned them."

"I can make you a real good deal on one," Jesse offered with a conspiratorial wink.

"Sorry, I don't have room. My pool takes up my whole back yard."

The lots were large in her neighborhood and Jesse could easily visualize her owning an Olympic-size pool. "You live in that big house all by yourself?"

He had relaxed considerably since they had first spoken that evening, and while Aubrey had too, she still wasn't inspired to break her standing rule about confiding in others. Opening her menu, she was glad to find her eyes had adjusted sufficiently to the dim light to read the flowery script.

"I thought you were starving. Hadn't we better order?"

For the second time that day she had slammed the door of her impressive home right in his face, and Jesse reacted far more negatively than he had before. "Sure, we're bound to run out of conversation in another couple of minutes anyway."

Aubrey peeked around the edge of her menu to check his expression and saw instantly by the depth of his scowl that she had hurt his feelings. "I'm sorry, I didn't mean to be rude. It's just that with *The Mind's Eye* being so popular, I've found I have to guard my privacy jealously or people will take advantage of me."

"Like my aunt and me?"

"Not exactly," Aubrey contradicted, but her tone lacked conviction.

Jesse swore under his breath. "So you do think we tried to take advantage of you?"

"Didn't you? Didn't you use the fact I'd once been a student of your aunt's to get me to her house? She didn't want to see me for old times' sake, but in hopes I could locate her missing son."

"Her son's body," Jesse corrected sharply. "Everyone is certain Pete and his family are dead."

"Let's not argue." Aubrey stuck her nose back in her menu and tried to find the seafood selections.

Jesse stared at her right hand since that was all he could see. While they were having tea he had noticed she had beautiful hands, with slender fingers and carefully manicured nails coated with a pale pink polish. They were her own nails, too, not the long acrylic daggers that women had all too often raked across his back. A silver ring in the shape of a calla lily was wrapped around her third finger in a graceful swirl. It looked as though it had been custom-made to fit her hand.

"You're a real strange person, you know that? You talk about following your heart and getting in touch with our higher selves. But all you're really doing is condoning selfishness if you don't give a damn about anyone else."

Aubrey set her menu aside with deliberate care. "It's not that I'm not concerned about other people. It's just that I've had some bad experiences with people who wished to use my methods to better themselves. I know your aunt was sincere in wanting my help, but there's nothing I can do to locate her missing loved ones. Now can we please just drop this subject and order dinner?"

Jesse slammed his menu shut, "Fine, I know what I want."

Had Aubrey driven her Volvo, she would have walked out on him. Unfortunately it had been a long day and she didn't feel like walking back to Edith Pursely's to get her car. She sat back, took a deep breath, and hoped the shrimp scampi would be better than the company.

Chapter II

On Sunday afternoon, Jesse rang Aubrey's doorbell, listened for the sound of approaching footsteps, then sighed in frustration when he heard none. He leaned on the bell again and when the effort still failed to yield a response, he scanned the jasmine and petunia-filled flowerbeds for one of the small metal signs from a home security company. Finding none, he turned the corner of the house and ambled on down the driveway with the self-assurance of a man who had every right to be there.

The garage door was closed so it was impossible to tell if Aubrey was at home. The afternoon was too pretty to waste running errands, however, and just as he had hoped, he found her in the corner of her patio trimming a bougainvillaea heavy with magenta blooms.

Wisely, she was wearing work gloves as protection against the plant's thorns, but the rest of her garb consisted of an oversized T-shirt covering a hot-pink bikini. Her curls were caught atop her head in a ponytail that was pulled farther askew each time it became entangled in the long curving branches. Impatient to finish her work, Aubrey batted the obstreperous boughs aside before chopping them short with clean, vicious strokes.

Amused to have caught her in such an unguarded moment, Jesse decided to wait at the wrought-iron gate until she turned his way. He stood six feet two inches tall without his boots and he guessed Aubrey was about five feet eight. Like most tall women, she had long legs. Hers weren't simply long though, they were also slender and shapely. In fact, they were downright gorgeous.

Jesse tipped his hat back slightly. God, how he loved women with legs like hers. He closed his eyes to savor the delicious vision of those lightly tanned limbs wrapped around him. A superbly proportioned pair of legs was definitely worth concentrating on, but he knew Aubrey wouldn't be pleased if he confessed that was the only type of creative imagery he considered worthwhile.

"Mr. Barrett?"

Jesse's head came up with a jerk. "Good afternoon, ma'am." He thought he had recovered quite nicely from his momentary lapse of manners, but Aubrey continued to regard him with a quizzical stare and failed to invite him to come into her patio. From the far corner of the yard a small, blonde dog came running, barking furiously in a valiant attempt to make up for its failure to alert Aubrey to Jesse's presence.

Ignoring the ferocious imp that more closely resembled an animated mop than a hound, Jesse favored Aubrey with the wide grin he had found to be enormously effective at melting feminine resistance. "I tried your bell," he called out.

"Sorry, I can't hear it back here."

Jesse waited as she laid down her clippers and removed her gloves before approaching the gate. The soft fabric of her pale pink T-shirt hugged her breasts with an alluring

subtlety he found difficult to ignore. He bet she wore a
size 34 bra, or maybe even a 36, but definitely a C cup.
He knew inches weren't all that important. It was the heavi-
ness of a full breast as he cradled it in his palm that mattered most.

Aubrey misread her visitor's lust-filled expression completely. "Are you feeling ill?" She swung open the gate
and motioned for him to come inside. "I was about to take
a break and have some iced tea. Would you like some?"

As she turned away Jesse was treated to a spectacular
view of the slow, undulating motion of her hips as she
preceded him up the walk. He couldn't take his eyes from
the trim curve of her butt. Her bikini bottom had the high-
cut French legs and he wished she would remove her T-
shirt so he could fully appreciate her slim figure. When
they had parted after a dinner during which neither of
them had spoken a single word, he hadn't cared if he ever
saw her again. Now he knew he hadn't seen nearly enough.
She might be over thirty, but he had seen plenty of
eighteen-year-olds who didn't look nearly as good.

"I'm fine, but tea would be nice, thanks," he finally had
the presence of mind to reply as they reached her side
door. The dog was still barking, running around them in
circles, and when Aubrey bent over to pat the furry pooch,
Jesse had to wipe his mouth to keep from drooling. Knowing Aubrey Glenn was definitely not the type of woman
who could be grabbed from behind when she bent over
to shush her dog didn't keep him from wanting to do just
that. He jammed his hands in his hip pockets when he
couldn't think of a better way to fight the impulse.

Jesse didn't understand what had gotten into him that
day but he hadn't been so damn horny since his sopho-
more year in high school. Maybe it was just the fact it had
been more than a week since he had slept with a woman.
For him, that was a major deprivation. That was it, he

decided. He was suffering from withdrawal symptoms, nothing more. Aubrey was very attractive, but certainly not irresistible. Or at least she wouldn't have been had he had another woman handy. Unfortunately, he didn't.

"Guinevere is all bark and no bite," Aubrey assured him. "You needn't be afraid of her."

"Me? Afraid of that pitiful excuse for a dog? No way."

"Of course," Aubrey replied as she straightened up. "A man who rides bulls for sport would never be afraid of a mere dog."

Jesse doubted that she was teasing him, but responded with a smile as though she were. "You guessed it." Even without an invitation, he followed her through the screen door into a sunny breakfast room separated from the kitchen by a cooking island. While he knew the house was far from new, it appeared to have been recently remodeled. Decorated in powder blue and white with delicate floral wallpaper, the two adjoining rooms were spotless.

"You like to cook?" he asked.

Aubrey had already taken two glasses from the cupboard and opened the freezer compartment to get the ice. "Not anymore."

Jesse waited for her to elaborate, but as usual she did not. "I know what you mean," he volunteered, although she hadn't given him a clue. "I like to cook for company, but not just for myself. I've found several microwave dinners that aren't half bad."

Aubrey took the pitcher of tea from the refrigerator and filled their glasses. She then added lemon slices and sprigs of fresh mint. "I try to avoid processed food myself. Let's go back outside. It's too pretty a day to sit indoors."

"Sure." Jesse took the glass she handed him and followed at a slow enough pace to allow him to take a peek into the large formal dining room. It was far too much house for one woman, and he wondered if she was lonely.

He opened his mouth to ask, and then thought better of it. When Aubrey sat down at the glass-topped table, he chose the place opposite her, thinking he would be smart not to get too close and spook her.

"I'm sure you must be surprised to see me again."

"Very." Aubrey pulled an empty chair around in front of her so she could prop up her bare feet and get some sun on her legs. "I thought we had said everything we could possibly say last night."

Jesse ignored the sarcasm in her voice. "I tried an experiment after I got home. I'm hoping you can explain what happened."

"What sort of experiment?"

Jesse pulled a snapshot of Peter Ferrell and his family from his shirt pocket. "This same photo was in the paper, but it didn't look nearly as clear. It's the one Pete and Marlene sent out with their Christmas cards the last year they were around to celebrate the holidays. Pete wrote the date on the back, and maybe the fact he had handled it has something to do with what I felt. Anyway, last night I sat down with the file my aunt showed you, and when I came across this photo I got the strangest sensation. You know how you shiver sometimes and people will say someone's stepped on your grave? It was like that."

"Perhaps you were seated in a draft."

"Hey, you're the one who says intuition can be enhanced. Don't laugh at me."

That he appeared sincerely insulted astonished Aubrey. "I'm sorry. It's just that you made no secret of what you thought of my ideas yesterday. I find it difficult to believe you've changed your mind overnight."

Jesse nodded. "I can understand that. I was rather obnoxious yesterday and I apologize for it." He wasn't about to beg for forgiveness though, and abruptly changed the subject. "Have you ever been to Andersonville?"

"No, why?"

"It was a Confederate prison and a notoriously barbaric one. About thirteen thousand Union prisoners died and were buried there. It looks like a park now, but when you walk through it," Jesse paused, then shrugged slightly. "It's difficult to explain, but it's as though all those men are screaming still, even though all you really hear is silence."

Aubrey took a long swallow of tea, then set her glass down on the table to make room for a large black cat who appeared out of nowhere and jumped into her lap. "This is Lucifer," she said as she gave the big tomcat an affectionate cuddle.

"That your familiar?"

"I don't practice witchcraft, Jesse."

That she had at last used his first name pleased him. "You've got to admit that's a black cat that would make any witch proud."

"True, but I'm no witch." As she stroked her pet, Aubrey mulled over what he had said about Andersonville. Surely the poor souls buried there would be uneasy. That their screams would still echo more than a hundred years after they had died wasn't impossible.

"Perhaps you did feel something unusual at Andersonville. Are you saying that you experienced a similar eerie sensation from the photograph of your cousin's family?"

"Yeah, I sure did. I tried to put it back in the file, to get rid of it, to get it out of my mind, but I couldn't. The feeling was too intense. I figure if I can sense something strange when I don't believe in intuition, let alone psychic phenomenon, then you ought to be able to detect a hell of a lot more. Here, will you try?"

Reluctantly, Aubrey held out her hand. "I don't claim to be psychic, Jesse. How many times must I remind you of that?"

The instant she raised the snapshot to get a closer look,

Lucifer let out a howl and leapt from her lap. "So much for his opinion," she quipped. She closed her eyes for a moment, took several deep breaths, and exhaled slowly. When she opened her eyes, what greeted her was not the smiling faces of Peter Ferrell and his family, but a hideous scene of torture and death. She stared at it, fascinated despite the horror. The images sharpened with terror and then blurred into a bright blood red which dissolved into glowing flames.

Chilled clear to the marrow despite the warmth of the sun, Aubrey swallowed hard before she spoke in an anguished whisper. "They were murdered," she assured her rapt companion. "The parents were shot in the head, and the boys beaten to death. Then all the bodies were tossed in a shallow grave and set on fire. The killers panicked though. They filled in the hole too soon. There's enough left of the bodies to identify them all."

Jesse waited for her to say more, not really believing Aubrey could actually extract so much grisly detail from the photograph. At the same time, her obvious fright assured him that she could. She hadn't gone into a trance, nor done anything odd. She had simply viewed the snapshot with intense concentration. When she set it on the table and looked away, he picked it up, half expecting to see the images she had reported, but he didn't.

"They disappeared one evening about suppertime. Marlene had made a salad and put water in a kettle to boil for spaghetti. At first the police tried to convince us that the family had just skipped town to avoid paying debts, but they didn't have any unusual debts and nobody goes to the trouble of starting dinner on the night they plan to run away.

"Pete was a successful accountant. Marlene did a lot of volunteer work and was on the PTA board at the boys' school. They were all involved in AYSO soccer and Little

League. They weren't the types to just pick up and leave without packing any of their belongings or telling anyone good-bye. But wait a minute, you said killers. We told you the only suspect was Harlan Caine, but the police failed to tie him to the Ferrells' disappearance. Are you sure there were two men involved?''

Aubrey nodded as she rubbed her upper arms briskly, but she couldn't shake the awful chill. ''I couldn't see their faces clearly. They were just menacing blobs, but there were two of them.'' She gagged as a wave of nausea began to assail her. ''I'm sorry, I'm going to be sick.''

Startled, Jesse turned as Aubrey leapt to her feet and sped by him into the house. She had looked a little pale, but her comments had seemed so matter-of-fact he hadn't realized she had been sickened by what she had seen. He waited five minutes, then five more before leaving his Stetson on the table and following her inside. He knew she wouldn't want him snooping around, but he could always say he thought she might have passed out and wanted to be sure she was all right.

He didn't bother to call out her name as he walked through the dining room. There was a study on his left and he paused a moment to look over the crowded book-cases that filled one whole wall. Several shelves were devoted to New Age philosophy and, while the subject had never interested him in the past, he was greatly intrigued now. He hoped Aubrey would let him browse through her collection to see what he could find out about psychic abilities. An Apple computer and printer sat on a desk by the windows, and he realized he would be wise to ask to read the book she had written before he borrowed any others.

His most immediate task, however, was to find her. His boot heels echoed with a dull thud as he walked on into an entry hall. It opened on his left into a spacious formal

living room. He then glanced up the wide staircase on his
right and wondered if he should search the second floor,
but seeing there was another room past the stairs, he tried
it first.

Like the rest of Aubrey's home, the den was as exquisitely
decorated and as neat as a furniture showroom. Besides
the door leading to the hall, the den had two others. The
first opened into a large walk-in closet, the other led to
what he assumed must be a bathroom. He knocked lightly.

"Aubrey? Are you okay?"

"No, I think I just died. Please go away."

"Come on out and lie down on the couch. That will
make you feel better."

Aubrey doubted that her sudden attack of queasiness
would ever abate. She splashed her face with cold water
and reluctantly opened the door. "I think what I need is
fresh air. Let's go back outside."

Because she still looked far from well, Jesse didn't challenge her on that request. That was the second time she
had rushed him out of her house that day, and he had
the distinct impression that she didn't feel comfortable
having him there. Hell, he wouldn't hurt her. If she wanted
to invite him upstairs to see her bedroom, he would assume
she wanted him to try out the bed with her in it, but he
wouldn't have tossed her over his shoulder like a caveman
and carried her upstairs.

It was clear Aubrey wasn't going to ask him to share her
bed, though. He had never met a woman who displayed
so little interest in him as a man. That wasn't at all flattering
to his masculine pride, but he could scarcely utter the
complaint aloud.

When they reached the patio, Aubrey sat down and again
propped up her feet. She picked up her glass of iced tea
and held it against first one flushed cheek and then the
other. "Intuition provides only subtle hunches. Sometimes

I hear a voice which offers a brief warning, such as, 'Don't forget your umbrella,' or it might urge me to buy something in the market I'm sure I don't need. Then when I get home, I discover it's precisely the item I require. I've never experienced anything like this, though. I feel as though I've come down with the plague.''

Jesse wasn't certain how to take her comment about voices, but decided to let it slide for the moment. ''Is this the first time you've tried something like this?''

His eyes were lit with a sympathetic glow, and she found it surprisingly easy to confide in him. ''Yes. I wasn't lying about not being psychic. I'm not, or at least I wasn't until today.''

''Maybe you just never tried.''

''I've done experiments with Trisha where we've taken turns going into another room and drawing pictures for the other one to reproduce. I'm better at sending images than receiving them, but neither of us has particularly impressive ESP.''

Extrasensory perception was something Jesse had always put in the same catagory as magic tricks. He thought it was the work of clever illusionists, nothing more. When Aubrey fell silent as she tried to compose herself, he felt an annoying twinge of guilt. Maybe he had tried to take advantage of her by asking her to look at the photograph, but he had never expected it to make her physically ill.

Her lashes were spiked with tears, but there were no dark smudges beneath her eyes. Maybe she wore waterproof mascara because of the pool. What kind of woman bothered to apply mascara and lipstick before going out to trim her bougainvillaea? he wondered. Then he knew: one with the class to take the trouble to look her best even when no one else was around.

His earlier preoccupation with her legs now made him ashamed. Guinevere was curled up nearby, but still observing him with a wary glance. He smiled at the dog, then felt silly for caring what she thought of him.

"Actually, being able to sense vibrations, to pick up meaning from objects is called psychometry, not ESP," Aubrey remarked, softly reminding herself, rather than instructing him.

"Well, whatever it's called, I believe you saw something I didn't." Jesse tapped the edge of the photo on the table as he thought out loud. "They had to have been killed at home and then taken somewhere else and buried. My aunt can't sell their house because it can't be proven Pete and Marlene are dead. They'd owned it for a number of years so the mortgage payments aren't large and they're being paid out of the estate. It's a nice day for a drive. Why don't we go out to the valley and see what kind of vibes you can pick up there?"

Appalled by his suggestion, Aubrey swung her feet off the chair and turned to face him. "What a wonderful idea! If I get sick to my stomach looking at a photograph, what sort of reaction do you hope I'll get at a murder scene? Do you know how to treat someone having convulsions, or can you do CPR? Maybe we should just telephone ahead and have the paramedics meet us there."

"I'm sorry. That didn't sound very nice, did it?"

"No, it certainly didn't."

"Like I said, I'm sorry. It's just that my Aunt Edith is the only relative I have left, and I'd like to see her son's killers get the justice they deserve. If you can help us, then I'm going to continue to encourage you to try. Don't accuse me of using you either. It's just the only possible way I can see to trap the killers."

Aubrey was exasperated that Jesse was so dense. "Look, I might see the murderers' names written in a bloody scrawl ten feet high, but if the police can't read that gruesome graffiti too, what good is it going to do? They need evidence and witnesses. Unless we can provide those, there's no point in going any further with this.''

While Jesse flinched at her gory imagery, he was not a man who was easily discouraged. He simply took a new tack. ''What were you planning to do today, just work in your yard?''

''Yes, and there's lots more to do.''

Jesse disagreed. ''Your yard is so damn perfect it could be on the cover of a seed catalog. What you need is to relax, lady. Go on upstairs and change your clothes. You're coming with me out to Pete's house. I'll promise you now that if you feel even the slightest bit of discomfort I'll let you sit in the truck, but I want to take a look around myself.''

As he rose to his feet and plunked his hat on the back of his head, Aubrey sent an appraising glance up Jesse's impressive frame. He was again wearing Levi's and a blue plaid Western shirt that came close to matching his eyes. The look in those bright blue eyes was now an extremely determined one.

''Just what are we playing here, the old 'Me Tarzan, you Jane' bit?''

That question made Jesse laugh. ''No. I guess the type of women I know like taking orders. I didn't mean to insult you though. Will you please come out to Pete's house with me? Even if we don't find anything of value, I can promise you a nice afternoon.''

That he would change his tone so quickly surprised Aubrey. Now that he was being so polite, she was reluctant to refuse his request. There was another consideration, too. What if she really did possess a psychic talent she had never before been called upon to use? Didn't she owe it to herself to test its range? Besides, he was right, it would be nice to get away from home for a change. She spent far too much of her time there, and all of it alone.

"Do you promise I won't have to get out of your truck if I can't handle visiting the house?"

Jesse held up his right hand. "You have my word on it."

"All right then. Give me a few minutes to dress. If you'd like to swim, there are some men's trunks in the cabaña."

Jesse turned to note the small structure at the far end of the pool. It was easily large enough to hold a dressing room and bath as well as the pool's heating system. "Yeah, maybe I will."

"I won't be long."

Jesse knew women though, and thinking that unlikely, he went to get himself a pair of trunks.

Aubrey took a couple of aspirin, then hurriedly showered and washed her hair. When she entered her bedroom to choose something to wear, she couldn't resist crossing to the window that faced the pool. Jesse was swimming laps, and she sat down on the window seat as she continued to towel dry her hair. He was an excellent swimmer, and she soon became so fascinated by his effortless rhythm she completely lost track of the time.

He had the fluid grace of a natural athlete, and she thought it a great pity that he had not taken up baseball, tennis, or golf—any sport but bull riding which she still thought must only appeal to the mentally deranged. Jesse didn't seem the least bit deranged, though. He was so attractive it was no wonder Edith Pursely was so proud of him.

As for her own opinion, she still felt numb where men were concerned. Jesse was handsome; she could appreciate that fact, but he didn't raise her pulse rate. When he paused at the shallow end of the pool and looked up at her, she was embarrassed to have been caught spying on him, but managed to wave as though her actions had been perfectly natural.

Jesse broke into a wide grin when he spotted Aubrey at

the window. Apparently she was a lot more interested in him than she let on, and that pleased him no end. She had a purple bath towel wrapped around her, and with her damp curls she looked so delightfully feminine he was immediately inspired to climb out of the pool and walk toward the house. When he stood directly below her window, he called out in a stage whisper.

"Do you know why cowboys make such good lovers?"

"I hadn't heard that they did," Aubrey replied. The question was such a silly one she couldn't help but laugh as she sent an admiring glance down his barely clothed body. If appearance meant anything, then she knew Jesse would be incredible in bed. He was not only tall, but well built—so perfect a physical specimen he could easily have earned a living as a male model, or a stripper, which she thought he might find more suited to his talents. She was wise enough to know looks weren't all that a man needed to please a woman, though.

"I'm the one trying to tell the joke here," Jesse complained with all the righteous indignation he could muster.

"I'm sorry. All right, why do cowboys make such good lovers?" Aubrey held her breath, hoping he wouldn't have the audacity to claim they were all hung like bulls.

Jesse again flashed his most charming grin. "It's because we only have to stay in the saddle eight seconds to be a champion."

Relieved that his answer was merely suggestive rather than just plain dirty, Aubrey broke into lilting peals of laughter. "That's absolutely awful. In a rodeo, does a cowboy only have to stay on a horse or a bull eight seconds to win the prize money?"

"It would be the longest eight seconds of your life," Jesse shouted.

"Is that part of the joke?" Aubrey called down to him. It was Jesse's turn to laugh then. "No, it wasn't supposed to be." He shook his head as he began to back away. "Hurry and get dressed. We can't waste the whole afternoon fooling around here."

Aubrey watched him walk around the pool to the cabaña. The man had great buns, she thought with a small knowing smile. "Eight seconds," she whispered to herself as she got up. "That might be long enough for a bull, but certainly not a woman." She was smiling though, and that was an expression she seldom wore outside of her seminars. And when she joined Jesse downstairs ten minutes later, she was smiling still.

"Why do I get the feeling this is only the second time you've ridden in a truck?" Jesse asked as he turned up the volume on the radio. It was tuned to KLAC, and the Judds' song playing was one of his favorites.

"I must have ridden in a truck more than twice," Aubrey argued, although she couldn't recall when. Because Country/Western music was too melancholy for her taste, she wished Jesse had the sense to turn it off rather than up. Thinking suffering through such dismal accompaniment was the price she would have to pay for traveling with a cowboy, she held her tongue, but it was a real challenge to do so. Her only consolation was that he wasn't talking on his CB radio.

"Twice," Jesse mused aloud. "I think knowing me is going to provide a real education for you."

"In what way?" Aubrey scoffed.

"We'll just have to wait and see," Jesse replied. She seemed too restless to enjoy anymore teasing so he let the matter drop. He hoped she wasn't worried that visiting the house would make her sick again.

Jesse had been in the Los Angeles area often enough to drive the freeways with confidence. He took 134 west to the 405, then followed it up to Northridge. There was the usual amount of Sunday traffic, several places where their progress slowed to a crawl, but he was grateful he didn't have to fight the traffic on a daily basis and didn't swear about it. Aubrey seemed uncomfortable the whole drive, and while he didn't want her nerves to get the better of her, he failed to think of a way to reassure her, so he just hummed along with the radio rather than try. When finally she spoke, he jumped at the sound of her voice.

"You said Harlan Caine was a developer. What sort of projects does he undertake—hotels, office buildings, subdivisions?" Appearing interested in his reply, Aubrey leaned over to turn down the radio.

"No, he builds shopping malls, or at least he makes people think that he does in order to get them to invest in his company. I'm not sure he ever actually completed one, though. Why do you ask?"

"A construction site would make an excellent place to dispose of bodies."

"That it would," Jesse agreed. "But I don't think Caine had any projects under construction at the time Pete and his family disappeared. I guess that's what their argument was about. Pete had invested in a project that didn't look like it was ever going to get off the drawing board. He'd mentioned to a friend that he was going to hire an attorney, maybe start a class action suit against Caine. He didn't get the chance."

"The threat of a lawsuit might provide Caine with a motive for doing away with Pete, but to slaughter his whole family, that's the act of a lunatic."

"That's what my aunt and I think, but until we find a way to prove it, it's only opinion."

Jesse found his cousin's home easily and pulled up at the curb. Located in an attractive subdivison, the house was hidden behind a six-foot wall. Only the tile roof of the one-story structure was visible from the street, but a crape myrtle tree with bright fuschia blossoms growing beside the gate made the entranceway inviting.

"Some of the homes in the area suffered damage from the earthquake in 1994, but Pete's didn't. Doesn't look like a murder scene, does it?"

Aubrey shook her head, then grew apprehensive and took a deep breath. "Not yet. But if it is, I can't help but think there would have been enough blood splattered around for the police to be certain there had been a killing."

Jesse got out and walked around to open her door. He took her hand to help her step down to the sidewalk, then didn't release it. "That's a good point. Maybe I'm way off base thinking they died here.

"The next door neighbors have a teenage son who looks after the yard. I'll have to tell them we're here so they won't worry someone's broken into the place. Come on, let's see if they're home."

Aubrey was surprised when Jesse continued to hold her hand. His grasp was firm, but it wasn't an unpleasant sensation. Rather than pull away, she tried simply to appear indifferent to his touch as they walked up to the neighbors' door.

Roberta Smaus remembered Jesse and greeted him warmly, but the instant she glanced toward Aubrey, she gasped in astonishment. "Aren't you Aubrey Glenn? I loved your book! Absolutely loved it, not that I've had the time to try much creative imagery myself, but your book was wonderful. Would it be an imposition to ask you to sign it for me?"

Aubrey noted Jesse's impatient frown, but agreed. "Of course not. I'll be happy to do it."

When Roberta hurried away to find her copy of *The Mind's Eye*, Aubrey raised up on her tiptoes to whisper in

Jesse's ear. "I'm sorry, but this will only take a few seconds and it's never wise to disappoint a fan."

There had been a time when people had clamored for his autograph, so Jesse knew exactly what she meant and didn't argue. He knew from watching others just how quickly fans could turn on a celebrity who didn't respect them. Even without provocation, fans tended to be fickle, and he didn't want to see Aubrey lose any of hers.

"These people have been real nice about looking after Pete's house. Take your time."

Jesse dropped Aubrey's hand when Roberta returned with a pen. She invited Aubrey to come inside where she could sit down to write and he waited outside on the porch trying not to feel left out. He wasn't used to being seen with a woman who got more attention than he did. Of course, Aubrey wasn't anything like the women he usually dated. She was a far more complex individual than any of his girlfriends had ever been. She wasn't really a date, either, he reminded himself. She just happened to have a talent he needed, that was all.

"No, that's not all," he scolded himself, for despite that Aubrey shared little information about herself, he was becoming increasingly intrigued by her. There was an air of mystery about her that he was eager to strip away, as eager as he was to strip away her clothes. As soon as she reappeared, he took her arm and hurried her next door.

"I want to read your book. If you have any extra copies at home, I'd like to buy one. If not, I'll pick up one at a bookstore tomorrow."

Aubrey stared at him for a long moment before responding. "I always have a few copies on hand for promotion and I'll be glad to give you one. I'll even autograph it for you."

"Thanks." Jesse reached over the gate to pull open the latch. "Let's walk around to the back first. I think you'll like the garden. There's a fish pond and so many plants the place looks like a jungle. We can sit down there for a moment, and if you'd like to stay there while I go inside, I'll understand.''

The small backyard garden was every bit as lovely as Jesse had promised, and in the warm afternoon sunlight it proved to be wonderfully serene. Obviously laid out by a master landscape architect, the yard was terraced to give it added depth and planted with an abundance of delicate pink azaleas, lacy white forsythia, and fragrant gardenias.

"This is a miniature paradise," Aubrey exclaimed. She strolled down the flagstone walk to the pond where gold-fish darted among the shadows to catch the insects landing on the water's surface. "The Ferrells must have been a very nice family. Anyone who would take the trouble to create such a beautiful garden couldn't have been other-wise.''

The ends of Aubrey's loose curls were tossed lightly by the afternoon breeze, and as she turned toward Jesse he thought her as pretty as a model who had been purposely posed in the garden. She was wearing a pale aqua shirtwaist whose sheer fabric glistened with a silken sheen. Barelegged and wearing tan leather sandals, she looked as though she might have spent hours to achieve a look of careless elegance, but he knew for a fact it had taken her only a few minutes.

No longer able to ignore the desire that had plagued him all afternoon, Jesse walked up to her, cupped her face gently in his hands, and gave her a long, slow kiss whose tenderness was carefully calculated to dissolve whatever lingering doubts she might have about him. "Most women think I'm very nice, too,'' he whispered when he finally drew away.

Aubrey found it difficult to catch her breath, and while she hadn't thought it possible, Jesse had definitely managed to set her pulse racing, and then some. She felt betrayed by the warmth of her body's response though, rather than pleased by the awakening of long-dormant emotions. She hadn't asked for his affection, and she didn't want it. It terrified her, in fact, and her reaction was an extremely hostile one.

"Is this why you brought me here? Did you merely want to take advantage of the romantic atmosphere rather than test whatever psychic ability I might possess?"

Her response was so contrary to the one Jesse had antici- pated, his temper also burst into flame. "Hell no! I just wanted to kiss you, so I did. What's the matter with that?"

Aubrey scarcely knew where to begin. She was sorely tempted to shove him into the fish pond to cool him off, and she barely restrained the impulse. "I'm certain there are scores of women who think you're far more than nice, but what we have is a professional relationship, not a per- sonal one. I should have made that abundantly clear before I went to dinner with you last night."

What Jesse had envisioned was that she would pull him back into her arms for a near endless series of kisses. He had hoped for another chance to impress her at dinner, and after that, well, he couldn't recall the last time a woman had sent him home before dawn. He knew Aubrey was reserved, but he hadn't thought she would be all that different from other women once they had broken the ice. His kiss had been meant to do just that. Obviously it had failed to achieve the desired effect, and he was not a man who could accept failure gracefully.

"If you're so damn anxious to see the house, I have the key. Let's go inside."

Aubrey marched past him, then had to wait for Jesse to fish the key from his pocket when he reached the back door. She knew the whole trip had been pointless now that she was too angry to feel anything other than rage.

She walked through the service porch and into the kitchen, but she didn't really see it before she went into the dining room. The table and chairs had been covered with sheets, as was the furniture in the livingroom. The house was still fully furnished, but her footsteps echoed as though it were vacant. When she came to the hallway leading to the bedrooms, she stopped and turned around.

"I don't want to see anymore. I'll wait for you outside."

"What's the matter? Are you afraid of what you might feel, or of what I might do?"

"Either way I'd get sick to my stomach and I'd rather avoid that." Aubrey slipped by him and returned to the garden where she sat for more than thirty minutes before Jesse reappeared. His expression was as dark as her own, and she didn't speak as they left the yard. There was a red Toyota parked in front of the house now and two men, one carrying a camera, quickly got out and blocked their way to the pick-up truck.

"Can you give me a quote for the morning paper, Ms. Glenn? Have the police asked for your help with the investigation of the Ferrells' disappearance?"

Unaccustomed to being badgered by reporters, Aubrey shrank back as the cameraman's flash went off in her face, but Jesse simply brushed the men aside. He yanked open his Chevy's passenger door, helped Aubrey up into her seat, then slammed the door shut with a possessive flourish.

"Ms. Glenn has no comment," he shouted as he lunged by them again before circling the truck to get in on the driver's side. He gunned the engine as he pulled away from the curb, but the photographer succeeded in getting several more shots.

"Son of a bitch!" Jesse swore. "Your devoted fan, Mrs. Smaus, must have tipped them off that you were here."

Aubrey thought that was too obvious a point to argue and kept still. That Jesse was too angry to turn on the radio was the only thing that kept her from shrieking hysterically the whole way home. The aggressive reporter had upset her badly, and coming right on the heels of her argument with Jesse, he had flayed her nerves raw. She wanted out. She would never be able to discover what had happened to the Ferrells, and even if she had that hope, there was no way she and Jesse could continue to work together.

It took only one glance at the fierceness of his frown when he pulled up in front of her house to convince her that he agreed. When she climbed down from the truck unassisted, she didn't bother to say good-bye.

Chapter III

When Aubrey went out her front door to get the newspaper at seven o'clock Monday morning, she found Jesse Barrett seated on her doorstep. He leapt to his feet and handed her the Metro section of the *Los Angeles Times*.

"It's about time you got up," he greeted her excitedly. "In another ten minutes I would have rung your bell. What do you think of this?"

The photograph for the lead story showed the two of them leaving the Ferrells' house. Aubrey was named, but Jesse was referred to only as an unidentified male escort. A quick glance at the accompanying article revealed it to be a brief review of the Ferrells' strange disappearance combined with a summary of Aubrey's success as a motivational speaker emphasizing creative imagery.

"It must have been a slow day for news," Aubrey remarked. Seeing Jesse had a bag from Winchell's in his hand, she felt a sharp pang of remorse for her hostility when they had last parted. He seemed to bring out the

worst in her, but she couldn't excuse her continual failure
to control her temper around him.

She had also had time to realize he could never have
predicted how negative her reaction to his kiss would be.
She was probably the only woman he had ever met who
had nearly punched him in the nose rather than ripped off
his shirt. She was responsible for her actions, she reminded
herself; he wasn't. He shouldn't have kissed her, but her
response had been wildly out of proportion to such a slight
offense.

"You brought donuts for breakfast? That was very
thoughtful of you. Come on in and I'll make some tea."

"I don't suppose you have any coffee?" Jesse asked as
he followed her through the door. Tea was simply not a
man's drink, in his view. Iced tea was passable on a hot
afternoon, but he needed more than a cup of steeped
herbs to get going in the morning.

"I think I have some instant. Do you mind if it's decaf-
feinated?"

"Don't bother looking for it," Jesse responded with a
shudder. "I might as well drink the tea."

Jesse slid into a chair at the breakfast table and hung
his hat on the back of the one next to it. Aubrey filled the
tea kettle and set it on the stove. She was wearing a white
cotton robe sprinkled with violets and decorated at the
neckline and cuffs with eyelet ruffles. Her hair had been
brushed into its usual flattering mop of curls, and her
features had been prettily accented with the light touches
of makeup he was used to seeing her wear.

"Are you going somewhere this morning?" he asked.

Aubrey brought plates and napkins to the table and
opened the Winchell's bag. "Yes, my assistants and I are
beginning a three-day seminar for the Wells Fargo Bank.
Glazed donuts are my favorite. Are they yours, too?"

Jesse frowned, not pleased to learn she had plans. "Yeah, glazed and jelly filled. Will you be gone all day?"

"Until the late afternoon, why?" Aubrey went to the refrigerator for a glass jar of cranberry juice and brought it and two small glasses back to the table.

Jesse tapped the newspaper. "I don't like this at all. 'Unidentified male,'" he sneered. "You went there with me, not the other way around."

Aubrey sat down opposite him and smoothed out the lavender and blue floral tablecloth before she poured juice for them both. "Do all cowboys have such inflated egos?"

"It's not a question of ego," Jesse said. "It's a question of giving the killers, and I'm sure they'll read this article, the impression you are going to provide clues to the Farrells' disappearance. If you'd murdered four people and gotten away with it, what do you think you'd do if you learned there was a psychic on your trail?"

Aubrey shook her head. "How many times must I swear I'm not psychic before you'll believe me? Yesterday's vision was probably no more than a strange fluke. It never happened to me before, and I sincerely hope it won't ever happen again."

Recalling how sick she had gotten, he understood her concern. "Whether or not you have psychic talent isn't really the issue. It's what the killers think that will count."

The tea kettle gave its first faint sputtering whistle. Aubrey got up, took a canister of imported tea bags from the cupboard, and went to the stove. "My publisher will be delighted I got a mention in the *Times*. It will undoubtedly sell a few more books, but I've learned not to pay any attention to the publicity I receive. Anyone who kills a whole family can't be frightened easily. I don't think today's story will faze them."

When she returned to the table with two blue earthenware mugs filled with orange spice tea, Jesse tried again.

"Where do your parents live? Could you go home and stay with them awhile?"

Aubrey took one of the donuts and began to pull it apart with her fingers. She never bought pastries for herself because they lacked even a hint of nutritional value, but she couldn't deny how delicious they were. "This is my home. My folks moved up to Seattle a couple of years ago, and while I'm sure they would love to have me visit them, I have too many commitments to get away now."

His apprehension mounting, Jesse leaned forward slightly. "What sort of commitments? Seminars, or more personal ones?"

Aubrey's glance cooled noticeably. "Let's leave my personal life out of this discussion. I'm very well paid for the seminars and when I contract to do one, I never cancel. What if your name had been in the paper? Would you be high-tailing it back to Arizona this morning?"

Jesse responded with a derisive laugh. "That's different."

"Why? Because you're a man?"

"You guessed it."

Aubrey watched him finish his first donut and start on another. Why she had expected him to recognize his opinion as blatantly sexist, she didn't know, but she realized there would be no point in belaboring the issue with a man who was obviously blind to such an important point.

"I don't suppose there's even the slightest possibility that your relatives actually did leave town on their own?"

"None," Jesse assured her. "They were either murdered at home or kidnapped and murdered elsewhere." He tapped the newspaper photograph. "And now whoever did it is going to be looking for you."

Before Aubrey could respond, Trisha Lynch came through the back door. "Ready to go?" she called out as she walked through the service porch and into the kitchen.

When she found Aubrey seated at her breakfast table with the good-looking cowboy from Saturday's seminar her mouth fell agape.

Jesse quickly rose to his feet. "Good morning, Ms. Lynch. It's nice to see you again."

Aubrey also stood, and while she had absolutely no reason to be embarrassed, her cheeks grew warm with an incriminating blush. "I'm sorry, Trisha. I lost track of the time. Just give me a minute."

"Take your time," Trisha called out as Aubrey left the room.

"Would you like something?" Jesse offered graciously. "Tea, juice, or a donut?"

"No thanks, I've already eaten." Trisha joined him at the breakfast table and motioned for him to be seated. She looked extremely pleased by what she had found and reached out to give Jesse's arm an encouraging squeeze. "I would never have believed this if I hadn't seen it with my own eyes."

Jesse leaned back in his chair. "Believed what?"

"Have you or have you not just spent the weekend with Aubrey?" the dark-eyed young woman inquired with unabashed glee.

Jesse considered several responses before he chose a deliciously ambiguous one. "Yeah, you could say that we spent the weekend together." He handed her the newspaper. "Did you see this?"

"No," Trisha scanned the photograph, then read the article hurriedly. "Great publicity, I'd say. What were you two doing out at the Ferrells' house? Are you a detective?"

"No, I'm Pete Ferrell's cousin, and I'm afraid I've gotten Aubrey into more trouble than she can handle if the killers assume she has some psychic ability."

"What killers? There's no proof of a murder." Trisha handed the paper back to him. "That's the whole point of the story. The police haven't a clue as to what happened to the Ferrells.''

"How many of your relatives have disappeared without a trace?"

"Well, none, but—"

"But, nothing," Jesse countered harshly.

Trisha regarded Jesse more closely. She would never have thought him Aubrey's type, but now that she had discovered how serious a man he was, she reconsidered her initial impression. Then she began to suspect his motives.

"You were at Saturday's seminar, so you know Aubrey teaches people how to create magical visions and set the goals to achieve them; she makes no claim of being psychic. If you're using her to try and solve a crime that has baffled the police, then you're making two grievous errors. First, she can't see into the future or the past, and second, you ought not to be sleeping with her. It's cruel to play with her emotions like that and she doesn't deserve it. No woman does.''

If there was one thing Jesse absolutely could not abide, it was having a woman lecture him, especially when he didn't deserve it. "What Aubrey and I do is our business and not yours," he said, not about to admit that he was no closer to sleeping with Aubrey than he had been when he walked into her seminar.

Aubrey entered the room a moment later to find Jesse and Trisha silently observing each other with equally suspicious glances. "Oh Jesse, I'm sorry, there are some copies of my book in a carton beside my computer, but I haven't time now to sign one for you as I promised.''

Jesse rose to his feet with a lazy stretch. "That's all right. Would you mind if I hung around awhile and looked through your other books? If I find anything I want to read I'll do it here. I won't take any of your books home with me.''

Aubrey was conscious not only of Jesse's earnest gaze, but of Trisha's curious glance, as well. She had intended for their relationship to remain strictly business, and here he was again asking for personal favors, but this time she managed to hold her temper rather than lash out at him. "Stay as long as you like. Go swimming again if you want, and then just press the button in the doorknob when you go out the back door. Lucifer and Guinevere have already been fed and put out in the backyard. Just be firm with Guin and she won't bother you."

"Thanks. I'll watch out for the pets and I won't leave the house unlocked," Jesse assured her. Aubrey was wearing a peach-colored outfit and looked so pretty that as she walked by him he couldn't resist reaching out to catch her hand. He leaned down and gave her a quick kiss on the cheek, then lowered his voice to a seductive whisper.

"Be real careful today. I'll talk with you later."

Aubrey was too startled by Jesse's affectionate farewell to scold him again and she hurried on out the back door. The man was absolutely impossible, but how could she criticize him for kissing her good-bye when his warning had sounded so sincere?

As soon as Aubrey had started her car's engine, Trisha began to pester her for information. "Tell me exactly what happened between you and the cowboy and don't you dare omit a single lurid detail."

Aubrey glanced over her shoulder and began to back out of the driveway. "Calm down, there's nothing exciting to tell."

"Don't give me that," Trisha argued. "When was the last time you spent the weekend with a man?"

What Trisha assumed was so far from the truth that Aubrey couldn't help but laugh. "You really mustn't let your imagination run wild." She continued to insist nothing of a romantic nature had transpired between her and

Jesse Barrett. That wasn't the complete truth, but she wasn't about to give Trisha a different impression. Still, Jesse had mentioned speaking with her later, and she could not help but wonder what their next encounter would bring.

She stopped to pick up Shelly Sandler and had to wait while Shelley gave her three-year-old daughter a good-bye hug and spoke a final word with her mother, who looked after the little girl during the day. As soon as Shelley had climbed into the back seat, Aubrey noted something was amiss. Shelley was always subdued, but today she appeared to be on the verge of tears.

Aubrey turned to face her. "If your daughter's ill, Trisha and I can handle the seminar on our own."

"No, Annie's fine. It's just that Ricky's back in town and he came by yesterday."

"Drunk or high, I assume?" Trisha asked.

"No. He was sober."

"Well, that's a first," Trisha said.

"That's enough, Trish," Aubrey scolded. They were running late and she preferred to talk on the freeway as they drove into Los Angeles. She wished Ricky Vance were merely some sleazy character on one of the daytime soaps rather than her shy assistant's demon lover. "Did he spend any time with Annie?" she asked.

Shelley searched through her large leather handbag for a tissue and wiped her eyes. "No. She was already asleep when he came by the house."

"Looks like he won't make father of the year again this year," Trisha scoffed.

"Do you actually believe you're helping?" Aubrey asked Trisha.

"Yeah. I do. One of the these days Shelley is finally going to be struck with a blinding glimpse of the obvious and she'll tell Ricky to go to hell and stay there."

"I love him," Shelley insisted softly.

Aubrey glanced at Shelley in her rearview mirror and saw only pain rather than the bright sheen of love in her tearful gaze. "Love feels good, Shelley. Does Ricky ever give you anything but grief?"

They had reached the Pasadena Freeway, and after speeding along the first few miles of its serpentine curves, they came to the point where the traffic had backed up with people commuting to work. It would be slow going from here into town, but Aubrey had expected it. "You're an excellent assistant, Shelley," she complimented her sincerely, "but I can't wait for the day when you find the courage to bring your own dreams into reality. Then you'll finally let Ricky go, for Annie's sake as much as your own."

Shelley sent a wistful glance along the small houses backed up against the freeway. "I never knew my father and I do so want Annie to know hers."

"That's all well and good," Trisha interjected, "but a responsible, loving stepfather would be better for you both. What about Gardner? He's nearly as quiet as you are. Don't you like him even a little bit?"

Shelley wiped away the last threat of tears. "Don't be ridiculous, Trish. Gardner's in love with you."

Trisha swung all the way around in her seat. "You have got to be kidding. She's kidding, isn't she, Aubrey?"

Aubrey shot Trisha a knowing glance. "Well, I don't know if he's in love with you are not, but I think it's safe to say he has a very serious crush on you. Haven't you ever noticed how eager he is to sit beside you at lunch or bring you a soft drink during breaks?"

"He does that for everyone."

"True. He's very considerate," Aubrey agreed, "but just watch him today. Maybe if you weren't so busy flirting with all the men in the audience, you'd notice how he always looks after you first."

Trisha slumped down in her seat. "I'm so embarrassed I don't think I can even look at him today. He's very sweet, but not my type at all."

"He's male," Shelley offered, clearly believing that was all Trisha required.

Aubrey laughed, but Trisha wasn't the least bit amused. "I'm not that obvious, am I?"

Keeping a close eye on the slow-moving traffic, Aubrey nodded. "Yes, Trisha, I'm afraid you are." For a brief instant she was tempted to offer Jesse Barrett as an attractive alternative to Gardner, but at the last moment decided it wouldn't be wise. She really didn't know him well enough to recommend him to a friend, and even without being able to foretell the future, she sensed in him a chance to learn more about herself. Unwilling to give away that opportunity, she focused her attention on the day's seminar and urged her companions to do the same.

Harlan Caine tossed the Metro section of the newspaper across his desk to John Gilroy. "Waste the bitch, but don't be so goddamned messy this time. Be creative. Make it look like a freeway sniping or a gang shooting. If she has a pool, help her drown in it. Hell, steal a car and see she dies in a hit and run accident. Just get rid of her before she comes nosing around here. We've got the police stumped and I want them to stay that way."

As John read the article, his lips moved slowly as he silently pronounced each word. "What about the dude with her? You want him dead, too?"

"I've no quarrel with him. Just take care of her as soon as you can and make it look like an accident. I don't want anyone connecting her death to the Ferrells."

"I know some guys who make pornos. Maybe they'd kidnap her for a snuff film."

"We can't trust perverts like that. Take care of this your-self. I'm trusting you to handle it."

"Sure, boss, the next time Aubrey Glenn's name is in the paper it'll be her obituary."

"I can't wait to read it." Harlan laughed at John's joke. John was as loyal as an old dog. He was the perfect employee. It was a real shame he couldn't afford to keep him around much longer.

Chapter IV

When Aubrey arrived home that afternoon, Jesse's truck was still parked out front. With Trisha's continual sly innuendos and Shelley's propensity for tears, it had not been the best of days, and by the time she reached her back door, her temper was creeping dangerously near the boiling point. It was one thing for Jesse to ask to peruse her library, but quite another for him to make himself at home there.

"Jesse?"

"In here!" he called from the study. He hadn't realized it was so late and wore a puzzled frown as he looked up from the book he was reading. He had read *The Mind's Eye* first and was astonished to discover the first half was a revealing autobiography. He couldn't help but wonder what had prompted Aubrey to share so much of herself in the book, when she would admit so little in person.

She had written what he considered a damn good book which clearly described a troubled young woman's journey to personal fulfillment through creative imagery when the real people in her life failed to appreciate her needs. She didn't mention her husband by name, or explain why their marriage had failed, but that only made Jesse all the more curious about what had happened.

Aubrey found Jesse sprawled across a brown leather armchair with his feet propped on the matching hassock. He was surrounded by stacks of books in which he had left scraps of notepaper to mark items he wanted to discuss. "My goodness, it looks as though you've been busy." It was obvious he had put his time to good use rather than just lying out by the pool all day as she had suspected. She had not realized he might have the capacity for serious study and cautioned herself not to underestimate him again.

"I read your book this morning," Jesse informed her as he straightened up. He was about to rise when she dropped into the chair beside him.

"If you'd rather not offer an opinion, I'll understand," Aubrey suggested diplomatically.

Jesse was keenly interested in her private life, but chose to discuss the other aspects of her book first. "No, I really enjoyed it. Perhaps I was too preoccupied at the seminar to appreciate the similarities, but it wasn't until I read your comments on creative imagery today that I realized it was exactly what I used to do when I was competing in rodeos."

Aubrey sincerely doubted it. "You're not serious."

"Oh, but I am. All the guys do it. I'd say half the sport is mental, maybe even a higher percentage. You have to imagine yourself having the best ride of your life long before it's your turn."

"Really?" Aubrey stared at him, amazed to find he was sincere.

"Yes. There's no margin for error. People think riding a bull is a test of strength, but it isn't. If it were, the damn bull would win every single time. It's a matter of rhythm and balance and that's something the cowboy has to control. You can't control anything about the ride with your mind distracted by the noise of the crowd or some pretty girl you're trying to impress or thoughts of how you're going to spend the prize money. You'll find yourself lying in the dirt long before your eight seconds are up. You have to be totally focused on dominating the bull with all the style you can muster. It's something you rehearse in your mind again and again so when you actually do ride, the bull's beaten before he leaves the chute."

Aubrey could not help but be impressed. "I had no idea being a successful bull rider required anything more than endurance." And the stupidity to do it in the first place, she was too considerate to add.

"Endurance is a big help, believe me it is, but the most important factor is always mental."

"So what happened? Did you lose your concentration and get thrown the day you were injured?"

"No, I'd done real well that day. I won, as a matter of fact, but my glove got caught in my rope and I had to fight to get free. That's why I slipped. I should have made it to the ground on my feet easily, but instead, I landed on my ass and like they say, the rest is history. A bucking horse won't go out of his way to stomp a cowboy, but a bull will. A bull will keep coming after you again and again and his hooves are like meat cleavers and," Jesse watched the color fade from Aubrey's creamy complexion and thought better of continuing with such a vivid description.

"I was laid up a long while and couldn't get my timing back. I wasn't about to compete if I had no chance of winning. It would have been too hard after having been the World Champ three years straight."

"Why Jesse, you never mentioned you were a World Champion. I ought to call the *Times* and tell them, so they can identify you correctly when they print a retraction of today's story."

"Can you make them retract it?"

"I'm going to try. I'm not worried about being stalked by Pete's killers, but I don't want people contacting me for help in locating their missing relatives. Just think of all the runaways in the country. If parents thought I could find their kids, I'd be besieged with heartrending requests."

"I'd never thought of that."

Aubrey gestured toward the books that surrounded him. "It looks as though you've been busy."

Before Jesse could respond, they were interrupted by the doorbell. "Better let me get that," he warned.

"My number's not listed in the telephone book. There's no way someone could have found my home address unless I'd given it to them."

"I found it, didn't I?" Convinced she might be in real danger, Jesse followed Aubrey from the room. "Look to see who it is before you open the door."

"Worry wart," Aubrey complained, but she ducked into the living room to catch a glimpse of the visitor through one of the front windows. "Relax; we're not under attack."

Not wanting to intrude, Jesse hung back, thinking she would invite the caller to come in, but she didn't. He could hear a man's voice and, curious as to who he might be, he stepped down into the living room so he could also get a look at him through the window.

There was a new black BMW parked out front, and the dark-haired man on the doorstep looked as if he could easily afford to drive it. In Jesse's opinion, he looked too perfect, and he supposed the guy was a bank president or held some other suffocating executive job that required him to look like he had just stepped off the cover of *Gentleman's Quarterly*. Just the thought of wearing a suit and tie made Jesse gag. As Aubrey's voice took on a strident note, he was inspired to come to her defense no matter what had caused the argument between her and her well-dressed caller.

With a devilish chuckle, he tugged his shirttail out of his Levi's and with a yank, unfastened the mother of pearl snaps. Then, certain he was showing off enough bare chest to provoke the man if he had a romantic interest in Aubrey, he walked up behind her.

"You have some kind of a problem here, honey?" he asked nonchalantly. He rested his left arm on the doorjamb and struck a casual pose.

Aubrey knew exactly what Jesse was doing, and why, but it was scarcely called for in this instance. "Jesse Barrett, I'd like you to meet my ex-husband, Larry Stafford. Larry was just admiring your photo in the paper, but I'm certain he's thrilled to meet you in person."

Jesse stuck out his hand. "Pleased to meet you," he lied without the least effort to sound sincere. He was shocked by how handsome a man Larry was, but his eyes were so cold a gray they reminded him of marbles. He had never met a man with such a frosty gaze.

In return, Larry Stafford studied Jesse with a contemptuous glance that focused first on his casual apparel and then on his hairy chest. He grasped Jesse's hand only briefly and then cut him out of the conversation as though he didn't exist. He was holding the Metro section of the *Times* and shook it as he continued to argue with Aubrey.

"I don't know why I'm surprised by this, but for some reason I thought you'd have more sense than to become involved in crimes the police are unable to solve. Do you plan to begin reading palms next?"

Aubrey had very little patience where Larry was concerned, and he had already exhausted it. She straightened up proudly. "You no longer have a say in anything I do. How many times must I remind you of that?"

"You ought to be grateful that I don't charge you for my advice."

"I wouldn't pay the bill if you did," Aubrey responded smugly.

Delighted Aubrey could hold her own with her obnoxious ex, Jesse began to laugh. "Actually, we're thinking of franchising a string of tarot card parlors. Perhaps you'd like to invest. They're sure to be a veritable gold mine and you obviously have expensive tastes."

Larry's steel-gray eyes narrowed to menacing slits. "You couldn't possibly know what my tastes are."

Jesse slipped his arm around Aubrey's waist and pulled her close. "I'd say I've got a real good idea what pleases you."

Rather than respond, Larry sent an insolent glance roving over Jesse's muscular frame. When he finally lifted his eyes to Jesse's, his grin was mocking. "You might be surprised." He turned, then and left without bothering to tell Aubrey good-bye.

Aubrey walked back into the house, but the way Larry had looked at Jesse had made his skin crawl and he was too stunned to move for a moment. Finally, he closed the front door and followed her into the living room. "Is Larry gay? Is that why you're no longer married to him?"

Aubrey sat down on the sofa and folded her hands primly in her lap. "No. He's not gay. He was just playing with your mind, and it obviously worked. But please, I don't want to agrue with you about him."

"We're not arguing," Jesse denied. "I just asked you a simple question. You make only vague references to an unhappy marriage in your book. Now that I've met Larry, I'd really like to know what happened. Hell, I'd like to know why you married a man like him in the first place."

Aubrey bit her lower lip to force back the tears that thoughts of Larry always brought. "You've no right to ask such personal questions, Jesse. I think you'd better go."

"Oh no, I'm not going anywhere," Jesse promised as he walked around the sofa to face her. There was a slate-topped coffee table in front of the sofa and after deciding it would support his weight, he sat down on it opposite her. Easily capturing her knees between his own, he reached out and took her hands in a gentle clasp. "Neither of us is going anywhere for a good long while."

Aubrey wasn't afraid of Jesse, merely embarrassed to tears by the years she had wasted trying to please a man who had refused to be pleased. She shook her head and glanced away.

Jesse tightened his grasp. Aubrey was again wearing the calla lily ring, and he took care not to gouge the petals into her finger. "I want the truth, lady. All of it and right now."

Aubrey responded with a surprisingly defiant tear-brightened stare, but despite her stubborn effort to exclude him, Jesse knew he had every right to learn her secrets, even though he had known her only three days. On Saturday he had been prepared to dislike her quite thoroughly, but he had soon discovered that was impossible. She was far too exciting a woman to dislike, even if they did clash wills far too often.

"How do you reconcile the fact that you don't always practice the same open, caring attitude that you preach in your seminars?"

"It's not a question of not practicing what I preach," Aubrey insisted obstinately. "It's a matter of maintaining my personal privacy."

"The hell it is!"

Aubrey recoiled as though he had struck her, but she still didn't begin the tale he was so anxious to hear. Jesse was regarding her with the same hostile stare she had seen at the seminar, but this time she fully understood the cause. He challenged her constantly, but he had every right to hold opposing opinions. Still, she wasn't convinced she ought to trust him as completely as his demand required.

"All right," Jesse conceded. "I apologize for the foul language, but I was sorely provoked. Let's start over from where you got home this afternoon. How did your seminar go?"

Aubrey was surprised by his sudden change of direction, but gave him credit for at least attempting to understand her. "Corporations hire me to conduct stress reduction workshops for their executives. That's what we were doing today. My presentation is slightly different than the one you attended, but the message is essentially the same: what we can imagine, we can achieve. People impose a great deal of stress on themselves when they try to live up to the unreasonable expectations of others, rather than striving to fulfill themselves."

"That's certainly true," Jesse agreed, and his hold on her became a smooth caress across her palms.

The warmth of his touch was distracting, but too pleasant for Aubrey to want to pull free. "I encourage people to find their strengths by following their hearts. I help them stop making excuses and begin setting realistic goals. When people dare to live their dreams, they become far more relaxed and confident. Confident employees are more productive, and so the whole company benefits from my seminars."

Jesse nodded thoughtfully. "You're a very persuasive speaker, but I can't help but wonder what type of goals you've set for yourself. Do you hope to remarry someday and have a family?"

Aubrey smiled slightly. "Yes, of course I do."

"But I'm not what you had in mind, am I?"

His cocky grin was very appealing, but Aubrey refused to fall into the trap she was positive he wished to set. She leaned forward slightly and spoke in a husky whisper. "Has it never occurred to you that not all women want to fall into bed with every blond hunk they meet?"

"No, because that's impossible," Jesse scoffed, amused by the roundabout way she had chosen to pay him a compliment. "Besides, it's not me we're talking about here, but you. I still want the truth."

Aubrey sat back. "Let me see. Where was I? Oh, yes. We were discussing today's seminar. My part went rather well. Trisha has a date with one of the bank's vice presidents, but I believe everyone above teller has that title so it may not be as impressive as it sounds. Shelley's boyfriend cruised back into town, but he's a worthless slime who hasn't paid a nickel in child support for their daughter. As for Gardner, he just watched Trisha flirt her way through the men in the audience, but it was plain he was dying inside. Now is there anything else you'd like to know?"

"I know Trisha's a flirt, but I barely noticed Gardner. I'm surprised Shelley has a daughter. She looks as though she just graduated from high school."

"She's twenty-four, but her vulnerability makes her appear younger. She does the graphics for my brochures, and I'd hoped that working at the seminars would boost her confidence. Unfortunately, she's still painfully shy."

"Well, it's nice that you're concerned about her and your other employees. Now let's get back to your husband. He's obviously successful. Why didn't he make you happy? Tell me."

His relaxed manner invited her confidence, and yet she caught the faint hint of a threat in his voice. "Or else?" she asked.

Jesse gave a sly chuckle. "Oh, yes, or else I'm going to assume that all you need is a man who'll treat you like a woman and I'll make love to you right here on the sofa instead of taking you upstairs."

"You wouldn't dare," Aubrey hissed.

Jesse let go of her hands and released his silver belt buckle with one hand. "Try me."

Aubrey stared at the teasing light in his eyes. He wasn't threatening her with physical violence, but he was making a promise he looked determined to keep. If he made love as well as he kissed, then that was no threat at all, she realized with a small sigh of surrender. "All right, I'll talk."

"Smart girl."

Aubrey tried to find somewhere to focus her glance other than Jesse's taunting grin, but he was much too charming to ignore. "My book was purposely vague not only to guard my privacy, but to avoid a lawsuit from Larry. He's an extremely successful attorney. I was twenty-four and teaching art in high school when we met. He was thirty, and more sophisticated than any man I'd ever dated. I was too thrilled by his attentions to give his proposal more than a few seconds consideration. We drove to Las Vegas and were married that very night."

When Aubrey suddenly fell silent, Jesse encouraged her to continue. "Come on, you're just getting to the good part. Don't stop now."

"I should make some tea or something."

"You can't be that thirsty. Just tell me what happened. Couldn't he get it up on your wedding night?"

"He had no trouble at all," Aubrey shot right back at him. "It was just that he was always very mechanical, as though he were following a script. Trial attorneys tend to have a theatrical nature, and he was as slick in the bedroom as he was in a courtroom, but there's a vast difference between technique and honest emotion."

That remark hit Jesse real close to home because it fit his relationships with women as well. He didn't like that fact at all. "I can understand that," he managed to say, consoling himself that he had never received a complaint from any of the women he had taken to bed. Of course, it was highly possible none of them had possessed the brains to make the comparison Aubrey just had.

Aubrey was beginning to feel a little sick to her stomach. Certain Jesse wouldn't believe that excuse, she hurried to finish her story. "He had been wonderfully attentive while we were dating, but once we were married, he became increasingly distant. He was never openly critical, but he managed to find fault with everything I did. He would say, 'Oh, you're wearing the blue dress to the party? I'd hoped you'd wear the green.' He would never mention a preference before I was dressed, however.

"At first I did my best to please him, but the harder I tried, the less success I achieved. I was attempting to live out his fantasy of the perfect wife, you see, and it just wasn't me. We appeared to have the perfect marriage, but I felt abandoned. I didn't know what I'd done wrong, or to whom to turn."

"Until you chanced upon creative imagery and wrote *The Mind's Eye?*"

"Yes. Larry dismissed my book as New Age nonsense and didn't bother to read the manuscript. By the time it sold, I'd seen our marriage for the sham it was and asked for a divorce. I'd intended to return to teaching until my book became a surprise bestseller.

"Larry blamed my sudden success and the pressures of his job for our problems and begged me to give our marriage another try. I had loved him dearly once and thought I should, but the very next week he mentioned how disappointed he was that I wasn't content simply being his wife, and we were right back where we had started. I saw his attempt to manipulate my thoughts and emotions for the abuse it was, left the house we had shared, and never went back. My parents were planning to move, so I bought this place from them and came home."

Aubrey looked down at her hands and realized they were trembling badly. "You were right when you teased me Saturday night about not going out much. I haven't dated at all since the divorce. Conducting seminars keeps me from being lonely, and quite frankly, I think it will take a long while for the disillusionment of my failed marriage to fade."

Jesse reached out to tilt her chin and forced her to meet his gaze. "There's no reason for you to be ashamed to tell that story. Larry wanted a cardboard cutout of a woman, not one who could think on her own, let alone one who believes in following her heart. Now when a kid falls off a horse, he's always told to get right back on again so he's got no time to be afraid. After such a lousy marriage, I don't blame you for avoiding men for a while, but it's high time you got back in the game. Come on, let's go upstairs. Someone else might come to the door and I don't want to give them an eyeful."

When he pulled her to her feet, Aubrey panicked. "Oh no, you can't expect me to regard making love to you as therapy."

"Why not? It sounds like a hell of an idea to me."

"NO!" Aubrey yanked her hands from his. "I divorced a man for trying to make me into something I'm not, and I'm nowhere near ready to make love to you." There was such little room between the sofa and coffee table she couldn't get by him. She glanced over her shoulder and wondered if she could leap over the back of the sofa without falling on her face.

"Hey, take it easy," Jesse called softly. He drew her into his arms but his hold was feather light. "If you're not in the mood, all you have to do is say so. Fortunately I'm always in the mood, so whenever you feel the time is right, we're sure to connect.''

His shirt was still open, and Aubrey found the warmth of his bare chest beneath her cheek as reassuring as his words. He smelled very good. The first time he had pulled her into his arms they had been outdoors and she hadn't noticed he wore such an intoxicating scent. Damn the man, she cursed silently. Why did he have to be not only handsome, but so wonderfully understanding? An amorous cowboy was the last thing she needed on that, or any other afternoon.

"I'm all right," she assurred him as she moved to the side.

Jesse released her instantly. "Make yourself some tea. I'll go to my aunt's house and get my things."

"What things?"

"You want a list? Let's see, there's my clothes, and—"

"You are not moving in here, Jesse Barrett." Aubrey put her hands on her hips, her mood instantly turning defiant.

"Look, this was your parents' house. Glenn is your maiden name. It's not going to take the killers any great amount of time to find out where you live. If you think I'll leave you here all alone, when you don't even have an alarm system or a dog that could bite anyone higher than the ankles, you're just plain crazy.

"As I see it, I placed your life in jeopardy by taking you over to Pete's house, and I'm not going to leave you to face the consequences alone. We don't have to sleep together if you don't want to. Just think of me as a bodyguard. We can keep our relationship strictly professional. That's what you want, isn't it?"

"Yes," Aubrey was quick to assure him. "But you can't live here indefinitely. If the police haven't been able to prove there has been a murder, much less catch the culprits, how do you think we're going to do it?"

"I don't know yet, but I've got a line on several interesting possibilities. I'll tell you all about them later. Now lock the door after me and don't let anyone else in before I get back. Just leave all the books where I left them so I can find what I want to show you."

In the space of three days' time, Aubrey's well-ordered life had gotten completely out of control. As she stood at the front window and watched Jesse drive away, she feared things were going to become a lot more complicated before they improved. It had begun so innocently, with a cowboy turning up in her seminar, but a sinking sensation filled the pit of her stomach as she recalled the chilling photograph of the Ferrells. That had been imagery of the very worst sort, and she didn't want any repetition of it.

While she hadn't admitted it to Jesse, she frequently let herself dwell on sharing the future with a man. She had given him all the traits of good character, but had purposely kept his physical appearance vague because any creation of a particular ideal would exclude men who might better fulfill her desires. A swaggering Brahma bull rider was absolutely out of the question, however.

She went into the kitchen to brew some soothing herbal tea, but as she sat down to sip it, her mind filled with taunting images of a blue-eyed cowboy with a wicked grin. Some bodyguard he would make! She might be in far greater danger from him than from the murderers he was so determined to catch.

"We'll just have to solve the crime and send him home," she promised herself, but she had little faith that they could succeed when their only clue was a ghastly photograph she refused to view a second time.

Chapter V

Jesse returned to Aubrey's within the hour, stowed his gear in the den downstairs, and joined her in the kitchen. She had an assortment of greens spread out on the counter at the end of the cooking island and was making a colorful salad, but he wanted something more substantial and quickly surveyed the contents of the refrigerator. When all he found were fruits, vegetables, juices, whole grain breads, and nonfat milk, he closed the door with a careless shrug.

"Don't bother making a heap of that healthy stuff for me. I'll order us a pizza."

Aubrey had resigned herself to having his company, but that didn't mean she would alter her eating habits. She continued ripping up bits of lettuce. "I prefer to have a salad in the evening, but go ahead and order whatever you'd like for yourself."

"If I make it a cheese pizza, will you share it?"

"I seldom eat cheese because it has too much fat, so order whatever you want."

She had set the kitchen table for two, but occupying the same space and sharing a meal were two entirely different things in Jesse's view. "I'll make you a deal. I'll eat some salad, if you'll take a slice of pizza."

Aubrey was amused by his effort to strike a bargain, but saw no reason to agree. "Salads are filled with delicious nutrients, while the only nutritional value in a pizza is in the sauce and crust. In fact, eating high-fat meats like pepperoni or sausage and cheese could actually contribute to a slow form of suicide."

Jesse was used to women watching their weight, but he thought Aubrey was taking her choice of food to obnoxious extremes. "What if I order a pizza topped with mushrooms, olives, bell peppers, and just barely sprinkled with cheese?"

"Well, that would be a significant improvement," Aubrey agreed reluctantly.

Jesse grabbed the telephone to place his order before she qualified her answer. The pizza arrived as quickly as the company promised, and while Jesse would have preferred Canadian bacon or Italian sausage, he was too hungry to regret his compromise. Aubrey had a fat-free ranch dressing that enhanced the flavor of the salad sufficiently to make it palatable, and as he bit into his first slice of pizza, he decided the vegetarian special wasn't half bad.

Aubrey took only a single slice of pizza and began with her salad. She hadn't invited anyone to have dinner at her house for a long time, and it was rather nice having company again. Still, she didn't really believe she needed a bodyguard and hoped after Jesse followed her around for a couple of days, he would be bored witless and go home. She took a sip of water and struggled to find a subject for conversation that wouldn't lead directly to an argument.

As soon as Jesse had taken the rough edge off his appetite, he explained his day's explorations. "I looked through the books you'd mentioned in *The Mind's Eye*, but I didn't find much on ESP, so I searched through your bookshelves. I found a volume from the Time/Life series on the *Mysteries of the Unknown* that has a test for ESP. It uses cards with symbols and is supposed to be an accurate test of psychic ability. Have you ever taken it?"

"Yes, but it was nearly a year ago, and my score was lower than what anyone would correctly identify by chance."

Jesse appeared perplexed. "How can that be possible?"

"To score lower than chance? Well, I suppose it requires some sort of talent, but obviously not the one we're looking for."

"That's discouraging," he murmured between bites. "After dinner, let's make a set of the symbol cards and try it again."

"Jesse, really. Please don't get your hopes up." Or anything else she thought to herself. She took a quick mouthful of salad to hide her smile, tickled by the joke she dared not speak aloud.

"Did you try the test with Trisha?" When Aubrey nodded, Jesse assumed she had been distracted by her vivacious assistant. "That's reason enough to take it again."

Aubrey couldn't imagine why, but his scowl provided a ready glimpse into his reasoning. She rested her fork on the side of her plate. "You don't like her for some reason?"

Jesse shrugged slightly. "She's just not my type is all. I'm too tall to go for petite women. I'm afraid I might inadvertently suffocate one with an enthusiastic hug."

There wasn't even a hint of clumsiness in any of Jesse's actions, so Aubrey thought the danger of his killing a woman with affection extremely remote. "I thought we were talking about ESP testing. Can't you think of women as anything other than sex objects?"

Jesse groaned as though he had been harpooned. "Oh, please. You can't expect me to willingly admit to being a male chauvinist."

"I think you already have." Aubrey picked up her slice of pizza and bit off the tip. She couldn't recall the last time she had eaten a pizza, and layered with vegetables, this one was awfully good. "Where do you suppose a person gets a preference for a certain physical type? I've never understood it myself. I don't want to be limited by some absurd preconception of perfection when an attractive appearance can mask hideous character flaws."

Their conversation had taken such a dark turn, Jesse began to suspect Larry Stafford had not simply been controlling, but physically abusive, as well. He also sensed this was not an appropriate time to pursue such a personal line of questioning. *A warning from my intuition,* he recognized with a surprising burst of satisfaction. He had a hunch now and then which proved to be correct, but they occurred too seldom to be of much use.

He watched Aubrey finish her salad and was grateful she didn't glance up before he had thought of a response. "American men are programmed from infancy to lust after leggy blondes, although I've always harbored a weakness for redheads," he admitted with a sly grin.

Aubrey ignored his last remark rather than encourage him. "You believe our preferences are due to media influences then, rather than innate?"

Jesse winked at her. "Sure. Boys are bombarded with sexual stereotypes from the time they're old enough to notice mommy doesn't look like dad. It's no wonder the swimsuit issue of *Sports Illustrated* is their biggest seller, but damn few women live up to that ideal. But what about women? Fabio has no shortage of fans, but not many men are bodybuilders, and maybe the few who are can't carry on a decent conversation."

On a roll, Jesse gestured with his fork. "What type of man fulfills your fantasies?"

Aubrey had to finish chewing another bite of pizza

before she replied. "Are you asking if I have a dream lover?" Jesse nodded, encouraging her to go on. She laughed to herself and then made a halting confession. "I've always been partial to the Indians in films. Now that they're hiring Native Americans to play those parts, they're even more appealing."

She glanced away for a moment. "There's something about a tall, lean man with golden skin and a wild mane of ebony hair that's incredibly sexy. I can't say that I've ever met such an individual, but still, if a film has lots of handsome Indians, then I'll definitely go to see it."

"Ah yes, the noble savage," Jesse agreed. "What sort of horse does your favorite brave ride?"

"I've never really thought about a horse, but a black and white pinto would be nice."

Aubrey's eyes had taken on a lively sparkle, inspiring Jesse to continue. "Does your Indian wear a warbonnet that trails eagle feathers to his moccasins?"

"No. Warbonnets are certainly impressive, but it would cover his hair and prevent it from whipping about his shoulders as he rode across the plains."

"He'd be hunting buffalo with a lance, I suppose?"

Jesse was studying Aubrey's reactions much too closely, but for once she didn't mind and smiled warmly. "What else?"

Suddenly the thought of her riding double on any man's horse annoyed Jesse so badly he brought their game to an abrupt close. "I don't know, maybe a rampaging herd of prairie dogs. Would you like more pizza? If not, do you have any notecards we could use to make a deck to test your ESP?"

It was Aubrey who felt like groaning now, but she suppressed the frustrated moan. "Are we back to that?"

Jesse assured her that they were, got up, and carried

their plates to the sink. "I'll help you clean up later. Let's do the test first."

"No. Let's clean up now. As I see it, this is my kitchen, and I make the rules," Aubrey insisted firmly. She left the table and wrapped the last of the pizza in foil before placing it in the refrigerator. She then donned a pair of rubber gloves and rinsed off their plates, glasses, and utensils.

"Do you always wash your dishes before placing them in the dishwasher?"

Jesse stepped out of her way as she pulled open the door and placed each into the appropriate slot or rack.

"Of course. It might not be necessary, but I don't want to leave globs of cheese crusted on the plates."

"God forbid."

Aubrey wiped off the counter. Jesse's expression made it plain he considered washing the dishes twice sheer lunacy, but she doubted he did his even once. "Do you use paper plates at home?"

"No, of course not. I have nice dishes and a woman to take care of them."

Aubrey yanked off the gloves and draped them over the edge of the sink. She hadn't stopped to consider what Jesse's home situation might be, but obviously his aunt didn't realize he lived with someone. She felt a twinge of jealousy and, sickened by the bitter sensation, endeavored to hide it.

"Is she a particular woman, or just any female passing through?"

Jesse was delighted that she cared enough to ask. "Lupe's been my housekeeper for years. Both she and her husband work for me. I told you I owned a ranch. Did you think I handled all the chores alone?"

Aubrey swept him with an admiring glance. From the tips of his boots to his sun-bleached curls, he appeared to be thoroughly capable. "You look as though you could handle whatever challenges ranching might entail."

"Yeah, I probably could, but I'd be worn out long before sundown. Now where are those notecards?"

Aubrey hadn't been intentionally attempting to distract him from exploring whatever slight ESP she might have, but she was sorry he had remained so firmly focused. She went into her study, and found a pack of watermelon-pink index cards. When she returned to the kitchen, she reached for the ruler and scissors she kept handy.

"The 4 by 6 cards are really too large. Let's cut these in fourths."

"You measure and mark the lines, then I'll cut," Jesse offered. "We'll have to draw the symbols in pencil, otherwise you'll be able to see them through the back of the card, and that will completely defeat our purpose."

Aubrey had such little faith in their experiment, she doubted it mattered how they created the symbols. Within a few minutes, they had their improvised deck cut and drew five of each symbol: a cross, circle, square, wavy line, and star. Jesse shuffled the small cards, then laid them in front of Aubrey face-down in five rows of five.

"The directions in the book simply say to concentrate on a card and record your impression," Jesse reminded her. He grabbed a notepad from beside the telephone and picked up the pencil already on the table. "Just call out the symbols, and I'll write them down."

Aubrey stared at the cards, but because she did not want a repeat of the horrible sensation she had felt while viewing the photograph of the Ferrell family, she was too uneasy to produce the necessary level of concentration. All too aware of Jesse's expectant glance, she lifted her hands to rub the day's tension from her shoulders. "Give me a minute, and then I'll get started."

Jesse rose to his feet. "I'll help you relax." He moved

behind her chair, waited for her to drop her hands into her lap, and then rested his hands on her shoulders. He used a light, easy touch, but feeling just how tense she was, he began to knead her muscles with his thumbs. "You're supposed to be an expert on stress reduction. How do you usually relax when you get home? Do you imagine colorful fields of wildflowers, or that renegade Indian tearing across the plains on his pinto?"

"Neither, actually." Aubrey closed her eyes and leaned into his soothing caress. Jesse had taken her hand several times, so she had known his touch would be pleasant, but the warmth of his fingertips was absolutely blissful now. It had been so long since a man had touched her body, or emotions. Too long.

"Sometimes I swim," she revealed in a contented whisper.

Jesse leaned down and, inspired by the sweetness of her smile, kept coaxing the stiffness from her neck and shoulders. He was tempted to offer a full body massage, but feared he would be pushing his luck. "I used to be so sore after competing in rodeos that rather than a leggy blonde, my ideal woman was an amorous chiropractor."

"Did you find her?"

Jesse replied with a deep chuckle. "Not yet."

Aubrey let her head drop forward. Larry had never given her backrubs, and she was thoroughly enjoying Jesse's attentions. She could not recall the last time she had been pampered by a man with slow hands, and it felt so good she soon began to crave even more. That she could be so starved for affection a backrub at her kitchen table turned her on embarrassed her terribly. When Jesse's thumb grazed her throat, she shivered clear to her soul and quickly straightened up.

"Thank you. That really felt good. Now let's give the cards a try."

Jesse had been enjoying himself, too, but slid back into his seat without complaining that he was a long way from through. "Any time. Maybe you ought to touch the cards rather than simply look at them. Perhaps you're only able to sense impressions by holding an object, and that's why you didn't do better with Trisha."

"I suppose that's possible." Aubrey laid her fingertips on the first card and closed her eyes to heighten whatever awareness she might possess. "It's a star, I think." She moved on to the next one. "A circle, then a wavy line, another star, and a square."

Aubrey paused to make certain Jesse was keeping up with her. He had drawn the figures in a row, and satisfied his tally was accurate, she continued touching the cards and offering what were really no more than wild guesses about their symbols. When she reached the final card, she waited for Jesse to record it, then turned over the first to check the symbol.

"Let's see how I did. Oh no, it's a circle, and I thought it was a star."

The second card was a square, and she had called it a circle, but she had correctly identified the wavy line and star in third and fourth place. She was wrong again about the last card, however. "I only got two right." Positive she had just confirmed a total lack of ESP, she sat back in her chair.

"Don't apologize yet," Jesse urged. "Let's score the whole set before we add up the number correct."

Still considering him overly optimistic, Aubrey turned over the cards in the second row and found she had made only one correct guess there. She had identified three symbols correctly in the third row, however, one in the fourth, and two in the last for a total of nine correct choices. "Well, what do you think?" she asked Jesse.

"I think nine is damn good," he said. "That's nearly double what you would have gotten merely from chance."

"It was another fluke is all. Let's repeat the test. I'll bet if we do it five times, we'll find my average is much lower."

"Don't downplay your ability," Jesse ordered. "Imagine yourself as the world's most talented psychic, and you'll probably boost your score this time." He quickly shuffled the cards and replaced them face-down in front of her.

"Maybe I need a turban like Johnny Carson's Karnac the Magnificient."

Jesse grabbed his Stetson from the chair where he had left it and plunked it on her head. It fell down over her eyes, but he quickly adjusted the fit so that she could see. "There, now you're Aubrey the Magnificient and you're about to do amazing things."

"I'll be more amazed than you if I do." She had great faith in creative imagery, but that involved fanciful inner visions of dashing Indians, or whatever else might strike her fancy. Attempting to read what couldn't be seen was completely out of her realm of expertise, as she fully expected this ESP test to show.

She scored ten matches on her second try, then fell to eight accurate responses on the third. She recovered and identified eleven correctly on the fourth, and ten for a second time on the final try. She removed the Stetson and watched as Jesse added her scores and computed the average.

"Nine point six is much better than I did in the earlier test. Maybe touching the cards is the key. Why don't you try it?"

Jesse gave the cards a lazy shuffle. "You're the one who saw the murder in the Christmas photo."

Aubrey reached for the pencil and tapped it on the table in a distracted rhythm. "In my seminars, I encourage people to stop giving excuses and put their energy into making their dreams come alive. You described an eerie sensation when you handled the photograph, so you must possess some ESP, too."

"Maybe you ought to lay out the cards." Jesse handed her the deck. He sat back in his chair, folded his arms over his chest, and waited while she arranged them in front of him. He closed his eyes to get focused, then peeked up at her through his lashes. "Don't I get a backrub, too? Maybe that's what boosted your score."

Aubrey hesitated a moment, then left her chair and rested her hands on his shoulders. He hadn't touched her hair, but she ruffled the curls dipping over his collar. 'You're already relaxed, Jesse. You don't need me to do this."

"You're wrong. I do," he assured her softly.

Aubrey had no way to refuse, but the warmth radiating through his shirt soon made her long to touch his bare skin. He had precisely the lean, muscular body she had described for her Indian fantasy, and it took no effort at all to strip him nude in her mind. She drew in a deep breath and released it slowly, but the usual relaxation techniques failed to quell her desire.

It was fast becoming impossible for Aubrey to concentrate on what she was doing, and when Jesse reached up to catch her hand and brought it to his lips, she lost all hope of delivering a friendly massage. He placed a kiss in her palm, then ran his tongue through the center. She shivered and quickly pulled free of his grasp.

"Stop it. That tickles," she complained. She scratched her palm, but the delicious sensation refused to fade. She reached out for her chair, meaning to sit down and put a safe distance between them, but Jesse pulled her down on his lap and caught her lower lip between his teeth in a light, teasing bite.

He released her with a low moan and then wrapped

his arms around her tightly. "I'd like to be more than a bodyguard," he murmured against her hair.

Only that afternoon he had offered a strictly professional relationship, but he hadn't kept his vow for a single day. He was bright, attractive, and his easy affection was so tempting Aubrey ached to agree, but she wanted more from a man than a few days' loving. The instant Jesse relaxed his hold, she hurriedly slid off his lap.

"Let's do your test another time," she suggested as she began to back away. "Conducting seminars wears me out and I'd like to go up to my room."

She didn't look tired, though—she looked terrified. Jesse cursed under his breath. "I'm sorry if I was out of line."

He sounded sincere, but his expression was a long way from contrite. Trisha would have been all over him by now, but Aubrey wouldn't settle for a casual affair that would end as quickly as it had begun. She shook her head. "No, you're not sorry at all," she told him and, unable to remain with him a moment longer, she left him to entertain himself for the rest of the night.

She locked her bedroom door, kicked off her shoes, and began to pace with a long, restless stride. The anguish of longing for something she could not have was nothing new, but she had thought she had escaped that torment when she ended her marriage. She felt hollow, and knew sleep would not ease the emptiness in her heart.

She filled her days inspiring others to live their dreams, but she would sleep alone that night and awaken tomorrow with an all too familiar yearning for more. She ran a bubblebath and soaked in its fragrant warmth, but the image which filled her mind was of a cowboy's slow, sweet smile, and she knew she had been far better off daydreaming of black-eyed Indian braves racing across the plains.

* * *

Jesse was already up and dressed when Aubrey came downstairs the next morning. She was wearing a navy blue suit with bright white piping and matching spectator pumps. She looked extremely professional, but he saw the faint shadows beneath her eyes and knew she had not slept any better than he had. He had already set the table, poured the juice, and was heating water in the tea kettle.

"I'm coming with you today," he announced in a voice that brooked no argument.

Aubrey raised her hands in an emphatic gesture of refusal. "Absolutely not. It takes a great deal of planning and effort to make my seminars appear to unfold at a relaxed pace, when in fact they're carried out on a strict schedule. You'd merely be in the way." The subject closed, she went to the cupboard and removed a plastic container filled with a popular whole grain cereal.

Jesse blocked her path when she crossed the kitchen to get a bowl. "Just introduce me as one of your assistants. Gardner could use some help setting up, and I can run the machine to copy tapes as easily as he can. I don't know what you're paying him, but you work him twice as hard as you do Trisha and Shelley."

"I do not, now get out of my way."

Rather than obey, Jesse reached into the cupboard and handed her a ceramic bowl for her cereal. "You take advantage of him," he insisted. "He arranges the chairs, totes the boxes of journals, and if there's anything heavy to be moved, you call on him. Then the poor guy has to handle the sound system, make recordings, duplicate tapes, and keep the money for them straight. I noticed the fond glances he sent Trisha's way on Saturday, so on top of everything else, he's working under the handicap of a broken heart. He needs an assistant almost as much as you need a bodyguard."

"Do you honestly believe that I could be attacked in a bank building? Wells Fargo has excellent security, and I'll be at absolutely no risk." Aubrey pulled open the refrigerator and removed the carton of nonfat milk.

Jesse had brought in the paper and, not giving in, he waved the Metro section. "If you called the *Times,* they didn't bother to print a retraction, so you're still neck-deep in the Ferrells' disappearance."

Aubrey filled her bowl with cereal, added milk, and carried it to the table, where she sat down and grabbed a napkin. "I called, but because all the *Times* had reported was that I was at your cousin's house, which I was, there's nothing for them to retract. At least that was their view."

"Did you give them my name?"

Aubrey nearly choked on her first bite of cereal. When she caught her breath, she waited until Jesse had joined her at the table. He was wearing Levi's and a navy blue shirt with a cavalry-style bib front. Certain it was no accident, she regretted telling him how much she admired Indians.

"While I know you must be disappointed in my failure to arrange any free publicity for you, I didn't want to get the killers off my trail by putting them on yours."

Jesse nodded appreciatively. "Thanks. It will make my job easier if they don't know my name. You want some toast?"

Aubrey took a long sip of cranberry juice. "Yes, please. Two slices, but I don't use butter, just jelly. Regardless of how helpful you are, I still don't want you coming with me today."

"Not only am I coming along, I'm going to drive your Volvo." Jesse left the table to fix the toast, but he knew the instant he returned Aubrey would start in on him again.

For the life of him, he couldn't imagine why he was looking forward to it.

Trisha knocked before coming in the back door. "Anybody home?" she called out.

"I left the door open for her," Jesse told Aubrey, "but don't leave it unlocked when you're here alone."

"I was doing just fine before I met you."

"Sure you were," Jesse teased, clearly unconvinced. "Morning, Trish. How was your date with the banker?"

Trisha saw Jesse spreading jelly on toast and Aubrey scanning the headlines on the *Times*. They looked like a superbly happy couple to her, and she knew instantly that Aubrey hadn't told her the truth about the weekend. She sat down at the table and smiled happily. "The banker's okay, a little on the conservative side, but that's to be expected, I suppose. It looks as though you two are getting along well."

Aubrey glared at her assistant. "We are barely speaking," she confided, "and Jesse has the absurd notion that I need him to come with us today."

"Great. I think having another man along is a terrific idea. You can help Gardner, Jesse. He's always swamped."

"Trish!" Aubrey picked up her bowl and carried it over to the sink. "Forget the toast. We're running late, and—"

"Well, if you aren't going to eat this, I will," Jesse replied. "Are we late, Trish?"

"No. We've plenty of time."

Trisha's sassy smile made Aubrey want to puke. "Need I remind you who signs your payroll checks?" she asked pointedly.

"We've always been like a family," Trisha reminded her.

Having finished the toast, Jesse rinsed off his hands. "Every family needs a black sheep, so it looks as though I can serve a useful purpose after all."

Aubrey eyed him with a cold stare, then decided because he was so insistent about accompanying her, she would agree, but as soon as she opened the seminar, she would call on him to relate what an important factor creative imagery had been in his career. She was taking a chance he might enjoy the attention, but with an audience of bankers, it was far more likely that he would make a complete fool of himself. Still appearing reluctant, she nodded slightly.

"All right. Come along if you must. I'll even let you drive, but you've got to promise you'll be a real help rather than merely in the way."

Jesse gave a mock bow. "Your servant, ma'am."

"This is going to be fun!" Trisha enthused.

As he straightened up, Jesse captured Aubrey's gaze and held it. He intended to make himself indispensable, and then he would lure Aubrey out to Pete's house for another try at discovering some much-needed clues. He hadn't pushed her to test her ESP simply to pass the time. He needed her in several important ways, but for the time being, he would let her assume his only concern was her safety.

Chapter VI

John Gilroy walked the German shepherd through Aubrey's neighborhood for half an hour before turning down her street. Dressed in khakis, a dark green windbreaker, and Raiders baseball cap, he drew no attention from the locals. He gave a warm greeting to an Asian woman struggling with a brown-faced Akita, and an elderly gentleman strolling with a honey-colored cocker spaniel, but hurried on before their leashes became entangled in his.

Several joggers ran by, but they gave his dog a wide berth and took little notice of him. He nodded politely to a woman clad in her bathrobe who had come outside to pick up the morning paper. He moved with a brisk stride, for all appearances a man out for exercise before leaving for work, but he didn't miss a single detail that might prove useful.

As he neared Aubrey's home, he made a mental note of every tree and hedge where a man might conceal himself. With a quick glance, he checked which neighbors had a clear view of her property from their front windows and which might only catch a glimpse of her house from the side. When he drew even with her driveway, he saw a Chevy truck with red and white Arizona plates parked just outside her garage. He remembered it from the *Times* photo and figured it must belong to the man he was supposed to avoid.

The dog paused to sniff a jacaranda's exposed roots, and not wanting to loiter outside Aubrey's house, John gave him only a few seconds to enjoy the mingled scents of the neighborhood's other canines. A pale green Geo Metro was parked at the curb, but he doubted it belonged to Aubrey Glenn. That meant there were at least three people in the house that morning. He hadn't counted on her having so many visitors.

He gave the dog's leash a quick yank and continued on down the sidewalk. The fact that the neighborhood was so damn quiet would make it difficult to do anything imaginative, but he was still confident he would erase Aubrey Glenn's name from his boss's list of worries in no time at all.

Jesse followed Aubrey's directions to Shelley Sandler's house. It was one of eight small bungalows built around a central courtyard. The exterior had been repainted recently a sunny yellow with white trim and it looked as cute as the day the first resident had moved in in 1922. Shelley, however, looked hopelessly forlorn as she came walking out to the car with her head bowed.

Aubrey turned toward her as she slid into the back seat. "Is Ricky giving you a bad time?"

Confused by Jesse's presence, Shelley responded with a questioning glance, and she didn't relax when Aubrey assured her he was merely serving as their chauffeur.

"Annie stayed at my mother's last night to give us a chance to talk. He wants us to get back together."

"Well, you sure don't look happy about it," Trisha observed pointedly. "Is he finally ready to settle down and get a job to support you and Annie?"

Shelley shrugged slightly and pulled the collar on her pink sweater up around her throat. "He says he has something in the works."

Jesse couldn't bear to see anyone as miserable as Shelley appeared to be. "Excuse me if I'm speaking out of turn, Ms. Sandler, but this Ricky of yours doesn't sound like much of a catch for a young woman as pretty as you. He had to support his child, but—"

"Ricky claims Annie isn't his," Trisha informed him. "That proves what a prince he is."

Jesse glanced over at Aubrey, who simply shook her head in disgust. He knew Shelley had to put her own life in order, but he couldn't resist offering another bit of advice. "You're bright and have a good job with Ms. Glenn. There's no reason for you to let anyone in your life who doesn't make you happy."

Shelley sighed sadly. "I know, but I've loved Ricky since we were in the seventh grade."

"And he denies your daughter is his?" Jesse asked incredulously.

Shelley hugged her oversized purse to her chest. "He knows that she's his. He just isn't ready for the responsibility of raising her is all."

"Then he sure as hell wasn't ready to make love to you," Jesse swore. "Can't your father talk some sense into him?"

Exquisitely uncomfortable, Shelley sank down a little lower in her seat. "He died of cancer when I was twelve. Ricky was real sweet to me then. The other boys laughed at him for walking me home after school, but he didn't care."

"Well, at least he had some character at one time," Jesse mused aloud.

Trisha leaned forward. "Maybe he did, but that was before he started spending all his time boozing and getting high. Now he's completely worthless."

"Trisha, please," Aubrey scolded. "Shelley's well aware of Ricky's faults."

"Then why doesn't she do something about it?" Trisha countered.

Jesse was having a difficult time keeping one eye on the morning traffic and another on the pair in the backseat. Trisha was adamantly opposed to letting Ricky anywhere near Annie, while Shelley kept mumbling something about a father having the right to see his little girl. Jesse had heard one too many pretty young women swear they loved some weasel who never gave their feelings a moment's thought.

"Do you ever give seminars strictly for women?" he asked Aubrey. "You'd be performing a valuable service if you taught them how to recognize a decent man when he comes along so they don't waste their whole lives tagging along after some bum who probably can't even recall their name let alone their birthday, or anything else that matters to them."

Aubrey wondered what had inspired that hostile outburst. Clearly Jesse didn't see himself as that type of man, but she was certain he must have broken his share of hearts. Perhaps he was protesting too much. After all, he had come on to her with a haste that made it difficult to believe he used much restraint where women were concerned.

"Didn't you have groupies when you were on the rodeo circuit?" she asked.

Growing defensive, Jesse shot her an accusing glance. "Yeah. Plenty of them, but I never promised more than I intended to give. I was also extremely careful not to father any children. But if I had, I would never have denied they were mine."

The hushed silence in the back seat made it plain Trisha and Shelley were waiting for Aubrey's answer, but she didn't want to spar with Jesse in front of them. "That's commendable of you. I think you'd do just as well giving seminars on how to choose a man as I would. After all, my track record proves just how little expertise I have. Now let's abandon the personal topics in favor of concentrating on today's seminar. It should go according to plan, but let's not risk having it sound stale."

Jesse thought they could make better use of their time coaching Shelley to bolster her self-esteem, but fell silent as Aubrey and her assistants reviewed the day's exercises. When they reached the bank, he pulled into the underground parking, and Aubrey handed him a placard to place in the window which would allow them to park in a convenient spot for the entire day. As they walked toward the elevators, he could not help but notice the way Aubrey was eyeing his suede jacket. A natural golden tan, with long fringe dripping from the sleeves and yolk, it would have made an Indian proud.

"I bought this last year," he bent down to confide, "long before I met you or knew about your passion for Indians."

Embarrassed that she had ever mentioned it now, Aubrey forced a smile. "It's a handsome jacket. That was my only thought. Honest."

"Sure," Jesse replied with a knowing wink, and he thought Aubrey's resulting blush utterly charming.

The conference room where the seminar was being held was painted a stately forest green. The matching carpet and upholstered chairs also conveyed the impression of old money, but none of the executives gathered for the second day of Aubrey's stress reduction seminar was over thirty-five. Eager for the session to begin, they found their chairs as soon as she called them to order. Evenly divided between male and female, they were fashionably dressed in well-tailored suits or classic, slim dresses. They were well groomed, but gave the appearance of extras assembled for a commercial extolling the benefits of their institution's services, rather than real human beings with varied and distinct personalities.

Gardner had arrived first to set up the sound and recording systems. He looked surprised to see Jesse with Aubrey and her assistants, but welcomed his help when Aubrey explained he was there specifically to be useful. Gardner's horn-rims continually slid down his nose, but he gave them a quick nudge into place before he extended his hand.

"Have you worked with audio equipment in the past?" Gardner asked.

Jesse purposely turned his back to the bankers. "Never, but if you'll just tell me what to do, I'll be happy to give you a hand."

Before Gardner had the opportunity, Aubrey opened the session and he had to monitor the recording. She introduced Jesse and provided a flattering summary of his success on the professional rodeo circuit. "Mr. Barrett has been using creative imagery for years, and I'd like to call on him now to share some of his experience with you. Then I'm sure he'll be happy to answer whatever questions you might have."

Caught off guard and completely unprepared, Jesse nevertheless raised his right hand and sent Aubrey a lazy salute as he walked toward the front of the room. There had been plenty of time for her to ask him to speak as they rode into town, and that she had preferred to surprise him made him wonder if she had a malicious streak she kept well hidden. He glanced out at the three dozen men and women who were obviously at home in the corporate world and thanked them for their welcoming applause.

He hooked his thumbs in his belt and began to pace up and down slowly. "Ms. Glenn is absolutely right, but rather than rediscovering creative imagery as an adult as she did, you might say that I simply refused to allow the schools to suppress the lively imagination that is any child's natural birthright. I was born in Montana, in a town so small the people used to go down to the railroad station on Saturday nights in hopes someone interesting might be coming in on the train."

He paused and looked out at the crowd. "As far as I recall, no one ever did." He waited for a ripple a laughter to die down, then continued. "My father was a copper miner by trade, and when he decided he couldn't take another Montana winter, he moved my mother and me down to Arizona. The town wasn't much of an improvement when it came to excitement, but at least we enjoyed warmer winters. We had always kept a few horses, and so I knew how to ride almost from the time I could walk.

"Being the new kid in town, it took me awhile to make friends. Until I did, I'd go out riding alone and I'd make up adventures: pretend I was a U.S. marshal tracking desperados one day, and play a desperado's part the next."

Aubrey had wanted to put Jesse in his place, but his relaxed manner and gentle humor captivated her as quickly as it did the audience. As he explained how he had gotten into competing in junior rodeos, first riding bucking broncos, and later moving up to bulls, she thought his addition to the day's program definitely worthwhile. Then as he detailed how he had visualized each ride beforehand, she noticed how intently both Trisha and Shelley were watching him, and had second thoughts.

She already knew Trisha wasn't his type, but Shelley, while painfully shy, could easily be described as a leggy

blonde, and the possibility of her becoming involved with
Jesse was simply appalling. She could see it all in a flash
of brilliant clarity. Jesse would shower Shelley with attention, give her the confidence to finally jettison Ricky Vance,
and then leave for Arizona without a backward glance.
Shelley would be devastated, and she didn't deserve any
more heartbreak.

Jesse noticed Aubrey's slight frown and assumed he had
been talking too long. He ceased pacing, turned to face the
audience squarely, and tried to offer a coherent summary.
"Now you may think you've nothing in common with a
rodeo rider who's seen better days, but let me assure you
the very same imagery which kept me in the prize money
for a number of years can make your dreams come true.
You've got to want something so bad you can't simply taste
it, but catch the scent, and luxuriate in its silken texture.
It's not easy, and it forces you to make difficult choices,
but you can believe me when I say it's well worth the effort.
I own a ranch just outside Sedona to prove it, and I wish
you good luck in realizing your dreams."

Pleased with his presentation, if not Shelley's worshipful
gaze, Aubrey quickly moved to Jesse's side. "Thank you so
much. Are there any questions?"

An auburn-haired man in the second row raised his
hand. "Can you describe what it feels like to ride a bull?"

Jesse laughed. "Sure. Have you ever rolled your car?"
When several people nodded and groaned, Jesse offered
another image for those who hadn't. "If you've ever tossed
ice cubes into a blender to make Margaritas, you know
they get ground into mush. It's just that brutal, but I swear
I loved it, and it wasn't just the rush. It was also the joy of
knowing I could succeed at something few men have the
guts to try, and the bruises were a badge of honor."

An attractive brunette in the first row raised her hand.
"May I have your autograph, Mr. Barrett?"

"It's Jesse, and I'll be happy to give you one during the break."

The man beside her quickly asked, "What did your father think of your riding bulls?"

"He thought I was a damn fool, which I expect a lot of you must think, as well. It wasn't until I started winning prize money on a regular basis that he warmed to the idea. After I put myself through the University of Arizona and bought land for a ranch, he was very proud of me.

"I hope all of you are wise enough to know you can't live your parents' dreams. That attempt traps too many good people. Banking is a respectable profession, but don't let the money you're making keep you at a job you hate. You probably don't want to become rodeo riders, but don't wait until you reach retirement age to do what you'd love to be doing right now."

Aubrey saw the appreciative nods in the audience and hoped the entire group wouldn't be inspired to quit their jobs that very day. She asked for another round of applause for Jesse, then opened her portion of the seminar with a challenge for everyone present to connect as deeply with their dream as he had with his. "Open your journals and make a list of the things that bring you the greatest pleasure in life. Don't be embarrassed to put making love in first place. After all, it's wonderful for relieving stress, and that's what we're here to discuss."

Jesse walked back to Gardner's table where he found the sound engineer gaping at him as though he had just revealed he was an alien visitor from another galaxy. He lowered his voice to a conspiratorial whisper. "I'll bet impressing Trisha would be high on your list."

Jesse surveyed Gardner's frizzy hair, plaid shirt, knit vest, and baggy trousers with a reproachful gaze. He wasn't a bad looking young man, but he sure didn't do much with what he had.

"You could use some fashion advice, a good haircut, and contact lenses. Then I'll bet you'd be as good looking as the rest of the men here." That Jesse included himself in that catagory was plain in his teasing grin.

Gardner hurriedly busied himself checking out an extension cord. When he straightened up, his face was still flushed with embarrassment. "Who told you I liked Trisha?"

"Hell. No one had to tell me. I could see it every time you glanced her way."

Gardner gave a strangled moan. "I didn't know it showed."

"Don't worry about it. Now I've only seen Trisha a couple of times, but I can guarantee you she's the type who likes to chase men until they stop running. After work tonight, go to one of the big department stores and ask a clerk in menswear to help you pick out some new clothes. Tell them you have to look sharp for a job interview. Get your haircut and make an appointment with an optometrist for a pair of soft contact lenses. You won't even be able to tell you're wearing them."

Gardner was five foot ten if he stretched real hard, which he did. A runner, he had no problem with weight, but that didn't mean he was eager to take on a man Jesse's size. Still, he couldn't just stand there and calmly accept his criticism no matter how it was intended. "I don't believe that was the type of help Aubrey intended you to give."

"I never do anything halfway," Jesse confided softly. "Now, when the next seminar begins, I expect you not only to look like a new man, but to act like one, as well. You're going to ignore Trisha, and in no time at all, she'll be chasing you. Take your time about letting her catch you."

"I think you've ridden one too many bulls," Gardner replied. "That will never happen."

"Aren't you listening to anything Aubrey says? Practice a little creative imagery and make her your adoring slave in your mind. Just follow my advice and it will happen."

Grasping a sudden insight, Gardner turned the tables. "Is that what you're doing with Aubrey?"

Jesse moved back a step and, while his expression was still friendly, he refused to answer that question. "I think Aubrey is about to introduce the next segment. We'll have to talk later."

As soon as the morning break began, Jesse was surrounded by those who wanted him to sign their journals. He moved to one of the chairs in the front row and signed each book he was handed. It had been awhile since he had been asked for an autograph and he was ashamed by how quickly he had dashed them off in his glory days, never realizing how soon the adoration would end.

Shelley brought him a cup of coffee, and he was pleased by her smile. Thinking her work must distract her from her personal problems, he didn't realize he was the cause of her improved mood until Aubrey pointed it out at the lunch break. "Oh, Lord," he sighed. "Don't worry. She's just a kid, and I won't take advantage of her."

"I hope you won't," Aubrey replied. "But when a girl loses her father either through death or divorce, she often falls into a predictable pattern and pursues only distant men who'll abandon her. Ricky is a perfect example. He just divebombs her life, leaves her heartbroken and convinced that if only she tried harder, the next time he might stay."

Again Jesse got the uncomfortable feeling that his lack of interest in permanent commitments might be described in the very same way. "What are you saying? If I'm distant, she'll like me all the more?"

"I'm afraid so. Now I always bring my lunch, but you go on and catch up with the others. Yesterday everyone said the food in the bank's cafeteria was actually quite good."

"Are you just going to sit up here all alone?"

Aubrey was surprised by his dismay. "I enjoy having a few minutes to myself during a seminar. Now go on. Don't worry about me." She walked over to the table in the front of the room where she had left her purse and the canvas bag holding her lunch.

"Wait a minute," Jesse called and Aubrey turned back toward him.

"I don't want you staying in here alone. Is that what you did yesterday?"

"Yes. Obviously I survived unharmed." She sat down to enjoy a carton of nonfat lemon yogurt and several pieces of fresh fruit.

"I don't like this." Jesse hesitated a moment, then joined her at the table. "I'll stay with you, then go out for lunch when the others come back."

Aubrey was exasperated with him, but the firm set of his jaw warned her she would be wasting her breath to argue. He hadn't complained about the way she had forced him to speak without notice, and grateful her ulterior motive hadn't been transparent, she decided to allow him to win this one, and thanked him again. "The group enjoyed your contribution immensely. I don't want to sound as though I'm delivering these seminars by rote, and whenever I can add something new, I don't hesitate to do so. Thanks for being such a good sport about it."

After moving his chair away from the table slightly, Jesse stretched out his legs to get comfortable. "I didn't really have much choice now, did I? I didn't want to embarrass you, or myself, either."

Aubrey peeled an orange and offered him a section. "Somehow, I doubt that you ever embarrass yourself."

"Constantly," Jesse admitted. He slid the bite of orange

into his mouth and wiped his hands on the paper napkin Aubrey offered. He had not been in the kitchen when she packed her lunch, but it was plain from the scant amount of food she had brought that she had not intended to share it. He was too stubborn to let her get away with snubbing him, whatever her excuse.

"Let's get back to Shelley," he suggested. "I've no desire to be anything other than friendly. Will that turn her on?"

"Probably, but if she finds you attractive, maybe she'll realize she's outgrown Ricky Vance."

Jesse accepted another orange slice. "I think Gardner is more her type. Have they ever dated?"

"Gardner?" Aubrey thoughtfully considered the pair as a couple. "Unlike most work situations, my team and I are together only a few times a month, not every day, so I don't follow their personal lives closely. They have their friends, and I have mine. It's possible that Gardner and Shelley could have seen each other after the seminars, but if they have, I don't know about it."

"Trisha would know though, wouldn't she?"

"She might not be as observant as you think. She seemed shocked yesterday when Shelley mentioned that Gardner had a crush on her. He's an excellent engineer, by the way, but I'm afraid Trisha just dismisses him as a nerd."

"With good reason." Jesse took the half of an apple Aubrey handed him and chewed his first bite slowly. "You're probably wise to avoid getting involved in your assistants' lives, but what about all the people who read your book and attend your seminars? Do they expect to have a personal relationship with you?"

"Yes. They most certainly do. My publisher forwards fan mail, and I was completely overwhelmed with it at first. Because of the subject of my book, people were inspired to confide all sorts of intimate details of their lives and I thought the least I could do was offer an encouraging comment or two."

Jesse assumed she must have received a mountain of mail and, for some bizarre reason, his first thought was of her sitting on a high stool and using a quill pen like Bob Cratchett in Charles Dickens's *A Christmas Carol.* "Did you actually answer every letter personally?"

"I tried to at first, but it just got to be too much for me. Trisha was doing freelance secretarial work, and I hired her to help me handle my mail. She quickly convinced me that I need only respond with a postcard which had an illustration from *The Mind's Eye* on one side and a brief acknowledgment of their letter on the other. I still feel it's rather impersonal, but I know I can't become a close friend of everyone who reads my book."

"Will you settle for being mine?" Jesse asked.

He had tossed his Stetson aside as soon as he had come through the conference room door that morning, but he was still wearing his fringed jacket. The gleam in his eye as well as his choice of attire made it plain he wasn't really looking for anything as tame as friendship, and Aubrey wasn't certain how to respond. "You are a most unusual man, Jesse Barrett."

"And you are stalling, Ms. Glenn." He was tempted to lean over and kiss her, but delayed just a second too long and Gardner came through the door, ruining what little opportunity Jesse might have had to be more than a friend. He rose with a languid stretch.

"Show me how to copy the morning tape, and I'll get started on them," Jesse offered. He turned to smile at Aubrey. "Thanks for sharing your lunch."

Rather than being pleased by his courtesy, Aubrey was sorry she hadn't thought to bring something more for him.

Jesse had an annoying way of insinuating himself in her life, and she still didn't know quite what to make of him. He had seemed to be genuinely interested in her assistants' romantic dilemmas, and she could not help but wonder just what qualified him to be an expert on love.

When they returned to Aubrey's that afternoon, Jesse waited for Trisha to leave and then suggested a swim. "If that's how you usually relax, you needn't change your routine just because I'm here."

The air-conditioning at the bank had made the conference room positively chilly, but on the ride home they had been bathed in the late afternoon sun and it had been sufficiently warm to make the pospect of a swim enticing. "That does sound good. Did you plan to join me?"

"Sure, but I promise to stay on my side of the pool and swim laps so I won't be in your way."

Jesse had such an expressive glance, Aubrey had no difficulty whatsoever reading what was really on his mind. Still, she really did want to swim. "Do I have your word on it?"

Jesse raised his right hand. "It's your pool, ma'am. I'll have to abide by your rules."

Aubrey was tempted to present an extensive list of prohibitions, but knew it wouldn't do a bit of good. "Last one in the pool is a rotten egg," she said instead, and dashed for the stairs before the astonishment had left his face. She knew better than to wear the pink bikini, and after tossing her clothes aside, slipped on a modest aqua tank suit. When she reached the pool, Jesse was just leaving the cabaña wearing the swimsuit he had borrowed on Sunday, but with a running dive, she beat him into the pool.

Jesse had no idea what had inspired Aubrey's playful

mood, but considering it a great improvement, he slipped into the water in the shallow end and, as promised, began to swim with a carefully measured stroke. When he reached the other end of the pool, Guinevere ran up barking loudly. He flicked water in her face and waited for Aubrey to complete her second lap and also reach the deep end.

"Your hairy hound has a real short memory. I fed her this morning, but she acts as though I'm a complete stranger."

Aubrey called Guin over and hushed her indignant yaps. "She's an excellent watchdog, so I'll not scold her." Loving the gentle caress of the warm water on her skin, Aubrey turned away and again swam for the shallow end.

Aubrey was fast, but Jesse's greater size gave him the advantage and he easily beat her down to the end of the pool. When Aubrey began her turn, he caught her eye. "Want to race?"

Guinevere had run alongside the pool and was again barking furiously. "I think we just did," Aubrey called, hoping to be heard above her pooch. "Do you want to try for distance?"

While he was sorry she wasn't wearing the bikini, the way her wet tank suit was molded to her slender curves wasn't at all disappointing. "I don't think I can keep track of my laps," he admitted honestly.

"Then you lose, because I'll have no trouble keeping track of mine." Aubrey pushed away from the side and swam toward the deep end.

Jesse cursed under his breath, then decided all he had to do was float and let Aubrey wear herself out swimming. He didn't want to be too obvious about what he was doing, however, and began swimming up and down the pool at such a lazy pace he could have kept it up all night. When at last Aubrey paused to rest in the deep end, he came up beside her and tried to sound surprised.

"Are you quitting already? I've barely had time to warm up."

Aubrey hadn't been fooled by his relaxed pace. Crystal droplets clung to his lashes, brightening his gaze, but she saw past his ploy and shook her head knowingly. "Do the women in Arizona actually fall for your tricks?"

"Every single time," Jesse admitted with a deep chuckle. "But I relish a challenge."

"Yes, I just bet you do." Aubrey grabbed the side of the pool and pulled herself out of the water with a graceful lunge. She turned to sit on the tile lip and smiled sweetly. "Go right ahead and finish your swim. I'll keep watch so you're in no danger of drowning."

She had such beautiful legs, Jesse couldn't resist placing a kiss on her knee before he also pulled himself out of the pool. Seated beside her, the prospect of drowning himself—in her—was incredibly appealing. He slipped his arm around her shoulders and gave her a hug. "We forgot about towels. Are you cold?"

Aubrey was about to shove him back into the pool when she noticed the long scar that curved up and over his right knee. Unable to stop herself, she reached out and the instant her fingertips brushed his skin, she heard the roar of the crowd, and through a swirling dustcloud, saw him astride a huge bull. She knew exactly what was going to happen but Jesse's hand covered hers before she could pull away. She saw him slip, and then heard the sickening crunch as the bull's hind feet came down on his knee.

She felt the nausea well up in her throat, broke free of his grasp, and lurched to her feet. She ran for the house, nearly tripping over Guinevere, who raced along beside her. She made it into the bathroom off the den with no more than a second to spare, but she was even more terrified than when Jesse had shown her the photograph of his cousin's family.

She did not know how she could explain to him, or to anyone else, what she had not merely seen, but felt clear to her marrow. Shaken, she sank to the floor. She now feared it was Jesse who carried the hideous visions. She doubted he would find that premise any easier to believe than she did, but somehow the intuition she had learned to trust convinced her it was true.

Chapter VII

Jesse followed Aubrey into the bathroom, knelt by her side, and stroked her wet curls. Water dripped down her back and trickled off her suit to dampen the thick terra cotta carpet. He grabbed a navy blue towel off the rack on the shower door and cuddled it around her shoulders.

"What happened this time?" he asked.

Aubrey shut her eyes and shuddered, but the ghastly scene she had witnessed out by the pool refused to fade. "When you were hurt, the bull you were riding was a black-faced chocolate brown. The tip of his right horn was broken off so it was perhaps six inches shorter than the left. Clowns came running to distract the bull, but they reached him too late to save you."

When she looked up at Jesse, her frightened gaze stared straight through him. She hadn't asked a question, but instead described a terrifying inner vision that had clearly filled her with a nearly suffocating dread. He tightened his grasp on her shoulders.

"How do you know so much?" he asked. "I didn't go

into detail when I told you what happened, nor when I spoke for your seminar today."

Aubrey wrapped her arms around her bent knees and rocked gently. "I saw it all clearly when I touched your knee. Had I actually been there that awful day, I couldn't have felt it any more deeply. I still don't believe I'm psychic, though. I think you're the one who's creating the awful visions, and I'm merely receiving them."

That bizarre notion convinced Jesse that Aubrey must be becoming hysterical. He rose and hauled her to her feet. "I want you to take as hot a shower as you can stand." He yanked open the glass door on the shower enclosure and, holding on to her towel, eased her inside. He turned on the hot water, but afraid he might scald her, adjusted the temperature by adding some cold before closing the door.

The bathroom had the same rust and navy color scheme as the den. Jesse had thought it both elegant and soothing but as he twisted the damp towel, the colors swirled around him with a jarring clash. If Aubrey had caught one of his worst memories in an eerie flash, it certainly had not been his doing. Perhaps they were playing with a power that couldn't be controlled, but he had never expected their attempt to solve a baffling crime to take such a puzzling turn.

He left the bathroom to shuck off his wet trunks and pull on a pair of Levi's. Afraid Aubrey wasn't herself, he quickly returned to the bathroom, which was rapidly filling with steam. "Aubrey? Are you okay? Shall I bring you a robe?"

When she failed to respond, he slid open the small cabinet along the wall and removed another towel. He then opened the shower door just a crack to peek inside and found Aubrey huddled in the far corner. She hadn't removed her bathing suit, which he thought was probably lucky for them both in the state she was in. He reached in to turn off the water, and then wrapped her in the clean towel before turning her around and leading her out.

"I'd like to sweep you off your feet and carry you upstairs, but my knee would probably buckle and we'd go bumping right back down. I'll just walk you up like this." He slipped his arm around her waist and guided her through the den and up the stairs.

When they reached the second floor, he paused at the doorway of the master bedroom. The thick comforter on the white enameled Victorian bed matched the dainty violet print of the robe Aubrey had worn Monday morning. A heap of pillows covered in the same pretty floral pattern, trimmed with white eyelet and purple ribbon, nearly obscured the fancy scrollwork of the headboard. A matching dust ruffle brushed a white rug with a deep purple border. The window overlooking the pool where Aubrey had waved to him was draped in gathered puffs of the violet print.

The armoire and dresser were handcrafted pine and painted the same creamy marshmallow shade as the walls. An easy chair and ottoman covered in a luscious purple velour faced a wall unit with a television set, collection of curios, and profusion of potted plants. Warmed by the afternoon sun, their glossy leaves were as bright as those scattered across the bed linens and curtains.

It was a delightfully feminine room, filled with the faint aroma of vanilla incense. Jesse found it difficult, if not impossible, to imagine Larry Stafford sharing it, then recalled Aubrey had moved here after her divorce, so he never did live here. The whole house was beautiful, but he still thought it a terrible shame she occupied it all alone.

"You're going to have to take off that wet bathing suit," he coaxed gently. "Shall I help you?"

Aubrey glanced down and seemed surprised to find she

was still wearing the aqua tank. Without replying to Jesse's offer, she slipped away from his grasp and walked into the adjoining bathroom. She left the door slightly ajar, revealing a glimpse of sparkling white tile and wallpaper with a narrow purple stripe.

Jesse debated following her, not wanting to again find her collapsed on the floor, and he would have, had she not swiftly reappeared wearing a short lavender sleepshirt. Her hair was wrapped in a purple hand towel, and she did not bother to remove it before climbing onto the high bed and slipping down under the covers.

Perplexed, Jesse moved to the end of the bed and rested his hands on the curving footboard until he was certain Aubrey was resting comfortably. Then he walked around to the other side of the bed and stretched out beside her. He wanted an explanation, not only for Aubrey's strange ability to scan his past as though it were an old movie, but also for the disastrous consequences she had suffered. He propped his head on his hands and stared up at the white ceiling fan. Its four tulip bulbs would give plenty of light, but he didn't want to have to wait until dark for his answers.

When Aubrey awakened, it was nearly eight o'clock, and Jesse was sleeping soundly beside her. A thin stream of light shone from the partially open bathroom door, but curled up facing her, his face was in shadow. He was still lying on top of the comforter, while she was underneath, but she didn't recall inviting him to share her bed. She was about to give his shoulder a rude shake to send him away when she remembered why she had come upstairs to her room, and quickly yanked her hand away.

She eased herself up into a sitting position and removed her towel turban. Her hair was still slightly damp, and she gave her head a hasty shake to fluff out her curls. She had touched Jesse before that afternoon with no ill effects. He had held her hand, kissed her, even given her a leisurely back rub without clouding her thoughts with hideous visions. Why had that day been different?

"Jesse, wake up," she urged loudly, and he immediately opened his eyes.

Jesse sat up and squirmed to get comfortable amid all the pillows. "Do you usually sleep with all of these?" he asked, clearly tempted to toss several to the rug.

"No, most are merely decorative but that's not really our problem, is it?"

Jesse also thought her mattress was too damn hard, but he was so relieved she was speaking calmly that he let the matter of his comfort, or lack thereof, slide. He reached over to turn on the bedside lamp. "No, but I'd prefer arguing about pillows to watching you become so upset again. Are you really all right?" He reached out to touch her forehead, but Aubrey raised her arm to block the move.

"Just keep your hands to yourself, please. When you showed me the photograph of your cousin and his family, what were you thinking?"

Insulted by her harsh rebuff, Jesse crossed his arms over his bare chest and tried to recall. "I thought they'd been kidnapped and murdered. I was hoping you'd receive the same eerie sensation from the photo that I had, and perhaps some tangible clue. It didn't even occur to me that you would provide the details you did." Jesse waited, and wondered if she would again accuse him of creating the bloody vision she had had, but she simply nodded.

"And when I touched your knee? What were you thinking then?"

Jesse knew telling the truth was always best, and smiled slyly. "I was thinking what beautiful legs you have, and I was worried about your being cold. Believe me, bull riding was the farthest thing from my mind.''

Aubrey believed him and softened her tone. "Was the description I provided accurate?"

"Sure was. That's what startled me so, and it obviously did worse to you."

Aubrey thought they ought to be having this conversation elsewhere, but still felt too shaken to move. She hadn't invited another man up to her bedroom, but then, she hadn't invited Jesse there, either. She knew she ought to complain that he had exceeded the limits of her hospitality, but he looked so at home beside her. He provided precisely the comfort she so desperately needed.

"I wasn't thinking about anything when I touched your scar. I was just going to trace its curve, then *wham.* I felt as though I'd been tossed right into the dusty arena with you, and that's the last place I'd ever want to be."

"Is that why you kept me from touching you just now? Are you afraid it might happen again?"

"I don't know what to think," Aubrey confided truthfully. "I felt as though I'd been turned inside out and shaken like an old rug. It was all so quick. I was seated at poolside one moment, and the next, I'd been plunked down in the middle of a rodeo. To say that was frightening in itself doesn't come close to explaining my terror. I knew something awful was about to happen and I was powerless to prevent it.

"Nothing like this has ever happened to me prior to meeting you." She turned to face him squarely. "That's why I think it's you who's creating all the havoc."

Jesse thought her assumption just plain crazy, but that was scarcely a helpful opinion. "Let's think about this a minute," he counseled. "You're the one who's been looking inward, searching your heart for your own sacred path, and attempting to rely more on your intuition. Isn't it possible that you've achieved more than you'd realized before I came along and gave you the opportunity to test your newfound abilities?''

A low, frustrated moan poured from Aubrey lips. "Trusting my intuition and being able to relive your experiences are two entirely different things. I've only wanted to know myself better, not to spy on others in such a painful way.''

Her anguished expression touched Jesse deeply. He longed to hold her close, but left his hands tucked firmly against his sides. "I can understand that, and believe me, there's a whole lot I hope you can't see just by touching me. But I came awfully close to losing my leg, so it's not surprising if getting stomped by a bull isn't imprinted in every cell of my body. Maybe it's violence that registers with you, and while that's obviously terrifying, some good might come of it.''

"I still think it's you," Aubrey protested. "Maybe it's some chemical link, or perhaps a psychic tie.''

"You think we're plugged into the same cosmic socket?'' Jesse was tickled by that idea and started to laugh.

Exasperated that he would make light of something so serious, Aubrey swung at him, but Jesse caught her wrist before her hand connected with his bare shoulder. She had forgotten how reluctant she had been to touch him just a few minutes earlier, and stared at the slim, tan fingers encircling her arm. Fearing the worst, she held her breath, but other than an almost exquisite awareness of his size and strength, she had no sickening result.

Jesse studied her frown. "Is it happening again?''

Aubrey released a deep sigh. "No. Thank God. Now let me go, before it does.''

Jesse released her, but he was badly disappointed that she was so afraid of his touch. After a brief hesitation, he proposed a solution. "Let's try an experiment. I'm going to concentrate on an image. You'll have to trust me that it's not violent, but let's see if you can picture what it is in your mind. Now give me your hand."

Aubrey swallowed hard, but wanting answers as badly as he, she extended a trembling hand, and he took it in a fond clasp. She closed her eyes and, shutting out her fears, swept aside all thought save those of him. The earlier images had been instantaneous and she waited, not at all patiently, for this vision to come to life in her mind's eye. She deepened her breathing in an attempt to create a relaxed, meditative state, but still, nothing came to her.

Then she realized that Jesse might be deliberately attempting to trick her. She opened her eyes and found him studying her closely. "Are you really concentrating, or are you simply making your mind a blank?" she asked accusingly.

"What kind of experiment would that be?"

Aubrey tightened her hold on his hand. "Just answer me!"

Jesse had been concentrating on a kid's birthday party because they were such colorful, happy events. He had been silently singing "Happy Birthday," and considered the fact that she hadn't heard it ringing in her head ample proof there was no exchange of thoughts occurring between them.

"I was working real hard to make you see something pleasant. Let's try again and maybe we'll have better luck."

Aubrey's gaze narrowed suspiciously, but she reluctantly closed her eyes and fought to cast aside any doubt of his sincerity. In a moment she saw a familiar grassy plain and a clear, azure sky. Way off in the distance, a rider was coming her way. When he drew near, she recognized him as an Indian brave in fringed buckskins. Astride a huge black and white pinto, he was racing straight for her, his jet-black hair whipped by the wind. Soon she could hear his stallion's labored breathing and the thud of his hooves pounding across the verdant prairie.

The Indian's right hand was raised; his feather-trimmed lance balanced in his fingertips, ready to throw. Aubrey stared in rapt wonder, fascinated by the sheer beauty of the moment. The instant the brave released the lance, the steel tip caught the sun's rays, blinding her. Frozen in place, she sucked in her breath and waited for the razor-sharp blade to pierce her chest.

Frightened by Aubrey's gasp, Jesse yanked her toward him. "What did you see? Tell me."

Mesmerized by his searching gaze, Aubrey was surprised to find his eyes a radiant blue rather than dark brown. The Indian brave was still with her, and she shook her head to send him away. "That was totally unfair," she complained. "I'd never have confessed to having a weakness for Indians had I known how quickly you'd use it against me."

Jesse had given up on the birthday party in favor of visualizing making love to her right there in a bed that was much too hard and cluttered with frilly pillows for his tastes. With both of them nude and hot for each other, his images had perhaps been lewd, but they certainly hadn't involved any Native Americans. "I wasn't thinking about Indians," he swore convincingly, "which proves I've absolutely no talent, nor responsibility, for the awful visions you've had."

Had he not been so adamant about it, Aubrey might have questioned him further. Instead, she pushed away from him and rolled out of bed. "Fine. Maybe it isn't you, but that discovery doesn't explain what caused the visions, or how to prevent them from happening again." As she rounded the bed, she reached out for the ornate footboard and challenged him again.

"What if I can't learn how to control this, Jesse? It must

be like having flashbacks to bad acid trips, or the hideous trauma of war. What if it happens when I shake hands with someone at a seminar? Or, God forbid, just bump into a stranger on a crowded street?''

Jesse wished for a way to lure her back into bed and bring his erotic fantasy into reality, but that hope was too remote to pursue. He swung his feet over the side of the bed and pushed off. "Scientists claim our minds have a vast, untapped potential. If there's a name for what you did, psychometry, wasn't it? Then you're not the first person to have the ability."

"Ability? It's a curse!" Aubrey strode past him into the bathroom and slammed the door.

Jesse made a face at the closed door. He would have appreciated a thank you for helping her into the shower and upstairs to bed, but clearly she was too self-absorbed to offer one. He went back downstairs. His clothes were still out in the cabaña, and as he went out the back door to get them, he flipped on the patio lights which brought Guinevere running and barking.

"Some help you are," he scolded. "All you're good for is a mop. How'd you like me to dip you into the pool and scrub the patio with your hairy hide?"

Guinevere reacted as though she had understood Jesse's threat, veered away, and took cover beneath the patio table where Lucifer lay enjoying a lengthy nap. The tomcat opened one eye, recognized Jesse even if Guinevere hadn't, and responded with a bored yawn before resuming his slumber.

Jesse slipped on his shirt as he returned to the house, and carried his pants and boots into the den. He doubted Aubrey would feel like eating, but having had only a few bites of fruit for lunch, he was famished. "Maybe we can cook up a big caldron of porridge," he muttered under his breath, but when he walked into the kitchen Aubrey was already making dinner preparations.

She had pulled on a T-shirt, jeans, and sandals and not bothered with makeup. "There's some homemade vegetable soup in the freezer. Will that be enough for you with cornbread and a salad?"

That she had even recalled he was there surprised Jesse, and he thought better of refusing her offer. "It would be just fine. Do you get CNN news?"

Aubrey told Jesse the channel, and he turned on the small set facing the kitchen table. There was the usual assortment of disasters, and updates of the conflicts which simply shifted location over the globe without ever being resolved. "Do you ever have the feeling that they're merely broadcasting the same news day after day and none of us is smart enough to catch on?"

Although surprised by his cynicism, Aubrey readily agreed. "Constantly. Only the scores on the sports segment change, and sometimes I'm not sure about those."

Jesse set the table and sat down to watch the rest of the news. With the aid of her microwave, Aubrey soon had dinner on the table, and while he would have preferred to cut into a steak, Jesse thought the soup was good, and said so. Aubrey made an appropriate murmur of thanks, and that exchange was their only dinner conversation. Jesse understood Aubrey's worries, but with no way to allay them, he just kept still.

Having dinner with a silent companion was a bitter reminder of the last days of her marriage, and Aubrey left the table as soon as politely possible. "Just leave your dishes," she called to Jesse as she started out of the room. "My cleaning woman comes tomorrow, and she'll take care of them."

"Good night," Jesse responded, but Aubrey had already started up the stairs and he doubted that she had heard

him. He didn't do dishes at home, but having nothing
better to do with himself, rinsed theirs and put them in
the dishwasher rather than let them sit. They had finished
the soup, and he returned the remaining square of cornbread to the refrigerator. He swept the crumbs from the
table and tossed them in the sink.

"There, everything looks great. You'd make some lucky
woman a fine husband," he told himself. Then he leaned
back against the counter and cursed the fact that he
couldn't do more for Aubrey than keep her kitchen neat.

Aubrey tried to read, but couldn't concentrate on the
printed page and set the novel aside. She checked the
television schedule but none of the programs appealed to
her. Thinking she would be better off to make it an early
night, she went downstairs, put her pets on the back porch,
and fed them. As she started back up the stairs, she heard
the theme music for a popular drama coming from the
den and was relieved Jesse had found something to watch.

Suddenly overcome with a longing for company, she
paused momentarily, then decided it would be a mistake
to bother him when he could so easily misinterpret her
interest. He was attractive and charming, but had created
a problem for her she had not even suspected might exist
before he strode into her Saturday seminar. How she was
going to get through the next day's seminar was problem
enough at the moment, and she continued on up the
stairs, intent upon reviewing her notes.

More than an hour passed before she turned off her
lights, and then try as she might, she couldn't get comfortable. She heard Jesse pull his truck into the driveway, and
hoped he would have a better night. Here she was, an
expert on stress reduction, and she felt as though her limbs
had not merely been tied in knots, but looped into a

decorative macramé plant holder. Leaving her bed, she paced the darkened bedroom.

Before she grew sufficiently tired to rest, a distant siren reminded her of the presence of the outside world. Fearful she might begin receiving random visions, she stood still for a moment, but other than the emergency vehicle's faint wail, nothing came to her. "Courage," she admonished herself, then went to curl up on the windowseat, gazing out at the night.

The crickets' chirp was magnified by the silence of the neighborhood, but Aubrey preferred their cadence to the heartrending throb of her fears. What if Jesse was right, and she had somehow crossed into a new realm where psychic impressions became a daily occurrence? She would have to stop giving seminars, and do all in her power to limit her contact with others or risk being destroyed by the dark visions that plagued her. Would it be selfish to refuse to share a gift that might possibly bring the justice Jesse sought? Or would it simply be a matter of self-preservation?

Even deep in thought, she noted the change in the crickets' rhythm. It had been a quick break, as though someone had moved through the yard and interrupted their frantic communications, but she hadn't heard the scrape of a shoe across stone. Alarmed, she closed the window and went downstairs to check the doors, but she had locked the back after putting the pets to bed, and Jesse had locked the front after reparking his truck. The side door to the patio was also locked, and because she always left the light on in the kitchen as a security measure, she doubted anyone would seek to force an entry there.

It could have been a stray cat, or even an opossum lumbering along close to the ground, but as Aubrey returned to her room, she took comfort in the fact that Jesse would be there to help her should she need it. The lights had been out in the den, but she felt certain he was a light sleeper, and would respond should she call. Fears of a prowler were ridiculous in a neighborhood frequently patrolled by the police, but Aubrey trusted her intuition.

She opened the journal she kept in one of the bedside tables, and made a note of the date and time. Then deciding the day had been extraordinary in many respects, she confided her fears in the silent pages of her diary. By the time she was finished, she was ready for sleep, but certainly not looking forward to tomorrow.

Chapter VIII

Trisha arrived at Aubrey's house a few minutes late Wednesday morning and dashed up to the Volvo as Jesse was backing out of the garage. She peeked inside, and relieved Aubrey wasn't already in the car, she stepped back and waited for him to cut the engine. "I hope I didn't keep you waiting," she said.

Jesse got out of the station wagon to close the garage, and then leaned back against the left fender. "You work for Aubrey," he reminded her. "You needn't apologize to me."

Trisha flashed a knowing grin. "You two make a swell team. Unlike the banker and me. The first time we went out I thought he was merely conservative, or perhaps shy. After last night though, I realize he's just plain dull. I won't be seeing him again."

Jesse wasn't certain which of the men in the seminar had been her date, and he didn't care. She was dressed in red, and as usual, her skirt was well above her knees. She could have posed for a Valentine poster, but he didn't believe she knew much about love. "If you liked him well enough to date in the first place, maybe you ought to take a little longer to get to know him."

Trisha took a step closer and looked Jesse up and down through fluttering lashes. "I'd just be wasting my time, and misleading him, so it wouldn't be a good idea. Besides, I've already learned from experience that the magic is either there at first glance, or it never comes."

Jesse shook his head knowingly. "Sometimes that kind of magic doesn't last longer than a single night. Aren't you looking for more?"

"Of course. Isn't everybody?"

Jesse wondered about Ricky Vance, but didn't consider Shelley's boyfriend worth mentioning. He wished Aubrey would hurry up, and glanced toward the house. "Not everyone," he replied. "Believe it or not, there are men and women who just love to flirt but somehow never seem to find what they're looking for and quickly move on. Perhaps you know someone like that."

Trisha considered Jesse's stare just a bit too intense and, certain he was making a pointed reference to her dating habits, became defensive. She straightened her shoulders proudly. "It's never wise to jump to conclusions," she replied.

"That's exactly my point. It's difficult to really get to know someone in a couple of dates. Why don't you give the banker another chance?" Jesse began to smile as he remembered the advice he had given Gardner. He sure wasn't helping out the bashful sound engineer by advising Trisha to date someone else, but it was easy to see by the fierce grip she had taken on her patent leather purse that she didn't like being told what to do, so maybe it didn't matter.

Also running late, Aubrey hurried through the back door, quickly locked it, and got into her car without noticing Trisha's sullen pout. When Trisha slid into the back seat, she wished her a good morning, but didn't turn to look at her before reviewing her notes. "I want to do more with positive affirmations this morning," she told her assistant. "Then move into creative imagery. It's possible people would like to work on other areas of their life in addition to their careers, so I'll end the day with reinforcement for that."

Aubrey was dressed in a burgundy silk tunic with burgundy and gray pinstripe pants. It was a striking outfit with her fair coloring and she had caught her hair at her nape with a burgundy chiffon bow to create a more sophisticated hairstyle. As Jesse backed out of the driveway, he found it difficult to concentrate on the road rather than on her. When they reached Shelley's bungalow, he was surprised not to find her waiting for them on the porch.

"Should I honk the horn?" he asked Aubrey.

"No. Just give her a minute." Aubrey was trying hard to focus on the final day of the seminar, and she didn't need any additional problems.

"I'll go and get her," Trisha quickly volunteered. She left the car, and when she reached Shelley's door, she turned back and waved.

"Looks like we're all running late," Jesse said. "You look real pretty in that outfit, by the way. The color is just plain luscious."

Aubrey didn't look up from her notes. "It's comfortable. That's why I like it."

Jesse was afraid he had embarrassed her and didn't try to take the exchange any further, but he wished she had thanked him for noticing how good she looked. He thought he looked pretty good himself that morning, but obviously she hadn't noticed.

"Here they come." Jesse sat up and started the engine.

As usual, Shelley was wearing pastels. Her tunic sweater

was a medley of pale hues over a gauze skirt the color of orange sherbert. Her expression was no happier than the previous day, however, and her eyes were swollen from crying. Her voice sounded husky as she entered the car and greeted them.

As soon as Trisha closed her door, she spoke in an anxious rush. "Prince Charming stood Shelley up last night. Do you believe that? He isn't in town a week before he's up to his old tricks, all of them nasty. I hope the bastard stays lost this time."

Jesse glanced into the rearview mirror and feared Shelley was too depressed to be of much help that day. "Would you rather stay home?" he asked. "I know enough to take your place today."

Surprised by his offer, Aubrey turned toward Shelley. "It's your call. Shall we drop you off at your mother's so you can get Annie?"

"No, please. I'd rather go to work. I'll be all right there, and if I stay home with Annie, I'll just end up crying all day and that won't be any good for her."

"Nor you, either," Aubrey stressed. She studied her blonde assistant's averted gaze and, as always, was touched by her plight. "I'm proud of you for thinking of Annie's welfare, but what are you going to do tomorrow, or the next day, when you'll be home with her? Will you try to pretend you're not heartbroken over the way Ricky treats you, or will you finally come to terms with making a life for yourself without him?"

Tears welled up in Shelley's eyes and spilled over her lashes. "I knew it was over last night," she confided softly. "He'd said he wanted to take me out to Tony Roma's for ribs; it's our favorite place for dinner. Then we were going to the Old Towne Pub to hear Rifficus Rose, a band we both love. He sounded so excited. He even told me what to wear, but then he didn't show up. If I'm not even worth a telephone call to cancel, then it's plain I'll be better off without him."

"You never had him," Trisha complained, "not in any real, important way, or he would have married you when you got pregnant with Annie. You never should have had her."

"Trisha!" Shelley cried. "How could you? Annie's the best thing that ever happened to me."

"Yes, she is," Aubrey agreed. "And you owe her something a whole lot better than the continual misery Ricky Vance provides. Now let's get going or we'll be later than we already are."

"Yes, ma'am." Jesse looked over his shoulder as he drew away from the curb and spotted a gold Corvette parked about half a block away. The Corvette also pulled out into the road, but with everyone going to work, he did not think it anything other than coincidence.

The traffic was slightly heavier than the previous day, but they still arrived with a few minutes to spare. As soon as Jesse entered the bank's underground parking lot, he reached out to take Aubrey's hand. "If you want me to speak to the group again, will you tell me now so that I'll have a moment to plan?"

Aubrey was ashamed that she hadn't shown him that courtesy yesterday, and quickly pulled her hand from his. At least touching him hadn't sparked any grostesque visions, but she did not want to take any chances. "I'm afraid that was a spontaneous gesture yesterday," she claimed, knowing full well it had been no such thing. She had been angry with him for forcing his way into the seminar, but he had proven his worth, and after a restless night, she was actually grateful to have him along with her today.

"Have you ever used creative imagery for something

other than your career?'' she asked as soon as he had parked the car.

"Does seducing women count?" he teased, but Aubrey's eyes widened in shock rather than amusement and he realized the remark had been in extremely poor taste. "I didn't mean that," he insisted, but it was too late to take back the remark. "Give me some time to think about it, and maybe I can come up with something."

"Yes, please do." Aubrey left the car and started for the elevators with a long, sure stride. She slapped the button, but was still waiting when her assistants and Jesse caught up with her. "Let's just get through today as best we can," she told them. "Then we can rest until Saturday."

"What's happening Saturday?" Jesse asked before he recalled the seminar he had attended had been the first of six. "Never mind. I remember." Aubrey looked tired, and he wondered how many seminars she had given recently and whether she had any vacations planned. Before he could ask, the doors slid open on the elevator, several bank employees rushed up to catch it, and the opportunity was lost.

Gardner always arrived before Aubrey and the rest of the team, but he had been even earlier than usual that morning. Yesterday, he had left for home angry with the way Jesse had talked to him, but then found himself driving straight to the Santa Anita Fashion Park. Two hours later he had walked out of the sprawling mall with a stylish haircut and a whole new wardrobe.

It wasn't until he started to get dressed that morning that he began to feel foolish. But wanting more than anything to get Jesse off his back, he had worn a new pair of gray slacks, loafers instead of Nikes, and a pale blue dress shirt with a brightly patterned silk tie. He hadn't made up his mind about getting contacts, but just having to push his glasses into place every time he bent over was so reassuring, he doubted he would go that far.

"My God!" Trisha squealed. "What have you done to yourself, Gardner?"

Gardner had heard the door open, and braced himself, but as usual, he couldn't think of anything clever to say. "It hasn't been that long since I got a haircut," he muttered under his breath.

Trisha walked up to him and, clearly approving of his new look, slapped him on the back. "You look terrific," she exclaimed. "You ought to keep your hair that length so that it curls rather than shoots out as though you'd stuck your finger in a light socket. Your new clothes are a big improvement, too. Doesn't he look cute, Shelley?"

Shelley barely glanced Gardner's way, but when she did, she smiled shyly. "Yes. He always does."

"Always?" Trisha repeated in an astonished gasp that swelled into a delighted giggle. "Did you hear that, Gardner?"

Gardner caught Jesse's eye and frowned. He had wanted to impress Trisha, not send her into hysterical laughter, and he felt as though he had failed miserably. So much for getting a haircut and buying new clothes. He was still the same man, and clearly she didn't want anything to do with him.

"Would you please step out of my way," he scolded. "I need to finish setting up."

Startled by that burst of assertiveness, Trisha spun on her heel and walked away, but she was intrigued, and glanced back over her shoulder. In the baggy clothes Gardner usually wore, he had looked pudgy, but now she realized he actually had a trim, athletic build. The men she dated often spent as much effort on their looks as she did on hers, but no one would ever accuse Gardner of being conceited. She was surprised by the sudden change in his appearance, but not at all disappointed.

Shelley had sworn he had a crush on her, but Trisha sure hadn't seen any evidence of it that morning. In fact, Gardner had been downright rude, when all she had done was tease him a little bit. Obviously Shelley didn't know what she was talking about. But Trisha glanced toward Gardner again and decided it was high time they got to know each other better.

On the last day of a seminar, Aubrey was usually relaxed, but she feared she would have a difficult time projecting an air of tranquility that day. She greeted the participants warmly, but she was relying on experience rather than any true sense of enthusiasm. "I'd like to spend a few minutes this morning talking about magic," she began.

"We've all marveled at the cleverness of magicians' tricks, but we know they're masters of illusion, rather than extraordinary beings with true supernatural powers. There's a very real temptation to visualize the life we wish to live, and then expect it to come about as if by magic, without any effort of our own. I want to caution you against falling into that trap, because that's exactly what it is. When we want something very badly, but don't actively work to do whatever it takes to bring that dream into reality, we've forged our own chains and kept ourselves stuck in lives that will never be truly satisfying."

Jesse understood exactly the point Aubrey was making, and from the appreciative nods coming from the audience, it was plain the bankers did, too. He glanced over at Gardner, who had probably heard this same speech dozens of times, and wondered if he had ever really grasped Aubrey's meaning. Then there was Shelley, who was caught in a relationship as predictable as a merry-go-round, and while it might provide an occasional thrill, it would never take her anywhere she wished to go.

As for Trisha, she would probably just continue skipping over the hearts she crushed beneath her tiny feet, and Jesse didn't wish her on anyone, least of all Gardner. Since reading *The Mind's Eye*, he would never accuse Aubrey of avoiding her problems and expecting solutions to appear magically, but he knew despite her obvious sincerity, she was still hiding something. *What a group!* he moaned silently, and decided right then and there to speak on the wisdom of working on one's own problems rather than attempting to solve someone else's.

He was about to tell Aubrey that he did indeed have something to say when it occurred to him that she had been hired to present a method for overcoming career-related stress. Thinking he would be smart to stick to that subject, he searched his mind for a pertinent anecdote, and soon found one. When she glanced his way, he came forward.

"I told you yesterday how hard I worked to visualize a prize-winning ride before I took it. Well, bulls being the unpredictable beasts they are, sometimes my best efforts didn't win me anything but a mouthful of dust. Considering the alternative, even that could be called lucky." He paused while everyone caught his meaning and either laughed or cringed.

"What I'm getting at here is that there's a real temptation to come down hard on ourselves when we fail, even though it may not be our fault. I've certainly done it, and I'll bet most of you have, too." He was interrupted then by several enthusiastic comments which sounded very much like amen!

"Good. I'm glad you understand what I mean. Just having a peaceful place in your mind, a retreat, if you will, can help you get over the discouraging setbacks we all suffer. For me, it's the memory of the first snowfall each winter in Montana. I've no desire to shovel off a walk ever again, but the silent beauty of a snowy night is something I'll never forget.

"Next time your plans don't work out as you'd hoped, take a few minutes to create your favorite image—be it the warm waters surrounding a tropical isle, a snowy mountain top, or anything in between—and just enjoy it. Then when you get back to work, you'll feel refreshed rather than defeated."

Again pleased by Jesse's sensible advice, Aubrey thanked him and pushed his suggestion a step further. "Those of you who love nature will easily take comfort in the scenery Jesse described, but others of you might prefer remembering a time when everything went right. It could have been a holiday when you felt especially close to your family. Perhaps you recall a joyous wedding, maybe your own, or a favorite aunt who never failed to make you feel special."

Jarred by that reference, Jesse felt guilty for not even telephoning his Aunt Edith since he had moved in with Aubrey on Monday. It had only been two days since he had last seen her, but he knew she must be worried about whether or not he was making any progress investigating his cousin's disappearance. He would call her at the break, but he sure didn't have much to report, other than a plan to lure Aubrey back to his cousin's home tomorrow.

Aubrey was pleased with the morning session, but unwilling to spend another lunch hour alone with Jesse, she went with the others to the cafeteria. She ate a fruit salad, while Jesse ate a hamburger and fries with so many appreciative murmurs she was embarrassed to think she had not provided enough in the way of meals. "I think we should dine out this evening," she suggested as they returned to the conference room.

Jesse had been hoping he could talk her into returning to the Barkley for another steak. "Yes. Let's do. Do you ever take your whole team out to celebrate the end of a seminar?''

"I haven't yet, but it's a nice idea. Let's not do it tonight, though."

Aubrey moved away from him to speak with Gardner, and Jesse marveled at how easily they had fallen into a comfortable routine. He was used to spending time with women, that was nothing new, but never as much as he had spent with Aubrey in the last few days. Rather than feeling the restlessness that usually drove him from a woman's arms, he just wanted more of her. He wasn't so fascinated by her, however, that he forgot he was supposed to be looking out for trouble.

The afternoon session was relaxed, but productive, and as the seminar drew to a close, everyone attending seemed genuinely pleased by the experience. "I hope this will be a yearly event," someone offered, and the suggestion was met with enthusiastic applause. Then a slender young man seated in the rear rose to his feet.

"I've been appointed the group's spokesman, and while we've all enjoyed your seminar, we've had a difficult time waiting to ask about the photograph that appeared in the *Times* on Monday. Would you tell us what prompted your visit to the Ferrells', and how you plan to solve the case? Can you do it with intuition and creative imagery alone?"

Aubrey supposed she should have expected the question and had an answer prepared. She felt Jesse move up behind her and knew he was about to respond for her, but able to take care of herself, she spoke first. "The Ferrells are Jesse's cousins," she explained. "We'd stopped by merely to check on the property, but unfortunately, the reaon for our visit was completely misinterpreted. I've no involvement in the case whatsoever."

She turned and looked up at Jesse, her steady gaze a clear warning to be still, and while his eyes narrowed slightly in a silent dare, he nodded on cue. Relieved, Aubrey turned back to the audience. "Now I'd like to thank all of you for being so willing to experiment with creative imagery. You're the ones who've made the seminar a success."

After another burst of applause, a few of the executives left immediately, while others lingered and presented copies of *The Mind's Eye* for Aubrey to autograph. Shelley was used to working primarily behind the scenes to guarantee everything ran smoothly, and as the last of the bankers finally moved toward the door, she went to Gardner's side to offer help.

"Is there anything I can do?" she asked. "You're always the first to arrive and the last to leave and that's never seemed fair to me."

"I don't mind," Gardner exclaimed, and rather than thank Shelley for her kindness, he followed Trish's progress toward the door. She was speaking with a tall blonde who looked as though he must have played basketball in college, and Gardner was surprised he didn't just grab her around the waist and pluck her off her feet so that he could look her in the eye while they talked. The way he was bending down was not only awkward, it looked painful, but the man was giving Trisha such rapt attention he obviously didn't feel a single twinge of back pain.

"Looks like Trisha's made another conquest," Gardner complained.

"Perhaps, but she's not interested in him, so it doesn't matter." Shelley waited a moment, but when Gardner continued to watch Trisha's extended farewell, she walked away. He had a dolly to tote his equipment out to his van, and plenty of experience doing it, so she wasn't really surprised he didn't need her.

As they drove home, Aubrey noted how frequently Jesse's glance strayed to the rearview mirror, and turned to look over her shoulder at the traffic trailing them. "Is something wrong?" she asked. "I don't see anything."

Jesse was sorry she had caught him being so vigilant, but figured if she were unaware of a possible danger, then she couldn't look out for it. "There's a gold Corvette two cars behind us that I saw near Shelley's house this morning."

"So what? Plenty of people drive into LA every day to work."

"That's true, but I've got a bad feeling about the car. Give me some credit for having a smidgen of intuition, will you? Shelley, do any of your neighbors drive a gold Corvette?"

Shelley turned around to get a look at it but the Buick Regal between them blocked her view. "I haven't paid much attention, but I don't remember seeing one."

Jesse pulled off the freeway an exit early, at Orange Grove, but the Corvette kept right on going toward Pasadena. Aubrey promptly dismissed it as a threat, but Jesse remained suspicious. "If that's the same car I saw this morning, then he knows where we're headed. Let's everyone keep an eye out for him."

They dropped Shelley off at her mother's house, which was right around the corner from hers, then took a circuitous route to Aubrey's, and didn't sight the Corvette on the way. Jesse let Trisha and Aubrey out of the Volvo before he drove it into the garage, and Trisha promptly drew her boss aside while they had a minute to speak privately.

"I thought Gardner looked awfully cute today, but if he has a crush on me as Shelley claims, he hides it well. He didn't even sit beside me at lunch. Do you think I ought to call him and ask him out?"

Aubrey regarded her assistant with a befuddled stare. She couldn't imagine a more spectacular mismatch than the self-conscious young man and the supremely confident Trisha, and hesitated to encourage it. "Why don't you wait until Saturday, and make a few friendly overtures. If he's interested, he'll respond."

"And if he doesn't?"

"Well, what would you do if it were anyone else?"

Trisha waved to Jesse as she started down the driveway toward her car. "I'd forget it. Thanks, I'll do just that."

"What's she going to forget?" Jesse asked.

Aubrey waited until she had unlocked the back door to respond, and then did so in a hushed whisper. "Asking Gardner for a date on Saturday, if he doesn't seem any more interested in her than he was today."

"She'd ask him out?"

"This is the nineties, cowboy. Don't women ask men for dates in Arizona?" Aubrey went into the kitchen and opened the refrigerator to get a drink of water. "I want to take a shower before we go out."

"Take your time, and yes, women do invite men out in Arizona, but I told Gardner to play it cool with Trisha. I thought once he improved his looks that she'd go into her attack mode, and apparently she has, but we ought to coordinate our strategies so we don't have those two working at cross purposes."

"I can't even coordinate my own life, let alone theirs, Jesse. Let's just stay out of it. Please."

Jesse nodded, but he had plans aplenty for them both.

Not wanting to surprise her in the morning, he was just about to broach the subject of a return trip to the Ferrells' house while they were eating dinner, when Aubrey surprised him by mentioning his cousin first. He carefully chewed his bite of steak and laid his fork on his plate. They were seated side by side in a comfortable red leather booth, and he hoped the mellow surroundings would influence her mood.

"I was surprised by the question about the photograph today," Aubrey confided, "but only because it hadn't come earlier. It's been three days since it appeared, and while I may have let you frighten me into allowing you to stay at my home on Monday, I really don't feel that I'm in any danger because of it." She paused to make certain he understood how serious she was.

"I don't want to regard every rustle in the bushes or car I see twice in a single day as a threat."

"Wait a minute. What rustle in the bushes are you talking about?"

Jesse appeared alarmed, and Aubrey hadn't meant to scare him. "Oh, I'm sure it was nothing. I thought I heard someone in the backyard last night, but Guinevere was on the back porch and she didn't bark. It was probably just an opossum. They're nocturnal and they wander the neighborhood, foraging for tasty leftovers in the trash."

Apparently completely unaware of the pain she had just caused him, Aubrey took another bite of scampi, but Jesse was so angry with her he shoved his plate away. "Why didn't you tell me about this last night? Did you think the killers would walk up and ring your doorbell?"

"Will you please keep your voice down," Aubrey asked. The couple dining in the next booth hadn't turned to stare at them, but if Jesse continued to berate her that loudly everyone in the dimly lit restaurant was sure to turn their way. "No. I did not expect danger to plunk itself down on the doorstep, but still, you're making too much of this, which is exactly why I didn't wake you last night."

Jesse shook his head. "When did you plan to call me, when you felt the cold edge of a knife at your throat?"

Aubrey had also lost her appetite, laid her fork across her plate, and blotted her mouth on her napkin. "I think we ought to continue this discussion at home. Then you can pack your things and go back to Edith's."

"Like hell." Jesse didn't know which was worse, that she hadn't called him when she had heard a suspicious noise, or that she wanted him gone, but he wasn't about to leave. "The only way to settle this issue to our individual satisfaction is for you to come out to the Ferrells' house again tomorrow. This time, I want you to pump up that intuition of yours, or whatever else it is that painted the clear picture of my last ride in your mind, and get us some real clues as to what happened to Pete and his family."

"I'll do no such thing."

Jesse wrapped his fingers around her wrist. "Yes, you will, or I'll feel obligated to serve as your bodyguard forever. Look at it that way, Aubrey. The only way to get me out of your life is to find the Ferrells, or what's left of them, and catch their killers."

Aubrey didn't fight his confining hold, she simply stared at his hand and waited for the awful images she was sure would appear, but other than outrage, she felt nothing. "I think we better leave," she ordered in a hushed voice, "or I'll ask the manager to call the police and have you arrested."

"What's the charge? Caring more than I should about a stubborn redhead who doesn't know enough to report a prowler?"

Aubrey didn't know what to make of his sudden declaration that he cared about her. Completely confused, she said, "Let's straighten this out at home."

Jesse brought her hand to his lips, then released her. "That's fine with me, but now that you've become so agreeable, I think I'll finish my steak."

Aubrey leaned back against the soft, red leather and hoped it took him long enough for her to think of a convincing way, other than summoning the police, to send him away. Where was an Indian brave when she needed one, she wondered, but that bit of wildly creative imagery brought her no peace that night.

Chapter IX

They had gone to dinner in Jesse's truck, and when they returned to Aubrey's, he parked in the driveway. "Just a minute," he warned when she reached for her door handle. "Let me go in first and check the house."

Aubrey doubted there was any need, but tried not to sound as annoyed as she felt. "My parents lived here more than twenty years and never had a break-in. I've never had one, either."

Jesse frowned slightly. "The Ferrells only disappeared once. That's all it will take for you, too. Now stop arguing, give me your keys, and wait here while I go in and take a look around."

Aubrey balked, then decided they could settle things a lot faster if she let him have his way for the time being. She already had her keys in her hand, and slapped them into his palm. "Fine. Search the place to your heart's content."

"Do you actually think I'm enjoying this?"

"Oh yes, I most certainly do. How often do you get to

masquerade as the Caped Crusader, or whatever superhero's popular now?''

Jesse couldn't believe she didn't know. "It's the Power Rangers, and there are five of them. But that's beside the point. I don't want to play a superhero; I just want to make certain you'll be safe."

"Aren't you concerned about yourself?"

Jesse shot her a condescending glance, and Aubrey immediately recognized her mistake. "Of course. You rode bulls for a living. How stupid of me to forget that you don't even know the meaning of the word fear."

Jesse took care not to slam his door so loudly he would wake every baby in the neighborhood, but he certainly didn't appreciate Aubrey's sarcasm. It was true he had gotten her into the mess she adamantly denied being in, but he did not believe cooperation to get her out was too much to ask.

Guinevere was inside, and started yapping at him as soon as he unlocked the door.

"Okay, rag mop. You've impressed me with how fierce you are. Now come on, back me up here." Aubrey had left several lights burning in the house, but Jesse flipped on a lot more as he moved through the downstairs. He didn't see anything out of place, nor find a window unlatched, but remained alert as he climbed the stairs. He paused outside Aubrey's bedroom, but neither heard nor felt anything odd. When he toured the room, the only scent was vanilla incense, and he felt sure no one had been there since they had left.

There were three other bedrooms on the second floor, and this was his first chance to see them. All were just as beautifully furnished as hers, but without the clutter that would have come from even occasional use by a guest. There were also two bathrooms in addition to Aubrey's, one decorated in pink, the other sky blue. The towels hanging on the racks were new, and the rolls of toilet paper unused. The couch in the den folded out into a bed, so he hadn't had to sleep on the floor, but it now struck him as insulting that Aubrey hadn't offered him the use of one of the spare bedrooms.

"This is a damn movie set," he remarked under his breath, and the sound of his voice echoing off the walls was enough to send Guinevere into another barking fit. Fearing Aubrey might worry that something had happened to him, he hushed the dog and hurried back down the stairs, but when he opened the back door, he found Aubrey leaning against his Chevy, gazing up at the stars, obviously completely unconcerned about his welfare. Still aggravated that she apparently didn't trust him enough to give him a room upstairs, his voice had a graveled edge. "I should have told you to stay in the truck with the doors locked."

"Why? I don't recall anyone being attacked in the driveway near here."

"Want to be the first?" Jesse scoffed. The dense cloud cover which so often blanketed Los Angeles was missing that night and the stars beckoned with a sparkling brilliance. He paused only a moment to enjoy the spectacular view, then coaxed Aubrey inside.

"Let's make some tea," he suggested, thinking he probably needed the soothing brew more than she did. While Aubrey lit the fire under the teakettle, he went to the refrigerator, opened the freezer compartment, and knelt down to survey the contents. "I knew you'd have frozen yogurt. Would you like some?"

"That's wonderful, Jesse. I'd like you to leave, while you're just making yourself more at home. Aren't you needed at your ranch?"

Aubrey was sorting through the tea canister looking for a particular type of teabag rather than facing him, but she was making no effort to hide her frustration, and Jesse readily picked up on it. "I'll take that for a yes." He grabbed the carton of strawberry frozen yogurt, closed the freezer, and stood. He knew where the bowls and spoons were, and quickly got them out.

"My ranch will survive a couple of weeks without my being there to supervise, so I'm not worried that I'll find nothing but tumbleweeds when I get home. Now that we've gotten my ranch out of the way, let's try to concentrate on the real problem." Jesse didn't want to lecture her, but he had a difficult time speaking in a relaxed, conversational tone.

"You're so different at the seminars that it's hard to believe you're the same person," he mused aloud. Not sure how much yogurt she wanted, he gave her the same generous portion he scooped out for himself and returned the carton to the freezer. He leaned back against the counter while they waited for the water to boil.

"At the seminars, you're supremely confident," he explained, "but at the same time you exude warmth. You're approachable there, and the audience responds positively. Once you bring the seminar to a close, however, you retreat into yourself. Or maybe you're simply a consummate actress, and the Aubrey Glenn people see at the seminars is an act."

Aubrey fought not to be insulted by what she considered an extremely unflattering description of her behavior. "We all have multifaceted personalities," she argued. "Just because I choose to show one side during seminars, and another in more private settings, doesn't mean either is an act. I'm no phoney."

"I didn't say you were." The water was hot, and Jesse waited until she brewed their tea to suggest they move into the living room to talk. He picked up the bowls of yogurt and led the way. Expensively furnished in fine antiques, the room had a twenty-foot ceiling with exposed beams.

It was a charming setting decorated in lush shades of cranberry and gold. Certain she would take the wing chair in
the far corner, he turned to block her way.

"Come sit with me on the sofa so we don't have to shout
across the room." He set the yogurt on the coffee table
and waited for her to make herself comfortable. That she
chose the far end of the cranberry velvet sofa didn't surprise him, but he took care not to crowd her and sat toward
the other end. He stretched out his legs to get comfortable.

"I truly believe we can use your talents to solve my
cousins' disappearance." Aubrey opened her mouth, but
already knowing she would argue, Jesse raised his hand.
"Hold on a minute. Just let me finish. I'm way past making
an appeal to your sense of citizenship, and I never meant
to use your fondness for my aunt to coerce you into working
on the case. Please believe me.

"Trisha thinks we make a good team, and so do I. That's
why I want us to work together: I truly believe we'll make
a difference. We might also discover something important
about ourselves." His voice softened. "Or something more,
I should say."

Self-discovery was the theme of *The Mind's Eye,* and that
Jesse would quote her book in an effort to impress her
struck Aubrey as incredibly low. She watched him take a
spoonful of yogurt and hoped that he would choke. He
didn't.

"You already know how highly I value self-discovery,"
she responded as calmly as she could, "but you're not the
one who's had to face the frightening visions. To expect
me to willingly repeat that experience, for whatever reason,
is simply too much to ask."

Jesse let the yogurt slide down his throat. Cold and sweet,
it helped him keep a firm hold on his temper. He took
another bite and nodded to acknowledge Aubrey's point.
He really didn't care if he had to keep her up all night,

he was going to win her cooperation; that's all there was to it.

A sudden hideous screech from the backyard brought Aubrey to her feet. "My God. What was that?"

Jesse set his yogurt aside and stood. Guinevere had heard the strangled cry, too, but the dog was cowering at her mistress's feet rather than barking. "Does Lucifer ever get in cat fights?"

"He's neutered, but occasionally he does. Tomcats exchange low, threatening moans before they sink their claws into each other, and I didn't hear anything that sounded like him."

"Stay here," Jesse ordered, but as he slipped past Aubrey, she followed right behind him. "I should have known," he murmured under his breath.

"This is my house," Aubrey reminded him, "and I'll go wherever I please."

Jesse reached the side door first and flipped on the patio lights. "Shouldn't the lights be on in the pool?"

Aubrey ducked under his arm to look out. "Yes. They're on a timer." She pushed the door open, then recoiled slightly. "What is that awful stench?"

Jesse eased open the screen door. "It smells like burnt fur. I sure hope Lucifer wasn't playing with matches. Do you have a flashlight?"

Aubrey ran to the other side of the kitchen to grab one off the counter. "Let's go together." She waited until Jesse had stepped out the door, then turned on the flashlight. The patio was well lit by a single bright bulb on the side of the house, but the pool and surrounding area lay in shadows. She swept the yard with the bright beam. It made an eerie circle on the well-tended shrubbery, but there was nothing unusual to see—until she aimed the light at the pool.

"There's something floating in the water," she whispered.

Jesse took Aubrey's hand to ensure a cautious approach. In another couple of steps, he recognized the victim. "It's the opossum you claimed you heard last night. He's obviously dead and he didn't have time to drown."

Gripped by terror, Aubrey pulled Jesse back from the edge of the pool with a frantic jerk. "Don't get any closer. He might have been electrocuted."

"What?" Jesse felt as though the patio had taken a fast five-foot drop and it took his stomach several seconds to catch up. "Of course. The poor critter must have sidled up to the pool for a drink and zap, he was toast. We're calling the police right now, Aubrey. This was no accident, and if we'd stopped for a swim before going out to dinner, we might have lost more than our appetites."

Aubrey had refused to believe Jesse's claims that she was in danger, but clearly someone had wanted her dead badly enough to rig the lights in the pool to electrocute her. That thought was far worse than any vision could ever be, and she didn't intend to let the culprit get away with it. She backed away from the pool with a shaky step, but she had never been more determined.

"I'll help you, Jesse," she promised in a breathless rush. "You have my word on it. The visions were horrifying, but they were no more than sickening images. This threat is real."

Jesse let out a startled howl as Lucifer brushed up against his leg. "Here's your cat. Let's bring him inside before he gets thirsty."

Aubrey shut off the flashlight and scooped up the affectionate tomcat in her arms. "My cleaning woman was here this morning, and I've never known her to take time out to swim, but my God, what if she had? The pool man comes tomorrow. If that poor opossum hadn't been killed tonight, we wouldn't have known the pool wasn't safe and it could have been him we found floating face down. What kind of monster sets a deadly trap when he can't be certain who'll be the victim?"

Jesse held the screen door open for her. "The kind who wipes out whole families without batting an eye. I wonder if anyone saw a gold Corvette parked nearby today."

Aubrey set Lucifer down in the kitchen and went to the telephone. "I don't know what to tell the police."

Jesse moved to her side and took the receiver. "Don't worry. I'll just get them over here, and they'll be able to see the problem for themselves." Jesse dialed 911 and reported a strong suspicion someone with deadly intentions had tampered with Ms. Glenn's pool. The police station was only a mile away, and as he replaced the receiver, he heard sirens in the distance. "Can't ask for better service than that. They're on the way."

"Our frozen yogurt's melting," Aubrey murmured absently, and Jesse drew her into a comforting hug. Without a thought of what tricks her mind might play, she slid her arms around his waist to return it. For a brief instant she felt safe, then embarrassed to need his warmth so badly, she backed away and went to the front door to wait for the police.

Aubrey's street was soon blocked by police cars and fire engines, their motors running with a deep, throaty hum. Lured by the noise and flashing lights, neighbors, who hadn't spoken to each other since the last major earthquake, came outside to mill about on the sidewalk and speculate on what had prompted such an impressive response from the city.

With so much excitement going on, no one took any particular notice of John Gilroy walking the German shepherd through their midst. He was simply mistaken for someone who lived nearby, and curious like them, had been drawn their way to investigate. "That's Aubrey Glenn's house," Cecile Blanchard told him. "She wrote a bestseller not too long ago."

"Did she now," John replied. He focused his attention on his dog, thereby shielding his face from her view. "Was there a fire?"

"No. I don't think so. Can't smell any smoke. Do you remember that big blaze up on Old Mill Road a few years back? Took the whole roof right off that English Tudor home."

"Is that a fact?"

"It lit up the whole sky. That was really something to see. Not much to look at here, though."

"Guess not," John agreed, and moved on. Up the block he overheard a mention of the man who drove the Chevy truck parked in Aubrey's driveway, and paused, hoping to learn something useful, but gleaned only sly innuendos about what his relationship to the author might be. The paramedics had accompanied the fire engines, but they were standing at the back of their ambulance, chatting with a couple of little boys. Disappointed they hadn't carried Aubrey's lifeless body out on a stretcher, John was about to leave when he caught sight of her silhouetted against her open front door. She was speaking with a police officer and the tall dude who seemed to be her constant companion was right beside her.

Knowing Harlan Caine was going to be furious with him, John swore under his breath. He pulled the dog along beside him and left the scene at a near run. He had been positive he had come up with the perfect plan to get rid of Aubrey Glenn, but since it hadn't worked, he would quickly devise another. "That bitch is history," he promised himself.

He had parked his Corvette three blocks away, and after unlocking the door, he slapped the dog's rump and urged him into the passenger seat. "You're not half bad," he told him. "Maybe I won't take you back to the pound after all."

Responding to John's encouraging tone, the dog licked his hand and turned to the window to enjoy the ride back to his new home.

It was nearly midnight before the last of the police and fire personnel left and Aubrey and Jesse were again alone. She put her pets to bed, then carried their dishes into the sink and turned on the water. Just as quickly, she shut it off. "What if the whole house has been booby-trapped? Am I going to pull a book from the shelves tomorrow and set off explosives?"

"I certainly hope not. Whoever rigged the pool must have expected it to be effective. I doubt that he would have set back-up traps, but if you like, we can call the police department again in the morning and have them send someone to search the house thoroughly. We were here nearly an hour before going to dinner, and if anything had been wrong, you probably would have sensed it then."

"Not if it happened while we were at dinner rather than during the day."

Jesse stepped close and rested his hands on her shoulders. "Stop it. I wanted you to be more aware of the danger we're in, but I don't want you to make yourself sick imagining exploding books or poisoned salt shakers."

Aubrey sent an anxious glance toward the breakfast table. There was a set of salt and pepper shakers by the napkin holder, but she never used them. "I don't salt my food."

"That's probably real healthy," Jesse commented before

tightening his hold on her. "My point was simply that while we have to be cautious, we ought not to be paranoid. Now I searched the house when we came home and nothing seemed out of the ordinary but if you're really afraid to sleep here tonight, let's go over to my aunt's."

"She can't possibly still be awake, and I'd not want to impose on her anyway." Aubrey focused her attention on the pearl snaps running down the front of his shirt. How had she come to be standing in a cowboy's arms worrying about being murdered? It was absolutely absurd, but he smelled delicious and as she forced her gaze up to meet his, his confident smile was so wonderfully reassuring that her fears melted into the anguished temptation of desire. When he dipped his head, she no longer wished to escape him and reached up to meet his kiss. His mouth was warm, and the pressure of his lips so tender she clung to him, silently encouraging far more—and he gave it willingly.

When he at last broke away to take a ragged breath, Aubrey understood the question in his eyes without being asked. This wasn't about simply being afraid to sleep alone, but about wanting, needing to be with him. She began to unsnap his shirt with careless tugs, and when he laughed way back in his throat, she knew she wasn't the first woman to undress him. "I bet you're real popular in Arizona."

"Honey, I'm popular everywhere I go." Jesse laughed out loud at that arrogant boast, then wrapped his arms around Aubrey's waist and lifted her clear off her feet. "That doesn't mean I'm easy, though."

Aubrey slid her arms around his neck and ruffled the curls at his nape. "Liar, but you're a long way from the rodeo, and I expect more than eight seconds from you."

Jesse silenced her laughter with a kiss he deepened until whatever doubts she may have had about his prowess as a lover were dissolved in a languid sigh of surrender. He set her down on the edge of the counter, stepped between her legs, and slid his hands under her pale blue skirt. She had not bothered with pantyhose and he ran his hands up the inside of her thighs. Her bare skin warmed to his touch, and the sweet, silken softness of her felt so good to him that he took his time working his way up to her panties.

Aubrey drank in Jesse's lavish kisses with a moan of abandon. She had learned as a teenager that some boys took the time to make a kiss sublime while others ruined the affectionate gesture with a single hasty tongue thrust. Jesse's kisses were hot and sweet, a luscious, sensual caress he had raised to an artform. She cupped his face in her hands and slid her fingertips over the smoothness of his jaw. With her eyes closed, she still saw him clearly and was bewitched by his teasing grin.

They were an improbable pair, but the intuition she cherished told her this was right. She shut out all thoughts save those of him, and the only vision that filled her mind was one of heavenly bliss. She slipped her hands inside his shirt and ran them over the smooth, muscular planes of his back. As her fingertips brushed his skin, she felt an almost musical tingle.

She leaned into him as he moved his hands to her hips, then down again over the satin barrier of her panties. He traced lazy circles with his thumb between her legs, teasing her senses with a mere hint of the erotic possibilities they might explore until she shuddered with longing. He stepped back a moment to remove her panties, but neither could bear to end their deep kiss. He quickly pressed close, his belt buckle cool against the flatness of her belly, before he brought his hand up between them.

Aubrey was already wet, and Jesse used her salty essence to ease the taunting trail of his fingertips. With a touch that was both feather-light, yet knowing, he dipped into her, then slowly moved up, caressing her most sensitive flesh with a leisurely grace that brought her to the brink of rapture before he withdrew to deliberately create a craving for more. All the while, his kisses bestowed an affection mere words could never express.

He slid his fingers into her again and with a fluttering rhythm delved deep, while using his thumb to tease the bud at the peak of her cleft. Then once again he stilled his intimate caress and waited for the joyous sensations he had coaxed forth to subside. Filled with an aching need, Aubrey wrapped her legs around him, but with a response that was carefully timed, Jesse remained still a few more seconds.

Then all he had to do was brush his thumb across her and the delicate motion set off a tumultuous climax that rocked Aubrey clear to her soul. She stiffened in his embrace, and Jesse tightened his hold on her as she relaxed completely and went limp in his arms. He cradled her head against his shoulder and waited until he thought she wouldn't still be so sensitive that he would cause her pain before he reached for his belt buckle.

The pleasure rippling through Aubrey was so intense that it was an effort to breathe, let alone think, but when she felt Jesse unbuttoning his Levi's, she put her hands against his chest and shoved hard. "No. Wait."

A look of stunned disbelief crossed Jesse's face. "Don't you want more?"

That was most definitely not Aubrey's problem. "I'll probably die in your arms, but yes. I do want more, but you told me you were careful not to father any children. And that's not the only risk if we're not careful."

Jesse had condoms in his shaving kit, but he sure as hell didn't want to take the time to go looking for them. He rested his forehead against Aubrey's and took a deep breath in a valiant attempt to cool down. As he straightened up, he noticed his reflection in the window and realized anyone could be standing in the driveway peering in at them. After all the commotion they had had there that night, he didn't put it past a nosy neighbor to do just that.

He quickly buckled his belt, then plucked Aubrey off the counter and eased her down on her feet. "I've tested HIV negative several times, but you're right, I ought to protect you."

Aubrey bent down to pick up her panties, then looked Jesse in the eye to make a painful admission. "It's you I'm worried about, not me, but let's talk about it upstairs."

Jesse grabbed her arm as she tried to move past him. "Dear God in heaven, you're not HIV positive are you?"

Aubrey hadn't meant to frighten him so badly, and his anguished expression touched her deeply. She covered his hand with her own. She had not thought she would ever be able to relate the whole humiliating episode to anyone, but it was surprisingly easy with him. "Not yet, but Larry cheated on me so often that I've no idea what the future might bring. When you sleep with me, you'll be sleeping with all the women he had sex with, too, and I can't bear to think being with me might rob you of your future."

Only a moment ago, her gaze had shone with the soft light of perfect contentment, and Jesse wanted to create that marvelous expression again and again. He pulled her into his arms and hugged her with a fierce passion. Had they gone swimming that evening, they would have no future, and he could not bear to think of either of them dying now. He had pushed whatever store of luck he might have to the limit when he was riding bulls, but he prayed he had enough left to give Aubrey Glenn the chance to live a long and happy life.

As for Larry Stafford, her snake of an ex-husband, he

sure hoped he had the opportunity to shorten his lifespan by a decade or two. He was going after Harlan Caine to avenge a terrible wrong, but dealing with Larry would be pure pleasure. He stepped back and took Aubrey's hand. He would be happy to continue their discussion upstairs, but he planned to do a hell of a lot more than talk.

Chapter X

Jesse detoured by the den, then went upstairs to Aubrey's bedroom. He had intentionally given her time to change into a lavender satin negligee dripping with lace, but sadly that was his fantasy, and not hers. She was still dressed in blue, and sitting cross-legged in the center of her bed. While he was disappointed, he couldn't help but wonder if she had replaced the satin panties he had removed with a most ungentlemanly haste. He hoped that she hadn't and walked over to the window to hide his grin.

The pool was again lit with a serenely inviting aqua glow, but Jesse doubted either he or Aubrey would want to use it any time soon. Whoever had tampered with the pool lights had created the perfect conditions for a deadly swim. The police and firemen had quickly discovered the source of the problem, but found no clues as to the culprit's identity. An electrician had been summoned to make emergency repairs, but nothing could soothe Jesse's sense of outrage. Clearly someone wanted them dead, but without evidence, they couldn't lay the crime at Harlan Caine's door. Neither of them had mentioned the developer's name, but it still rang with a menacing clang in his mind.

Turning away from the window, Jesse sat down on the softly cushioned windowseat and smiled invitingly. Whether or not he cared to hear it, he sensed Aubrey needed to tell him about her ex-husband's affairs. He had absolutely no intention of providing the lengthy list of his own. "I find it difficult to believe you'd stay with a man who was unfaithful to you."

"I didn't know," Aubrey replied. "Perhaps that sounds ridiculous, but while I was well aware that nothing I did ever really pleased Larry, I didn't realize his dissatisfaction went that far."

She twisted her calla lily ring as she attempted to express the depth of her dismay, but it all seemed so long ago now and the pain which had stabbed through her then was no more than a faint memory. "As I told you, Larry is an ambitious and successful attorney. He frequently worked long hours preparing for a case and he'd always have his secretary call to tell me not to bother making dinner or wait up for him. It was one of the few thoughtful things he did—or so I thought at the time."

Jesse leaned back against the windowsill and crossed his ankles to get comfortable. He already had the whole picture, but again, didn't want to rush Aubrey into bed when he planned to keep her there a very long time. "But he wasn't really working late, was he?"

Aubrey glanced up at Jesse only briefly. His expression was filled with sympathy rather than pity, and that warmed her clear through. "A good deal of the time he was, but several evenings a month it was merely an excuse to keep me from growing suspicious. Frequently he'd have to take trips out of town, and apparently they weren't strictly business. He always told me they were, however, so that I'd not ask to come along. I know you must think me incredibly naïve, but my parents have such a close, loving marriage that I'd been raised to expect fidelity.''

Jesse didn't pause to reflect upon what he had been raised to expect from marriage, but it wasn't the idyllic partnership she described. Now there was a tale, he thought, but not one he had ever shared. ''I can understand that.''

Seated on the violet-strewn bed, Aubrey looked very small and sweet, but Jesse had frequently glimpsed her strength, and while he waited calmly for her to draw upon it, he offered some encouragement. ''Tonight wasn't the first time I've accused you of not being nearly as open in private as you are in your seminars, but there's really only a small portion of yourself that you won't share. I asked you for the truth the afternoon Larry was here. You told me part of it then, and I appreciate your having the courage to tell me the rest now. How did you find out about Larry's affairs?''

''I told you that I'd asked him for a divorce, then reconsidered. It was during that time. I was taking a couple of Larry's suits to the cleaners, and in the pocket of one found the travel agents' flight schedule from his last trip. There was a woman's name, Karen West, on it in addition to his. I didn't want to believe that he'd been unfaithful and thought she might possibly be an associate of his firm who'd also had reason to make the trip.

''At the same time, my intuition chided me for not accepting the truth while I was holding the blatant evidence in my hand. Still, on the off chance Karen West was with Larry's firm, I telephoned and asked for her. The receptionist gave a startled gasp, which in itself revealed a great deal, then said she had never heard of Ms. West. I found her name in the telephone book and left a message on her answering machine. I merely gave my name and said we really ought to discuss our mutual acquaintance.

"Larry came home early that afternoon, and I'd never seen him so angry. I already had my bags packed and didn't respond to his hostile accusations that I'd been spying on him. That outraged him all the more because there had been a time when all he had to do was raise his voice in a slight reproach and I'd dissolve in tears. When he realized that he'd no longer get such an emotional response from me, he lost his temper completely. He didn't just admit that he'd had an affair with Karen, he bragged about it, then began spewing out names of the other women he had slept with during our marriage. A couple were attorneys I'd actually met, but most were women he'd simply picked up in hotel bars when he traveled."

Aubrey remembered that horrible afternoon vividly. "At the time, I'd already detached from the heartache he had caused me and it was as though I were watching some ghastly confrontation in a movie." She whispered the last of it very softly. "Of course, he claimed it was all my fault, and that if I'd only done more to please him, he'd never have strayed."

Jesse straightened up. "That's bullshit."

Aubrey shrugged. "That's precisely what I thought at the time. It was a last ditch effort to undermine my confidence in myself as a woman, and even seeing it for exactly what it was, the words still hurt. But a feeling of betrayal was my primary emotion, and I could barely recall how much I'd once loved him. All I loved was the illusion he had created before our marriage, not the man who truly was my husband."

Aubrey released a poignant sigh. "I consider myself lucky that he didn't bring home any sexually transmitted diseases while we were married, but who knows what the future might bring? Perhaps there's something even worse than AIDS that also has a long dormant period and has yet to be discovered."

She was studying her ring rather than looking up at him, but Jesse couldn't allow her to live another minute expecting a death sentence that might never come. He yanked off his boots and set them aside before walking over to the bed where he sat down beside her. He raised his hand to her shoulder and began to rub her back in gentle circles.

"I think you'll create a spectacular future, one without a bitter legacy from your ex-husband. I've read that Don Juan-types are such insecure individuals they have to constantly pump themselves up with new conquests. That's really pathetic. I'm not even sure marriage is still a viable institution, except for those who want children, but you're far too much woman to be alone. You mustn't let anything Larry said make you doubt just how desirable you truly are."

When he leaned down to kiss her, Aubrey had no doubts at all. She reached up to encircle his neck and pulled him down with her on the bed. She knew as well as he did that they were a mismatched pair if there ever was one, but it didn't matter tonight. He hadn't buttoned up his shirt, and she slid her hand down his belly, tracing the thin line of blond curls that disappeared beneath his belt buckle. She drank in his scent, and then leaned back to ask what it was.

"It's Lagerfeld. I don't know what kind of clothes he designs, but I like his cologne."

Aubrey raised up slightly. "So do I, but I didn't realize cowboys would bother with it."

"You've been watching too many Westerns. We're quite civilized now." Jesse pulled her back into his arms and kissed her long and hard. She relaxed against him with a fluid grace, but he wanted her closer still. He shrugged off his shirt and hung it over the foot of the bed. He usually didn't waste much time undressing a woman, but he was still worried about spooking Aubrey.

"I don't want to wrinkle your clothes," he whispered against her throat.

His mustache tickled her skin in the most delightful way, and Aubrey arched into his caress. She would not have cared had he ripped off her dress, and wrinkles were not even a minimal concern. When he eased his hand up her leg, she tensed slightly. She had tossed her panties in the hamper, and he nearly choked on the delicious rush when he found her bare. He moistened his fingers in her wetness and began to tease her again with a whisper-soft touch that was now achingly familiar.

"One of us is going to have to get you out of that dress," Jesse promised with a lazy chuckle. "If you don't want me to stop what I'm doing, then it will have to be you."

There was no question as to whether Aubrey wanted him to continue, and she fumbled with the single button at the neckline of the soft knit dress, then yanked it off over her head and tossed it aside. She unfastened the center snap on her ice-blue bra, and quickly discarded it as well as the matching half-slip. Barefoot to begin with, she was now nude, but felt no embarrassment under Jesse's admiring gaze. He moved up slightly to lap at her breast, and she ran her fingers through his hair to hold him close to her heart.

It had been so long since she had made love, really made love as they were now, and she closed her eyes to drift on the luscious sensations. There was a magic to being with Jesse that mere chemistry didn't explain, and yet she didn't want to analyze it for fear of spoiling its spell. She giggled when he trailed kisses down to her navel, then gasped with delighted surprise when he shifted position to move lower and brought his mouth down on her.

His intimate kiss was incredibly sweet, and she reached

for his hair, guiding him with subtle hints to make his lavish affection even more arousing. He rolled his tongue and drank up her nectar with an excruciating tenderness that was almost more than she could sanely bear. The instant he slid his fingers inside her again, her body responded with an explosive climax that ricocheted down her spine and rebounded clear to her fingertips and toes.

Her spirit soared, then spiraled to earth in a glorious freefall. She felt Jesse leave the bed to slip out of his Levi's, but could barely lift her hand to welcome him as he rejoined her on the bed. He slid up over her, caressing the whole length of her body with his hardened cock before pausing to pull on a condom, and spreading her legs with his knee. Aubrey watched him through a pleasure-drugged haze as he balanced himself above her on his elbows. Then he kissed her and began to probe with such shallow thrusts that she wrapped her legs around him to encourage him to plunge deep.

She was slippery wet, but tight, and Jesse was filled with a delicious tension he stoked with each stabbing thrust. He stretched her with a slow, relentless rhythm, burrowing deeper and deeper until finally he filled her completely. He lay still for a moment, his tongue sucking hers into his mouth until her body began to contract around his cock as another orgasm caught her by surprise.

She turned her head to call his name in an ecstatic gasp, and he began to move again. Chasing his own release, he rode the waves of rapture coursing through her until neither of them could stand more. It was only then that he abandoned himself to the joy he had given Aubrey so freely. It seared through him with a blistering heat that left him too weak to leave her arms even after the fiery warmth had faded to a faint afterglow.

At perfect peace, Aubrey wished she had dimmed the lights and lit incense before Jesse had come upstairs to her room, but even without those romantic touches, their passion for each other had made the night sublime. She ran her fingertips up over Jesse's broad shoulders and down his back, memorizing the feel of him to fuel her dreams after he was gone. She savored every enchanting second, and offered a soft moan of protest when he at last moved aside.

"I don't want to crush you," he called over his shoulder as he went into her bathroom.

"You won't," Aubrey assured him. When he returned to the bed and pulled her back into his arms, she splayed her fingers across his hairy chest, then combed the coarse curls with her nails. His skin was deeply tanned, except for a jagged white scar that crossed his left hipbone. It was too low for her to have noticed it before, and curious, she sent him a questioning glance.

Jesse laughed and shook his head. "You don't want to hear it."

"Does it involve another woman?"

"Absolutely not," he swore. He waited a long moment, but when she continued to regard him with a pointed glance, he reluctantly gave in. "All right, fine, but don't say I didn't warn you. I was seventeen, and had been riding bulls just long enough to get real cocky." He paused then and took hold of her hand. "Why don't you just touch me there. Maybe you'll be able to see what happened for yourself."

Aubrey immediately jerked her hand away. "I'd rather just hear it, thank you."

Jesse hadn't meant to force another experiment on her. "Whatever you like," he said. His glance swept her delectable figure and despite the intensity of the climax they had shared, he already wanted her again. Burgeoning desire was such a terrible distraction that for an instant he couldn't recall why they were talking, let alone about what.

"Where was I?" he asked. "Oh, yes. I was riding what was only my eighth or ninth bull, a white Brahma with wicked horns."

Aubrey didn't need to hear any more. "My God. You were gored?"

"Well, let's just say the bull gave it his best shot, but his horn bounced off my hipbone rather than ripping through my intestines, so I walked out of the arena waving to the crowd. I got a real roar of applause. Then I collapsed. The wound wasn't deep, but that didn't make the scar any less nasty. That's why I told you it's not the horns you have to worry about, but the bull's hooves."

Aubrey didn't want to ever touch the scar now, then realized that while they had made love, he had been stretched out over her. Every inch of his magnificent body had been aligned with hers, and pleasure had been the only result. Still, she could not help but wonder if he had a deathwish. "And you kept right on riding bulls?"

Clearly she thought him just plain nuts, but Jesse smiled agreeably. "Not until my side healed I didn't, but when I went to my next rodeo, I was a lot more focused and rode better than ever. In fact, my career really took off then, and I never looked back."

From what she knew of him, she doubted that he ever dwelt on the past, but she hoped he would remember her as fondly as she would recall the time they spent together. "I'm not certain if you're very brave, or merely foolish. At least you didn't take up bullfighting. That's sheer lunacy."

"Yes, indeed." Jesse leaned over to lick Aubrey's breast, and the pale pink nipple tensed into a flavorful bud. "You taste awfully good."

Aubrey was delighted by his compliment, but laid her hand on his shoulder. "Turn the lights down a bit, will you, please?"

Jesse searched her face and willed her to want the same thing he did. "I like being able to look at you."

Aubrey had never been so delightfully uninhibited with a man, but still, she preferred a less brilliant light. "I didn't say I wanted it dark, only dim and seductive."

"I think I've already been seduced," Jesse countered, but he got up, found the dimmer switch, and muted the overhead lights. "There, is that better?"

Aubrey watched him walk toward the bed. With broad shoulders, narrow hips, and long legs, he had the elegant proportions of a classical statue, but he was very much alive. "You're very handsome," she offered in a contented purr, for indeed he was better looking than most male models, and unfortunately he knew it.

Even in the muted light, Aubrey's luscious curves invited lengthy lovemaking, and Jesse made his intentions plain as soon as he stretched out beside her. He ran his hand down over her hip, then up her inner thigh, before invading the moist heat between her legs. He kissed her lips lightly as he began to trace slippery trails with his fingertips to again lead her into a paradise entirely of their own making.

Aubrey had never slept with such a generous lover, and matched his every kiss and caress with one of her own. Jesse was as responsive to the touch of her fingertips and lips as she was to his, and by the time they finally fell asleep locked in each other's arms, neither could have asked for more. It wasn't until Aubrey awakened near noon, and alone, that what had been so real during the night seemed little more than a splendid illusion.

She savored the memory and fought an overwhelming sense of loss. Jesse had come into her life for a purpose, and she doubted it had anything to do with the tragedy that had befallen the Ferrells. Instead, it might only have been to give her the courage to trust her heart again—

and trust it she did. She would have to thank him for that extraordinary gift and forgive him for causing her pain when he left.

She quickly made up the bed, showered, and then dressed in jeans and an apricot silk shirt. She rummaged through the floor of her closet and found a pair of tan boots to complete the outfit. Projecting the same air of confidence she drew upon for her seminars, she strode into the kitchen and greeted Jesse warmly. Then she yanked open the refrigerator as though having breakfast were the only thing on her mind.

Jesse had been perusing the sports section of the *Times*, but quickly folded the paper and set it aside. He hadn't known quite what to expect from Aubrey that morning, but he was grateful that she sounded so cheerful. "I won't ask how you slept because I know, but there is something else I need to say."

Aubrey set the bottle of cranberry juice on the counter and closed the refrigerator with an easy shove. Way ahead of him, she delivered the expected speech before he could. "Please. You needn't tell me how sorry you are you'll soon be going back to Arizona. We both know this isn't going anywhere, but that won't make it any less enjoyable while it lasts." She filled a glass with juice and raised it in a silent toast.

Aubrey Glenn continually amazed Jesse, but he doubted that she could really regard sleeping with him as casually as she had just made it sound. Still, it was a hell of a lot better than being greeted with a tearful demand for his intentions. "Thank you, but I was about to mention my plan to revisit my cousin's house, rather than give you the, 'It's been fun, but—'speech. You're a whole lot better than just fun, by the way."

Jesse's teasing grin was already imprinted on her heart, and Aubrey smiled easily in return. Some things weren't meant to last, but that did not mean they weren't precious. He had already had a bowl of cereal, and not really hungry, she grabbed an apple to eat on the way. "We've gotten such a late start, let's get going."

"That's fine with me." Jesse carried his bowl to the dishwasher and dropped it into an empty slot. He wanted to hold Aubrey for a moment, but before he could reach for her, she left the kitchen to get her purse and sunglasses and the moment was lost. He had left her bed because he couldn't think straight with her cuddled against him, but now he thought it might have been a mistake not to wake her and make love again.

He wasn't used to women treating him as though he were no more than a momentary diversion, and while he was too proud to admit it to her, it hurt. Then again, she had told him that she hoped to remarry and have a family, and as a father, he would have damn little to offer a child. He carried that distressing thought outside and looked up at the cloudless sky. Guinevere ran up to the wrought-iron gate. He had fed her and Lucifer that morning, and she recognized him now, and twisted in a welcoming wiggle rather than bark.

Aubrey locked the back door on her way out, but before she and Jesse could climb into his truck, a man and woman appeared at the end of the driveway. The woman was tall and reed thin. A brunette with close-cropped hair, she was dressed in a beige jacket and slacks and carried an over-sized canvas handbag. The man looked to be several years her junior. Slightly overweight, his navy blue suit jacket was stretched over his bulging belly, and the effort to keep up with his slender companion as she hurried up the drive-way left him gasping for breath.

"Ms. Glenn?" the woman called. "May we have a few minutes of your time?"

"Reporters?" Jesse asked softly.

"I'll handle them," Aubrey assured him. "I'm sorry, but I don't give unscheduled interviews."

The woman responded with a hoarse laugh and produced a badge. "I'm Detective Helen Heffley, and this is Detective James Kobin, L.A.P.D., Devonshire Division. How's your time now?"

Jesse took a step forward. "What happened here last night has to be out of your jurisdiction. Is this about the Ferrells?"

Helen and James exchanged a startled glance. "We've no idea what happened here last night. We've been assigned to the Ferrell case and are merely following up on the story that appeared in Monday's *Times*. Are you Ms. Glenn's attorney?"

Jesse had left his Stetson in his truck, but dressed in a Western shirt, Levi's, and boots, he sure didn't think he resembled an attorney. "I'm Jesse Barrett," he announced proudly, "and no one has ever mistaken me for a lawyer."

Helen swept him with a bored glance. "You'd be surprised at the people who pass the bar exam. Now let's cut the chitchat and get on with it. Could we go inside?"

After the way Aubrey's privacy had been invaded last night, she didn't feel up to inviting them into her home. "It's a pleasant day, let's just use the patio." She opened the gate and hushed Guinevere, who had begun to bark the instant the detectives came into view.

Once they were all seated at the round glass table, Aubrey waited for Kobin to mop his forehead with his handkerchief, then chose her words with deliberate care. "Jesse is Pete Ferrell's cousin. He mistakenly believed I possessed some talent as a psychic, but I don't. We went out to the Ferrells' home, but I didn't see it all."

"Did you?" Helen asked Jesse.

"Yes, but my aunt gave me the key, so it was perfectly

legal. There's no yellow tape strung around the house, nor notice on the door that it's a crime scene.''

Helen glanced toward her partner and rolled her eyes. "Do I detect a bit of hostility here, Mr. Barrett?''

Jesse laughed. "You're the detective, you tell me. You've had more than two years to find out what happened to my cousin and his family, and failed to make a single arrest. Meanwhile, Harlan Caine has probably kept right on attracting unsuspecting investors for projects he'll never build.'' He offered a brief summary of the pool incident, then glanced toward Aubrey.

"I didn't intend to use Ms. Glenn as bait to trap Caine, but I suppose even that would be better than what we've seen from the police.''

Helen bristled at Jesse's sarcasm. "There's a vast difference between having a suspect, and granted, Harlan Caine is one, and proving his guilt. Frankly, there are a few psychics who've actually solved crimes, but that's been an extremely rare occurrence, so we didn't really expect any concrete leads from Ms. Glenn. However, we do want to caution you both about any further involvement in the case. Last night certainly sounds like an attempt on your lives, and you mustn't push your luck any further. Stop whatever amateur sleuthing you've been doing and leave crime solving to the professionals.''

Jesse leaned forward. "At the rate you're progressing, you'll retire before you discover what happened to my cousin's family—so don't ask, nor expect, me to butt out.'' He rose and stretched to his full height. "Did you have any other questions, Detective?'' Jesse slurred the title into an insult.

Helen rose and handed Aubrey her card. "Here's my number should you need help reining in Wild Bill.'' She summoned her taciturn partner with a quick nod and strode out of the patio with him again tagging along behind her.

Aubrey tapped the card on the table. "Interesting pair. Do you suppose Kobin ever has anything to say?"

"Would she allow it if he did?"

"I certainly hope so." Aubrey picked up her purse as she left her chair. "I've no intention of attempting to rein you in, by the way. Caine made a very bad mistake last night, and I think he ought to pay for it."

"Yeah, it's never wise to attack an enemy on his own turf."

Aubrey opened the gate and held it for Jesse. "That wasn't what I meant," she told him. "His mistake was that he failed."

Shocked by the determined tilt to her chin, Jesse decided Helen Heffley had also made a grave tactical error. It was Aubrey, not he, who had the wild streak and needed to be reined in. Fortunately, he had already found an effective way to do it.

"What are you grinning about?" She paused beside his truck.

Jesse opened her door and waited for her to get in. "Nothing at all, sweetheart." Before he closed her door, he leaned in and kissed her soundly. "I should have done that earlier. You look awfully pretty this morning and I should have said so."

"Thank you. You look damn good yourself, but we're wasting time and if I end up sick again, I want to be able to get over it before tonight."

"Something good on TV?" Jesse asked as he slid into his place behind the steering wheel.

"Maybe, but I don't intend to watch it."

"Damn, but I love a woman who knows what she wants."

Aubrey responded with a knowing smile, but she wished he hadn't mentioned love. She refused to give what they shared such a tender name when it would be over as quickly as it began. Instead, for the present she would concentrate her energies on searching the Ferrells' house for clues, and pray she did not find anything too hideous to endure.

Chapter XI

Jesse turned on the truck's radio as soon as he pulled onto the freeway, but Aubrey was too preoccupied to care that his taste in music didn't match her own. She drummed her fingers in a restless rhythm on the armrest as she recalled her first visit to the house. The beautiful backyard had held an inviting serenity, but she doubted a second tour through the interior would provide such a pleasant respite.

"Do you always do that when you're nervous?" Jesse asked.

Startled by the sound of his voice, Aubrey shrugged slightly. "Do what?"

"I wouldn't mind if you were just drumming your fingers with a steady thump, but your nails are clicking like *castanets*." He reached for her left hand and gave her a fond squeeze. "It'll be over before you know it."

"I certainly hope so." When he released her, Aubrey clasped her hands in her lap. "I didn't mean to bother you. It's just that as Detective Heffley said, there's a vast difference between having a suspect, and proving his guilt. I'm not sure this is the right approach, but it appears to be the only one we have, unless—''

Jesse noted Aubrey's pensive frown, and waited for her continue. When she didn't, he prodded her. ''Unless what?''

''You mentioned you hadn't intended to use me as bait, but that's obviously what's happened, so maybe we ought to be playing that angle rather than searching for invisible clues at Pete's place.''

''Oh no. Absolutely not.'' Jesse had to keep his eyes on the road as he changed lanes to pass a crate-back truck, then shot Aubrey a glance laced with the same strident authority which rang in his voice. ''I feel terrible about the danger I put you in unwittingly. To deliberately goad Harlan Caine is out of the question.''

Aubrey adopted a forced calm. ''You don't regard what we're doing as dangerous? After all, there have been people who've been so traumatized by witnessing the horror of death in an accident or wartime that they've never recovered. Now I'm willing to push whatever ability I might possess to the limit to pay Caine back for trying to kill us, but that doesn't mean I'm discounting the risk.''

Ashamed that he had, Jesse apologized. ''I'm sorry. You've gotten sick twice on my account and I'd not even considered that what you might find today could be a whole lot worse. I sure hope it isn't, but I should have considered it. You have every right to be nervous. I'm sorry I complained about the noise of your nails.''

Aubrey reached over to grasp his thigh and felt his muscles tense beneath her touch. It quickly brought to mind how much she had enjoyed being with him last night. More than enjoyed, really, but she was at a loss for the correct superlative. ''Hush. For all we know, I might not sense anything, and this trip will be a total waste of our time.''

An Alan Jackson tune came on the radio and Jesse turned up the volume slightly. Women had told him that he resembled the tall, blond singer, but Jesse couldn't see it. "I'll stay with you," he promised. "I should have thought to bring a tape recorder. Then even if the police won't accept your impressions as evidence, you wouldn't have to repeat them endlessly."

Aubrey leaned down and rummaged through the purse she'd set between her feet. In a moment, she withdrew a palm-sized tape recorder. "I grabbed this from my office on the way out. I don't use it anymore because Gardner is always there to record my sessions, but I thought using it would be easier than relying on memory."

"Have I ever mentioned how much I admire your intelligence?"

"I believe that was one of the few things you overlooked last night."

Jesse winked at her. "Then I'll be sure to mention it tonight."

Aubrey hoped she would feel up to making love again, then rushed to distract herself from the possibility that she might not. "When I was growing up, I'd often guess what a gift contained before I'd unwrapped it. It was merely a game, but I was usually right. Of course, the size of the box limited the possibilities and was in itself a strong clue. I got so good at it I finally had to stop announcing my guess because whoever had given me the present would be disappointed that it wasn't a surprise."

"If that's the case, then I was wrong about your acquiring the ability to sense information. You've always possessed the talent."

"Yes, but without positive reinforcement, I didn't pursue it. Now it seems a shame. Then again, perhaps I'm making too much of it."

The wistful lilt to her voice stirred Jesse's conscience,

but they were in too deep to simply turn around and go home. He reminded himself that they weren't safe even there with Harlan Caine's sinister intentions—if it really was Harlan Caine who was the culprit. If he wasn't, then Jesse would be at a complete loss for what to do.

By the time they reached the Ferrells' home, Aubrey was eager to get the ordeal over with. She bounded out of the truck without waiting for Jesse to help her and then remembered the woman who lived next door. "Roberta Smaus called the newspaper the last time we were here and that visit was more innocent than this. Do we dare alert her to our presence again?"

Jesse took hold of Aubrey's arm as they moved through the gate. "No. There's nothing illegal about our being here and I don't want to provide anyone with more photo opportunities. Let's hope we can come and go today without causing a ripple of notice."

"Stay with me," Aubrey urged.

"Don't worry. I won't stray." Jesse had the key ready when they reached the front door.

They had come through the service porch on their first visit, and Aubrey paused in the entryway. The house was chilly despite the warmth of the day, and the air uncomfortably still. She swallowed hard, and pressed the button to start the tape recorder. "The house seems undisturbed since we were here on Sunday. Because Marlene meant to boil water for spaghetti, I'd like to begin in the kitchen."

The family room was on the left, but Aubrey walked right through it to reach the kitchen. Only a cooking island separated the two rooms, and while the family room's furnishings were draped with sheets, she could easily envision Marlene working in the kitchen and talking with her sons while they were doing their homework in the adjoining room. "Let's uncover everything, so we can see it exactly as it was the last time the Ferrells were here."

"Makes sense to me," Jesse agreed, and he began pulling the sheets from the comfortably worn maple sofa, chairs, and low coffee table. The television set was recessed into a wall unit, but it had also been covered, and he pulled away the sheet. Not really knowing what to do with the bundle of linens, he carried them out into the entryway and dropped them on the glossy tile.

Aubrey stood at the stove, set down the tape recorder, and then gingerly rested her hands on the counter. "I don't feel anything yet," she revealed softly. "Give me a minute or two."

"Take all the time you need."

Aubrey closed her eyes. On Sunday, she had not merely been apprehensive about the wisdom of their mission, but angry with Jesse for kissing her. She had been horribly uncomfortable, but now she wondered if she hadn't been reacting to her own foul mood rather than responding to any possible distress the Ferrells might have suffered.

She took a deep breath and released it slowly. Perfectly relaxed, she welcomed whatever sensation might come, but when the wait grew tiresome, she looked up at Jesse. "I don't feel anything, but let's tour the whole house, and maybe something will strike me." She picked up the tape recorder.

Jesse preceded her into the dining area at the end of the formal living room and again whisked the sheets from the furniture. The house was decorated throughout in a cozy Early American style with braided rugs and a liberal use of maple and tiny prints in shades of wine and blue. Marlene had loved to needlepoint, and there were attractive examples of her work on decorative pillows heaped on the sofa. Currier and Ives prints were featured on the walls, along with Aububon's magnificent birds.

"It looks as though there was a great deal of love here." Audrey picked up a handcrafted pillow from the sofa and pressed it to her chest. "Perhaps that's what's lingered here, Jesse, rather than the frightful evening they all disappeared."

Jesse felt only the chill, and wished he had worn his jacket. "Are you cold?"

"A little, but it's all right." Aubrey replaced the pillow with a gentle pat, then turned toward the hallway leading to the bedrooms. She spoke clearly into the small tape recorder. "I'm facing the wing with the bedrooms. This is as far as I went the last time."

"I remember." Jesse kept his distance so as not to distract her. "Marlene's and Pete's room is to the left. The boys' rooms are on your right."

Aubrey entered the master bedroom and helped Jesse remove the sheets covering the bed and dresser. Photographs of the family had been displayed on the dresser, but were now turned face down. She set the tape recorder down again and reached for the first frame. When she turned it over, she found two giggling infants in sailor suits. Her eyes flooded with tears, and she quickly replaced the photo on the dresser.

"I'm sorry, but I can't look at the other photographs. It's simply too sad." She crossed to the bed and sat down on the quilted spread. "There are people who die in natural disasters, or plane crashes, and random accidents wipe out entire families in an instant, but this crime is almost beyond imagining."

Seated with her shoulders slumped, Aubrey projected such an anguished mood Jesse couldn't bear it. "Come on. Let's get out of here. I can see what this is doing to you, and it just isn't worth it." He unfurled the sheet he had pulled from the dresser and hastily recovered it.

"What's a few minutes of discomfort compared to what the Ferrells suffered, or what Caine tried to do to us?"

"Enough," Jesse ordered. "There has to be another way."

"If there was, the police would have found it." Aubrey picked up the tape recorder as she swept by Jesse and went on down the hallway to the boys' bedrooms. She walked into the first, and held her breath, but like the rest of the house, her only impression was one of immense sorrow. She tarried only a minute in the second bedroom, and then turned to find Jesse waiting at the doorway.

"Nothing?" he asked.

Aubrey's brow furrowed slightly with concentration. "There's definitely a presence here, but it's merely a mist of sadness. It's as though the house knows it's empty and misses the Ferrells." Aubrey shut off the recorder. "Perhaps I'm romanticizing things, or projecting my own emotions into this."

Jesse had never wanted to hold a woman more to simply offer the comfort of his presence rather than sex, but the chill of the house was giving him the creeps, and he wanted to leave. "I've walked through the house several times, but if it's holding any clues, neither the police nor I could find them."

A math book was open on the desk, and Aubrey laid her hand on it, but felt only the cool slickness of the paper rather than the happy noise of a classroom. "The police have a substance in a spray that can detect the presence of blood even after it's been washed away. I saw it in a TV movie once, and the effect was stunning. Did they try it here?"

"I believe it's called luminol, and yes. It was used here, with absolutely no result. But there are plenty of ways to kill people without splattering the walls with blood."

"That's a pleasant thought." The chill had begun to sink into Aubrey's bones, and she rubbed her arms briskly. "Come on. Let's cover the furniture and go."

They completed the chore quickly, but as Aubrey made a final pass through the kitchen, she glanced out the window at the double car garage. "Let's go out the backdoor and check the garage."

Jesse felt as though he had already asked too much and reluctantly followed her outside. He was suffering from a strange combination of disappointment and relief, and was anxious to go. The garage was padlocked, but he sorted through the keys his aunt had given him and found one to unlock it. He then moved to the center, grabbed the handle, and raised the heavy wooden door. Two cars were parked inside, a silver Toyota van and a white Chevrolet Camaro.

"How many cars did your cousins own?" Aubrey asked.

"Just these two, which made the police's insistence that they'd probably skipped town all the more absurd. They checked the records of the taxi companies and airport vans, and none had made a pickup here. There were no airline nor bus reservations in their names.

"Their disappearance wouldn't have been noted as quickly as it was had there not been a PTA meeting that night. When Marlene didn't show up, one of her friends came by and saw all the lights on, but no one answered the door. When the boys didn't arrive at school the next day, she was so worried she called the police, but there's been no progress from that day to this."

"I'm sorry I couldn't find anything."

"You needn't apologize."

Aubrey had hoped to sense or find something others had overlooked, and hated to walk away without making every effort to do so. She took a step into the garage and shivered, but it was no longer due to the chill of the air. She closed her eyes, and after a moment, an eerie wail coiled through her mind. Something awful had happened

there, and the memory still mingled with the dust motes
floating in the air.

She turned and reached out for Jesse. "Come stand here
beside me and tell me what you feel. I swear I can hear
the silent screams you heard at Andersonville. Can you?"

Jesse came forward and gripped her hand tightly. He
closed his eyes in an effort to suppress the background
noise from the neighborhood. There was the annoying
whine of a leafblower as a gardener cleaned up a yard,
and farther up the street a dog was barking out low, lazy
howls.

The well-tended landscape at Andersonville had been
silent save for the chirping of the birds, and surrounded
by acres of low grave markers, Jesse had been immersed
in the site's former horror. The sorrow there had rolled
up against him in waves, but here, he had to fight all the
outside distractions to touch what couldn't be seen. He
deepened his breathing, coaxing the presence forth, and
just as he was about to give up the attempt as futile, he
heard it, too.

Tears instantly flooded his eyes. "It's Marlene. She's
begging them not to take the boys. Oh, God." What Jesse
felt then was a sorrow so intense he could barely remain
on his feet, and had Aubrey not pulled him back out onto
the sunlit driveway, he surely would have collapsed. Badly
embarrassed to have cried in front of her, he hastily wiped
away his tears, then bent over and rested his hands on his
knees while he struggled to catch his breath.

"I told you the power was in you, Jesse, but you didn't
believe me. Maybe we each have only a particle of what it
takes to function as a psychic, but together, it's enough
for brief flashes of insight."

When Jesse straightened up, he felt drained, as though
he had aged ten years in a matter of minutes while Aubrey

was as cool and composed as she was during her seminars. "Just what did you hear?"

"Merely an anguished cry. You're the one who identified the source, and understood the plea. We are dealing with monsters here, Jesse, and their own arrogance will be their undoing."

She projected a confidence Jesse envied, and he quickly closed the garage, then looped his arm around her shoulders as they walked to his truck. "Let's just go home and rest this afternoon. I don't know what to do next, but maybe something will occur to us tomorrow."

Aubrey had already volunteered to be bait, but Jesse was far too upset to remind him of that now. "Would you like me to drive?"

"Are you kidding? Hell, no. I'm not that shaken up." But Jesse couldn't recall another instance when he had felt so emotionally drained. He gave Aubrey's bottom a playful swat as she climbed up into the Chevy's cab, and then quickly circled around to the driver's side. As he unlocked his door, an engine's low rumble caught his attention and he glanced up in time to see a gold Corvette swing around the corner.

He yanked open his door, and leaped in. "Did you see that?"

"What?" Aubrey had been touching up her lipstick.

Jesse slammed the truck into gear and peeled away from the curb. "There was a gold Corvette parked up the street and that can't have been a coincidence."

"We're being followed?"

Jesse didn't respond, he just turned the first corner as sharply as he could and the next in a skidding slide. "If he beats us back to the freeway, we'll never catch him." He swore under his breath, but when they left the subdivision and turned out onto the thoroughfare, the Corvette was nowhere in sight. Jesse swore a bitter oath. "We've lost him."

"I should have been more alert."

"It's not your fault. At least we know that as long as whoever's following us stays close, he can't have tampered with anything at your home."

"That's some consolation," Aubrey mused, but she kept a close watch on the adjoining lanes as they drove back toward Pasadena. When they got home, she didn't argue with Jesse when he insisted upon going inside first, but as soon as he motioned for her to enter, she pulled a box of Pillsbury Lemon Cheesecake Bars from the cupboard and tied on an apron.

"You're going to cook?" Jesse asked incredulously.

"Yes. It's marvelous therapy. Besides these are delicious and I'm hungry. What about you?"

"Yeah. I could do with some lunch. Shall we steam up a bucket of squash?"

Aubrey was already greasing a retangular baking pan. "I've a can of tuna. I'll make sandwiches. "Just give me a minute to get the lemon bars in the oven."

"I can mix up a can of tuna," Jesse insisted. "I wouldn't have survived this long if I couldn't cook the basics."

"Tuna is definitely in that category." Aubrey moved out of his way so that he could get a small bowl, and soon he was prowling the refrigerator for things to add. "Bell pepper is good along with celery, and I always add a few pecans."

"Pecans?" Jesse winced. He liked just plain tuna and mayonnaise but apparently Aubrey couldn't open a can of tuna without turning it into a gourmet treat. "You're one hell of a woman, Ms. Glenn."

Aubrey slid the pan of lemon bars into the preheated oven. "Where did that come from?"

"It just popped out." He nudged her with his hip and began to chop celery on the counter. "My mother wasn't the best cook in the world, so I began fending for myself real early. To this day I can't stand the sight of meatloaf.''

"That wasn't one of her best recipes?'' Aubrey carried the mixing bowl to the sink and filled it with water.

"Hers more closely resembled an adobe brick than anything edible. It's a wonder we didn't bust our teeth trying to chew it.''

Aubrey couldn't help but be amused. "What did your father say about your mother's cooking?''

"Well, he wasn't what anyone would describe as particular, and I don't believe he ever noticed. He was fond of snacking on beef jerky, which will tell you a lot about his tastes.''

Aubrey tried to imagine what his parents must look like, but even observing him for inspiration, they refused to come clear. "Are your parents still living?''

Jesse diced a couple of slices of bell pepper before replying. "No. They're both gone. They died within a couple of months of each other a few years back. Hand me a spoon for this, will you?''

Aubrey quickly supplied a mixing spoon, then not wanting to hover, she sat down at the breakfast table and sorted through the paper. Larry had never expressed any interest in cooking, and it was a pleasant change to have Jesse help prepare a meal. She stole frequent glances at him as he finished making their sandwiches. He muttered about the mayonnaise when he discovered she had the fat-free variety, but once he sat down with her and took a bite of his sandwich, he ceased to complain.

"This is delicious,'' Aubrey said. "Thank you.''

"You're welcome. I have to admit the pecans add an unexpected crunch,'' Jesse replied. He would have liked a big handful of potato chips, but hadn't found any in the cupboard and supposed they lacked sufficient nutritional value to justify Aubrey's buying them. "I probably ought to go by my aunt's place this afternoon. I don't have much to report, but—"

"Don't tell her about the pool," Aubrey urged.

"I won't even be tempted, but I sure wish I did have something tangible to report."

Aubrey paused in mid-bite. She had always known Jesse would be returning home soon, but the prospect of his leaving in another day or two was surprisingly painful. They had made no real progress, however, and she knew he could not remain with her indefinitely. That she would even consider the possibility amazed her.

"I really enjoy your company," she suddenly blurted out, "but even if we had met under different circumstances, I doubt anything would have come it. So please don't delay your return home because of me."

This comment, coupled with her earlier one about their not having a future together, made Jesse wonder if Aubrey weren't saying what she thought he wanted to hear. "I don't know about that," he argued. "They say opposites attract, and we're about as opposite as two people can be."

Aubrey took exception to his sly grin. "I'll grant you that people can sometimes be attracted to a complete opposite, and those relationships are generally passionate, but they're also brief. It's people with similar interests and tastes who remain together."

"Doesn't that strike you as the perfect formula for boredom? I'd rather be by myself than with a woman who was exactly like me. Hell, she'd just get in my way." Jesse got up and carried his plate over to the dishwasher. "I like women with spirit, who'll teach me something new, rather than women who are so eager to please, they lose themselves in every man they meet. That's Shelley's problem. She's all wrapped up in that worthless rat. What's his name?"

"Ricky Vance."

"Yeah. Wouldn't it be nice if you could buy courage in a can and spray it up and down Shelley's spine?"

"Or Ricky's. He's the one who needs a boost of character in my view." Aubrey wasn't certain how they had digressed to Shirley's miserable lovelife, but having made so many mistakes herself with Larry, she did not want to pursue it. Fortunately the timer on the stove began to chime, and she had to get up to remove the lemon bars from the oven.

"These really need to cool slightly, but I think I'll just go ahead and cut them while they're still warm and you can take some over to Edith."

"They sure smell delicious. It's a shame all pretty girls can't cook."

"You made the sandwiches from scratch. I baked these from a mix, but what if I were to say what a terrible shame it is that all handsome men can't cook?"

As Aubrey picked up a knife, Jesse moved around to the other side of the cooking island. "Handsome men usually have other talents," he claimed in an engaging drawl.

"So do pretty girls, but why are we talking about men and girls, instead of men and women?"

"I think you better hurry and slap those cookies on a plate before I get myself any deeper into trouble here."

"You see? If we're not focused on finding your missing cousins, we don't get along well at all."

Aubrey ran the knife blade over the lemon bars, gently scoring the golden top before she began to slice. Jesse waited until she was finished to comment. "It's never wise to argue with a *woman,*" he stressed the word, "with a knife in her hand, but we sure didn't lack for compatibility last night."

Aubrey could feel the heat of a blush rise in her cheeks, but forced herself to be equally flippant. "No, we didn't, but I've already warned you not to make more of it than it was."

"Ah, yes, just one of those life-affirming lays after coming close to ending up dead like that singed opposum?"

Aubrey placed half a dozen lemon bars on a plate, and covered them with plastic wrap. That hadn't been her thought at the time, but she let him believe that it had. "You guessed it." She shoved the plate toward him and he took it. "Please tell your aunt hello for me."

Jesse looked down at her, his expression mirroring his confusion. He had never wanted anything permanent with a woman, so why was he arguing with Aubrey when she dismissed the possibility? That was just plain stupid, unless she was a whole lot more clever than the women he usually met and was using reverse psychology on him. Because that theory was flattering as well as probable, he flashed a ready grin.

"I won't stay long, sweetheart. Keep the doors locked and don't let anyone in." He grabbed a lemon bar and moaned with contentment on his way out.

"I'll be fine," Aubrey called after him, but he hadn't been gone ten minutes before she picked up the telephone, dialed information, and got Harlan Caine's number. She made a note of it, then ate a couple of the delectable lemon bars while she gave what she wished to do thorough consideration. Jesse had not offered a revised plan when their visit to his cousin's house had failed to yield more than heartrending cries no one else could hear. Therefore, it was now up to her to proceed.

With that justification well in mind, she dialed the number and greeted Harlan warmly. "Mr. Caine? My name is Aubrey Glenn. I know you've undoubtedly been questioned innumerable times about the disappearance of the Ferrell family, but I wonder if you have time tomorrow to speak with me about them? It's a mere formality, really. The family asked my help in locating the Ferrells, but I've no training as a detective, and as soon as I can assure them I've done what little I could without result, they'll be content.''

She wrote down the time and address Harlan supplied, and thanked him profusely before saying good-bye. Her hand shook as she replaced the receiver, but the appointment was made, and she knew Jesse would go with her. The only problem would be in admitting that she had called Harlan without discussing it with him first, but she felt certain he would eventually come around to her way of thinking. *Eventually.*

She still didn't have a clear plan, but any effort was better than calmly waiting for a second attempt on her life. She slid the lemon bars into the refrigerator, then went upstairs to put on her bikini. It was a lovely afternoon, and she didn't want to waste another minute of it.

Harlan Caine stared at the telephone for a long moment before turning the full fury of his anger on John Gilroy. "The bitch called me!" he shrieked. "I told you to get rid of her, and here she is calling me as sweet as a cherub. You bet I have time to see her.

"That pool stunt was pathetic. If you can't do any better than that, I'll find someone who can, and you can file for unemployment. There's got to be plenty of work at other firms for bungling fools; there's so damn many of you."

John moved to the front of his chair and gestured helplessly. "Calm down, Mr. Caine. Give her a tour of the construction site. There are a million ways for her to break her neck there."

Harlan left the chair behind his desk and began to pace alongside it. "Don't you think that's a bit obvious? The police can't pin a damn thing on me, but if corpses start piling up there, they're bound to get suspicious!"

John cowered back in his chair. "Give me a few days to come up with something good."

Harlan came to a halt and fixed him with a threatening stare. "You have until eleven o'clock tomorrow morning, and not a minute more. Now get out of here. I'm sick of looking at you."

John bolted out the back door, then slowed so that it wouldn't slam shut behind him. Harlan couldn't stand to have his door slammed, and he didn't dare upset him any further than he already had. He wiped the sweat forming on his brow on his sleeve and squared his shoulders. Harlan was just loud, that was all. The man couldn't possibly want to replace him when he knew so much.

Buoyed by that thought, John strode out into the sunlight, certain he would have a damn good plan ready long before tomorrow.

Chapter XII

Jesse planned to take Aubrey out to dinner, so he parked his truck in front of her house and walked up the driveway. When he saw her stretched out on a chaise longue on the patio, he was annoyed with himself for not being more specific with his order to keep the doors locked. Then he realized that she was sound asleep, as was Guinevere. He was totally infuriated.

He opened the gate without making a sound, and then tiptoed across the patio. Guinevere awakened when he drew near, but she got up and came to him without barking. He patted her head, then knelt beside Aubrey and planted a sloppy kiss in her navel.

Caught by surprise, Aubrey's shriek evaporated into bubbling giggles until she calmed down sufficiently for Jesse's furious expression to register. She sat up then, and with him still on one knee, was level with his gaze. Because he could not possibly know that she had called Harlan Caine, she couldn't imagine why he looked so angry.

"What's wrong?" she asked. "Is Edith upset by our lack of progress?"

Jesse hadn't expected her to play innocent, but it was a convincing act. "No. She's grateful that we've tried to do what we can, so she's definitely not the problem. You are," he stressed. "Hasn't it occurred to you that I could just as easily have been Harlan Caine just now? What if he had caught you napping and rather than a kiss, plunged a knife clear through your belly?"

Jesse had just given Aubrey the perfect opening to reveal that she had made an appointment with the developer, but knowing he was unlikely to be pleased, she dared not do so when he was already upset with her. "Guinevere would have barked had a stranger come to the gate, and he wouldn't have caught me napping."

"She didn't notice my presence the first time I came here until you spoke to me."

Aubrey leaned down to scratch her hairy pet's ears. "That was unlike her."

Exasperated that he was getting nowhere, Jesse got to his feet. "I suppose I should be grateful I didn't find you in the pool."

Aubrey glanced toward the sparkling water and found it wonderfully inviting. "Well, now that you're here to call the paramedics, should I need them, I think I will go for a swim."

Aubrey rolled off the opposite side of the chaise before Jesse could catch her, entered the pool with a flat, racing dive, and started swimming toward the deep end with quick, graceful strokes. She had more problems than she cared to count, but forgot them all in the simple joy of exertion. When she returned to the shallow end, she looked up to find Jesse removing his shirt. She turned and continued swimming. It wasn't until he overtook her that she swiftly discovered he hadn't bothered to don trunks.

"What are you doing?" she gasped.

"What does it look like?" Treading water, Jesse came close and with a couple of rapid tugs, untied the top of her bikini and tossed it up on the deck. "This is a private pool. Why do we need bathing suits?"

He had seen her nude, so feigning modesty seemed absurd, and yet Aubrey feared things were already dangerously out of hand. "Let's hope the pool man was here this morning, or the pool won't be nearly as private as you've assumed."

Jesse tossed his head to flick the water from his hair. "I'll risk it." He dipped beneath the surface and pulled Aubrey down with him. His hands circled her waist, and when she struggled to get free, he yanked away the bottom half of her bikini. When they came up for air, she swung at him with a playful swat, but he just waved the bright pink bikini bottom like a flag.

Aubrey would have relieved him of his trunks had he been wearing them, but unable to turn the tables on his trick, she dunked him with a savage lunge. She then swam out of his reach and headed for the shallow end. He overtook her again, grabbed her foot, and pulled her back down under the water, but his grasp was light, and she easily escaped him.

Aubrey circled, intent upon revenge, and when Jesse continued to elude her, she dived deep, and coming up under him, grabbed his knees to pull him down with her. They rose to the surface in a lazy spiral, but the gleam in Jesse's eyes warned Aubrey she was in trouble. She hit the water with the heel of her hand to splash him in the face. "You started this!"

"I'll finish it, too!" Jesse surged forward and caught Aubrey in a bear hug. He kicked to propel them to the side of the pool where he could still stand easily, while she couldn't touch bottom with her toes. He pressed up against her, molding his body to hers, and nibbled her earlobe. She tasted faintly of chlorine, but that scarcely diminished his pleasure.

Aubrey had to hang on to Jesse's shoulders to keep her head above water. They were so close she could not mistake his state of arousal. "Jesse, please. This isn't a good idea."

"It's the best one I've had all day," he breathed against her lips. He kissed her before she could offer any further protest, and slid his hand down her thigh to encourage her to wrap her legs around his waist.

Aubrey grabbed a handful of Jesse's hair, but slippery wet, it slid right through her fingers. "Not here!" she scolded.

"Perfect place," Jesse argued before kissing her again, and again.

Surrounded by the seductive warmth of the water and Jesse's fiery heat, Aubrey was tempted to give in to the madness of his desire, but she could not forget, as apparently he had, that the consequences could be dire. "Jesse," she hissed. "Stop it!"

Jesse leaned back slightly to search her expression for more than her words revealed. "Why?"

"Damn it. You know why. Let's go inside where we can protect more than our reputations."

Jesse moaned way back in his throat. Aubrey's whole body was caressing his with what he had mistaken for abandon, but when he raised his hand to cup her breast and brushed the tightly puckered nipple with his thumb, her steady gaze didn't soften. He knew she was right, but being right had never been much fun.

"Okay," he gave in reluctantly. "I'll let you go if we can go straight to your room and continue this there."

"It's a deal, but try not to drip too much water on the rug."

Jesse stepped back and pulled her along with him toward

the shallow end. When she stood, he watched the smooth undulation of her hips as she climbed the steps to the deck and thought no artist's version of the birth of Venus had ever been more enchanting. She stopped to grab the towel on the chaise, dried off quickly, and then, apparently comfortable nude, tossed the towel to him. He wrapped it around his hips and followed her in the side door.

"Do you want something to drink?" she asked as they entered the kitchen.

Jesse took hold of her upper arm and guided her toward the stairs. "Better keep right on walking, or I can no longer be responsible for my actions." He almost asked if she paraded around nude when she had been married to Larry, but caught himself before he ruined her enticing mood with wretched memories.

As they entered her bedroom, Aubrey tried to recall the last time she had made love in the afternoon, if ever. Jesse began to sling the pillows heaped on her bed every which way, and she reached out to grab one as it came flying by. "Careful," she chided, but he ripped back the beribboned comforter with the same urgency and then turned toward her with a desperate glint in his eye.

She threw the pillow at him, and their game began anew with skillful dodges and sudden dashes around and then up and over the bed. They were both laughing, and their spirits so high that when Jesse finally caught up with Aubrey and pulled her down on the bed, she made no further attempt to elude him. Instead, she yanked away his towel and slid down over him, spreading a trail of kisses that brought him to the brink of rapture before allowing him a moment to grab one of the condoms he had left on the nightstand.

Their lovemaking had been slow and sweet last night, but that afternoon they came together in a heated rush that spun them with a tornado's fury, and then left them fully sated in each other's arms. Aubrey clung to that shared bliss as she fell asleep to the comforting rhythm of Jesse's breathing, but when he awakened her later, the loving warmth of their erotic interlude was quickly chilled by thoughts of Harlan Caine. She sat up slowly and pushed her tangled curls from her eyes.

The sunset's last rays lent the bedroom a rosy glow but her mood was no longer mellow. Jesse was already dressed, and feeling at a distinct disadvantage, Aubrey pulled the sheet up over her bare breasts. Thinking she would be better off to get her confession over with quickly rather than draw it out, she made a hasty announcement. "I made an appointment with Harlan Caine for eleven tomorrow morning."

A look of horrified disbelief crossed Jesse's face. "You did what?"

"You heard me. We were out of ideas, so I called him after you left for your aunt's. I doubt we can inspire him to admit to his crimes, but something good might come from meeting with him face to face."

"Is your husband still the beneficiary on your life insurance?"

Jesse was taking Aubrey's news better than she had expected, or so she hoped. She knew he had been making a pointed joke, but she provided a serious answer. "No. I removed his name when I filed for divorce and changed it and my will to leave everything to my parents."

"I doubt the money will brighten their retirement." Jesse was so angry he didn't know what to do with her. "I should just wring your neck and be done with you. I told you we'd not goad Caine, but you went behind my back and did just that."

"It wasn't behind your back. You weren't here, and I didn't know when you might return."

Jesse swore a particularly bitter oath. "That's a damn lie

and you know it. Why didn't you tell me this when I first got home? No. Don't bother to answer, because it's plain you knew I wouldn't sleep with you if you did."

"Jesse, really. That wasn't what I thought at all, and you're the one who's to blame for distracting me."

"Yeah. Right. Blame everything on me." Jesse started for the door. "I wanted to take you out to dinner, but I've lost my appetite. I don't care whether or not you get up. In fact, why don't you stay in bed until tomorrow, and it will save me the trouble of avoiding you."

Jesse strode out of the room, leaving Aubrey to ponder the wisdom of her actions alone. Certain she had had little choice about confronting Caine, she got up and went into the bathroom to shower, then dressed in aqua leggings and a matching sweater. She and Jesse were both stubborn and independent, so it wasn't surprising that their partnership had swiftly degenerated into a power struggle, but as she made up her bed, she could not help but be sorry.

As she came down the stairs, she noticed Jesse reading the *Times* in the living room and went into the kitchen to fix herself some supper without bothering to ask if he would like to join her. He had already made it plain that he wouldn't, but still, she thought it ridiculous for them to eat separately. She looked through her refrigerator and cupboards and decided to make a salad and pasta.

She diced some celery, bell pepper, and onions, and browned them in a saucepan before opening a jar of thick tomato and herb sauce. While she boiled the water to cook the pasta, she made the salad, taking care to make plenty, should Jesse deign to join her. She really didn't want him staying in her house if he wasn't going to speak with her. It was her house afterall, and she had every right to boot him right out of it.

Despite his earlier protests to the contrary, the delectable aroma wafting from the kitchen teased Jesse's senses and his stomach began to growl. He was going to have to eat, and that meant either having something delivered, or dining on whatever Aubrey was preparing.

Getting up was the hardest part, but once he was on his feet, he managed a nonchalant stroll into the kitchen. He sent a deliberately casual glance toward the stove. "What are you cooking?"

"Meatloaf," Aubrey lied, "and because I know it isn't one of your favorites, I'll forgive you for not joining me."

"You don't eat meat, Aubrey, or have you forgotten?"

"No, but for some reason, I was overcome with a perverse desire to bake a meatloaf."

Aubrey hadn't looked at him once, and while Jesse knew she was the one who was in the wrong rather than he, he decided to be gracious. "I'm still angry with you, but what do you say to calling a truce for the dinner hour?"

Aubrey had a difficult time controlling the width of her smile. "Then what? Do you plan to again ignore me the minute you finish dessert?"

"Let's just play it by ear."

"You're choosing convenience over principle merely until your stomach's full; is that what you're saying?"

Jesse hadn't realized how his offer had sounded, and backpedaled a bit. "No, not exactly. I don't approve of what you did, but you can't take it back, so why don't we just make the best of it?"

Aubrey carried the pot of boiling water over to the sink and stained the pasta through the waiting colander. "I doubt that you'd like spinach pasta anyway."

"Spinach pasta?" The very thought made Jesse gag, but he walked over to the sink and eyed the green noodles. "How do they taste?"

"Delicious." Aubrey handed him a fork and observed his expression closely as he sampled one. He flinched slightly, but chewed, and swallowed without any ill effects. "Well?"

"I guess they're all right."

"Is that a real 'all right,' or an 'all right' as in they'll do when you're trapped playing bodyguard and there's nothing else to eat?"

She had him there, but Jesse refused to admit it. "Isn't it the sauce that makes the dish?"

"Sure is. Would you care to taste it?"

Jesse didn't like the evil gleam in her eye, and feared she had cooked up something godawful just to spite him. He leaned over the stove, dipped his fork in the bubbling sauce, and took a tiny taste. When he found it wasn't laced with enough garlic to curl his eyelashes, he nodded appreciatively.

"I do believe I mentioned earlier that you're one hell of a cook."

He had called her one hell of a woman, but Aubrey didn't correct him. She took the compliment to mean that he would join her for supper, and she quickly set the table for two. She divided the tossed salad in half, then asked him to serve his own plate so that he would be sure to have enough. He took a more generous portion than she had expected, and she again wondered if he was getting enough to eat. Not wanting to hear a sarcastic answer, she kept the question to herself and sat down at the table.

Jesse slid into his place beside her. "Do you usually eat alone?" he asked.

"I don't mind. I watch the news or read. I'm never lonely."

"Never?" Jesse caught her gaze and held it.

"Let's put it this way, I'm not nearly as lonely now as when I was married."

Jesse thought that was one of the saddest comments he had ever heard. "You have friends though."

Aubrey kept her attention focused on her plate. "Yes. I'm blessed with several really close friends and we try and keep in touch even if we aren't able to get together as often as we'd like."

"Sure. Everyone's busy with work and family."

"Hmm." Aubrey had much less, but ate more slowly than Jesse, and they finished dinner at the same time. "Help yourself to the frozen yogurt and lemon bars. I'm going to wait until later. I need to look over my outline for Saturday's seminar."

She left the table before he could stop her, and found containers for the leftover pasta and sauce. Jesse brought their dishes to the sink, and she tugged on her rubber gloves and began to rinse them. She wasn't used to having someone else in her kitchen, and bumped into him as she reached for the dishwasher.

"Sorry." Jesse moved over to the stove, then again felt in the way when Aubrey came over to collect the pot and pan. "You did all the cooking. I should be doing the dishes."

"They're no trouble." Aubrey didn't want another angry confrontation, nor did she want to lose herself in him again, but she was exquisitely aware of his presence. He was a larger than life figure in so many ways, and the two of them filled the kitchen no matter where they stood. Finished cleaning up, she yanked off the gloves and laid them on the counter, but when she turned away from the sink, Jesse blocked her way.

"Wait a minute," he asked. "I'm not sure what's happening here, but I got you into this, so I suppose it's stupid of me to be angry with you for getting ahead of me. I'm fairly good at reading people, so I'll meet with Caine tomorrow. That way you needn't become involved with him afterall."

"That's very considerate of you, but completely mis-

guided. I'm the one who made the appointment, and while
I assumed you'd go along with me, I won't let you go alone.
That's absolutely out of the question. Besides, if you leave
me here, who's to say Caine won't send someone to try
and harm me again while you're gone?''

Jesse released a frustrated sigh. He couldn't argue when
everything Aubrey said made sense. ''I wish I had some
alternative plan to propose, but you may be right. Confronting Harlan Caine is the only option we have.''

Aubrey flashed a delighted smile. ''I knew you'd come
around to my way of thinking.''

If there was anything Jesse hated, it was being outsmarted
by a woman. ''Oh, really? Well, you're never going to get
me to say that I actually liked that weird green pasta. What's
the matter with plain spaghetti?''

Aubrey knew enough not to continue to gloat over her
victory, and quickly stepped by him. ''Nothing. Now you'll
have to excuse me. I really do need to study my notes. I'll
see you in the morning.''

Jesse's eyes widened in surprise, but Aubrey left the room
before he could think fast enough to stop her. He had
been too angry earlier to consider their sleeping arrange-
ments, but clearly she had just banished him to the den
and he didn't like that one bit. He picked up the rubber
gloves and whacked them against the counter with a vicious
slap, but that didn't do nearly enough to cool his temper.
Consoling himself with frozen yogurt and lemon bars, he
went into the den and flipped on the television, but after
sleeping with Aubrey, he knew the entertainment on the
tube was going to seem awfully tame.

Aubrey did indeed need to review her notes. She used
the same basic outline for each of her seminars, but
because the character of each group was slightly different,

she always revised her presentation to better serve the particular audience's needs. She didn't allow herself to think of Jesse until she had finished preparing, and then she found herself exactly where she had been that morning.

Jesse had such an appealing exuberance. She had never met anyone who even remotely resembled him. Knowing him was definitely going to be a memorable experience, but bittersweet in its brevity. "Don't let him get to you," she cautioned herself, but deep down, she feared that he already had.

She left the study, went up to her room, and read before preparing for bed, but it took a long while to get to sleep. She awakened once, long after midnight, and found Jesse standing in her doorway silhouetted against the soft glow of the nightlight burning in the hall. His face veiled in shadow, his mood was impossible to discern; but clad only in low-slung Levi's, he was a stirring sight. A fierce longing welled up inside Aubrey and she hoped he would come to her, but she remained motionless, observing him through her lashes until he at last turned away and went downstairs.

She could have called out to him, but didn't. There was too great a risk he had merely been restless and wanted to make certain she was all right, nothing more. She burrowed down under the covers and wondered if the open door had in itself been an unconscious invitation. Obviously Jesse had not considered it such, or had refused it. She was glad then that she hadn't spoken and necessitated an embarrassing exchange with a polite invitation and an equally polite refusal.

Jesse wasn't Larry, she reminded herself, but it was so difficult not to be overwhelmed by the old hurts. She longed to be held and loved with all the tender promises Larry had made and not kept. Jesse was unlikely to be moved to make promises of any kind, and she refused to coax lies from his lips with affectionate words of her own. Jesse was the kind who reveled in his freedom, and while the idea of scorching her initials on his butt in a loving brand was incredibly appealing, it belonged in the realm of fantasy with her dashing Indian brave.

Jesse was again waiting in the kitchen when Aubrey came downstairs for breakfast. She was wearing a pair of white pants with a watermelon-pink shell and a black shirt with a deep V-neckline and high side slits as a jacket. Fashioned of sandwashed silks, it was a stunning outfit, and she nodded to acknowledge Jesse's low whistle.

"I'm trying to appear attractive in a soft, non-threatening way. From your reaction, I'd say I've succeeded."

"And then some. Do you suppose you could take that little tape recorder of yours and use it without Caine catching on?"

"I can try. I was hoping that you'd help me frame some apparently innocuous questions to put him at ease. If he's relaxed rather than wary, perhaps he'll let something slip. This has to be preying on his mind. Doesn't it?"

"If he were the squeamish type, he wouldn't have murdered four people in the first place."

"I suppose you're right. Do you think he drives a gold Corvette?"

"I seriously doubt it. I'll bet he has some flunky following us."

"An accomplice?" She had seen two vague shapes in the vision prompted by the Christmas photograph.

Jesse left the table and came over to the counter. "Could be. There's still time for you to back out, and I'll take him on alone. He can't be any worse than an enraged bull."

Aubrey refused to even consider staying home. She carried a glass of juice to the table, then brought a small notebook from her study. "I'd like to know what became of the money your cousin invested."

Jesse refilled his juice glass and then returned to his place at the table. "So would I, but let's not hit him with that question first. Let's begin with how he happened to meet Pete, and then get a description of the project in which he invested."

Aubrey made a few quick notes. "Right. Then the question about money seems more natural. We ought to have a signal so if either of us wants to leave, the other will understand and go along."

Jesse glanced out toward the patio. Lucifer was again asleep on the glass table. "Doesn't that cat do anything but sleep?"

"Not much. Cats have a high-protein diet and it requires a great deal of their energy simply to digest their food. I know, let's say we have to leave to take Lucifer to the vet."

"Yeah, that's good, but let's try to keep Caine talking for fifteen to twenty minutes at least. Then when we go back to the parking lot, remind me to check underneath the truck for a bomb."

Aubrey shuddered. "God help us."

"This was your bright idea, remember?"

Aubrey couldn't deny it, but she knew if she had to walk into the lion's den, she couldn't ask for a better champion to defend her. "Does Caine know you're Pete's cousin?"

Jesse frowned slightly. "I don't see how he could. I wasn't identified in the recent *Times* article, and we've not discussed the case with anyone except the police. Some of Pete's neighbors, like Roberta Smaus, might remember that we were related, but what are the chances that Caine's talked with any of them?"

"I wouldn't put anything past him, but if he doesn't know you're Pete's cousin, and therefore have a more urgent need to know what's become of the Ferrells than I would, let's not volunteer the information."

"You want me to just play the 'unidentified male escort' again?"

"Think about it. If we don't appear in the least bit threatening, it should work to our advantage."

"Yeah. It could," Jesse reluctantly agreed. He recalled how difficult it had been to get Aubrey interested in finding his cousins, but now that she was, she sure wasn't letting anything get in her way, including him. While that wasn't a pleasant thought, he was desperate enough to give anything a try.

Harlan Caine's office was in a two-story business complex shared by a savings and loan and an insurance firm. A modern structure of natural wood and glass, it was beautifully landscaped with wide banks of pink and white azaleas, while towering eucalyptus trees softened the sharply angled roofline. To anyone else coming to visit, the offices were undoubtedly inviting. Aubrey took a deep breath and hoped she wouldn't faint the instant she met Harlan Caine.

"Pretend you're at a seminar," Jesse whispered. He took her arm and gave her a fond squeeze as they entered the developer's door.

A statuesque blonde dressed in a form-fitting black sheath left her desk and came forward to greet them. "Good morning. Are you Ms. Glenn?"

Aubrey nodded and introduced Jesse as a friend. She checked her watch for the hundreth time that morning. "I realize we're a couple of minutes early. Is Mr. Caine running behind schedule?"

"No, but he's taking a long distance call at the moment." Obviously impressed, the blonde sent an eager glance roaming over Jesse's trim build before focusing on his face.

Her smile widened seductively. "I'm Rachel McClure, Mr. Caine's personal secretary. May I get you some coffee or tea while you're waiting?"

Jesse nodded appreciatively, then spoke in a lazy drawl. "That's real nice of you, ma'am. I'd like coffee with two sugars, and enough cream to make it resemble chocolate milk. How about you, darlin', you want some tea?"

Jesse didn't usually have much accent, but Aubrey was amazed by how natural it sounded coming from his mouth today. She attempted to appear perplexed. "I usually bring my own teabags with me." She opened her roomy purse and made a hasty search. "Oh no, I seem to have forgotten them. Do you have anything exciting, peppermint or orange spice?"

"Yes, which would you like?"

Aubrey licked her lips. "Orange spice I think, no wait, make it the peppermint."

"Just give me a moment." The secretary gestured toward the black leather sofa beneath the windows. "Please make yourselves comfortable. I'm sure Mr. Caine won't be long."

Aubrey took a seat, but Jesse remained standing to study the architect's drawings displayed along the wall. A mix of commercial and residential buildings, they were all handsome structures with clean, crisp lines. When the secretary returned from the workroom off the outer office with their drinks, he gestured toward the first rendering. "Has Mr. Caine built this, or is it just in the planning stage?"

"Those are all future projects. You'll see some of the firm's completed developments in Mr. Caine's office."

"I look forward to it." Jesse took a sip of his coffee. "Perfect. What about this pretty building we're in? Is it one of Caine's?"

Rachel returned to her desk before replying. "No. We merely rent the offices from the savings and loan." She

answered a soft beep on her telephone and smiled graciously. "Mr. Caine will see you now."

Aubrey had to set aside her tea to stand, and then picked
up the styrofoam cup. She sent Jesse a frantic glance, but
he responded with a good-natured grin and started toward
the inner office. Harlan Caine's name was written on the
highly polished brass plaque on the door, and as Jesse
swung it open, the developer came forward to meet them.

Aubrey had expected the man to look like evil incarnate,
but Caine's appearance was deceptively appealing. He was
in his early forties, stood just under six feet tall, and had
the broad shoulders and narrow hips of a bodybuilder.
His dark brown hair was thick and curly, and his brown
eyes alight with intelligence. Ruggedly handsome, he was
dressed in a pale blue shirt with the sleeves rolled up and
light gray slacks, but he could have modeled the jungle
fatigues in *Soldier of Fortune* magazine and been completely
convincing.

Harlan flashed a charming smile, but waited until
Aubrey introduced Jesse as a close friend before extending
his hand. "Glad to meet you, Mr. Barrett. I'm sorry it's
under such sad circumstances. I can't believe the police
have had such little success discovering what's become of
the Ferrells. I don't know how many people disappear
from Los Angeles each year, but the Ferrells have been
sorely missed."

Harlan had gripped her hand only briefly, but Aubrey
felt a numbing chill beneath the warmth. She placed her
cup on his desk and sank down into one of the deep leather
chairs facing it. She reached into her purse and fumbled
around, searching for her notebook. As she removed it,
she switched on the tape recorder. She waited until Harlan
had returned to his chair behind his desk, and then gave
him a well-rehearsed opening.

"You have the advantage here, Mr. Caine. I've never

met the Ferrells, and it seems unlikely now that I ever will."

"Call me Harlan, please." He picked up a paperclip and began tapping it on his blotter.

"Harlan, then." Aubrey smiled shyly. She repeated her complete lack of expertise in the field of investigation, and apologized profusely for taking his valuable time. "It's just that I want to have something to report, and Lord knows, the police are stumped."

"The crime rate appears to be soaring," Harlan complained with a sorry shake of his head. "The police are overworked."

"And underpaid for such dangerous work," Aubrey added. "How did you happened to meet Pete Ferrell?"

"I'd advertised for investors, and he was among those who responded. Unfortunately the project he invested in was delayed by the downturn in the economy, and rather than the fast profit he had anticipated, he feared he faced a big loss. The fault wasn't mine, of course, but I was an easy target for his frustration. The police know he was dissatisfied with the way I was running the project, but the fact that he disappeared before it finally got underway was merely a coincidence."

Harlan shrugged slightly. "The construction industry can certainly get cutthroat at times, but no developer kills off his investors."

He had stated the opinion as fact, and Aubrey nodded as though it made perfect sense. "What became of the funds Pete invested with you?"

"I still have them. It was only a few thousand dollars, but the project will be completed soon, and all my investors will show a healthy profit. I'll just keep Pete's share, and it will continue earning interest until the courts tell me what to do with it."

Aubrey found it difficult not to focus on the paperclip

he was still tapping on the blotter. It made only a soft, hollow tap, but revealed he was far more nervous about speaking with her than he wished her to believe. His lips had a decidedly sensuous fullness that drew her glance to his mouth, and yet repelled her at the same time.

Jesse left his chair to look at the drawings on display along the office walls. "You've built some spectacular projects, Mr. Caine. I did some framing when I was a kid, and I know a good design when I see it."

"Thank you. Perhaps you'd care to visit the construction site where Pete had invested?"

Aubrey turned to send Jesse a questioning glance, and he nodded. "Yes, I do suppose that would make my investigation look more complete," she replied. "I really appreciate your talking with me, Mr. Caine, Harlan. The next time someone presses me for a favor I can't possibly perform well, I am most definitely going to refuse. I teach the creative use of positive imagery, but I sure don't read minds and I couldn't catch a criminal unless he collapsed at my feet with a heart attack."

Aubrey took a last sip of tea, then rose. "If you'll just give us the address of the site, we'll go right over."

Harlan left his chair. "You'd find nothing but noise and dust today. If you're free Sunday afternoon, however, I can give you a personal tour."

Aubrey knew it was a trap the minute he delayed the tour until Sunday, but she smiled as though she were completely charmed by the idea. "That is so nice of you, Harlan. Who knows, I may want to invest in your next project myself."

Harlan took her hand between both of his. "Ah, you've seen through my ploy already, Ms. Glenn. Are you certain you can't read minds?"

Aubrey had to fight the nearly overwhelming urge to yank her hand free of his confining hold, but she had never experienced a more chilling grasp. At the same time, his palms were sweating slightly, so the frosty feel was entirely in her mind. She forced a laugh and finally managed to pull away, but she immediately reached for Jesse's hand and held on tightly until they reached the safety of the parking lot.

Chapter XIII

As they approached his truck, Jesse whispered an aside. "Drop your purse so that I can check underneath my Chevy without drawing any undo attention."

Aubrey released his hand, made a sweeping gesture toward nothing in particular, and then let her handbag's shoulder strap slip down her arm. She made a clumsy grab for the bag, then careened into Jesse and dropped it. "Oh dear," she exclaimed. "What an awful mess."

She bent down to retrieve her wallet, scattered pens, and the grocery coupons which had spilled out around her while Jesse knelt and appeared to be searching for belongings which might have rolled under the truck. "Do you see anything?" Aubrey called softly.

Jesse had palmed a lipstick as he bent down, and after satisfying himself on the question of their safety, he straightened up, helped Aubrey to her feet, and handed it to her. "Nothing that's not supposed to be there." He leaned back against the Chevy and hooked his thumbs in his belt.

"Caine was lying. He was fiddling with the paperclip for the same reason you drum your nails: we made him nervous. He was entirely too pretty, and none of it was natural. I'll bet he even perms his hair. He made my flesh crawl on sight, but shaking hands with him, well—" Jesse's disgust contorted his expression into a hostile sneer. "Tell me what you thought of him first."

Aubrey felt dizzy and weak as though she had been forced to leave her bed during a bout of the flu. "I'd like to go home and take a shower. Caine's touch was colder than death, but his palms were sweating. I agree, we definitely made him nervous, and he had no idea who you were. I tried to appear to be too silly and disorganized to pose a threat. Still, the instant he mentioned it, I got a very bad feeling about Sunday's tour."

"So did I. Come on, let's get out of here." Jesse walked Aubrey around to the passenger side of his truck and helped her in, but he did not begin to relax until they had returned to the freeway. "I can't believe Pete ever trusted Harlan Caine. He's just too damn slick. Do you suppose he's sleeping with his secretary?"

Aubrey had been rubbing her hands together in a futile attempt to remove the lingering unpleasantness of the developer's touch. "Please. I don't want to picture such a revolting possibility. Besides, he's undoubtedly too deeply in love with himself to provide much affection."

Jesse chuckled, turned on the radio, and began to hum along with a tune by Alabama. "No," he argued after a lengthy pause. "I'll bet you Harlan is a real accomplished lover. You'd probably describe him as mechanical, but he just might thrill Rachel clear to her toes."

"You want me to throw up in here?" Aubrey warned. She glanced into the sideview mirror and searched the traffic in the lanes behind them, but there were no Corvettes of any color.

"I've become too adept at creative imagery to enjoy imagining that fiend doing anything more than rotting in prison, and it ought to be a small, squalid cell where he has to fight huge rats for the putrid rations."

Jesse shot her a horrified glance. "I don't believe the criminal justice system in California allows for anything that primitive, but it's all he deserves. I was hoping a meeting with Caine wouldn't bring doubts as to his guilt, and it sure didn't. I've never had such a negative reaction to anyone before."

"Neither have I. Which will count for absolutely nothing in court."

"True, but it helps to know we're on the right track."

Aubrey also trusted their gut reactions to Harlan Caine. "Do you suppose we ought to call Detective Heffley and alert her to our plans?"

"So she can screw them up? Hell, no."

"We'll actually have a plan by Sunday?"

Jesse winked at her. "Of course, and a damn good one, too. Just leave everything to me."

Still feeling slightly queasy, Aubrey was prepared to do just that for the moment. "Let's stop for lunch on the way home. I need to sit in the sunshine awhile and pretend everything's normal."

That sounded awfully good to Jesse, as well. "I guess I have turned your life upside down, haven't I?"

Aubrey's smile was faint. "Inside out is more like it, but—"

"But I'm worth it?" Jesse teased.

"Don't push your luck, cowboy. Do you know where the Crocodile Cafe is on Lake Avenue?"

Jesse gave it a moment's thought and then nodded. "Sure do." He was afraid the popular restaurant would be crawling with yuppies in their shirtsleeves who had escaped their stultifying office jobs for the midday meal, but the restaurant's clientele included women out shopping with their friends, mothers and grandmothers with small children, young couples paying more attention to each other than the menu, and men of all ages and descriptions.

As soon as they were shown to a corner table on the patio, Jesse stretched out his legs and decided he might not move until sundown. He watched Aubrey scan the menu and hoped the place offered something more substantial than alfalfa sprout and avocado sandwiches. When he finally consulted the menu, he was astonished to find the selections among the most varied he had ever encountered.

"I can't decide between the pizza with barbequed chicken, sausage, and pepperoni, and the oakwood grilled steak," he said. "What are you having?"

"I'm awfully fond of their sauteed eggplant, but it's a lot for lunch, so maybe I'll just have a small Caesar salad."

Jesse couldn't blame Aubrey for not having much appetite, but if anything, meeting Harlan Caine had given him an almost desperate desire for the energy to defeat him. When a friendly young man appeared to take their order, he chose the steak and the fresh-squeezed lemonade, while Aubrey asked for the salad and passion fruit iced tea. When the waiter left, Jesse cast an admiring glance at the blue sky.

"The sky is always this sparkling clear in Sedona."

The wistful note in his voice made Aubrey's heart catch in her throat. She hated to think he was eagerly looking forward to telling her good-bye and had to fortify herself with a gulp of water before she spoke. "You're anxious to go home, aren't you?"

"I've never cared much for cities," Jesse confided easily. "There're just too many people bumping into each other on the sidewalks, and way too much noise. I guess you must like it here, though."

"I grew up here, but I'm more often at home alone than out mingling with crowds on the streets." Their conversation flowed easily, but while Jesse was intent upon comparing city and country living, Aubrey found herself simply studying him. He was serious one minute, then flashed a ready grin the next and began to tease her with a gentle humor. His comments were endearing rather than made at her expense, and she responded with relaxed smiles.

They broke off their conversation when their meals were served, and as Aubrey took a bite of salad, she noticed the women at a nearby table were eyeing Jesse with more than merely appreciative glances. There were exchanging giggles and hushed whispers which were clearly centered on him. Jesse, however, was intent upon eating his steak, and hadn't noticed them. Aubrey certainly wasn't going to point them out, although she knew he would enjoy their attention.

Jesse glanced up, noted Aubrey's preoccupied frown, and felt certain he was the cause of her distress. After all, he had dumped a whole lot of trouble in her lap, and then thoughtlessly made her think he was homesick. "Hey," he called softly. "I won't abandon you. I'm not going home until Harlan Caine's behind bars."

Aubrey had no idea what had prompted Jesse's promise, but smiled to acknowledge it. "Don't forget the accomplice. He might be the man who drives the gold Corvette, or he might be someone else entirely. Maybe Caine has a whole string of men with more muscle than character who'll do whatever he asks. Then again, maybe Ms. McClure has talents we've not considered."

Astonished by that possibility, Jesse sat back in his chair and wiped his mouth on his napkin. "That's good. I just considered her most obvious assets, but we ought to suspect everyone in Caine's employ. Damn. If we don't come up with anything new on Sunday, maybe you ought to pretend a real interest in investing with him. That might be our only way to keep going back.''

Aubrey speared a flavorful crouton. "Caine's an arrogant s.o.b. and he must believe he's committed the perfect crime. Still, he wouldn't have been so nervous if he didn't fear there might be a way for us to tie him to the murders.''

"The bodies," Jesse reminded her. "You said they weren't completely burned.''

Aubrey returned his steady gaze. "It's such a lovely afternoon and the food here is delicious. I can't believe we're talking about partially cremated bodies as though we were playing a game of Clue.''

"It is gross, isn't it? Want some dessert?''

"No. I think I'd just like to go home.'' Jesse arched a brow, and Aubrey found the unspoken invitation ever so much more exciting. She had every intention of glorying in the moment until she arrived home and checked her answering machine for messages. There was only one, but it was a frantic lament from her editor in New York. Aubrey played it twice and looked up to find Jesse standing at her study door.

"Did you hear it all?'' When he shook his head, she gave him the gist. "One of the tabloids ran the photo of us that appeared in the *Times* with some imaginative speculation as to my abilities to find missing persons. My publisher has been deluged with calls from those seeking my assistance to locate loved ones. Quite naturally my editor wants to know what's going on, but it's too late now to reach her in New York.''

Aubrey walked toward him. "This is exactly what I was afraid might happen.''

Jesse came forward to meet her. "The only thing I'm afraid of is that Harlan Caine might see it. Which tabloid was it? I'll go and get us a copy.''

Aubrey gave him the name, and as he drove away, her hopes for a romantic afternoon vanished in a mist of frustrated tears. The Ferrell case had a life of its own, and there seemed to be no way to avoid being sucked into it. She sank down into one of the brown leather chairs in her study, propped her feet on the hassock, and closed her eyes.

Up until now, she had been successful in separating her public and private lives, but no longer distinct strands, they had become hopelessly entangled. When Jesse returned, her only consolation was that the story wasn't on the front page. She read it through hurriedly and then handed it back to him.

"I'm surprised they didn't have your name before they went to press, but at least one of their devoted readers has to be a fan of rodeo, and will recognize you."

"So what? I've already given Harlan Caine my name, and this story doesn't really add anything new. I'm sorry about the calls to your publisher, and the people you'll have to disappoint, but other than a bit of unwanted notoriety, this doesn't change things." He extended his hand. "Come on upstairs. Let's look for the missing pieces of ourselves, and forget about Harlan Caine for a while."

His gesture was made with an enticing grace that promised more than Aubrey had any right to expect from a handsome cowboy who'd soon be on his way home, but she wanted him too badly to care. Tomorrow she would have to be a thoroughly professional motivational speaker, but for now, she could simply be herself, and there was nowhere she would rather be than with him.

"Still want that shower?" Jesse asked when they reached her room.

"Only if you'll join me." Aubrey removed her black jacket with a seductive shimmy and laughed when Jesse tore open the snaps on his shirt with a single tug. He moved toward her with a dancing slide as he reached for his belt buckle, and it was difficult to recall how quickly she had panicked when he had made the same gesture Monday afternoon. That she had known him less than a week mattered not at all when she trusted him so completely.

"Have you ever thought of dancing at Chippendale's?" she asked. "You've definitely got the looks, as well as the grace to flaunt it."

"Thank you, ma'am, but my knee wouldn't hold up for long under such strenuous exercise." He slid his arms around her and dipped her low. "Besides, I'd rather dance with you, than for a pack of screaming women I don't even know."

The teasing light in his eyes reflected the laughter in hers, and they soon had a colorful montage of clothing strewn about the white rug. Once nude, they danced into the bathroom and continued their play in the shower. Covered with soap bubbles and slippery wet, they soon found the glass enclosure much too confining. Jesse rinsed off, then stepped out to give Aubrey a turn beneath the warm spray. The instant she turned off the water, he wrapped her in a purple towel and hugged her close.

Aubrey had been too busy giving seminars to consider her life empty, but as she reached up to kiss Jesse, she saw with a sudden clarity just how lonely she had been. He had brought danger and troubling questions without answers, but more importantly, a delicious excitement she would always crave. She was lost in him before they reached her bed, and she gave her affection as generously as he. He coaxed forth a pleasure so intense it was nearly painful, but the only cry to escape her lips was a sibilant sigh of pure ecstasy.

Everything changed for Aubrey that sunlit afternoon. Jesse's passion was no less consuming than the first time they had been together, but now it was flavored with a tenderness that left her not merely wonderfully content, but perfectly fulfilled. She lay snuggled in his arms, instinctively knowing all she would ever need to know of him, and longing for an eternity in one blissful afternoon.

She had never known a man whose needs matched hers so superbly. Certain it was no mere accident of chemistry, she rested her hand lightly on his chest and savored every delicious nuance. After showering together, only a faint trace of his cologne remained beneath the musky aroma of sex and his own masculine scent. She drank in the mingled fragrances, hoping to make them an enduring part of her memories.

Jesse felt Aubrey moving closer still, pressing against him, into him, blurring whatever thin boundaries might still exist between them and could not even imagine a more exquisite sensation short of orgasm's blinding joy. He closed his eyes and relaxed into her, welcoming her spirit as well as her supple body. He had always drawn away from other women as soon as politely possible after they had satisfied his sexual needs, but with Aubrey he felt none of the nagging impatience for solitude others had always inspired.

They drifted lazily, neither speaking nor needing to, until Jesse brought her fingertips to his lips. "I want to try something new," he confided softly. Keeping her fingers laced in his, he drew her hand down over the flatness of his belly. He was hard again, and she needed no further coaxing to bring him to the edge of another climax.

He leaned over her then and smiled. "This should be just like dancing, only better. We need to get really close." He teased her with his fingertips. "And then just barely move. You take the upward stroke, and I'll take the down."

Aubrey wasn't sure what Jesse had in mind, but once he had entered her, he pressed close rather than propping his weight on his elbows. She wrapped her arms around his shoulders, and her legs around his thighs. After a few tentative adjustments, they found a pleasurable alignment that allowed for slow, deep penetration rather than fast thrusts. At first Aubrey felt only Jesse's weight, but the sensation gradually dissolved in delicious tremors the crept up her spine and made her cling to him more tightly.

They had found the perfect rhythm, and each stroke brought them closer to the ultimate union, until conscious effort was impossible and their bodies seized control. In a final surge, they crossed the threshold of paradise together in a climax that shook them clear to their souls. Barely conscious, Aubrey had to remind herself to breathe, but at that heavenly moment, she would have joyously welcomed death.

When at long last her mind cleared sufficiently, she wondered where Jesse had learned such a thrilling technique, and then just as quickly decided she didn't really want to know. She supposed there was a limit to the amount of time they could spend in bed, but she doubted she would live to reach it. Almost from the beginning of her marriage she had felt something was missing, and while she still could not give the exquisite ingredient a name, she had definitely found it with Jesse. When he at last moved aside, she still felt too sated to do more than smile.

Jesse took one look at Aubrey's beatific expression and regarded their latest experiment as a complete success. "That was good, wasn't it?"

"Better than good," Aubrey insisted sleepily. "There's a magic in you that just never ends."

"Well, let's hope not." Jesse drew her back into his arms and held her tight. She felt so good to him, and unlike mere magic, she was real. He couldn't see past that afternoon, but for now, it was more than enough for him.

* * *

The telephone rang just as Aubrey began to set the table for dinner. She let the answering machine in the study pick up, but reached for the extension in the kitchen when she heard Trisha's voice. "Hi, Trish." She glanced toward Jesse and rolled her eyes as her assistant began to talk in a frantic rush. "Give me a minute to think," she begged, then slid her palm over the receiver.

"Shelley just called Trish to tell her she isn't feeling well and wouldn't need a ride to the seminar in the morning. Trish says she heard Ricky Vance swearing in the background and doesn't know what to do."

Jesse was seated at the table, where he had been riffling though the tabloid he had bought earlier and entertaining Aubrey with a sample of the more audacious articles. He rose and tossed the tacky publication aside. "Tell her to sit tight. I've been dying to meet Ricky, and this is as good a time as any."

"You're not going anywhere without me," Aubrey replied, and after telling Trish she and Jesse would handle it, she grabbed her purse and followed him out the door.

No fool, Jesse took the time to make certain no one had tampered with his truck, then he and Aubrey drove to Shelley's bungalow. A Harley-Davidson motorcycle was parked by the porch, and Jesse began to laugh the instant he saw it. "I just can't picture sweet little Shelley riding on the back of that thing. Can you?"

"No. Ricky was driving a beat up Dodge the last time I saw him." Aubrey had refrained from asking Jesse what he intended to do. Because she was positive Ricky Vance deserved whatever grief Jesse gave him, she wasn't even tempted to ask him to go easy on the young man . As they started up the walk, Ricky stepped out on the porch with a bottle of Red Weasel ale in his hand. He drained it in a single gulp, then tossed the empty bottle into the flower-bed.

He was six feet tall, with a thin, angular build, and dark curly hair that brushed his shoulder blades. Dressed in a black T-shirt, Levi's, and boots, he thrust his hips forward in a menacing pose and glared at them. His cheeks were shadowed by several days' growth of beard, and while he may have once been a charming boy, there was nothing appealing about him now.

"Shelley's not working for you anymore," he called to Aubrey. "I'm taking care of her now."

Aubrey would have walked right up to the door, but Jesse caught her elbow to hold her back. "That's a commendable desire," she replied. "Where are you working?"

Ricky raked the sole of his right boot across the edge of the porch to dislodge a hunk of mud. "We'll get by," he boasted.

"We need to speak with Shelley," Jesse announced calmly.

Ricky eyed Jesse with an insolent glance, then dismissed him with a shrug. "If you have something to say to her, just tell me, and I'll give her the message."

"Let's start with a message for you," Jesse replied. He moved over to the Harley, raised the kickstand, and then gave the heavy motorcycle a shove to knock it over on its side where Ricky would never be able to right it on his own.

"What the hell are you doing!" Ricky screamed, and he came off the porch in a flying leap. He doubled his hands into fists and raised them in a clear challenge.

The commotion outdoors brought Shelley to the screen door. She was holding Annie on her hip. She had obviously been crying, and Annie was clinging to her with a terrified grasp. "Leave him alone, Ricky!" she screamed, and Annie began to cry in a thin, warbling wail.

"Close the door, Shelley," Jesse directed firmly. He tossed his hat to Aubrey, and knowing Ricky would count that split second of inattention as the perfect opening, he anticipated his blow and blocked it easily.

"I've yet to meet a punk who could fight," Jesse taunted him. "Do you really think bossing Shelley around makes you a man?"

Aubrey dodged around Jesse and hurried up the porch steps. Shelley pushed open the screen door to welcome her inside, but neither young woman wanted to miss the fight. Annie had burrowed her face into Shelley's shoulder, and couldn't see a thing.

"I told him I didn't want anything more to do with him, and he just wouldn't listen," Shelley explained tearfully. "He wanted me to leave Annie with my mother to raise and go away with him. I refused, and he was getting so loud I was afraid one of the neighbors would call the police. Maybe they already have."

Aubrey kept her eye on Jesse while Shelley described Ricky's demands. As usual, he had refused to acknowledge or provide for Annie, and wanted Shelley to follow wherever whim took him. Jesse was merely toying with the young man, and flailing wildly, Ricky couldn't land a single blow while Jesse struck him repeatedly. Ricky already had a bloody nose, and growing dizzy, slipped and went down on one knee.

Jesse leaned down to grasp a handful of Ricky's T-shirt and hauled him to his feet. "You are easily one of the most pitiful excuses for a man I've ever seen. You could have a beautiful wife and adorable daughter, and instead all you've got is grease under your nails." Jesse lifted the disheveled young man clear off his feet, and then dropped him in the grass where he lay sprawled in a heap.

"Do you want to have him arrested?" Jesse asked Shelley.

Shelley gave her head a frantic shake. "No. I'll just spend the night at my mother's, and he'll be gone by tomorrow."

Aubrey noted the confusion in Shelley's eyes and doubted she was thinking clearly. "Are you certain that's what you really want to do?" she asked.

Shelley hugged Annie more tightly. "He told me this was my last chance to come with him, and I'm not taking it. I want something better for us, and he doesn't even understand what that is."

Jesse knelt down beside Ricky and took hold of a hank of hair to lift his head off the damp grass. "I want you to pay real close attention, Rick." He waited until the look in Ricky's eyes cleared from muddled to an intelligent gleam. "Good boy. Now you can lie out here in the yard until you feel better, and then you're going to find some friends to help you get that Harley out of here. I'm going to keep a close eye on Shelley from now on, and if she has a reason to complain about you ever again, then we'll just have ourselves a re-match. You understand what I mean? You stay away from Shelley, or I'm going to make you real sorry that you didn't."

The sound of a distant siren filled Ricky with hope, and his battered features mirrored his relief. "Think you're going to be rescued?" Jesse asked. "Think again."

Aubrey sensed the violence welling up inside Jesse and called to him before he could give Ricky Vance a final reminder to stay out of Shelley's life. "Don't do it," she ordered as she came out on the porch. "He knows just how easily you could break his hands. You needn't do it. This time."

Jesse released Ricky and straightened up. He stared at Aubrey a long minute, then appeared to reluctantly concede the point. "Yeah, I guess you're right, darlin'. He'll need two good hands to ride that noisy machine out of town."

Aubrey hurried Shelley and Annie out to Jesse's truck and dropped them off at her mother's with the assurance they would return quickly should the need arise. "I do think you ought to take the day off tomorrow. We've nothing scheduled for the week, and I'll talk with you before next Saturday." Aubrey said.

"All right. Thank you. Just give me a minute." Shelley took Annie inside, then came back outside to speak with Jesse. "Ricky isn't mean," she stressed. "He'd never hurt us. He's just young is all, and too self-centered to take care of a family. By the time he grows up, Annie and I won't need him anymore, but we sure needed you tonight. I want to thank you again for what you did."

Jesse wasn't used to receiving such unabashed admiration, and he sure didn't want Shelley transferring her affections to him. He slid his arm around Aubrey's shoulders and hugged her close to make his choice plain. "You have a good night, Shelley, and kiss your little girl for us."

"Thank you. I will." Shelley paused beneath the porch light, looked back at them, and waved.

"Come on," Jesse whispered under his breath. "Let's get out of here before playing hero gets to be too much for me."

Aubrey was becoming adept at climbing up into his truck, and was as eager as he to get away. "How are your hands?" she asked.

"I can drive home," Jesse assured her, "then soak them a bit. Where did you get the idea that I'd break Ricky's hands? It was positively inspired, by the way, but did you really believe I'd have done it?"

Aubrey chose her words with care. "I sensed you were about to do something more to him. At least, that was the way it sounded and I didn't want to see it."

"I was just trying to scare him into behaving himself. I don't go around stomping defenseless men's hands. I hope the police do find Rick stretched out on the lawn and take him in. A night in jail would do him a lot of good.''

"Are you speaking from experience?''

Jesse chuckled way back in his throat. "It's been awhile, but yes, I've spent a night or two in jail and it was definitely a worthwhile experience.''

"I can't imagine how.''

Jesse pulled into her driveway, cut the engine, and set the brake. "Let's just say it gives a man the opportunity to contemplate the error of his ways.''

The light beside the back door provided enough illumination for Aubrey to read his expression clearly. He was teasing her again, and yet for a moment when he had had Ricky Vance at his mercy, she had felt more than a mere threat of violence meant to keep the young man in line. There was far more to Jesse Barrett than she had had time to explore, and while she had come to appreciate the side of him that gave so generously of love, she knew he must possess a dark side that she would be a fool to ignore.

She shivered and Jesse hurried her inside the house, but it had not been the temperature of the air that had touched her, but a premonition of something bad to come.

Chapter XIV

Aubrey walked into Saturday's seminar wearing a stylish apricot sheath and a radiant smile. Trisha took one look at Jesse's equally satisfied grin and felt certain they hadn't spent all of Friday night dealing with Ricky Vance. As soon as she had gotten caught up on that situation, she turned coy. "Are you going to introduce Jesse as Shelley's substitute, or give him a more intriguing title?" she asked pointedly.

Aubrey knew she would have to offer some explanation for Jesse's move from the last row of the audience to the front of the room, but until that moment, hadn't given it much thought. Then people began filing in carrying either their photograph from the *Times* article, or the tabloid, and the matter was easy enough to address. She waited until everyone had found a seat, then opened the second seminar in this series.

"Good morning. I hope you've all found time during the week to apply the techniques we practiced last Saturday. I'll ask you to share your successes before we begin today's presentation, but first I'd like to take a few minutes to discuss my week.''

Jesse cocked a brow, but Aubrey had no intention of revealing any of the intimate details of their budding relationship. Instead, she related only a request from a former teacher to look into the Ferrells' disappearance, and how inappropriate her talents were for such a task. "It's unfortunate that my effort to be helpful was misinterpreted by the media, but I'm sure many of you have had a similar experience when your actions were misconstrued, if not by the press, then by an acquaintance or friend.

"Indeed, we all have difficulty communicating with each other, whether it's simply in being understood, or in effectively making our needs known. Now I'd love to hear how some of you handled the stress you encountered last week. Were any of you better able to cope?"

Several hands were raised, and Aubrey guided the ensuing discussion to limit its focus to the relaxation techniques she had introduced. Some accounts were humorous, others serious in tone, but she succeeded in ending whatever speculation there might have initially been as to her psychic abilities. As for Jesse, she introduced him as she had at the seminar for the Wells Fargo Bank employees, and he repeated his experience using creative imagery on the rodeo circuit.

With the morning off to a good start, Trisha sidled up to Gardner Evans. "How was your weekend?" she asked softly.

The engineer was startled by the question, then shook his head to warn her he was too busy tending his equipment to chat. Trisha was dressed in a hot pink outfit he considered much too distracting for a workshop stressing creative imagery, but because Aubrey didn't seem to feel the bright colors Trisha wore were inappropriate, he had never offered his opinion. He had worn another of his new shirts and ties, but still felt as though he was wearing a disguise rather than his own clothes.

"You look very handsome," Trisha whispered, and then leaving Gardner blushing a bright red, she moved away. At the morning break, she again attempted to engage him in conversation, but still had no success in drawing out the shy young man. Giving up, she waited until the seminar adjourned for the day, then confided in Aubrey.

"Shelley was dead wrong. Gardner just seems annoyed whenever I try to talk with him. Maybe he thinks I'm cute, or likes my legs, but he doesn't care about me at all. I'm going out again with the banker tonight anyway. He makes no secret of his interest in me, and I can't help but be flattered."

"Even if he's a mite dull?" Jesse asked.

"You were right." Trisha squirmed with embarrassment. "I hadn't given myself enough time to get to know him. Now I can't help but wonder if I might have let Mr. Right slip by before I'd realized who he was."

Trisha looked sincerely pained by that prospect, and Aubrey was quick to reassure her. "Then he couldn't have really been the right man for you," she insisted, "or he'd have stayed."

Trisha shrugged slightly. "Well, let's hope he would have, but sometimes I'm afraid we're all hopelessly out of sync." She looked over her shoulder and watched Gardner pack up the last of his gear. "I wonder who Gardner's trying to impress. It sure wasn't me."

Jesse kept his mouth shut, but he thought it likely Gardner hadn't really expected his effort to enhance his looks to work so well with Trisha, and when it had, he had been intimidated rather than proud. Jesse didn't have the time to hold the young man's hand and talk him through a date, but after having prompted him to make a necessary change, he didn't want Gardner to slump back into his baggy clothes and painfully shy ways. He walked over to him and again offered his help.

"And I'm not talking about your equipment," he whispered. "I advised you not to warm to Trisha too quickly, but you're carrying your lack of interest to an obnoxious extreme."

Gardner slammed a bright orange extension cord on his dolly. He wiped his hands on his pants before he remembered he was wearing a new pair, then jammed them into his pockets. "I'm never going to have your finesse with women. It's useless to try."

Jesse had always regarded his success with women as a natural gift, and didn't believe finesse was the proper term to describe it. "It's sincerity that impresses women," he argued. "They want to feel they're genuinely liked, just the way men do. Now what's the real problem here? Did you only want Trisha when you thought you couldn't have her? Now I realize worshipping her from afar saved you the embarrassment of asking her for a date, but I can't really believe you enjoy being alone."

Unwilling to discuss his most private emotions, Gardner turned sullen. "Are you licensed to do counseling?"

Jesse laughed. "No, but I've definitely got the practical experience to qualify. Shelley had a real rough night last night, but I think she's finally seen the last of Ricky Vance. If you've no plans for tonight, maybe you could give her a call and cheer her up. Sometimes a man just needs a woman friend, and I know Shelley admires you."

Gardner looked dismayed. "Why?"

Jesse was ready for him, and slid his arm around Gardner's shoulders. "You're the kind of man a woman can depend on. That means a lot."

Gardner nodded slightly. "I'm reliable. So what? That's not very exciting."

"Not every woman craves excitement. In fact, that's

probably the last thing Shelley wants. I'll bet you could be real romantic if you put your mind to it, and Shelley deserves some sympathetic attention."

Pulling away, Gardner grabbed hold of his dolly. "Shelley has a daughter, and I don't want a ready-made family."

Instantly, Jesse saw Gardner for the fool he was and raised his hands. "Excuse me. I mistook you for someone with character. That's the last mistake I'll make with you." He walked away, but as soon as he and Aubrey were on their way home, he gave vent to his anger.

"I just can't understand that kind of thinking. If it can even be classified as thinking rather than a stupid prejudice," he fumed. "If Gardner doesn't have an obstacle, then he'll just build himself one. I'm sorry I mentioned Shelley to him because he's as big a flake as Ricky Vance. He'll probably die a virgin and it'll be his own damn fault."

Aubrey thought Jesse was taking her assistants' problems too seriously, and then wondered if he weren't creating a convenient diversion rather than expressing whatever doubts he might have about his involvement with her. As for herself, she harbored no doubts about them whatsoever. They were a fine, if not lasting match, and she intended to cherish every second they shared. She reached out for his arm and slid her hand down to his bruised knuckles.

"It's a shame Gardner lacks your insights, but he'll have to make his own mistakes and learn life's lessons in his own way."

"But he's not learning," Jesse argued. "He's stuck in his own stagnant pond. Trisha would have gone out with him if he had asked her today, but he didn't ask. Shelley's just as quiet and shy as he is, but he won't pursue her, either. The man's an idiot!"

"You're not responsible for his choices. Let it go," Aubrey advised softly.

Knowing she was right, Jesse reluctantly dropped the subject. "How did you get so smart?"

Aubrey answered as Jesse turned into her driveway. "I learned the hard way. Just like everyone else. There's always the risk of being hurt whenever we care about someone else. Gardner's afraid to take that risk. It's a shame, really, because life doesn't amount to much if we care only about ourselves."

"Well, I've never been one to choose the safe path," Jesse assured her.

His eyes were aglow with a mischievous twinkle, but Aubrey knew better than to expect him to put his feelings for her into words. He was definitely a man of action, but she hoped before they parted for the last time, that he would finally hint at love.

Between her passion for Jesse and her anxiety over meeting Harlan Caine a second time, Aubrey spent very little time sleeping Saturday night. When she awakened late Sunday morning and found Jesse nestled beside her, observing her with an amused smile, she quickly sat up. "From the width of your grin, I'd say you've either thought of a brilliant plan for dealing with Harlan Caine, or you're too distracted to care. Which is it?"

Jesse reached out to comb her curls off her forehead. "You are most definitely a distraction, but I've not forgotten today's appointment. Because I think it's likely Caine will lay a trap, we're not going to let him lead the way. No matter what he suggests, we're going to veer off in the opposite direction. We're going to keep him between us, so a sniper, if he's hired one, can't shoot us without a grave risk of hitting him. We're also going to rush him through the site, so if he's timed an accident, we'll throw him off schedule."

"We'll simply be the tourists from hell, is that it?"

"Yeah. You could say that. There's some risk involved, but we'll already be on our guard around him, and we should be able to sense whatever trouble he might cause us before it happens."

Frightened rather than reassured, Aubrey tried not to shriek uncontrollably. "Feeling uneasy around Caine, and being fast enough to sense and avoid danger are two entirely different things. I'll be happy to interrupt his conversation, and divert his tour so the route we follow is ours rather than his, but I wish we had a secret weapon or two just in case everything goes wrong."

Jesse didn't appear the least bit concerned. "The way I took care of Ricky Vance didn't impress you?"

Jesse's size and strength were not the issue in Aubrey's mind. "Oh, yes, it most certainly did, but the odds that you'll have to use your fists today are extremely remote. Do you remember the Russian defector who was murdered in London with the poison-tipped umbrella? It's the possibility of something that bizarre that scares me, not that Caine will challenge you man to man."

Jesse gave her a quick kiss, then rolled out of bed. "Maybe you ought to stay here, and then if I don't come back, you can call out the National Guard."

He was such an impressive sight nude, that Aubrey had a difficult time focusing her attention on his face as he pulled on his Levi's. Then she eyed him with a roving gaze. "It would take more than a National Guard unit to replace you," she murmured in a husky purr.

Laughing, Jesse crawled back up on her bed. "What a mind you have. Would you keep the troops to entertain you rather than send them out to rescue me?"

Aubrey struck a sultry pose. "Possibly, so you don't dare go without me."

Turning serious, Jesse left the bed a second time. "I

keep a knife in my right boot. Don't block my way if it looks as though I might need to throw it."

He left her bedroom with a proud swagger, and Aubrey did not waste her breath urging him to be cautious. She prayed Harlan Caine wasn't crazy enough to try to make them disappear on a sunlit afternoon, then wished she knew how to throw a knife, too. She threw back the covers and wondered what she ought to wear. By the time she joined Jesse downstairs, she had become positively inspired.

"My God. You look like Little Bo Peep."

Aubrey had caught her curls atop her head and donned a white blouse with puffed sleeves and a bodice richly adorned with tucks and lace. She turned to show off the generous folds of her blue floral skirt, then stamped her feet and clapped her hands in a graceful imitation of a Flamenco dancer. "Close enough. I've worn this outfit to parties whenever I needed a costume. Once I called myself Doris Day, and another time said I was one of the dancers from the musical "Oklahoma!

"Today, I'm just padding out my silhouette so I'll make a difficult target. I've read men used to fight duels in baggy suits for the same reason. I hope you're planning to wear that gorgeous fringed jacket."

As usual Aubrey was full of surprises, but Jesse considered her idea too good to pass up. "I hadn't considered that, but now that you've mentioned it, I certainly will."

He reached out to take her hand and spun her around. "Let's just dance our way through the construction site, and Caine will surely think we're too addled to cause him any problems. Usually all I have to do is use a thick accent and people mistakenly believe I'm not too bright, but I think we ought to go all out today."

Aubrey relaxed in his arms, but she did not forget their true purpose for a single second. She didn't like to think of herself as a tasty morsel, but bait was all she really was. "Let's decide right now that you'll keep an eye on Caine, and I'll watch for something, anything, peculiar at the site."

"All right, agreed."

Neither of them felt like eating, but thinking they should, each drank a glass of juice and ate a piece of toast before they left. Aubrey had a floppy straw hat, and while she wasn't comfortable wearing it in the truck, she plunked it on her head as soon as they reached Harlan Caine's office. On Sunday afternoon, the parking lot was empty except for a cream-colored Cadillac Seville, but she scanned the wooden building, searching for any sign someone else might be lurking nearby.

"I want you to wait here," Jesse ordered. He dropped his keys into Aubrey's hand. "Hang on to these in case you have to get out of here fast. I'll tell Caine it would have been silly for us both to make the trek to his office to announce we're here, so if he planned to nab us when we arrived, he can't. When I come back with him, I won't agree to riding in his car no matter how politely he offers, but of course, you should appear to go along with his invitation. Now give me a smile."

"I thought I was smiling."

"Not quite." Jesse bent down to kiss her, then ambled off toward the stairs leading up to Harlan Caine's office. He turned and waved when he reached them, then disappeared into the stairwell.

Aubrey had brought the tiny tape recorder again, but couldn't bring herself to record her impressions as yet. She knew Harlan Caine was evil, and she was scared to death. She had gum in her purse and was still unwrapping a piece when Jesse reappeared with the developer.

"Would either of you like some gum?" she asked.

Jesse reached out his hand, but Caine just shook his head.

"It's nice to see you again, Ms. Glenn," Caine stressed warmly. "We're only a few blocks from the site, and there's no reason to take two cars. Let's go in mine."

Aubrey shoved the gum into her mouth, and began to chew. She hadn't popped gum since high school, but thought the rude habit inspired now. "That's kind of you," she replied, and started toward the Cadillac.

"Darlin', you know I won't be comfortable in Mr. Caine's car. I'll either have to fold up my legs, or crush my hat and neither will make for an enjoyable ride. We'll just have to follow in my truck."

"Suit yourself," Caine offered agreeably. He was dressed in Levis and a pink knit shirt which showed off his muscular build as well as he had intended.

Aubrey removed her hat, and climbed up into the truck. "Did Caine say anything interesting?" she asked.

Jesse started his engine, and then slammed the truck into first gear. Without an audience, he had no need to affect a southern accent and used his normal voice. "If by 'interesting' you mean incriminating, no, he didn't. The gum's a nice touch, by the way."

Aubrey rolled her hat brim in a frantic clutch, and wondered why she had ever thought confronting Harlan Caine was wise. "We should have called the police."

"I had no idea you were so nervous. I'm really looking forward to this tour. You want to just throw up on my boots, and I'll tell Caine you overdid it at brunch?"

Aubrey glared at him. Caine had greeted her in a relaxed and friendly manner, but she was far too anxious to drop her guard. "Let's save that one for another time. Even in this frilly blouse I feel as though I have a target painted on my chest."

"Remember what I said about staying close to Caine?"

Aubrey nodded. "I remember the plan. I just wish we had an idea of what his is."

Just as Caine had reported, the construction site was less than a mile away. The wooden frames outline half a dozen buildings clustered around a central courtyard and parking lot. A large sign proclaimed it the future home of the Northridge Fitness Complex. The architect's name and Harlan Caine's were featured in bold script beneath an impressive illustration of the completed project.

"It doesn't look far enough along for anyone to find the necessary cover to shoot us," Aubrey whispered.

The plumbing and aluminum air-conditioning ducts were in place, but Jesse agreed they didn't offer much in the way of cover. "Let's just keep our eyes open," he cautioned. He took his time leaving the truck, then swung Aubrey down to her feet. "It sure is a beautiful day for sightseeing," he called to Harlan Caine.

"That it is. I'm sorry we're not further along in the construction, but things will go quickly from here on. What makes this project unique is its focus. The first building, the largest, is the gym. I'll unlock the security gate, and we can take a closer look at it. The swimming pool is already in."

Aubrey moved to Caine's right, and nearly struck him in the eye with her elbow as she adjusted her hat. "I'm so sorry. How clumsy of me. Is the gym going to be used by both men and women?"

Harlan unlocked the padlock and pulled open the gate in the chain link fence. "Yes, of course. It works well to mingle the sexes. If fact, a great many people belong to gyms simply to meet people of the opposite sex rather than to workout seriously. We'll offer everything from aerobic classes to weight training, so we'll have plenty of options for everyone. The beauty of this place is that we'll have shops selling sports equipment, clothing, and shoes in the same complex. We'll also have a restaurant which will specialize in delicious, low-fat healthy foods, and a facility for day care which will be staffed by credentialed teachers rather than mere babysitters."

His pitch well rehearsed, Harlan moved at an easy pace as they walked toward the gym. "With hours stretching from 6:00 a.m. until midnight, fitness should be within everyone's reach. Not that you two appear to need help in that area, but exercise is vital for staying in shape once you reach your goals."

"I couldn't agree more," Aubrey enthused. There was something different about the developer's manner that day, and it took her a moment to realize he was far more relaxed than during their previous meeting. He was wearing a sickeningly sweet cologne, but she refused to be repelled by it and stayed close. As they crossed the construction area, she stepped around a pile of rubble, and took note of a stack of lumber off to their right.

She heard Jesse ask a question about security for the site, and Harlan Caine's praise for a private security patrol. She turned her back to the men for a moment and concentrated solely on the unfinished buildings. There was the scent of raw wood and trampled earth, mixed with the faint aroma of oil from a nearby generator.

Traffic was light on the road behind them, and the pervasive atmosphere on the lazy afternoon was tranquil. If Harlan Caine had laid a trap, it wasn't here. And while relief flooded through Aubrey, she felt the sting of frustration, as well. She had told Jesse from the outset that she lacked the requisite skills to solve baffling crimes, but she hated to let him down.

She smiled shyly as she turned toward him, and he winked at her. The gesture brought an amused chuckle from Caine, but he continued praising what he was certain would be a successful venture. Jesse rushed him through the gym and along the other buildings just beginning to take shape.

"I'm awfully fond of frozen yogurt," Jesse exclaimed. "Is one of these places going to sell some?"

"Yes. In addition to the restaurant, we'll have a cafe which will carry nutritious snacks, juices, and yogurt. There will be umbrella tables scattered around the courtyard for those who'd like to relax outside."

Aubrey took note of the hazards at the site. The ground was uneven. Nails were sprinkled over the dirt, and there was an occasional oil slick, but certainly no imminent danger she had overlooked. Still taking care to avoid complacency, she moved away from the men, and then came back, before darting away in another direction. Finally, she reached into her purse and handed Harlan a business card.

"The mind and body must be in balance for optimum health. Once this wonderful facility opens, it will be a perfect location for one of my creative imagery seminars. Why don't you give me a call, and we'll schedule one. You might make attendance available as a prize to the first fifty or so who join the gym."

For a brief instant Harlan appeared surprised, then he responded with a near blinding smile. "Excellent idea, Ms. Glenn. I'll keep you in mind."

"Yes. That's where I belong," Aubrey teased with a gentle sway that sent her full skirt into a twisting swish. "I'm sorry we had to meet under such difficult circumstances, but let's not let that prevent us from having a profitable association in the future."

The developer grasped her hands between both of his. "Certainly not. I envy you, Jesse. Ms. Glenn is a remarkable woman."

The instant Caine touched her, Aubrey was filled with a dizzying sense of doom. She quickly broke away and grabbed hold of Jesse's arm to steady herself. Jesse was solid and warm, but she feared it would take several minutes for the despair Harlan Caine had caused to fade.

Jesse backed away with Aubrey in tow. "Yes, she sure is. I hope you'll forgive us for rushing off, but Aubrey has such a full schedule we have to make every spare minute count."

"I understand." Harlan walked along with them back to the gate. He quickly reattached the heavy padlock, then bid them a final good-bye and waved as he headed toward his car.

Jesse kept smiling until the Cadillac Seville pulled away. "I can feel you shaking. Here, just get in the truck, and we'll be home before you know it."

Aubrey removed her hat before getting in, then waited impatiently for Jesse to climb behind the wheel. "I didn't sense any danger here until Caine touched me. And then, well, I came close to throwing up right there."

Jesse reached out to give her hand a comforting squeeze. "Caine was different today. He was too confident if you ask me. But the real question is, why? Has he dismissed us as a threat, or cooked up something diabolical?"

"I've never touched a murderer before meeting him, so I can't say if the horrible sensation I got when he touched me is from what he's done, or what he intends to do to us. Either way, I don't want to be near him again. But what have we really accomplished today, other than satisfy our curiosity that Caine really is a developer?"

Jesse shrugged. "I'll grant you this looks like a dead end—"

"I wish you hadn't used that term."

"Whatever. It's only a temporary setback. I heard you tell Shelley that there's no seminar scheduled in the coming week. Do you have something else planned?"

Aubrey's mind refused to consider the coming week. She simply sat and stared out the window as Jesse turned onto the freeway. She had learned so much about herself in recent years, and had reveled in the resulting confidence she had gained. Now the pleasant world she had built for herself was suddenly atilt, and she didn't know how to set it right.

"Next week?" she finally mumbled.

"Yes. If you've nothing to do, I thought maybe you'd like to come home with me. It might help us to get away. Perhaps we'll find a new perspective on things."

"What things?" Aubrey asked, unclear about whether he was referring to Harlan Caine, or to what they meant to each other. When he didn't answer immediately, she turned toward him. In that same second, the truck's rear window was shattered by a single shot, bits of broken glass flying into her hair and spraying Jesse's shoulders.

Jesse had been struggling to put his feelings into words, and caught off guard, he cursed his own stupidity as he fought to remain in control of the Chevy. He saw a gold Corvette speed by on his right, and turned hard to cross two lanes to give pursuit.

"Are you all right?" he screamed.

Aubrey looked down, fully expecting to find her blouse soaked with blood, but it was as snowy white as when she had pulled it from her closet. She raised her hands to her hair, but they came away clean, as well. "I guess so. Are you?"

"I'm going to kill that rotten son-of-a-bitch!" Jesse knew his truck didn't have the Corvette's speed, but as the driver swung onto an off-ramp, he felt certain he had a good chance to catch him. There was no time to waste using his CB radio to summon the police, and he came barreling off the freeway with fire blazing in his eyes. The light was red at the bottom of the ramp, and a truck from a local nursery filled with six-foot palm trees and glossy green ficus was waiting to make a right turn.

The Corvette swung around the truck on the left just as a homeless man in a long, floppy overcoat pushed a shopping cart filled with aluminum cans into the crosswalk. The sleek sportscar struck the cart a glancing blow and sent a shower of colorful cans into the air. The driver slammed on his brakes to avoid running over the vagrant, giving Jesse a split second to overtake him. Tromping the gas pedal, he plowed the front of the massive truck up and over the rear end of the Corvette, trapping the driver inside.

Jesse cut the engine and leapt down out of his truck, but then had to fight to pull the irate man who had lost a cartful of cans away from the Corvette. With the passenger side of the vehicle jammed against the nursery truck, the driver was trapped in his seat with a German shepherd howling as though he were being beaten. Even knowing the man was armed, Jesse nearly tore the door off the Corvette to get at him.

With his arm almost wrenched from its socket, John Gilroy fell to his knees as Jesse yanked him out of his car. He tried to protect himself with his right arm, but Jesse punched him so hard in the face, he lurched backwards. Jesse then slammed his knee into John's groin and stepped back to let him fall forward on the pavement.

Terrified Jesse might light into him next, the homeless man began running around gathering up his scattered cans and tossing them into the shopping cart which was now so badly bent the wheels would barely roll. The two gardeners left the nursery truck and grabbed a shovel and hoe to contain what they feared might fast become a riot. Too frightened to leave the Corvette, the German shepherd continued barking in high-pitched yelps.

Aubrey watched the whole ghastly scene from the safety of the truck, but she couldn't stop shaking—even after the police arrived and arrested John Gilroy for attempted murder.

Chapter XV

Aubrey raised trembling hands to accept a cup of tea from Helen Heffley. She and Jesse had been asked to come down to the police station to provide statements. They had asked to see Detectives Heffley and Kobin, but thus far, Jesse had done all the talking.

As Aubrey brought the styrofoam cup to her lips, a tiny chunk of glass fell from her hair, bounced off her shoulder, and then hit the floor with a faint ping. She stared down at it, wondering if there was an effective way to remove the remaining bits of glass from her hair without shredding her scalp. She supposed the detective might know, but this seemed an inappropriate time to inquire.

Sensing Aubrey's distress, Jesse reached out to rest his hand lightly on her knee. "The man you arrested, John Gilroy—can you tie him to Harlan Caine?"

"Possibly, but we recovered the bullet from the padded sunvisor in your truck, and it will undoubtedly match one fired from the gun in Gilroy's car, so he's in enough trouble on his own."

Aubrey scarcely seemed to be listening, but Jesse didn't want his remark to be misinterpreted and moved forward cautiously. "No one would ever mistake Gilroy for a gangbanger cruising the freeway and shooting at cars for kicks. This was a deliberate attack on Ms. Glenn's life, and the only person with a reason to want her dead is Harlan Caine. Now if Gilroy was paid to get rid of Aubrey, it's likely that he was in on what happened to the Ferrell family, as well."

Helen Heffley was dressed in gray slacks and a loose-fitting gray silk blouse; her outfit was only slightly less forbidding than her expression. "We'll pursue that avenue," she promised without a shred of conviction.

Clearly the detective didn't like to be told how to do her job, but Jesse would not allow her to overlook the obvious. "Will the District Attorney offer Gilroy immunity in exchange for his testimony against Caine?"

"It's a possibility." Helen pursed her lips thoughtfully, then quickly wrote herself a note. "My partner and I would like nothing better than to get a conviction in the Ferrell case, so you may rest assured that we'll give it our best effort."

"Right." Jesse rose to his feet and glanced over at James Kobin who was nibbling a fingernail rather than following their conversation. Again dressed in the snug-fitting navy blue suit, he did not appear to pose a threat to any criminal's freedom. "Is there anything else?" Jesse asked.

Helen turned to check with her partner, and Kobin shook his head. "No. Thank you. That's all for today. We'll keep you informed."

"I'm taking Ms. Glenn home with me to Sedona. Let me give you my number there should you need us."

"Isn't Sedona where the spectacular red rock formations are?" Helen asked.

Jesse supplied his telephone number, and then answered. "Yes, it is. But I'd rather just relax in their

shadows than have to hide from the likes of Harlan Caine."
He spoke far more softly to Aubrey. "Are you ready to
leave?"

Aubrey took a last sip of tea before looking up. "What
happened to Gilroy's dog?" she asked the detectives.

"What dog?" Helen asked. She quickly flipped through
the arresting officer's report. "There's a mention of a
German shepherd, but Gilroy apparently referred to him
as a stray, so he'll go to the pound."

"Why would Gilroy be picking up strays?" Jesse asked.
"That doesn't make any sense at all. The dog must have
been in his car for a reason."

James Kobin finally stopped fretting over his nail.
"Maybe he expected the dog to bark and confuse anyone
who thought they'd heard gunfire."

Helen's brows shot up, but after a moment's hesitation,
she shrugged. "That's as good an explanation as we're
likely to get. The dog's probably still here. Do you want
him?"

Jesse watched a shadow cross Aubrey's expression and
knew she was seriously considering it. "That hound would
gobble up Guinevere in a single bite."

"He'd make a good watchdog though, wouldn't he?"
Aubrey replied. "I just hate to send any animal to the
pound, and from what I saw when you yanked Gilroy from
his car, that poor dog was as badly shaken as we were.
Maybe we should take him."

Jesse opened his mouth to argue, then decided he would
much rather watch Aubrey fuss over a dog than stare into
space as she had been for the last half-hour. "Where can
I find him?"

James Kobin lurched from his seat. "I'll go look."

Aubrey handed Jesse her cup to toss away, then directed
her attention to Helen Heffley. "Do you have any idea
how I might remove bits of glass from my hair? I'm afraid

I'll slice up both my hands and my head should I try to shampoo it out."

"That is a problem, isn't it?" Helen rose and grabbed her wastebasket. "Just come here and lean over. I'll pull the pins from your hair, and the glass should fall out as easy as rain."

"I'm going to have my rear window replaced with bullet-proof glass," Jesse swore. He had not thought much of Helen Heffley, but his opinion soared as the detective gently combed her fingers through Aubrey's curls to dislodge the remaining bits of glass. The shards fell into the metal wastebasket with the clatter of miniature hail, but in a matter of minutes, the last had been dislodged, and Aubrey straightened up.

"Thank you. This has been quite a day, hasn't it?" Aubrey murmured absently.

"Would you like to stick around for the rest of my shift?" Helen asked. "I can promise you plenty more excitement."

"We've already had more than enough," Jesse answered. When Gilroy had fired at them, Jesse had been intent upon masking his need to take Aubrey home behind a casual invitation. He had had more of his attention focused on her response than the traffic on the freeway, and he knew they were damn lucky he hadn't lost control of the truck and splattered them and several other cars along the center divider. He sure wasn't looking forward to the long ride home, but at the same time, he was anxious to get going.

James Kobin returned within minutes with the German shepherd on a long leather leash. A new choke chain dangled around the dog's neck, but it had no license identification tag attached. When the detective came to a halt, the dog quickly sat down at his side and glanced up at him as though he expected a treat.

"That's someone's dog," Aubrey said. "He's obviously been well trained, and his collar and leash are new."

"If you don't want him to take his chances at the pound, we can run an ad in the *Times* and see if anyone claims him," Jesse suggested.

Aubrey took the leash from Kobin. "Yes. That's a good idea. He must be someone's dear pet."

"Maybe not," Helen argued. "He looks young. Some breeders produce more pups than they can sell, and just send the extras to the pound. Some are adopted, but most aren't. I'd call that dog Lucky if I were you, because you're probably the best chance he'll have for a home."

"Lucky? I rather like that," Aubrey agreed. "Come on, Lucky. Let's go home."

The dog licked her hand and trotted along beside her toward the door. "I've never owned a big dog," Aubrey said as they walked toward Jesse's truck. "They eat a lot, don't they?"

"Yeah, they sure do. And let's hope he's housebroken."

Aubrey detoured around a tree, where the dog paused to relieve himself, and then led him to the truck. "Does he have to sit in the back?"

"With the rear window gone, he'd probably just climb in with us anyway; we might as well let him ride in the cab." Jesse still couldn't believe Aubrey actually wanted the dog, but the shepherd seemed to be good-natured, and he had complained that she needed more protection than tiny Guinevere could provide. As he pulled out of the Devonshire Division parking lot, he tried to recall just where he had been in the conversation when all hell had broken loose.

"When we get to your place, find someone to take care of your pets. Then pack a bag—you won't need much more than Levi's, a few shirts, and your toothbrush—and we'll leave for Sedona. If Harlan Caine hired John Gilroy, then he must be expecting him to report in, and when he doesn't, I don't want to give Caine the opportunity to come after you himself."

"I can't stay long," Aubrey argued. She had given Lucky the place by the window, and was scratching his ears.

Jesse had never taken a woman home, and thought he ought to just concentrate on getting her there for now. "Let's take it one day at a time. I'll call the detectives assigned to the case every morning and keep after them to arrest Caine."

Jesse usually drove in a relaxed slouch, but he was sitting up straight, and Aubrey hoped he wasn't blaming himself for what had happened. "You've torn up your hands again."

Jesse flexed his bloody knuckles. "It was worth it. I'm only sorry Gilroy passed out before I could beat the truth out of him." He glanced toward Aubrey. "Maybe we ought to go after Caine ourselves."

"That's easily the worst idea you've ever had. He'd have you arrested for assault, and then where would we be?"

Jesse conceded the point, but he wasn't happy about it. When they reached Aubrey's, he called his Aunt Edith, but told her only that he had to get back home and would keep in touch. He packed up his gear and was ready to go long before Aubrey got herself organized, but he dared not rush her. She decided to take Lucky along, but found a neighbor, who had been a good friend of her parents, to look after Guinevere and feed Lucifer for the few days she assumed she would be away.

When the woman arrived, Aubrey introduced her as Cecile Blanchard. Jesse greeted her warmly, and Lucky wagged his tail as though he knew her. Cecile took one look at the friendly dog and smiled. "I didn't realize you'd gotten a new dog when I saw him the night the fire department was here. I didn't recognize the man walking him, but we exchanged a few words before he continued down the street. He knew less than I did, which was odd if he was a friend of yours."

Jesse was as alarmed as Aubrey, but tried not to let it show. "There are a great many German shepherds," he reminded Cecile. "What makes you think this is the same one?"

Cecile leaned down and Lucky came to her. "You see? He remembers me. That's a smart dog. He seemed real eager to explore the other night, and the man kept yanking on his leash. That's the same leather leash. You don't see many of those anymore. Most people have switched to the colorful nylon variety, but maybe leather works best for him."

"Can you remember anything about the man?" Aubrey asked.

Cecile glanced away and tried to recall. "Can't say that I do. I think he was wearing a cap and windbreaker, but I'm really not sure. I guess I was distracted by the dog."

"There was a lot of excitement that night," Aubrey added, before gently steering the conversation to the care of her pets in her absence. She waited until after Cecile had left with Guinevere before she allowed herself to dwell on the most obvious possibility. "Do you suppose Gilroy just grabbed a dog, any dog, as an excuse to walk through my neighborhood?"

"It's a good theory, and there's only one way he knew which night to pick. It's a shame Lucky can't testify against him, isn't it?"

"It sure is. Come on. Let's get out of here." After changing her Doris Day outfit for jeans and a T-shirt, Aubrey had thrown what she thought she would need into a colorful canvas satchel. She was certain she must have forgotten something, but was too anxious to be on their way to make a comprehensive list and conduct an inventory.

There was still plenty of light when they finally got on the

road. Fortunately, the weekend traffic was thick streaming
back into Los Angeles rather than heading east, and they
made good time. Jesse felt no need to talk, and enjoyed
driving along in companionable silence. Lucky took up
too much room in the cab, but Jesse didn't mind having
Aubrey pressed close, and when she rested her head on
his shoulder and fell asleep, he was surprised by how good
it felt to be taking her home.

He refused to push his thoughts past the next few days,
but he intended to make them memorable. His home was
nothing like Aubrey's elegant house, but it was comfortable
and he liked to think it had a certain southwestern charm.
So did he, he supposed, and he stifled a dry chuckle before
he woke Aubrey. He wanted her to be well rested and he
didn't care how tired he was, he was going to provide an
enthusiastic welcome to his home.

They stopped for supper and gas in Blythe, then angled
north. Aubrey fell asleep again, but was awakened abruptly
several hours later when Jesse pulled off the highway onto
the rutted dirt road that led to his ranch. "Sorry," he
yelled above the clatter of the bouncing truck. "I'd pave
this road, but that would just encourage people to turn
down it, and you're all the company I need."

Aubrey peered ahead, but the Chevy's headlights illumi-
nated only a thin margin of chaparral on either side of
the narrow road, and she had no idea where they were.
They were sending up a cloud of red dust that spilled in
the open rear window and choked her as she tried to speak.

"I didn't realize you lived so far from town."

"I told you I owned a ranch."

"Well, yes. I suppose it wouldn't be a ranch if it were
in the middle of Sedona."

Jesse was too tired to do more than nod at that bit of
piercing logic. "We're almost there." He slowed to take

the next turn, and for the first time, a faint light shone in the distance. "There it is, just up ahead."

Aubrey had begun to worry about what she had gotten herself into, but when the headlights swept across a low adobe structure with a red tile roof, she relaxed. "Did you build the house yourself?"

"No, but I've added on and modernized until I might as well have." He swung the Chevy around the circular drive and parked beside the front door. "Let's postpone the tour until morning. Right now, all I want is some sleep." He left the truck and removed their luggage from the back.

Having napped a good deal of the way, Aubrey was more curious than tired, but after letting Lucky explore the front patio, she followed Jesse through the handcarved wooden door. Square terra cotta tiles not only lined the entryway but spread out to form the floor of the living and dining area. Jesse had turned on an occasional lamp as he headed for his bedroom, and she followed the trail of light.

Navaho rugs woven in bright earthtones were scattered across the floor tiles, and from what she could see of the furnishings, they were a mixture of overstuffed leather and ornately carved wood. It was an impressive home, and thoroughly masculine in decor. When she finally reached Jesse's bedroom, he was seated on a huge bed formed of rough-hewn pine logs joined together at the corners with the stark beauty of fence posts. It was covered with a terra cotta comforter with a deep black border.

"I don't have a guest room," Jesse teased as he removed his boots, "unless you want to count the bunkhouse. I'm assuming you'd rather sleep here with me than with half a dozen men who probably forgot to bathe on Saturday night."

Aubrey glanced down at Lucky. "What do you say, boy? Shall we flip a coin?"

The dog thumped his tail on the tile.

"Lucky's voting for the bunkhouse, but I'll stay here—at least for tonight."

Jesse nodded toward the adjacent doorway. "You take the first turn in the bathroom. I'll shut Lucky in the kitchen and put out a bowl of water. I doubt the scraps we fed him after dinner will hold him all night, but maybe I can find something for him to chew on in the refrigerator."

Aubrey handed him Lucky's leash, but as Jesse walked by her, she noticed him limping, and hoped he wasn't in too much pain. She had offered to take a turn driving, but he had stubbornly refused to consider it. Now that it was too late, she wished she had been more insistent.

She carried her satchel into the bathroom and was pleasantly surprised to find the room not only modern, but handsomely designed with beige fixtures and terra cotta tile accented with aqua trim. Thick aqua towels hung from wrought-iron racks, and a plush aqua rug covered the floor. Throughout the house bold earth colors and oversized furniture fit Jesse's personality and proportions well, but Aubrey found the complete lack of feminine touches a bit disconcerting.

She peeled off her clothes, stepped into the glass enclosed tub, and turned on the shower. The instant the warm water splashed her shoulders she wished Jesse had joined her, but because he hadn't, she hurried so as not to keep him waiting for his turn. She quickly toweled off, pulled on her lavender sleepshirt, and left the bathroom. She found Jesse already sprawled across his bed sound asleep.

Aubrey was positive she had not taken too long in the shower, so he must have been exhausted. Not wanting him to grow chilled, she covered him with the comforter, then climbed into the bed beside him. The mattress was too soft in her view, but she reminded herself she would not be there long. The beige sheets were crisply pressed and smelled of sunshine, inviting her to snuggle down under the covers. She wished Jesse had at least been awake enough to kiss her good night.

Late the next morning, faint strains of *mariachi* music spilled over into Aubrey's dreams. Slowly teased awake by the exuberant melodies, she stretched lazily, then raised up slightly. Jesse's bedroom was larger than she had realized last night, and bathed in the bright morning sun, the whitewashed walls had taken on a soft golden glow. In the distance, the red mountains were dotted with pine trees.

"I can't believe you didn't wake me," Jesse complained. "Did you really think I'd enjoy sleeping in my clothes?"

Aubrey turned to look at him. He was leaning on his left elbow, and his chest above the sheet was bare. He was trying to affect a menacing frown, but a teasing smile tugged at the corner of his mouth to give away his true mood. "It looks as though you survived."

"Just barely," Jesse replied. He had gotten up earlier, showered, shaved, and then been lured back into bed by Aubrey's angelic smile. He was amazed she could have such pleasant dreams after being shot at, but extremely grateful that she felt safe enough with him to have them.

Aubrey had no recollection of her dreams, but Jesse looked awfully good to her that morning. She reached up to caress his cheek, and he caught her hand to draw her near. She pressed against the length of him, boldly fitting her curves against the hardened planes of his muscular body, but she still didn't feel close enough. She pulled away briefly to toss her sleepshirt aside, then returned to his arms with a contented sigh that soon became a sultry invitation for something far more passionate than mere gentle cuddling.

Having fallen asleep long before he had intended, Jesse readily responded to Aubrey's desire. On the drive to Arizona, he had replayed the moments preceding the gunshot a thousand times. He was uncertain when it had become imperative to bring Aubrey home with him, but when he had first mentioned it, she hadn't sounded particularly eager to make the trip. In fact, he had feared he would have to talk all the way to her house to convince her it was a good idea.

He recalled glancing toward her, and she had turned to him. Their timing had been as perfect as the steps of the most intricate ballet. Then, boom! Gilroy had fired a shot at them, and the day had taken on a white-hot glow.

As a child, he had been at a movie theater one afternoon when the film had broken. Scorched by the projector's brilliant light, the image on the screen had faded as though doused with bleach. Then the celluloid had blistered and melted, creating a nightmarish landscape on the screen. He had rather enjoyed the grisly sight as a kid, but yesterday, the scene had been played out far too close, and he just wanted to forget it.

What if he hadn't spoken, and Aubrey hadn't turned? That was too horrible a possibility to explore even in his mind, but looking at the sweet, sleepy softness of her now, he needed her with a desperate passion. "God, how I want you," he moaned, his voice husky with desire. Intent upon having her, he moved over her, but rather than rush, took his time to feel every delicious inch of her.

Aubrey had succeeded in distancing herself from her emotions yesterday, but now the memory of her close brush with death brought a searing heat that infused each of her gestures with an unmistakable demand for more than Jesse had ever given. Her kisses burned his mouth, and her nails grazed his shoulders as she pulled him deep into her embrace. With a consuming surrender, she wrapped herself around him, and as she lost her heart, she longed to capture his.

It was afternoon before the hunger for more than each other drove them from the oversized bed. Arm in arm, and laughing happily, they wandered into the kitchen and found the housekeeper, Lupe Peña, putting away the groceries she had just brought back from Sedona. About to scold Jesse for failing to let her know when he would be home, she turned away from the refrigerator wearing an impatient frown. But the instant she saw Aubrey at his side, she broke into a wide smile.

"Finally!" she exclaimed, in a voice softly accented with the musical tones of her native Spanish. "I feared you would never find a woman to please you." She hurriedly wiped her hand on her apron, and extended it to Aubrey. "I'm Lupe Peña."

When Jesse had mentioned a housekeeper, Aubrey had imagined a plump, grandmotherly woman, who kept his house neat, and him well fed. Lupe, however, was closer to forty than sixty. A Hispanic beauty with beautiful dark eyes and thick, sable hair worn in a single braid, she was tall, slim, and dressed in Levi's, boots, and a red cotton shirt, rather than a prim uniform. It was only the wide gold band on her left hand, and a faint recollection that Jesse had mentioned her husband also worked for him, that gave Aubrey the courage to smile.

Sorry he hadn't been quicker, Jesse completed the introductions and then promptly dismissed Lupe's comment. "You're the first woman I've ever brought home, but considering the circumstances, I couldn't have done otherwise."

Lupe appeared greatly intrigued by that comment, while Aubrey wished it had been affection for her rather than fear for her safety which had inspired Jesse's invitation.

Her feelings hurt, she moved away from his side, then tried to hide her disappointment.

"What a pretty kitchen this is. I don't think I've ever seen a more colorful display of Mexican tile."

"You don't think it's too much?" Jesse asked.

The walls were white, as were the appliances, while the wooden cabinets were stained dark. The yellow tile counters were liberally accented with decorative Mexican tiles with intricate floral patterns in blue, white, and green. Windows above the sink let in plenty of light, along with a breathtaking view of the mountains, lending the kitchen a bright and festive mood. Lupe looked perfectly at home there, and was awaiting Aubrey's comment with an expectant glance.

"No," Aubrey assured Jesse. "This kitchen is absolutely spectacular. It suits you, and the house."

"You see, Jesse?" Lupe stressed. "He thought the tile should be as white as the walls, and I told him it would look like a hospital. Because I spend my time here, and he doesn't, I got my way."

Lupe appeared to be extremely pleased with herself, making Aubrey feel even more like an outsider. She remained silent while the housekeeper and Jesse discussed the menu for dinner, but hated to think she was causing extra work. "Please don't go to any trouble for me," she apologized.

"You're no trouble at all," Lupe assured her. "I cook for the men as well as Jesse, and the tiny portion you'll eat won't even be noticed. Now sit down at the dining table, and I'll bring you some fresh *pan dulce* and coffee."

"Aubrey drinks tea," Jesse advised, making it sound as though tea were a controlled substance.

When Lupe gave her a blank stare, Aubrey apologized again. "I should have brought some of my own. If you have any juice, I'll take that—or water is fine."

"I could send Fernando back to the store for tea," Lupe offered.

"No, don't bother," Jesse said. "I want to take Aubrey into town later, and we'll get some then."

"Really," Aubrey insisted. "Water will be fine."

"Why are you so nervous?" Jesse whispered as soon as they were seated at the heavy pine dining table. Placed at the end of the home's main room nearest the kitchen, the table and six ladderback chairs were as impressive as the rest of the furnishings.

"I didn't realize I was," Aubrey insisted, hating herself for the lie, but unwilling to reveal how little she appreciated being invited there out of a sense of duty. "Tell me something about this house. Was this center section with the fireplace the original structure?"

Jesse doubted Aubrey cared all that much about the architecture, but not wanting her to dwell on Harlan Caine, he supplied the answer. "Yes. The original owner came here to raise cattle around the turn of the century. He built this single room for living and sleeping, and cooked his meals outdoors. He had intended to add on to the house when he married, but the woman he had hoped to entice out here from Virginia kept postponing her trip, and then married someone else.

"The ranch was bought and sold several times, but apparently I was the first to want indoor plumbing and more than a single room. I rather like the old place, though. If and when I get real ambitious, I'm going to add on wings to give the house the shape of a C."

Lupe carried in a tray of flakey sweet Mexican pastries, coffee for Jesse, and glasses of orange juice for them both. "Perhaps I should have offered lunch rather than breakfast. Would you like something more?"

Aubrey waited for Jesse to assure her they were fine, and

then agreed. "Lupe seems very nice," she added when they were again alone.

Jesse smiled as he replaced his cup on the table. Lupe made the best coffee he had ever tasted, and even if she had not been able to do another thing, he would have kept her on the payroll. "Yes, she is. She's also a damn good cook, and I haven't found a speck of dust in here since the day she arrived. I think you'll like her husband. Fernando started working for me first, then I hired Lupe."

Aubrey hadn't eaten a *pan dulce* in a while and pulled off a flavorful bite. It had a hint of almond and almost melted in her mouth. "Lupe's very attractive. Is he?"

Jesse laughed at that question. "You'll have to tell me. He takes care of my horses, and you'll meet him later. You do ride, don't you?"

"Ride? You mean horses?" Aubrey's heart sank.

"Well, you're too big to ride one of the llamas."

Aubrey shrugged slightly. "Well, I have ridden a horse upon occasion."

It had not even occurred to Jesse that Aubrey wouldn't know how to ride, but now he couldn't understand why he had thought a woman who had been raised in the city would. "That's good. Did you enjoy it?"

Aubrey doubted that she had been more than twelve or thirteen the last time she had been invited to go horseback riding. "I've only ridden horses I've rented for an hour or so, and the trails, like those around Griffith Park, weren't demanding. I would like to see something of the area though, and you know I can't stay long. I've a seminar to lead on Saturday, so I'll have to fly home on Friday."

Jesse found it surprisingly difficult to think of her leaving so soon. "Well, I can't promise to turn you into a cowgirl in four days, but I'll give it my best try."

Jesse took a bite out of his second *pan dulce*, but Aubrey couldn't finish her first. If she flew home Friday morning, which she intended to do, they would have only four and a half days together, and then probably never see each other again. She was certain Jesse would promise to call her when he visited his aunt, and he might the next time he came to California, but then he would forget.

Large windows on either side of the stone fireplace provided another magnificent view. Knowing how brief her stay would be, Aubrey thought it very sad the home's original owner had not been able to share the marvelous scenery with the woman he loved. It was far easier to dwell on his heartbreak than her own.

"What do you suppose happened to the man who built this house?" she asked wistfully.

The story I heard is that he went on to California, became one of the first car dealers, and got rich. Now if you're finished, let's go. There's lots to see in town, and I want to have time to find you some tea."

Aubrey left the table with him, but she wished he weren't in such a terrible hurry, because it would make the few days they had to share go by much too fast.

Chapter XVI

As Jesse and Aubrey entered the kitchen, Lupe stopped chopping onions. "I sent your new dog out with Fernando this morning. We have too many dogs as it is, but if you must have another, you really should take care of him yourself."

"Lupe likes to pretend she's my mother," Jesse leaned down to tell Aubrey.

"I forgot all about Lucky," Aubrey exclaimed. Then badly embarrassed, she apologized to Lupe. "Lucky's my dog, and I'm sorry if he tore up the kitchen last night."

"No. He is very well behaved. He did not even spill a drop of water, but I'm glad to hear he is your dog rather than Jesse's."

"How many dogs do you own?" Aubrey asked.

"Well, this is a ranch, and with so much land a few dogs here and there don't make much difference."

Aubrey took note of Lupe's frown and knew the dogs must be a point of contention between them. "Just how many are there?"

Jesse looped his arm around Aubrey's shoulders and turned her back toward the living room. "I haven't taken a count since I got home, and the number may have changed. Come on. The truck's still out front. Let's get going or we won't be home in time for supper."

Aubrey glanced back toward Lupe, who was rolling her eyes, and decided Jesse must own at least a dozen dogs. "If you usually don't allow your dogs to come inside the house, we should have left Lucky outside last night."

"No. He's a guest, and he didn't hurt anything, so it doesn't matter." Jesse opened the front door for Aubrey and then followed her across the patio. "On the way into town, we'll pass Tlaquepaque, a real fancy shopping village built with Spanish Colonial architecture and filled with expensive boutiques. If you feel like spending lots of money, we'll stop."

Aubrey climbed up into the truck and waited for Jesse to walk around and get behind the wheel. "I'm sure they must have lovely shops, but I'd rather just drive around and enjoy the scenery."

Jesse reached over, wrapped his fingers around Aubrey's wrist, and pretended to take her pulse. "Are you feeling okay? I didn't think women ever got out of the mood to shop."

"In such a beautiful setting? Why would I want to spend my time indoors trying on clothes?"

"Beats me." Jesse stared the engine, and they were soon bouncing along the unpaved road on their way to the highway. Once they reached it, he was able to talk without having to shout. "The red rock formations were laid down as sediment when this area was below sea level. Fault lines created separate mesas, and erosion accounts for today's sculptured buttes. Each one has a name: Cathedral, Courthouse, Bell Rock, Coffee Pot, Sugar Loaf, Steamboat, and others. I'll point them out, but there are a lot of people who come here to experience a vortex rather than the red rock canyons.''

"A vortex?" Aubrey asked. "They're something like magnetic fields, aren't they?''

"You can look at it that way. The Earth is a giant magnet. A vortex is merely a spot where there's a change in the Earth's magnetic field. There may be lots of them, but there are four clustered near Sedona, and that makes this a major site. The energy here is positive, but there are places, like the Bermuda Triangle, where the energy is negative. Or so I've read. To tell you the truth, I've never paid much attention to the psychic claims for the area, but after meeting you, I've begun to wonder if I'm not wasting an opportunity to explore them.''

So that was why he had invited her home, Aubrey thought. Just as quickly, she dismissed the suspicion as unworthy of contemplation. She had come to Sedona with him because she had wanted to, no, needed to, and nothing else truly mattered.

"That's Bell Rock up ahead to our right.''

"It's aptly named, isn't it?" Aubrey leaned forward slightly to observe the butte whose knobbed summit flared out into a broad circular base. The layers of rock varied in color from a deep, rich red to a sandy terra cotta, and were sprinkled with sparse vegetation. "Could we stop?" she asked.

"Of course." Jesse pulled off onto the shoulder of the highway across from the Bell Rock Motel. He then led Aubrey over the rocky trail toward the domed butte. "We can sit down awhile, and give the spirits in the area a chance to contact you.''

Aubrey made her way carefully over the trail worn in the powdery, reddish soil. The dust clung to the toes of her boots, giving the tan leather a pink cast. "Just what sort of spirits are they?''

"Friendly ones," Jesse stressed. "I told you Sedona is known for its positive energy."

"The sky is such a vivid blue," Aubrey observed admiringly, "and the earth here is unlike anything at home. It's difficult to believe this is nothing more than a spectacular example of geology."

Jesse waited until they had reached a shady slope to speak. "The Yavapai believe this is where the world began. It's not the way I envision the Garden of Eden, but it's theirs."

Aubrey breathed deeply and, unlike Jesse, found it easy to imagine the colorful landscape as the birthplace of man. "I rather like the idea. The terrain is wildly primitive, and yet unbelievably beautiful. Could we stay here awhile?"

"The rocks are as soft here as anywhere," Jesse advised, and as soon as Aubrey had assumed a cross-legged pose, he dropped down beside her. He was about to take her hand when he remembered that the last time they had tried a mental link, they hadn't been successful. He did not want to risk being blamed if Aubrey's visions weren't pleasant, and kept his hands to himself.

Aubrey had gone on an occasional hike in the San Gabriel Mountains above Pasadena, but the view there was one of granite boulders and pine trees. Here, the vista was surreal, and yet calming. She closed her eyes and released her mind to float wherever it might take her. For a long while there was only a whisper of breeze and Jesse's reassuring presence, then a sandy plain formed in her mind's eye.

Drenched with sun, the soil sparkled with bits of mica. An Indian brave she recognized instantly stepped into view and began walking toward her. He came close, then turned, and motioned for her to follow him back across the desert. When she did not immediately obey, he came back for her and extended his hand. He was a handsome

man with a compelling gaze, but Aubrey did not understand why she should accompany him when his destination
appeared to be a vast, lonely desert.

"Why?" she called to him, and he pointed to her, then
to himself.

When she still did not follow, he bent down, raised a
handful of the sandy soil, and let it slowly trickle through
his fingers. He then rose, pointed in the direction of the
setting sun, and walked away. Confused, Aubrey called to
him to come back, but rather than respond to her plea,
like a mirage, he dissolved in a shimmering mist.

Startled, Aubrey sat up straight. She turned, hoping Jesse
might have felt something, but he was simply observing
her with a sly smile. "Apparently the local spirits aren't
interested in me. All I saw was the Indian brave who comes
to me at home."

"Really? What do you suppose he was doing way out
here?"

"He wasn't here, but off in some desert."

Jesse gestured widely. "This is desert land."

Aubrey rested her hand on Jesse's shoulder to gain the
leverage to stand. "Yes, I know. But the sand wasn't red.
I'm sure he's just a figment of a playful imagination and
nothing more. Whatever psychic talent I have must not
work here."

Jesse rose and rested his hands lightly on her shoulders.
"You're a lot better with touch. I should have told you to
pick up a rock. I'll bet that would conjure up more relevant
visions."

The Indian had pointed west, and Aubrey couldn't help
but wonder if he weren't urging her to return home. That's
all she needed: a spirit guide who hated travel. "Another
time," she begged. "Let's go on into town."

Jesse reached for her hand as they started down the trail.
"Whatever you like. Sedona is at the mouth of the Oak

Creek Canyon. It's named for Sedona Schnebly. Back in 1902, her husband became the first postmaster, but officials in Washington thought Schnebly Station was too long a name to fit on a postmark."

"I thought the name must be Indian."

"Nope. Sedona Schnebly was the inspiration, but you've got to admit, Sedona is a much prettier name than Schnebly Station would have been."

"Yes. It certainly is."

Jesse kept up a running commentary on the area as they rode into town, but Aubrey couldn't shake the image of the insistent Indian. He had thrown a lance at her in his last visit. Had that been a warning rather than a threat? If so, she had been mystified rather than enlightened. Then again, perhaps she had been foolish to bait Harlan Caine, and then not to be alert to every possible hazard.

Aubrey turned and looked back over her shoulder. They were being followed by a RV with camping equipment piled on top, but the sight of the heavily loaded vehicle failed to reassure her. "We should have called Detective Heffley before we left the house. John Gilroy might already be out on bail."

"I'll call them as soon as we get into town. That's Tlaquepaque on our left through the trees. Even if you don't want to shop, we might stop there sometime just to enjoy the art galleries, although there are several in Sedona proper. The place has been an artist colony for years."

"That must be a wonderful way to live."

The road curved just ahead, and Jesse could only shoot her a quick glance. "Aren't you happy with your life?"

"Now there's a question," Aubrey sighed softly.

"That wasn't an answer though, was it?"

Aubrey was well aware of how evasive she had been. "I'd like to just be a tourist this afternoon. Can we tackle the weighty issues another time?"

Jesse reminded himself that barely twenty-four hours had passed since Gilroy had taken a shot at her, and it was no wonder that she didn't want to concentrate on anything serious. "I suppose happiness is a relative term," he mused aloud. "I doubt I'll ever know the same sheer burst of joy riding a bull can bring, but I knew all along I couldn't follow the rodeo circuit forever."

"Are you certain you couldn't get your timing back if you trained hard?"

They had reached Sedona, and Jesse turned down a side street to find a place to park. Once he had set the brake, he answered Aubrey truthfully. "There are men who've ridden well into their forties, but getting stomped once was enough for me. Besides, could you bear to watch if I went back to bull riding?"

Touching his scar had produced such a horrifying vision, that Aubrey couldn't suppress a shudder. "No, I couldn't. But you shouldn't remain retired just to protect me, or some other woman. You have to please yourself first, Jesse, and then everything else will fall into place."

Jesse reached out to caress her cheek. "Hey. I've been to enough of your seminars to know what you believe, but I've never regretted retiring. That I was forced to retire sure hurt at the time, but I've done all right for myself, and like I said, happiness is relative."

Aubrey was happy with him, but underlying the joy he gave was the fear they were still in danger. Then came the longing for something more than the brief affair that appeared to be their only possibility. "That's why it's always wise to live in the moment," she murmured, and she quickly opened her door to begin the tour of Sedona before she turned any more maudlin.

"There's a pay phone at the corner. I'll call the detectives. Why don't you wander around the first couple of shops, and I'll catch up with you?"

"Fine." Aubrey entered a general store filled with quilts, handmade dolls, colorful clothing, and all manner of folk art. She tarried so long perusing the shop's wares, that she began to worry Jesse must have received bad news and been arguing about it. She stepped out on the walk and found him still standing by the telephone, but he wasn't using it. He was speaking with a young woman whose wild mane of blond hair brushed her hips.

She was dressed in faded Levi's which sculpted her curves to perfection, and a deeply fringed suede halter top. In boots, she was nearly as tall as Jesse, and standing so close, it was plain they were very good friends indeed. Edith Pursely had mentioned Jesse had plenty of girlfriends at home, and Aubrey did not need any psychic talent to recognize this exotic creature as one of them.

The young woman pressed closer, playfully rubbing her hip against Jesse's, and Aubrey had seen more than enough. She fought to suppress a painful burst of jealousy, but failed, and felt sickened to be so insecure. The adjacent shop window featured merchandise decorated with a riot of sunflowers, but as her vision blurred, the bright flowers took on the taunting gleam of cat's eyes.

Jesse hadn't spoken any promises of undying love, so there was absolutely no reason why he shouldn't enjoy flirting with someone as attractive as the statuesque blonde. It was completely illogical for her to feel betrayed, but she did. Tears filled her eyes, and she tried to blink them away, searching in her purse for a tissue.

"Did you find anything you like?" Jesse asked as he reached her.

"Lots of things," Aubrey replied as steadily as she could. "What about you?"

Mistakenly believing she was teasing him, Jesse replied in kind. "Don't play coy," he scolded. "If you saw me talking with Dory Pruitt, you must have noticed that every time she took a step forward, I moved two steps back.''

That wasn't how Aubrey would have described their exchange. "This is your home, Jesse. You needn't be embarrassed if you want to stop and talk to the women you date. I'm fully capable of entertaining myself. I won't be in your way.''

Aubrey was looking down, and Jesse brushed his fingertips under her chin to force her to look up at him. "There's not a woman in this town who matters to me in the slightest. If you sincerely believe that I'd ask you to duck out of sight to make it easier for me to flirt, then you don't know me at all.''

The sincerity of his expression was unmistakable, and Aubrey's emotions took an uncomfortable slide from jealousy to guilt. "Perhaps I don't,'' she replied, now believing her fears might have colored her perceptions. "Were you able to speak with Detective Heffley?''

Jesse took note of Aubrey's abrupt change of topic, and feared he had merely embarrassed rather than reassured her. "Yes, I did, and things are looking good. The DA has offered immunity in exchange for information on the Ferrell family and it looks as though Gilroy is going to take the deal. Apparently he's already served time for armed robbery and assault. With the new 'three stikes' law, he's looking at life for taking a shot at you.''

"So he has nothing to lose?''

"Not a thing.''

Although she had hated feeling like bait, at that moment, Aubrey could not help but think of herself dressed as a wedge of cheese. "If you finally get justice for the Ferrells, then the risks will all have been worth it.''

"This was a team effort,'' Jesse insisted. "Come on. There's an ice cream parlor just ahead. Let's order hot fudge sundaes and celebrate.''

Aubrey preferred non-fat yogurt to ice cream, but at that moment, a hot fudge sundae sounded divine. No longer caring about long-legged blondes, she looped her arm through Jesse's. "Terrific. Lead the way."

Once the good news about John Gilroy had lightened Aubrey's mood, she felt far more relaxed. She enjoyed every minute of sightseeing, and while she saw several magnificent paintings, she bought only gifts of sterling silver jewelry to take home to her assistants. It was nearly dusk when they started back toward the ranch, and she was tired but content. She raised a hand to cover a wide yawn.

"Perhaps it's the fresh air, but I'm already sleepy."

"Unlike Los Angeles, the air is too clean to see here, but I'd like to apologize for whatever part I had in causing your fatigue."

Aubrey knew he wasn't just talking about their extended walk through town, and smiled to herself. It was a shame they couldn't begin every day making love, but at least for this week they could. She reached over to squeeze his thigh and looked forward to caressing his bare skin later that night.

Jesse began to swear the instant he caught sight of the Jeep Cherokee parked in his driveway. "That's Dory's jeep, and I sure as hell didn't invite her here. Give me a minute to get rid of her, and we'll have the kind of night I'd planned."

"Sure. I'll wander out back and see if I can find Lucky."

As she grabbed her door handle, Jesse reached out to stop her. "You needn't hide. I don't enjoy Dory's company any more than you enjoy Larry's."

Aubrey's breath caught in her throat, making it difficult to form the question that had to be asked. "She's not your ex-wife, is she?"

Jesse howled. "Please. I've got a lot more sense than that.

Dory's the kind who'll wrap her legs around a barstool, or anything else that's handy. Find Lucky if you like, but I won't need more than a minute or two to send Dory on her way.''

When he leaned over to kiss her, Aubrey responded easily to his affection, but as she walked around the corner of the house, she still thought there was a very real possibility Jesse was merely shielding her feelings rather than telling the truth. Dory Pruitt looked as though she had stepped right off the pages of *Playboy*. Clearly she worked at being a male fantasy come to life, and Jesse was a man who craved all types of excitement. Would he really sidestep her kind?

Not wishing to pursue the thought, Aubrey paused to enjoy a carefully designed rock garden planted with a splendid variety of cactus, then rounded the house. The bunkhouse was off to her left, south of the house. A barn stood straight ahead, flanked by a corral where half a dozen horses appeared to be dozing in the late afternoon sun. A man with jet-black hair tied at his nape was leaning against the corral. He wore Levi's, an aqua Western shirt, and a straw hat pulled low to shade his eyes. Lucky was seated beside him, and Dory Pruitt—her hands shoved in her hip pockets, and her ample breasts thrust forward— was talking with him.

Aubrey assumed the man must be Fernando Peña, Lupe's husband. Having no desire to introduce herself to Dory, Aubrey was about to retreat to the cactus garden when Lucky caught sight of her and came bounding her way. Trapped where she stood, she bent down to hug the dog. He had become attached to her so quickly, she was very sorry she had forgotten about him that morning.

She looked up to find Fernando and Dory walking toward her. "Thanks for watching my dog," she greeted him. "I'm Aubrey Glenn."

Before Fernando could reply, Dory let out an ecstatic

squeal. "Not *the* Aubrey Glenn! I don't believe it! It is you, isn't it? Just wait until my mother hears that I met you. She loved your book, and now I'll be sure to read it, too."

Dory was even more striking up close. She was in her early twenties, her features were finely drawn, and her flawless skin was a healthy shade of lightly tanned peach. Her eyes were more green than blue, and her lashes were long and thick. Her teeth were very white, creating a dazzling smile. Aubrey had expected her to have a low, sultry voice which would match her exotic beauty, but Dory spoke in breathless bursts, in a high childlike tone that gave ample evidence of her immaturity. While there were plenty of men who would love to call her their baby, Aubrey was now positive Jesse would not be among them.

Enormously relieved, she replied with the warmth she showed all her fans. "Please give your mother my best."

"Oh, I sure will. Her name's Norma, and I'm Dory Pruitt."

"How do you do, Dory?" Aubrey felt Jesse approaching a second before she heard his boot heels goudge the dirt. She turned and smiled and drew him into their conversation before he could make his feelings known.

"Dory told me her mother's a fan. Isn't that wonderful? It's a constant thrill to meet people who've read my book and been touched by its message."

Jesse caught his jaw before it fell agape, and forced a smile. "Yes. I'm sure that's inspiring. Why don't you get along home, Dory, and tell your mother you met Aubrey. I'm sure she'll be delighted."

Aubrey watched Fernando bite his lower lip to stifle his laughter, but Dory seemed not to understand that she had just been dismissed. She gestured toward the corral with red-tipped nails and began questioning Jesse about a sorrel mare. Jesse replied that the horse wasn't for sale, but Dory wouldn't accept his decision as final.

"You'd sell her to me, though, wouldn't you?" she coaxed in a childish whine.

Jesse stepped forward, grasped Dory's upper arm, and wheeled her around toward the path Aubrey had followed. "Nope. I wouldn't. Now Aubrey and I have plans for the evening and we haven't another second to chat. Come on. I'll walk you back to your Jeep."

"But, Jesse," Dory argued. She wiggled and squirmed, but Jesse kept right on walking and pulling her along.

Aubrey didn't want to laugh out loud, but after hearing Fernando's low chuckle, she was sorely tempted. "You must be Fernando," she said.

Fernando nodded. "That I am. My wife told me you were very pretty, but she did not know how smart you are. I do not read many books. Would I enjoy yours?"

Besides his dark coloring, Fernando did not resemble the Indian in her visions, but there was something in the way he moved that reminded Aubrey of the elusive brave. He was flirting with her, which she hadn't expected, and certainly wouldn't encourage. "You'll have to ask Jesse. He's read it and can give you an unbiased opinion."

Fernando glanced down at Lucky, who was nestled close to Aubrey's side. "Jesse is no more unbiased than your dog, but I will ask him just to hear what he has to say. Do you like horses?"

Aubrey licked her lips nervously. "They're magnificent creatures," she replied, "but I've had very few opportunities to ride."

"You have the perfect one now." Fernando touched his hat brim, then turned away, leaving Aubrey with the distinct impression that he was advising her to apply herself. He entered the barn, and she strolled over to the corral to take a closer look at the horses. She spotted the sorrel mare easily, and thought her much too delicate for a woman Dory Pruitt's size.

In addition to the sorrel, there was a palomino, three bays with glossy black manes and tails, and dapple gray. Apparently looking for treats, the gray approached her and pressed against the rail. "Sorry, fella, I'm fresh out of apples, or whatever it is you eat."

Again she felt Jesse coming up behind her before she heard his footsteps. "This horse is spoiled," she told him. "I've apologized for coming out here emptyhanded, but he doesn't seem to believe me."

Jesse dropped a sugar cube into her hand. "Hold out your palm, and he won't nibble your fingers by accident."

Aubrey held out her hand and then laughed when the horse plucked the cube from her palm. "His whiskers tickle. Oh look, they're all coming over now."

Jesse pulled another sugar cube from his shirt pocket and handed it to her. "I've enough for everyone. Which do you like best?"

"They're all gorgeous, and I'm sure they must have distinct personalities. The gray is the boldest, but I'm not sure he's the most beautiful. What's his name?"

"Bluebeard," Jesse replied, "but he's a gelding and has never done away with any wives."

"I'm glad to hear it."

Jesse kept handing her sugar cubes for each horse in turn. "Thanks for being so gracious with Dory. I swear her bra size is above her IQ, and sometimes it's difficult not to become impatient with her. It wouldn't surprise me in the least if she didn't turn up here tomorrow with her mother and ask you to autograph her copy of your book."

Aubrey stroked the palomino's velvety muzzle before giving him a sugar cube. "I won't mind. It's really a nice tribute to the book."

"And you," Jesse stressed. Out of treats, he hugged Aubrey briefly, then took her hand. "Let's clean up before supper. Lupe feeds the hands first, then serves me the leftovers, but with you here, I might get first pick of the food for a change."

"You're teasing me, aren't you?"

"Yes, but it's fun."

He winked at her, and Aubrey remembered how serious he had been the first time they had spoken. She had been positive she couldn't help him find out what had happened to the Ferrells, and now it looked as though they were very close to learning the whole sad story. A couple of men appeared on the bunkhouse porch, but Jesse just waved to them rather than swing by to introduce them.

"Can we go riding tomorrow?" Aubrey asked with as much enthusiasm as she could muster.

Jesse held the back door open for her, and they were enveloped in the savory aroma of barbecued beef coming from the kitchen. "Damn, but that smells good," he sighed. "Yes. Let's go riding tomorrow, and I'll give you the complete tour. As for tonight, I promise to keep you entertained right here."

Aubrey reached up to kiss him, then quickly pulled away when Lupe called to them. She wasn't used to having so many people around, but Jesse was such a fascinating man, it was going to be very easy to ignore all the others. "I can hardly wait," she purred in a throaty whisper, and the desire that filled his glance warmed her clear through.

Chapter XVII

Lucky tried to follow them inside, but Aubrey gave the friendly dog a gentle nudge to send him back outdoors. She would have felt sorry for him had a spotted dog not appeared and trotted away with him. "What kind of dog is that?" she asked Jesse.

Jesse glanced out the window. "That's Freckles, our Blue Tick Coon Hound. Granted we don't see many raccoons in these parts, but he keeps busy chasing jackrabbits. Looks like he and Lucky have become friends."

The shepherd was making himself at home, which caused Aubrey a tinge of regret. If she took Lucky home, he would be confined to her backyard or house, while here, he would be able to run free. Her decision was made in an instant. "Jesse, would you mind terribly if I left Lucky here with you? I know I'm the one who wanted him, but he could have such an exciting life here, and I'm afraid he'd be bored to death at my house with only Lucifer and Guinevere for playmates."

There was a soft, sad light in Aubrey's eyes, and Jesse

wondered if she saw her own life as equally dull. "What about advertising for his owner? Have you given up on that?"

"Oh, yes. I'd forgotten we ought to at least try to find his home." Aubrey didn't understand how such a simple matter had become so complex. "I'm afraid I didn't think this through before we left home. My home," she quickly amended.

"Neither of us was thinking too clearly, and that's Gilroy's fault, not ours. Why don't I keep Lucky for a while? When you get home, place an ad in the *Times*, and if the owner responds, I'll buy a dog carrier, put Lucky on a plane, and send him out to you."

That suggestion solved their problem with Lucky, but Aubrey still felt uneasy. "There's something about that dog," she murmured.

Jesse watched Aubrey's frown deepen. "The Ferrells didn't own a dog. Is that what you were thinking, that he might have been theirs?"

"No, it's not that. It's just a feeling, but it won't come clear." The Indian's gesture toward the west had certainly been emphatic, but had only left her confused. "Something's going on, but I don't know what it is yet. Maybe I'll understand in another day or two."

"A premonition?"

Aubrey rubbed her arms. "Not yet. Have you ever had the feeling you've forgotten something, but you don't know what?"

"Yes. Then later when I remembered what it was, I felt like an idiot."

Lupe Peña came to the doorway and appeared mystified to find them conversing on the back porch. "There are better rooms in this house to entertain your guest, Jesse. Now you didn't answer my question. Do you want a green salad, or coleslaw tonight?"

Jesse vaguely recalled hearing Lupe's voice, but her question hadn't registered. Aubrey appeared to be too preoccupied to make the choice, so he answered for them both. "The green salad, and give us time to clean up, please."

Lupe gave a mock curtsy. "As you wish."

Jesse guided Aubrey through the house to the bedroom, and again sent her into the bathroom first. He then went out onto the front patio, sat down on the weathered bench, and stretched out his legs. Almost immediately, a brown and gold Collie appeared and rested his head on Jesse's knee.

"Hi, fella." Jesse scratched the dog's ears and ran a quick mental tally. Despite Lupe's protests, he didn't think there were more than ten dogs on the ranch, and one more wouldn't matter. But damn it all, Lucky was Aubrey's dog, and that was all there was to it. He didn't want to argue with her about it, but he sensed there was a damn good reason for her to keep Lucky. Perhaps he was picking up on the uncomfortable sensation she had described, but for the time being, he would be gracious about it, and abide by her choice.

After a scrumptious meal of barbecued beef, tossed salad, and hot, homemade flour tortillas, Jesse took Aubrey out on the patio to enjoy the stars. "On a night this clear, the whole galaxy beckons. How many stars can you name?"

Under the brilliant canopy, Aubrey recognized several distinct formations, but could name only the Big and Little Dipper, and was proud of herself for that. "I'm afraid I've not studied astromony as yet, but this is a marvelous place to begin."

"It was an extremely popular course when I was at the university, but I think a lot of the guys just wanted an excuse to cuddle up close to the girls."

Jesse was pressed against Aubrey's back, with his arms draped around her waist, and she could not imagine a better tutor. "That's the North Star, isn't it?"

"Sure is. Can you find any of the planets? They follow the path of the sun across the sky, and don't twinkle the way the stars do. Like our moon, they shine with reflected light."

The path of the sun, Aubrey repeated silently. Was that merely a fact, or another suggestion from an unexpected source that she ought to return home? She caught herself before the silence became unforgivably long. "I know Mars is red. Can you point it out?"

Jesse gestured. "Can you find it?"

With such a dizzying array of stars, it wasn't easy for her. "I think so. What about the others? Do they have colors, too?"

"Jupiter is pink, and Saturn's orange." Aubrey nodded, but she appeared to be only mildly interested, prompting Jesse to abandon the astronomy lesson. He used gentle pressure to turn her around. "I don't mean to push you in directions you'd rather not go. Just speak up if I'm boring you, and I'll switch topics."

Even in the pale moonlight, Jesse's expression was easy to read. He was teasing rather than serious, but Aubrey answered truthfully. "You've never bored me an instant. It's just difficult to concentrate. The night is gorgeous, but it will probably take me several nights to see everything as clearly as you do."

Jesse kissed her forehead, then trailed tender kisses over the softness of her cheek to her lips. "Whatever you wish," he murmured against the gentle curve of her throat. "Do you like to dance?"

"Yes, I love to, but I haven't danced in years," Aubrey admitted shyly. "Whenever Larry and I attended parties where there was dancing, he always had people to see, important cases to discuss, deals to make. He never set aside any time to dance with me."

"I swear I don't understand how any man can be that great a fool. Come on inside with me. I've got a Patsy Cline CD that's perfect for dancing."

Aubrey bit her lip rather than render an opinion on Country/Western music. But once she was snugly tucked in Jesse's arms, she was touched by the late singer's poignant music. Lupe and Fernando Peña lived elsewhere, and beyond the soft circle of music the house was hushed. With only a single lamp burning, Jesse had created a wonderfully romantic mood, and Aubrey shut out the day's distractions to soak up the sheer joy of being with him.

Jesse smelled delicious and moved in perfect rhythm to the slow songs. It was easy to imagine the same music playing in cowboy bars all over the southwest. Couples would be clinging to each other with the same loving warmth that flowed between her and Jesse, while men and women seated alone would remember past lovers and miss them with a terrible longing. It was all too easy to imagine Patsy Cline's haunting songs of love and loss as the perfect score for their affair. She doubted purchasing the CD would be wise, and yet made a mental note to buy one as soon as she returned home.

"It's a shame Patsy Cline died so young," Aubrey whispered softly. "I'll bet she would still be recording hits."

Jesse leaned back slightly. "I've always thought she was lucky to die when she did. Sure, she could have gone on singing a long time, but could she ever have sounded any better?"

"We'll never know." Aubrey laid her cheek on his shoulder and let the music bring them closer still. The more time she spent with Jesse, the more precious each second became. The lilting strains of "Sweet Dreams," captured the heartbreak of a lost love so beautifully, a mist of tears filled her eyes. Jesse wasn't lost to her yet, and she pushed the sadness away in an effort to make the night the best it could possibly be.

When the music ended, Jesse wanted Aubrey so badly he couldn't bear to play it again. "I know it's still early, but maybe we ought to call it a night."

Aubrey left his arms with a graceful turn. "Do I still have the choice between being with you and staying in the bunkhouse?"

Jesse shook his head. "Sorry. That was a one-time offer, and you have to abide by the choice you made last night."

Aubrey took his hand to lead the way. "Then I shall just have to make the best of it."

Jesse danced her into the bedroom. "I sure hope so, ma'am." He unbuckled her belt, then unbuttoned her soft silk shirt. He ran his fingertips along the smooth swell above the scalloped edge of her bra. "You sure have fancy underwear for a cowgirl."

"And you, sir, are no ordinary cowboy," Aubrey replied in a husky drawl. She was glad it was early, and grateful he was such a generous lover. It was so easy to become lost in him, and she abandoned herself to the love filling her heart. She thought it fortunate he had a sturdy bed, because no matter how rambunctious their amorous adventures became, they were in no danger of damaging it.

She slid her hands inside Jesse's shirt, and peeled away his clothes as he removed hers. She loved the smoothness of his deeply tanned skin, and the strength which flowed so easily from his muscular body. She trailed her fingertips through the crisp curls covering his chest, and leaned close to nip a leathery nipple. He flinched, but laughed and, after a graceful dip, swung her toward the oversized bed.

"You're a dangerous woman, Aubrey Glenn, and you can obviously read my mind."

Aubrey slid her hand down the rippled flatness of his belly. He was fully aroused, and she stroked him with a knowing touch. "No, I can't read your mind, but other parts of you are shockingly easy to understand."

Jesse eased her down on the bed and began to explore her body's secrets with a slow, taunting touch. She was dripping wet, and he shifted position to taste her. "I can say the same for you," he murmured before his tongue brushed her core.

Aubrey sighed and grabbed a handful of his tawny curls. No more words were needed when they were such a splendid match physically. She surrendered completely and accepted all he would give as though it were her birthright. Equally lavish in her devotion, she gave exquisite pleasure in return. When they at last fell into an exhausted sleep, she lay snuggled in Jesse's arms, too content to utter a murmur of complaint should she fail to live to see another dawn.

Her dreams were as lazy as her mood for several hours, then gradually lost their radiant colors and faded to the ivory and pale gold of desert sand. She was trudging through a wasteland, and tiring rapidly. She gazed out across the barren horizon where faint dustclouds heralded an approaching sandstorm.

With nowhere to flee, she was soon caught in the swirling sand. The wind gained a banshee's eerie wail, and unable to breathe, she fell to her knees and covered her face with her hands. Nearly faint from lack of oxygen, she would have pitched face forward into the dune forming around her had she not been plucked from the ground and carried high above the sandstorm.

Her hair whipped across her face, blinding her for an instant, but when she was able to brush it aside, she found herself in the Indian's arms. He had no wings, but flew with an eagle's grace. He was scowling angrily, and pointed down toward the desert from where he had just rescued her. "I know you want me to go home," she shouted against the breeze that still buffetted them. "But I don't understand why."

Rather than answer, the Indian swooped down low to carry her past the storm, and when he released her, she fell only a few feet. She quickly picked herself up. "Answer me!" she screamed, but again the Indian vanished without speaking.

Awakened by the anguished intensity of the dream, Aubrey raised up in bed. Jesse had left a lamp burning on the dresser, or she would have been too disoriented to recognize her surroundings. Desperately thirsty, she shoved the covers aside and headed toward the bathroom.

"Are you all right?" Jesse called.

"Yes. I just need a drink." Aubrey replied, and quickly got herself one.

"Bring me one, too," he answered. "I was just dreaming that I was lost in the desert, and—"

Aubrey stepped back into the bedroom. "The desert? Are you sure?"

"Of course, but it wasn't around here. It must have been the Sahara, or somewhere the sand's pale gold. Now do I get a glass of water or not?"

Aubrey quickly refilled the glass and carried it in to him. She watched him drain it, then set the glass aside. "What were you doing out in this unnamed desert?"

Jesse slicked back his curls with his fingers. "Just walking along. I was looking for something, but a sandstorm came up before I found it. I guess that's why I was so thirsty when I woke up. What woke you?"

Aubrey simply stared at him for a long moment, then certain they had been lost in the same desert, she described her dream. "There have been reports of people sharing the same dream. It's an uncommon phenomenon, but it does happen occasionally. Perhaps it occurs more often than we realize because most people don't discuss their dreams upon waking and miss the opportunity to discover similarities."

"I don't understand. Why didn't your blasted Indian rescue me, too? Was he just going to let me suffocate in the sandstorm?"

"I'd be happy to ask him the next time he appears, but he doesn't speak, or maybe he just doesn't speak English."

"This is making my head hurt. Come back to bed."

Aubrey slid in beside him and again felt at home in his arms. "I think I'm supposed to go home, Jesse. I know I planned to stay until Friday, but maybe I ought to fly home tomorrow."

"No!" Jesse shouted before he could catch himself. "Well, what I mean is, of course you can go home if you think you should; but isn't allowing an Indian who only appears in visions and dreams plan your life for you a bit much?"

Aubrey sat up slightly. "Is crazy the word you'd really like to use?"

"Hell, no. You're the sanest individual I've ever met." Jesse caught her hand and brought it to his lips. "It's just that no man enjoys being second choice, especially when the other man's merely a dream."

Aubrey nestled into the hollow of his shoulder. "You are a very sensible man, Jesse Barrett, but I'd like to remind you that you're the one who got me into this in the first place. I didn't have strange visions and weird dreams until I met you."

"What about the Indian?"

"No. I merely said that I liked films filled with handsome Indians. That's as far as it went. I didn't wile away lonely evenings fantasizing about bare-chested braves."

Jesse hugged her tight. "Good, now let's not waste another minute of tonight."

"I don't believe we have," Aubrey murmured in the instant before his mouth covered hers. With Jesse so warm and willing, it was easy to put aside confusing dreams, but not even the heat of their passion erased their memory.

After breakfast Tuesday morning, Jesse took Aubrey out past the barn to show her the enclosure where he kept the llamas. The shaggy beasts came over and stared at her, curiosity lighting their soulful eyes. "They're related to camels, but lack humps. Indians in the Andes weave their wool into all manner of beautiful articles, but I've not done more than collect it here."

"Do they bite?" Aubrey wanted to reach out and touch one, but feared the worst.

"No. When they get angry with someone, they spit. It's a real nasty habit, so I try to keep them well fed and happy. The largest is the male; the three smaller ones are his harem."

"Well, no wonder he's happy," Aubrey exclaimed.

"Frankly, I can't understand how the animal kingdom works," Jesse confessed. "One woman seems like more than enough to me, and I'd sure hate to have three chasing me around all day."

The llamas proved to be so friendly, Aubrey scratched their necks in turn. Their wool was soft, and she knew it must make marvelous sweaters. Tall animals, they looked her in the eye, and she wished she could read their thoughts. She was positive Jesse's comment had been spoken in jest, but it simply underscored their differences. A loner who reveled in the privacy his ranch afforded, he might want her to extend her stay, but that was a far cry from seriously pursuing her.

"Smart women make men chase them," she finally replied.

"Yeah. So I've noticed. I asked Fernando to saddle Blue-beard for you. Because you're not used to riding, we won't go out long. Then maybe we can tour the art galleries at Tlaquepaque this afternoon."

Jesse had the day all planned, but Aubrey didn't really feel like doing much of anything. She would rather have just sat out on the patio and let the hours creep by. She was a good sport though, and with Jesse leading the way astride the palomino, she rode out to explore the ranch. They passed by some of the hands mending fences, but Jesse just waved, rather than stop to introduce her.

"Are you afraid that if given the chance, I'll flirt with your men?" she asked.

Jesse was highly amused by that question. "It's not you I'm worried about. The hands are mostly transients. I've no desire to become best friends with any of them, and I doubt you'd want to know them at all. I raise prime rodeo stock, and that's their only concern. There's no sense dis-tracting them from their work."

They were riding along a narrow trail that curved through the chaparral. Expecting an enraged bull to charge them at any second, Aubrey kept glancing over her shoulder. "Just where are all your cattle today?"

"They're grazing south of here. Please don't beg me to ride a bull for you, because my best bulls are out on the rodeo circuit, and I'd feel ridiculous riding a calf."

"You needn't worry. I'd not even thought of it."

Aubrey listened as Jesse extolled the virtures of Samson, the bull he had retired from rodeo in hopes the beast would sire more of his powerful, unbeatable kind. So far the results of his breeding efforts had been very successful but Jesse let other men manage his stock on the road. She listened attentively, but didn't picture the bulls in her mind, or the cowboys who limped away after riding them.

"What's the name of that rock formation in the distance?" she called out.

"That's Cathedral Rock. It's farther than I thought you'd like to go, but if you want to visit it, we can."

Bluebeard was such a gentle, sweet-tempered mount, Aubrey felt adventurous. "Yes. Let's do. Are there spirits there, too?"

"All of Sedona is awash in them!" Jesse replied.

The ride was longer than Aubrey had anticipated, but after crossing Oak Creek, the craggy cluster of buttes known as Cathedral Rock grew near. Climbers could be seen scaling the southern face of the largest, and just watching them made her heart race. "Isn't that dangerous?" she asked.

"Compared to what?" Jesse swung down from his saddle, then waited to see if Aubrey needed help, but she didn't.

Aubrey supposed that was precisely the question. At home, an earthquake might kill her in her bed, so risk was probably always relative. "I don't understand how anyone can consider rock climbing fun. One slip and—"

"They're using ropes, Aubrey. If one guy slips, he'll just dangle until his buddies pull him up. Would you like to rest here awhile, or turn back?"

"We've come so far, let's rest a bit." Aubrey looked around for a good place to sit and found a natural rock bench where she wouldn't have to watch the climbers. "Although my home's quiet, I like the stillness here. I think if I were a spirit, I'd rather hang out here than float on the fumes above the freeways."

Jesse sat down beside her. "Amen to that. My aunt's home is as exciting as a tomb, and still, her rose garden doesn't compare to this."

Now afraid she would merely provoke another hostile encounter with the belligerent Indian, Aubrey kept her eyes open and surveyed the stark beauty surrounding them.

She had known Sedona existed, but she doubted she would have ever come there had Jesse not invited her. Knowing him had been illuminating in so many ways, and she hated to see their friendship end.

"Is something wrong?" Jesse whispered.

"With what?"

Her gaze was innocent, but Jesse doubted she had misunderstood. "I thought you wanted to commune with the spirit world."

"Hmm. I am," Aubrey insisted, "but the scenery here is so gorgeous I don't want to close my eyes." Jesse was most definitely a delicious part of the landscape, but she kept that thought to herself.

Jesse watched a hint of a smile touch her lips and hoped he was the cause. Not wanting to be accused of fishing for compliments, he just took her hand and sat quietly observing a lizard on a nearby rock. He had seldom felt more at peace with himself, and to achieve it while doing absolutely nothing was something new for him.

Aubrey sensed, without need for lengthy reflection, that this was easily one of the best days of her life. The serenity of the natural environment filled her with hope, and the touch of Jesse's hand was a constant reminder of how often she had advised others to follow their hearts. This perfect moment was all the evidence she would ever need to validate the belief which had been the inspiration for *The Mind's Eye*. Jesse had become her heart, but she would also have to become his for them to remain together.

Whatever lay ahead, she would have no regrets, and she smiled warmly as she gave Jesse's hand a fond squeeze. "Shall we go?" she asked. "I don't want to miss Tlaquepaque if the art galleries are worth visiting."

Caught by surprise, Jesse quickly got to his feet and pulled her up beside him. "Sedona must have about as many artists as spirits. When I get too old and feeble to hobble around my ranch, I may take up painting myself.''

In a flash of intuition, Aubrey saw Jesse fifty years hence, but there was nothing feeble about him. His posture was still ramrod straight and he was as handsome with white hair as he was blond. "You'll never be that frail, so if you truly wish to learn how to paint, you ought to begin now.''

"I'd swear you've told me half a dozen times that you can't see the future. Has being here in Sedona boosted your psychic powers?''

Aubrey stole a moment to think while she mounted Bluebeard. "Your future's plain in the bright sparkle in your eye, Jesse. Anyone could see it.''

There was a new calm to Aubrey's manner, and Jesse couldn't help but wonder if the spirits who called Cathedral Rock home hadn't whispered something meaningful in her ear. He was sorry they hadn't spoken to him as well, but shrugged it off and tried to make the ride home as interesting as the ride there had been. When they arrived, Aubrey went in the house to let Lupe know they were home for lunch while Jesse unsaddled the horses.

Fernando soon came to help him. "How long is your woman going to stay with us?'' he asked.

Simply out of force of habit, Jesse opened his mouth to deny there was anything serious between Aubrey and him that would qualify her for the term. He had never referred to any woman as *his,* and not merely because he refused to regard women as property, either. He enjoyed female companionship immensely, but had always kept things light and avoided making promises and plans. In fact, he had once bragged that he would rather link up with a sidewinder, whose deadly dose of venom he could always dodge, than have a permanent relationship with a woman.

Embarrassed by that callous remark now, he let Fernando's pointed reference slide. "She's leaving the day after tomorrow."

Fernando carried Bluebeard's saddle and blanket into the tack room and returned with a curry comb. "Is that what you want?"

"It isn't a matter of what I want," Jesse argued. "Aubrey's a popular author and motivational speaker. She had a full schedule before we met, and we were just lucky she could come home with me when she did."

Fernando began brushing Bluebeard's silver hide with long, sure strokes. "So you'll take her to Sky Harbor in Phoenix, put her on a plane, and wave good-bye?"

Jesse nodded, but he hadn't been prepared for the pain the thought of Aubrey's leaving brought. Startled, he began to back away. "Just take care of the horses, and Aubrey and I'll manage our lives."

"Pardon me, but if you plan to just kiss her good-bye, it sure looks as though you could use some help."

Jesse dismissed that comment with a rude laugh, and strode into the house.

Framed by towering sycamores, Tlaquepaque was a charming place Aubrey found utterly delightful. The graceful Spanish Colonial architecture was enhanced with flower-lined courtyards and bubbling fountains. The shops were filled with exquisite merchandise, and the overall mood was relaxed.

As she and Jesse toured the art galleries, she was drawn to the Native American art, but although many colorful paintings featured proud young men, none resembled the brave who had controlled last night's dream. Fascinated by the bold designs, she studied pottery and painted gourds, as well as beautiful sterling silver jewelry:

Jesse was having far more fun observing Aubrey than

shopping, but he couldn't understand her reluctance to purchase the things that caught her eye. "Aren't you even tempted to buy something?" he finally asked.

"Of course, but there are so many lovely things, and what would I do with them all?"

"Enjoy them, I suppose."

Ready for a break, Aubrey pulled Jesse down beside her on a bench near a beautifully tiled fountain. The gurgling water sent up a fine spray that created a shimmering rainbow in the air. She had always loved rainbows, and took this one as an omen of good things to come.

"I've been seriously thinking about simplifying my life," she revealed. "I've received more offers to travel and conduct seminars than I can accept at present, but the idea of just wandering the world, the way we have Sedona this week, is becoming more and more appealing."

Surprised, Jesse shook his head in disgust. "I traveled the rodeo circuit too many years to enjoy living out of a suitcase."

"Yes. I can understand that, but there must be a great many places you've still not seen. Australia, for example—have you ever been there?"

A little boy in bright red shorts ran by and splashed water from the fountain. Only a drop or two struck Jesse, and he brushed them away. "Australia is a very long way from here."

"Of course, it is. That's the beauty of it. It's a huge country and there's so much to see. If I've gotten that far, I might as well tour New Zealand, and Bora Bora, as well. The whole trip would be an adventure." The idea was really beginning to take shape in Aubrey's mind. After all, when she returned home, she was certainly going to need a distraction to keep her from missing Jesse terribly.

"Things have a way of trapping people," she continued. "They have to be cared for, protected, insured. I think it would be marvelous to travel with a couple of changes of clothes in a single bag, set out to explore the world, and not come back for years."

Until that moment, Jesse had never realized how restrictive Aubrey would find life on his ranch. Because he was so content there, it hurt. Fortunately, he was very good at hiding pain. "I'll bet you'd gather plenty of material for another book," he suggested. "Probably more than one."

"Yes. I just might." Aubrey glanced away. She had always known she and Jesse were too different to remain together, and there were some things love just couldn't change. Suddenly she felt a desperate need for a token of this glorious week.

"Do you remember which shop had the charm bracelet with the Indian symbols?"

"The one with the little bows and arrows, or the one with designs from the petroglyphs up at Canyon de Chelly?"

"The petroglyphs."

"Sure. I remember the place. If you've decided you want it, let my buy it for you."

That it had come from him would make the bracelet all the more treasured as a souvenir. "That's very sweet of you. Thank you."

"It'll be my pleasure, ma'am," Jesse insisted, but it was awfully hard to smile with the jagged splinters of his heart tearing him in two.

Chapter XVIII

At just under an hour, the plane trip home was not nearly long enough to allow Aubrey time to prepare answers Trisha Lynch would deem satisfactory. She had known what to expect when she had called and asked her assistant to meet her at the Hollywood Burbank airport, but had seen no reason to postpone the inevitable. Unfortunately, while flippant answers would have eventually discouraged Trisha's impertinence, Aubrey could not give them where Jesse was concerned.

Aubrey dodged a traveler's heavily loaded baggage cart as she and Trisha crossed the street to the short-term parking garage. "I'm sorry I couldn't do more than leave a message on your answering machine before we left town. I hope you've not been worried about me."

"*Worried?* Now there's an understatement," Trisha replied. She searched in her purse for her keys as they climbed the stairs to the second level of the concrete structure. "That John Gilroy took a shot at you was not only in the newspaper, it was also featured on all the local television news broadcasts. You always dismissed questions about the Ferrells with a nonchalant shrug, but you and Jesse could have gotten yourselves killed trying to find out what happened to them."

Aubrey didn't even want to think about such a dire possibility. "Obviously we survived. Can we please change the subject? Talking about murder makes we nervous."

"Do you honestly believe that I enjoy it?" Trisha wasn't at all pleased not to have heard a word from Aubrey until she needed a ride home from the airport, and her manner clearly showed it. "Let's talk about Jesse then. You said you had a fabulous week together. When are you going back to Sedona? Or is he coming out here again?"

Aubrey slowed down to let Trisha lead the way to her car. She hadn't taken much to Arizona, but her carry-on bag was becoming increasingly heavy. "We didn't make any plans," she insisted. "I know that must disappoint you, but it's a fact."

Trisha unlocked the door of her Geo Metro and helped Aubrey load her luggage. "Aren't *you* disappointed?" she replied. "Jesse had it all: looks, brains, charm so thick you could slice it, and a cattle ranch! What more could you want?"

After riding in Jesse's truck all week, Aubrey found Trisha's car uncomfortably cramped, but that was the least of the adjustments she would have to make. She recalled how Jesse had chided her for having both a public and private persona. While she hoped Trisha would not also accuse her of hiding her feelings, she had every intention of guarding her privacy now. Using them as worry beads, she rubbed her fingers over the delicate charms on her new silver bracelet. Whenever she moved her hand, the ten ancient symbols rang with a wind chime's musical tinkle.

"I truly believe meeting Jesse was a gift from heaven, but we both knew it couldn't last, and we didn't pretend otherwise. We might see each other again a time or two, but it won't be the same." She reached for her wallet. "Here, let me pay for the parking."

"Wait a minute. I might have been in the garage less than twenty minutes, and it will be free." Trisha handed her ticket to the attendant in the booth, who waved her through. "Yes! We made it. I really can't believe you're being so philosophical about this, Aubrey. If Jesse had fallen for me, I'd not have come home."

Aubrey was certain Jesse had cared for her, but fallen for her? No. He had been preoccupied on the ride to the airport, and almost brusque when he bid her good-bye. He had brushed her cheek with a brotherly kiss, then left her standing alone in the line to board the plane. Perhaps they had both gone to extremes to make their public parting friendly rather than intense, but she had not expected him to drop to his knees and propose.

No. She had not expected anything from him, and that was precisely what she had received. It was possible to visualize success in so many areas of life, but love, she sighed thoughtfully, was such a capricious thing. She would not trade a second of the time she had spent with Jesse, but she hated to believe she had been so lonely she had simply grabbed for the few days of happiness he had brought her way.

When Trisha turned onto the freeway, the San Gabriel Mountains provided a glorious backdrop to the drive. After the spring rains, the sharply angled slopes were cloaked in a bright emerald green that rivaled Ireland's rocky splendor. It was as spectacular a day as any Aubrey had ever seen, and yet she would much rather have come home to a gloomy, overcast sky where damp weather would have masked her tears.

The freeway traffic was light in the early afternoon, very much as it had been last Sunday when she and Jesse had driven out to the San Fernando Valley. Only she had changed. Sorrow encircled her heart, and she looked forward to getting home, where she would no longer have to feign the calm resolve she believed to be her only public option.

"How are you and the banker getting along?" Aubrey finally remembered to ask.

Trisha made a face. "I'm not sure. His name's Eric, by the way. We're still seeing each other, but it doesn't seem to be going anywhere. Oh, you aren't going to believe this, but Gardner called me on Wednesday to pump me for information on Shelley."

Now there's a surprise. "What sort of information?"

"The usual stuff. What does she like to do when we're not working? Where does she go? Whom does she see? I didn't get so much as a wink out of him, but please don't accuse me of being jealous about his interest in Shelley. It's just that Shelley's so vulnerable. I'd hate to see Gardner ask her out a time or two, then lose interest. Then again, Shelley might very well be the one to lose interest, and then Gardner would be hurt. That would create such an awkward situation at the seminars. Maybe you ought to institute a no dating policy for your employees. It might save everyone a lot of grief."

Aubrey had difficulty concentrating on Trisha's dilemma, but after a few moments consideration, she quickly dismissed it. "I can scarcely accept money for advising people to follow their hearts, and then forbid dating among those who work for me."

Trisha moaned softly. "Oh, yeah. I guess you're right. I called Shelley a couple of times myself this week, just to make certain Ricky Vance wasn't bothering her. She's doing okay, although she sounded rather sad. I wish Gardner could bring some excitement into her life, but I just don't think he can."

"I've had more than enough excitement for a while," Aubrey readily confessed.

Trisha's dark eyes lit with an impish sparkle. "Are you referring to John Gilroy, or Jesse Barrett?"

"They're responsible for two entirely different types of excitement," Aubrey stressed, but she would always welcome more of Jesse's delectable variety. "Have you given any thought to tomorrow's seminar? I don't want it to deteriorate into a question and answer session about Gilroy. I hope to simply dismiss the incident in my opening remarks so we can concentrate on strengthening intuition, imagery, and goal setting."

"Tell me something first. If you hadn't had tomorrow's seminar scheduled, would you still have come home today?"

Aubrey remained silent a moment too long. "I think we were lucky I had the commitment, as it saved us from having to choose a date on our own. Jesse's a free spirit, and he would soon have felt crowded had I stayed much longer. Everything worked out for the best."

"Well, don't you think you're being awfully detached about this?"

"About what?"

"See what I mean!" Trisha changed lanes to pass a slow-moving station wagon. "A couple of weeks ago you were spending all your time giving seminars and answering fan mail. Then Jesse Barrett appeared and your life was soon overflowing with sex and murder."

"Good lord, Trisha. That sounds like the introduction for a TV movie of the week."

"So what? It's true, isn't it?"

"No comment. Aren't the mountains gorgeous? I can't remember ever seeing them this green."

Trisha shook her head. She was getting absolutely nowhere with Aubrey. Giving up in disgust, she turned the radio to a rock station and cranked the volume up loud. When Aubrey didn't even seem to notice, let alone complain, she felt certain delicious memories of Jesse Barrett were to blame.

When they arrived home, Aubrey fixed Trisha a glass of iced tea, then hurried up the street to collect Guinevere. Cecile had fed Lucifer each day, but unlike Guin, who was shameless in her delight at seeing Aubrey, the tomcat feigned complete indifference. He left the glass table to sit in Trisha's lap and purred with a noisy contentment as she stroked his thick, ebony fur.

"I think we ought to have an early supper together after the seminar tomorrow," Aubrey suggested. "The four of us spend a lot of time together, but we're always busy with work, or hurrying through lunch. If you're available, I'll go and call Shelley and Gardner right now."

"Eric said something about a movie, but I'll still have time to have supper with you beforehand. It sounds like fun, actually. Maybe we can spike Gardner's glass of milk and liven him up a bit."

Aubrey responded to that suggestion with a forbidding frown. "Don't you dare pull a trick like that on Gardner, or anyone else. Let's just spend a relaxing hour or two together, and if Gardner and Shelley hit if off, fine. If they don't, we'll all still have had a good time."

"Let's go to the Claimjumper. It shouldn't be too crowded early, and their potato cheese soup is incredibly good."

Aubrey hadn't been to the popular restaurant, but thought it a good choice. When both Shelley and Gardner accepted her supper invitation, she gave Trisha one last warning. "Promise me you won't do any overt matchmaking. I don't believe either Shelley or Gardner get out much, and tomorrow should just be fun. In the morning, pick

Shelley up as you usually do, then I'll suggest Gardner might give her a ride home."

Trisha finished her tea. "Great plan. I'll be good. Cross my heart. Now I better get going and let you unpack. Is there anything else you'll need for tomorrow?"

"No. The seminar's all planned. The only challenge will be to keep it on track." Aubrey remained on the patio after Trisha said good-bye, but it was impossible to look at the pool without remembering the afternoon Jesse had stripped off his clothes before joining her in the water. She couldn't stop her tears then, nor could she deny how lost she felt. She had been living alone, without ever being lonely; but now she did not even want to go inside where surely Jesse's deep chuckle would still echo through every room to sharpen her pain.

Taking pity on his tearful mistress, Lucifer climbed into Aubrey's lap. She hugged him tight, and he quickly forgave her for disappearing for a week. "There isn't nearly enough love in the world," she told him, "and I'm not a bit sorry I met Jesse. I just wish that we could have been together longer than a couple of weeks."

A tear splashed Lucifer's paw, and he quickly lapped it up. He slid his raspy tongue across Aubrey's palm, then began to groom himself to lazy perfection. He eyed Guinevere snuggled at her feet with smug superiority and welcomed a return to the routine he cherished, while for Aubrey, nothing would ever be the same.

As soon as she entered the convention center Saturday morning, Aubrey spotted the television crews and knew she had been incredibly naïve not to expect demands for an interview. Bracing herself for the most obvious questions, she walked right up to the half-dozen reporters blocking the entrance to the room where her seminar was to be held. Dressed in crisp navy blue linen, she was the consummate professional.

"Good morning. If you've been waiting for a provocative soundbite, I'm going to disappoint you. I've been in Arizona all week, and have no idea how the case against John Gilroy is progressing. Now you must excuse me, I have a seminar to teach."

Rather than move aside, the reporters surged forward. "Ms. Glenn," a young woman shouted. "Is it true you've volunteered to use your psychic powers to locate the Ferrells' bodies?"

"I've no psychic powers to volunteer," Aubrey answered emphatically. "The detectives assigned to the case will make the necessary discoveries."

"Do you believe it's wise to grant John Gilroy immunity when it's likely he's one of the murderers?" another reporter squeezed by the others to ask.

"I'll leave that up the the District Attorney. Now I must ask you to stop blocking the hallway, or I'll have to summon the center's security guards to evict you."

Several more questions were directed her way, but Aubrey refused to acknowledge them. Unwilling to engage in a shoving match, she simply stood her ground and silently waited for the reporters to withdraw. It took them several minutes to realize she would not expand her remarks, and when the first turned away, Gardner thrust his shoulder through the opening and escorted her inside the conference room.

"I should have waited outside for you," he agonized.

"You needn't apologize. You're not a trained bodyguard. If this ever happens again," Aubrey advised, "just call the building security and let them handle it." She took a quick tally and found only a few seminar participants missing. It was still early, and she fully expected them all to appear. She was actually grateful for the unexpected

excitement as it kept her from brooding. She greeted Shelley and Trisha, and at the stroke of ten, opened the seminar
with her usual poise.

Yes, she informed her audience, she was a minor partici-
pant in a murder investigation, but today, she wished to
concentrate on them. "Life presents us with an endless
series of challenges, but if we regard each one as an opportunity to learn and grow, even the worst adversity will leave
us stronger rather than defeated. You all know what my
challenges have been recently. I'd love to hear some of
yours."

In the warm and sympathetic manner which came so
easily to her, Aubrey responded to comments from the
audience, and the seminar was underway. She truly
believed in the mystical power of intuition to improve lives,
took comfort in her established routine, and drew on the
enthusiastic support of the seminar's participants to make
the hours pass quickly. It wasn't until the last of them bid
her good-bye that she realized she had merely survived the
day rather than lived it.

The Claimjumper restaurant was new, but decorated to
reflect the rustic atmosphere of an early California mining
camp. With delicious food served in ample portions, it had
quickly become a favorite of many, including Trisha, who
came there often with her dates. Trisha and Shelly rode
over together, while Aubrey and Gardner arrived in separate cars.

As they were shown to an attractive booth, Aubrey made
certain Shelley and Gardner were seated side by side, and
she and Trisha faced them. As soon as they had placed
their orders, she handed out the presents she had brought
for them. Trisha slipped on the bangle bracelet and

hugged her, while Shelley offered a softly voiced word of thanks for hers.

Gardner unwrapped the silver roadrunner tie tack and promptly put it on. "Thank you. This is swell. It makes me glad I started wearing ties."

"You're welcome." It wasn't until that moment, when the four of them found themselves staring at each other, that Aubrey realized she had failed to prepare an intriguing list of topics for conversation. Now her mind was a blank, and as the hostess, she felt obligated to provide a good time. She didn't want to monopolize the conversation by discussing her week in Arizona, but felt safe in describing Sedona.

"The countryside has been used in countless Western movies, but I'd not realized how beautiful it truly is. The earth is a powdery red that turns everything pink, and there are several vortices believed to be sacred energy fields. I didn't actually feel anything special there, but it's definitely something worth investigating."

Shelley's eyes widened slightly. "Could we all go there sometime? It sounds like a wonderful place to conduct a seminar."

"That's a splendid idea," Aubrey responded, but she couldn't use such a transparent excuse to see Jesse again.

Gardner leaned forward slightly. "I was there with about five thousand other visitors in 1987, for the Harmonic Convergence. I didn't feel anything, either. I did talk to people who swore their hands and feet got hot near a vortex, but I was hoping for something a little more, well—"

Shelley waited, but when Gardner couldn't seem to find the word he was seeking, she supplied one. "Spiritual?"

"Yes. Exactly. It's a great place to go camping, but I'd still hoped for a tingle or two, but didn't feel them."

"Maybe you were with the wrong person," Trisha teased. "Do you like to camp out, Shelley?"

Shelley shrugged slightly. "I've never gone camping. Well, I did have slumber parties in the backyard a couple of times when I was a kid, but that doesn't really count, does it?"

"Sure it does," Trisha replied.

"No, it doesn't," Gardner argued. "The whole point of camping out is to get away from home and experience nature. You can't do that if you can run back inside the house every time you want a drink of water."

"Camping costs a lot of money though, doesn't it?" Shelley asked. "Don't you need a tent, sleeping bags, and cooking equipment?"

"Well sure, but I have all that," Gardner stressed proudly.

Aubrey saw Trisha open her mouth to offer a comment and elbowed her in the ribs to keep her quiet in hopes Shelley and Gardner would continue the conversation on their own. Trisha caught on, kept still, and it worked. Gardner explained how he kept his camping gear all packed and ready to go in an instant, and how much fun camping was, and then invited Shelley and her daughter to come with him sometime soon.

"Isn't Annie too young?" Shelley asked.

"No. She's the perfect age. Little kids love it, and they get so worn out you don't have to worry about putting them to bed. They just fall asleep as soon as it gets dark."

"Really? It does sound like fun. I didn't realize that you liked children."

Gardner nearly choked on a mouthful of lettuce, but quickly took a drink of water. "Sure I do. I was a kid once," he offered as proof.

The conversation flowed easily, but Aubrey missed Jesse so badly she could almost sense his presence. Her charm bracelet was a constant reminder of him, just as she had known it would be, and she doubted she would ever want to remove it.

No one could finish their entire meal, and when the waitress suggested the fabulous chocolate cake for dessert, they all groaned. Trisha was the first to ask to be excused to get ready for her date, and Aubrey stood to allow her to slip out of the booth. "This was fun," she declared. "Let's do this again soon."

"Next time you'll have to let us treat you," Trisha suggested.

"Absolutely not," Aubrey countered. "The boss pays for all company parties." She hadn't slept well, and had to hurriedly cover a yawn. "I'm sorry, but this has been a long day. I hate to rush you two, though. Why don't you stay and have coffee? Could you give Shelley a ride home, Gardner?"

A flash of panic filled Gardner's expression, but he quickly adjusted his glasses and forced a smile. "Sure. That's no problem."

Had Aubrey been curious about how often Gardner dated, she would just have had her answer; the poor guy didn't date at all. "We've nothing scheduled for next week, so I'll see you two again next Saturday." Shelley and Gardner thanked her again for the bracelet and tie tack, then Aubrey and Trisha walked out together.

As Aubrey paid the check, she looked longingly at the blueberry muffins on display in the bakery case. "Don't those look good?" she asked.

Trisha, however, was eyeing the chocolate cake. "Please. I want to walk out of here without carrying a bag of extra calories to consume tomorrow. Not that I'll feel like eating any time soon. Still, maybe I ought to buy a piece of cake for Eric to have later."

"I'll bet he'd enjoy that." Aubrey quickly added the

piece of cake and four muffins to her bill. She had purchased the muffins purely on a whim, but knew four was precisely the right number.

When she arrived home, she checked her answering machine, but there were no messages. She had hoped Jesse might have left one waiting for her when she got home yesterday, but had been disappointed then, too. Apparently he was confident she had made it home safely, or simply didn't care.

She had neglected her journal, forgetting to take it with her to Sedona, so catching up occupied her until bedtime. She was tired, but again had difficulty sleeping. The Indian brave hadn't visited her dreams again, but she continued to worry that his message, while vital, still eluded her.

She ate one of the plump muffins for Sunday breakfast, spent most of the morning perusing the Sunday *Times*, then worked in her yard. She thought about going to a movie that evening, but feared the romantic comedies playing in the local theaters would prompt tears rather than laughter. There was fan mail to read, but she couldn't seem to find the proper upbeat attitude required to answer, and so lay it aside.

Watching Jesse walk away at Sky Harbor had been heart-breaking, but she had not realized she would feel even worse once she got home. She checked her calendar, hoping for a luncheon date she had forgotten, but the days of the coming week were all blank. "There's always the Australian trip to plan," she murmured to herself. Guinevere perked up her ears, then went back to sleep when she realized Aubrey wasn't speaking to her.

Until now, Aubrey simply had not realized how focused she had been on her work. There was so much more to learn—new resources to explore and seminar topics to expand. The problem was, her heart just wasn't in it. A long vacation would occupy several weeks, if not months, and she could easily afford it. She wasn't fool enough to believe she would feel any different while she was away, however, or come home with the new scars on her heart healed.

It would take time to get over Jesse, but when time was all she had, it wasn't going to be easy. Creative imagery proved useless while bright visions of Jesse's smile filled her mind. She ached clear to her soul, and yet could think of no other way their relationship could have ended. Tears came often, but provided little solace, and she spent most of Monday sitting out by the pool, remembering other days when the water had sparkled with promise, rather than reflected tears.

Late Monday afternoon, Larry Stafford strode through Aubrey's back gate then slammed it shut with a loud clang. She had been napping on a chaise by the pool, and he shouted to her as he crossed the patio. "All hell's broken loose, and we've got to get you out of here."

Guinevere recognized Larry, gave an excited yelp, and began jumping up on his pantlegs to greet him. Never having cared for the shaggy little dog, the attorney stopped just short of kicking her out of his way. He leaned down to give her a fainthearted pat, then brushed her aside.

Aubrey yawned lazily as she sat up. "What are you talking about?" she asked. Uncomfortable around Larry in a revealing bikini, she reached for her pink T-shirt and pulled it over her head.

"I've friends in the DA's office, and naturally asked them to keep tabs on Gilroy because you were involved in the case. The man's no dummy. He demanded immunity not simply for taking a shot at you, but also against prosecution in the Ferrell case in exchange for providing testimony against Harlan Caine."

Aubrey swung her legs off the chaise. "And something's gone wrong?"

"I'll say. Apparently once Gilroy began talking, the DA had second thoughts and tried to renege on their deal. Gilroy's attorney promptly informed a judge, and the judge agreed the immunity promise had been improperly revoked. Gilroy was out on bail, and now he's disappeared. I assume you're smart enough to know what that means."

Although his condescending tone was nothing new, Aubrey found it especially grating that day. She pushed herself to her feet. "You're the one with the legal expertise, Larry, not me. Is there any way to tie Caine to the crime without Gilroy's testimony?"

Larry shook his head. "There's never been a shred of evidence against the man, but now that he knows Gilroy rolled over on him, he's sure to go after Gilroy. I think there's also a damn good chance he'll come after you. That's why I want you to come with me now. Just pack a couple of changes of clothing, and we'll buy whatever else you need once we reach Hawaii."

"Hawaii?" Aubrey responded in a shocked gasp. She had once been naïve enough to suggest a vacation there would be wonderfully romantic, but Larry had been too busy to get away. Now she knew just what he had been busy doing, and with whom. His charcoal-gray suit fit him as superbly as gift wrapping, but there was a worthless package underneath.

"I don't believe that's a good idea," she argued. "Getting out of town for a while might be wise, but no, thank you, not with you."

"You've someone else in mind? Where's the cowboy? I didn't see his truck."

"He's in Sedona, not that it's any business of yours."

Larry reached out to take hold of her arms. "I've no time to play games," he scolded. "I believe you're in terrible danger. If you'll recall, I'm not the one who wanted the divorce. I still care about you, Aubrey, and maybe if we went away together now, we could not only save your life, but resurrect our marriage, as well.''

"Resurrect is an interesting term, especially when you're the one who buried your wedding vows beneath a ton of lies." Aubrey couldn't bear to hear another word and broke free of his grasp. "I appreciate your warning me about Gilroy before I saw on it the evening news, but I can take care of myself just fine now."

"The man just missed killing you when he fired on you on the freeway!"

"Well, they say lightning never strikes twice in the same spot."

"This is the worst mistake of your life," Larry warned darkly.

Aubrey began to laugh for the first time in days. "Not even close. My worst mistake was marrying you." For a brief instant, a fiery rage flickered in his eyes and she thought he might actually strike her, but she didn't flinch. When he walked off, she heard him muttering an extremely uncomplimentary phrase, but no longer cared what he called her.

She did take his warning seriously, however, and brought both Lucifer and Guinevere inside the house. Her first thought was to call Jesse, and relying on her instincts to make the right choice, she quickly dialed his number. She expected Lupe to answer the phone if not Jesse, but it was Dory Pruitt's high-pitched whisper she heard.

She almost slammed down the receiver, then fought for control of her temper and won. "Hello, Dory. This is Aubrey Glenn. May I please speak with Jesse?" She heard an exchange of muffled whispers and wondered if Dory had simply reached over to pick up the extension beside the bed. When Jesse at last gave a startled hello, she had a ready response.

"Any port in a storm?"

"No!" Jesse cried. "It isn't like that here at all. Dory's mother was too embarrassed to come meet you in person, but she sent Dory over hoping to get your address so that she could write you a fan letter."

"That's inventive, but you needn't make excuses. I just called to let you know there's been a gigantic snag in the case." She quickly repeated what Larry had told her. "I may have to go away for a while."

"I'm leaving now. Just sit tight until I get there."

Just hearing Jesse's voice had created an almost unbearable longing, and Aubrey was almost afraid of what seeing him again would do. "I'm not your responsibility, Jesse," she countered softly.

"The hell you're not! I'll be there before midnight."

The line went dead before Aubrey could refuse to wait. She hung up, then began to shake. It wasn't the danger Harlan Caine posed that frightened her. It was the sure knowledge she would never be able to walk away from Jesse a second time. Rationalizations about the differences in their lifestyles still made perfect sense, but failed to soothe her aching heart.

Chapter XIX

As soon as darkness fell, Aubrey turned on every light in the house. Then fearing she had only enhanced her silhouette and created a better target, she turned them all out. Until the pool incident, she had always felt safe in her home. Now she felt exposed and vulnerable.

The police had responded quickly to a request for more frequent patrols of her street and had sent slow-moving police cars by at regular intervals. With John Gilroy undoubtedly on a flight out of the country, and Harlan Caine too visible a suspect, the likelihood of another attack on her life was extremely remote. But the Ferrell case had always defied logic, and she remained on guard.

Each time she glanced at a clock, she was disappointed to find only a few more minutes had crept by. Too anxious to eat, she made several cups of tea, but let each one grow cold. She had not meant to dump this latest disaster into Jesse's lap, and wanted to devise a coherent plan before he arrived, but did not even know where to begin.

She sat on the floor in the den to watch the evening

news, but there was no mention of the botched immunity deal with John Gilroy. Suddenly suspicious of her ex-husband's motives, she placed a call to the Devonshire Division, but Detectives Heffley and Kobin had already left for the day and she hesitated to discuss the complexities of the case with anyone else. The possibility Larry might simply have played a malicious trick on her added to her worries, and she wished she had had the presence of mind to demand proof of his story while he had been there.

For a long while she paced the dark house, then returned to the den and attempted to follow the intricate plot of a classic Bogart film on cable. Rather than providing a welcome distraction, however, the dark melodrama only intensified her fears. She knew this was the perfect opportunity to practice some of her most effective stress reduction techniques, but considered it foolhardy when her life might depend on her ability to remain alert.

She wondered if she ought to pack the essentials for a quick trip out of town, but dared not go upstairs where she might miss the warning noises of a ground floor break-in. No matter what she did, she feared she would be making a mistake, and finally ended up seated at the bottom of the stairs hugging her knees. Happy not to have been shut on the service porch, Guinevere and Lucifer kept her company but offered little in the way of protection.

The dark visions she had experienced with Jesse had been terrifying, but beckoned now as taunting evidence of a power she had no desire to possess, but surely did. With the law unable to touch Harlan Caine, how could she refuse to draw on the only resources which might tie him to the crime? she agonized. It was a wretched choice and not one she would make willing, but a fervent desire to seek justice for the Ferrells, and peace for herself, made it imperative. She dozed off more than once, but awakened the instant Jesse's Chevy rolled up her driveway with a low, throbbing rumble.

Jesse's hand was already on the knob as she unlocked the door, and he quickly yanked it open. He passed beneath the porch light as he entered, but his face was shadowed by his hat, veiling his mood. Aubrey had pulled on a pair of Levi's, but still wore her bikini and pink T-shirt. She had not even combed her hair, let alone applied makeup, and fearing she must look far from her best, she took a hesitant step backwards rather than leap into his arms.

Anxious to hold her, Jesse didn't catch a glimpse of Aubrey's dishevled appearance before the door closed behind him. He simply pulled her into a confining embrace and, in a wild show of affectionate enthusiasm, gave her a brusing kiss. She seemed almost to melt against him, and the sensation was so luscious he could not bear to pull away until they were both gasping for breath.

"I should never have let you come home alone," he moaned against her temple.

Not wanting the threat of danger to prompt the words of affection he had failed to speak on his own, Aubrey remained silent while Guinevere yapped excitedly at their feet. Before Jesse could offer a more tender thought, Lucky's husky bark pulled him away. Jesse went back outside to his truck to let the dog out of the cab, then walked him along the driveway before bringing him inside. Guinevere took one look at the shepherd and cowered behind Aubrey, while Lucifer made a hasty dash up the stairs.

"I was afraid Guin would still be terrified of Lucky, but you'll never need a watchdog more than now." Jesse released the leash, and Lucky lowered his head to give Guinevere a friendly sniff.

Aubrey rescued her quivering pet and shut her on the service porch but she was trembling just as badly herself.

"There, Guin's out of the way until morning, and I'll catch Lucifer later. Are you hungry? I could fix you something to eat."

Aubrey hadn't bothered to turn on any lights, but Jesse could feel how frightened she was without needing to see her expression clearly. "No, thanks. I grabbed a hamburger on the way. Have you just been sitting here in the dark?"

"I know it's stupid, but I couldn't think of anything else to do." Aubrey had missed Jesse so much, but now that he was here again, the few days they had been apart were quickly forgotten. Readily drawing on his courage, she straightened her shoulders. "You'd already left home before I realized Larry might have been lying, and—"

"He wasn't. I called Helen Heffley, and she confirmed his story. We're going to have to get Harlan Caine on our own, Aubrey, which puts us right back at square one. Now I'm too tired to plan strategy tonight. Let's go to bed and get an early start in the morning."

Jesse left Lucky in the kitchen, then rested his hand on Aubrey's shoulder as he guided her toward the stairs. "Maybe Caine left town as soon as he heard Gilroy had been arrested. With a week's head start, he could be anywhere in the world by now."

"No," Aubrey argued convincingly. "He's still close by. I can feel him."

Jesse followed her into her bedroom and lit a bedside lamp. He was shocked to find her looking so frazzled, and yet it was wonderfully endearing. He tossed his hat aside and peeled off his fringed jacket. "Is it him you feel, or are you just scared to death he'll come crashing through a window?"

"It's him." Aubrey slumped down on the side of the bed. "Do you believe in fate?"

"Yeah, I suppose I do. Why?"

"I'd like to believe everything happens for a reason. I never thought I possessed any psychic abilities until you appeared and insisted I use them to trap the men who killed your cousin and his family. Then all sorts of strange things began to happen. Were you and Pete especially close?"

"No. Edith Pursely is my father's sister, and he wasn't big on maintaining close family ties. Growing up, I only saw Pete a time or two, but when I joined the rodeo circuit, I always made a point of coming by to see my aunt whenever I was out this way. You know what a sweetheart she is."

Aubrey watched Jesse yank off his boots. He was certainly making himself at home, but she did not mind at all. "And Edith believed that I could find her son."

"We've come awfully close."

"No. We've just stumbled around. It was the ridiculous references to me in the press which must have alarmed Caine and flushed Gilroy out into the open. I can't take any credit for that. I still feel as though I've forgotten something vital, but it just won't take shape in my mind."

"You're as exhausted as I am." Jesse reached out his hand. "Come take a shower with me. After a good night's sleep and some breakfast, everything will look better."

Aubrey didn't believe a word of it, but rose wearily. "It was good of you to come."

"No. It was stupid of me to let you go."

Again Aubrey waited for him to mention a shared future, but Jesse helped her remove her clothes without adding to his comment. She was certainly a thoroughly modern woman, and believed couples ought to make plans together, but she wanted him to be the first to broach the subject. This was not the time, obviously, but still, she longed for a loving promise or two.

Jesse ran his fingertip along Aubrey's jaw. "I'm sorry it took me so long to get here. I could have flown, but then

I'd have had to rent a car, and I wanted to have my truck. I didn't realize you'd just be huddled in a dark corner waiting for me."

Aubrey hated how pathetic that sounded, and eluded his grasp to enter the bathroom and turn on the shower. "I've not been counting the minutes," she lied. "I've been busy trying to come to grips with whatever psychic talent I possess." She stepped into the warm water, and when Jesse followed, she relaxed against him.

"I'm so tired, but I'm afraid I won't be able to sleep."

Jesse began to soap her soft swells and gentle curves. "That's because you're too tense. I'll relax you soon enough."

Aubrey leaned into the spray peppering her breasts. "Promises, promises."

"I sure don't recall receiving any complaints from you before, ma'am."

Other than the lingering sorrow leaving his ranch had brought, Aubrey had none. Shutting out her fears, she responded to Jesse's tantalizing attentions with a slippery seductiveness. "You think mighty highly of yourself, don't you?" she teased.

"Well, now. As I see it, you deserve the best."

They continued to exchange playful compliments, but once out of the shower, Jesse dried Aubrey with unseemly haste and led her back into her bedroom. "I still wish we'd made love in the pool. Promise me we'll do it the first chance we get."

"Oh, no. That's far too risky. I want to be certain we'll have the privacy we need, in addition to sufficient time."

"A stickler for details, aren't you?" Jesse pushed her down on the bed and swept her with a hungry glance. "You look as good as a jelly donut, and I'm going to just eat you up."

As he rubbed his cheek along her thigh, a sandpapery

hint of beard tickled Aubrey's skin and she responded with
a sparkling giggle. She closed her eyes, breathed deeply,
and the joy he always brought soon flooded her senses in
surging waves. Together they created a magical splendor
unlike anything she had ever known, but even as Jesse fell
asleep in her arms, she longed for something even more
profoundly beautiful.

With sunrise still several minutes away, Lucifer jumped
on the bed and curled down into the comfortable hollow
in the small of Aubrey's back. Aubrey had forgotten the
cat, and yawned sleepily as she glanced over her shoulder.
She was about to get up and take Lucifer downstairs when
the telephone rang. Not wanting it to wake Jesse, she
grabbed the receiver as she rolled off the bed, and carried
the telephone into the bathroom before she spoke. Her
New York editor sometimes forgot the time difference and
called early, but this was an inexcusable intrusion.

"Ms. Glenn?" a male voice inquired in a hushed whisper.

Badly frightened, Aubrey tightened her grip on the
receiver. It wasn't her editor, and while she was positive it
wasn't Harlan Caine, either, she thought it might very well
be John Gilroy. "Yes, this is she, and it's too damn early
to call. What do you want?"

"I've no time to play games," the man cautioned in a
deep hiss. "I've left a map on the zebra marker in the
parking lot at the zoo. It will lead you to the bodies."

The line went dead before Aubrey could ask any questions, but she had heard the directions clearly. Shaken,
she carried the telephone back into the bedroom and
found Jesse sitting up in bed with Lucifer in his lap. She
quickly repeated the caller's message. "It could be a trap.
What do you want to do?"

Aubrey slid back under the covers, but not before Jesse

had had ample time to appreciate her figure. She was lightly tanned except for the pale expanse at her bust and at her hips, normally covered by her bikini. It was a tempting pattern he had explored with his fingertips and lips, but not nearly as often as he would have liked. Distracted by erotic thoughts, he delayed his reply.

"Let's think about this a minute. Did the man's voice sound anything like Harlan Caine?"

"No. He has such an ingratiating tone. This man's speech was more clipped, and direct. He sounded rushed, and spoke as though he feared he might be overheard."

Jesse continued scratching Lucifer's ears. "If Caine had called, it would definitely be a trap, but if it was Gilroy, who's already turned on Caine, then the map is probably genuine. Let's go and get it."

"Do you want to have Heffley and Kobin meet us there?"

"Are you kidding? In more than two years they've not had any success whatsoever finding the evidence to convict Caine. It took us to bring Gilroy out into the open, and then the DA screwed up his own deal. I'd say after that miserable record of failure they don't deserve to be in on anything. Besides, all we're going to do is check out the map. If it does lead us to the bodies, then we'll call the police and coroner in to make the recovery official."

"Yes. That's a good plan. I sure don't want to dig up the graves myself."

Jesse dropped Lucifer off the side of the bed. "It's early yet. Come here."

Aubrey snuggled down into his arms. "It's also too early to celebrate."

"I'm not celebrating," Jesse whispered against her throat. "I need you to survive."

Aubrey knew precisely what he meant, and wanting him just as badly, moved up and over him. Lowering herself down easily on his hardened shaft, she used a slow, sweet rhythm to coax him toward climax. With her hands on his shoulders, she watched as heightening rapture deepened the bright blue of his gaze to indigo. Flushed with a heady rush of power, she flexed deep inner muscles to increase the friction between them with every stroke. He bucked beneath her, but she pressed her knees into his sides and stayed with him until he grabbed her around the waist and forced her down under him.

Jesse was the one who controlled their erotic dance now, and he held nothing back. He reached for Aubrey's hands, and laced his fingers in hers as an ageless thrill churned through them, whipping desire to near madness. Through his own ecstasy he felt her release tighten around him in a blistering coil, and it pleasured him as deeply as his own. The resulting blissful aftermath was regrettably brief, however, and as his longing for more swiftly began to swell, he was appalled by his own uncontrollable hunger.

Jesse rolled off the bed and grabbed his Levi's on his way into the bathroom. "Let's get out of here," he said just before the door slammed closed.

Completely confused by his abrupt command, Aubrey struggled to sit up, and then collapsed among the pillows. "My God," she whispered. Jesse had a variety of moods— from playfully sweet to wildly passionate—but she did not know how to describe what she had glimpsed in him that morning. Had she not known him better, she would have sworn it was simply terror, but Jesse wasn't a man haunted by private fears. He was so good natured, and even tempered, and she could no longer pretend mere affection when she loved him so dearly.

Had he sensed the change in her feelings? she suddenly wondered. Had he recognized the desperate longing flavoring her passion and rebelled? Sickened that might be exactly what had happened, she left the bed. Jesse's scent clung to the sheets, making her dizzy with desire, but she hurriedly made the bed and tossed all the pretty pillows into place. Grabbing casual clothes suitable for whatever adventure the day might bring, she used one of the guest bathrooms to dress. Her intuition told her everything had changed between them, and she dared not hope it was for the better.

Jesse left the freeway at the exit for Zoo Drive. As the road curved, he kept a close watch on the rearview mirror, but with so little traffic at that hour, it was easy to tell they weren't being followed. That didn't mean they wouldn't be ambushed in the parking lot, however, and he scanned the lot searching for any sign of trouble. Again, there was none.

"Look," Aubrey called exitedly. They had brought Lucky along, and she raised her hand from his collar to point. "There's the zebra marker. Do you suppose whoever called us was reminded of prison stripes?"

"That's as good a guess as any." Jesse swung the truck around in a wide arc and came to a stop beneath the marker. Colorful animals were posted throughout the parking lot as location signs. They provided charming decorations and were a cinch to recall, but Jesse felt as though he had just driven onto the bull's-eye on a target.

"Let's just sit here a minute," he urged, but he left his motor running.

Aubrey searched the trees bordering the lot. "Do you think that's wise? If someone is waiting to get a shot at us, why should we provide him with the time to take careful aim?"

"That's a damn good point. Duck down while I get the map." Jesse bolted out of the Chevy, circled the pole, and found the map attached with several strips of masking tape. He reached up to yank it away, and was back in the driver's seat in less than five seconds. He slapped the map in Aubrey's hands, shoved the truck in gear, and tromped on the gas pedal.

Aubrey grabbed hold of Lucky as the truck careened into a tight turn. As Jesse sped toward the exit, she took a quick glance at the map, then looked back over her shoulder. The rear window had been replaced and she prayed that Jesse had asked for bullet-proof glass.

"There's no one following us. Pull over when you reach the access road so we can study the map. I can't make out anything at this speed."

Jesse complied, but he was as perplexed by the hastily scribbled map as Aubrey. "Damn the man. Why couldn't he have just Xeroxed a page from a Thomas Guide?"

Interstate 15 was little more than a rude slash across the crumpled paper, interrupted by a notation for the city of Barstow. Past the town, an area southeast of the highway was shaded and marked with four tiny Xs. Jesse turned the map to read the words scrawled beside them.

"Devil's Playground. That's rich. Do you suppose that's what the area's really called, or is this an example of black humor?"

"Interstate 15 is the road to Las Vegas, and if I'm not mistaken, the Devil's Playground is a vast area of sand dunes." The Indian brave's image flashed in her mind and her expression lit with sudden recognition. "That has to be the desert the Indian was walking though. There are sandstorms in the area all the time, just like in our dreams."

Jesse stared at Aubrey while he weighed her supposition, but he quickly came to the same conclusion. He reached into his glove compartment, yanked out a tattered map of California, and spread it across the dash. "What's the fastest way to Barstow from here?"

Aubrey quickly plotted their route. "Interstate 15 crosses

the 10 out past Ontario. We'll take it all the way. It will be a long drive. Better let me walk Lucky.''

Jesse left the truck with Aubrey and Lucky, keping a close eye on the road while she walked the dog. He had not argued with her about bringing him, and while he had thrown a shovel in the back, he thought the shepherd might find the gravesites a lot more quickly than he. It was still cool, but the day promised to be warm, and he hoped they would have everything settled by nightfall. Not everything perhaps, he chided himself, but everything concerning the Ferrells at least.

Jesse kept the Chevy at the speed limit until they reached the turnoff for Interstate 15. Then the road snaked and turned as they climbed up and over the San Bernadino Mountains and they couldn't make nearly as rapid progress. "How's Lucky doing? I've had dogs who got carsick in the mountains and I sure don't want to discover that Lucky's one of them too late."

Aubrey had rolled down the window, and Lucky was riding along with his nose pressed into the oncoming stream of air. He appeared to be enjoying himself immensely, although she felt a bit queasy. She had brought along a bag of fruit, but didn't feel up to eating anything. "Lucky's fine, but I've had better days."

"Do you want to stop?"

"No. I just want to get this wretched trip over and done." She had never been able to read in a moving car, but quickly checked the map. "This can't be drawn to scale. I'll bet the Xs aren't anywhere near the actual graves."

"We'll find them," Jesse assured her. "A metal detector might help, but Caine probably stole their watches and rings."

Aubrey wondered if the family had still been alive on the trek out to the desert, then hoped that they had not driven all those miles suffering from the terror she felt now. She reached over to squeeze Jesse's thigh. "You're a good man, Jesse Barrett. I'm sorry I couldn't have done more for you, but I'll do my best now to help you find the graves."

Jesse regarded Aubrey with an anxious glance. "You've been an enormous help. I've been trying to remember the desert dream, but there weren't any significant details in mine. Were there in yours?"

Aubrey shook her head. "Nothing helpful like a gnarled old tree with a hangman's noose dangling from it." She could not summon the Indian brave at will, but would certainly give it a try should their initial explorations prove fruitless. She hugged Lucky and rolled the window a bit lower for him.

"It's getting warm." She had brought bottled water for them all, but it was nearly gone. "Let's stop in Barstow. I don't want to run out of water."

"Right. We ought to eat something."

Jesse was excited, but relieved they at last had a tangible, if not all that precise, a clue to the Ferrells' whereabouts. Aubrey was simply withdrawn. He knew how hard on her the whole perplexing case had been, and hoped with all his heart they were finally at the end. Interstate 15 had replaced the historic Route 66, but he was still aware of how many travelers had passed that way and could not shake the feeling something deeply memorable was yet to occur.

"I'm not such a good man," he argued absently. "I just never had much in the way of family, so maybe losing what little I had hit me harder than it would have most people."

They had exchanged very little information about their families, but Aubrey was definitely curious enough to prompt him to continue. "You mentioned that your father and Edith weren't close."

"My dad wasn't close to anyone," Jesse admitted darkly,

"unless a bottle of booze qualifies as a best friend. People are a lot more aware of what's going on now than when I was a kid, but back then, my dad was simply a drunk, and my mother martyred herself keeping it a secret."

Aubrey had seen that same deeply suspicious expression on Jesse's face at their first seminar. She could only imagine how unhappy his home life had been, and no child raised with that kind of misery and shame was likely to survive it without scars. She knew just how badly he would react to pity, and strove to keep it out of her voice.

"Where were you while all this was going on, just out riding and making up the adventures you told us about?"

"Yeah, you could say that. Until his heart gave out, my father had a constitution of iron. He never missed a day of work in the copper mines, nor a night of drinking until he passed out in his chair. When I was little, my mother actually told me that he was having back trouble, and found sleeping in his easy chair more comfortable than the bed. I couldn't have been older than four or five, but even then I knew she was lying. It can't be good for a kid that young to see his father as a drunk and his mother as a liar."

"No, definitely not, but I think it's common in alcoholic families."

Sorry he had shared such a pathetic tale, Jesse straightened up. "I've made it all right on my own, but I do want my aunt to finally have some peace. Let's hope we can give it to her today."

Jesse may have effectively closed the door on his past, but he had just explained a great deal to Aubrey without realizing it. He did not associate a home and family with love and security as she did, but that did not mean he could not learn to accept them as his right. Thinking things might not be as impossible as she had feared, she hugged Lucky and began to enjoy the passing countryside.

Irrigated with well water, wide alfalfa fields blanketed

the desert land with green, and had their errand not been such a sad one, Aubrey would have found the agricultural setting a relaxing one. Willows and cottonwoods lined the farms, but as they neared the city, the landscape gradually changed to the familiar one of gas stations and convenience stores. Aubrey never ate fast food, but when Jesse pulled into his favorite place for hamburgers, she felt safe in having a chocolate milkshake.

After eating, they replenished their supply of bottled water, fed and walked Lucky, then passed on through Barstow, and continued northeast toward the Devil's Playground. Aubrey could not help but wonder if Harlan Caine had chosen the site for its evocative name, or simply because it was remote. They had to drive the better part of an hour before the first sign naming the area appeared.

Jesse pulled off onto the shoulder of the highway, and he and Aubrey consulted the makeshift map. "Other than to put us in the general area, this map is absolutely useless," he complained.

"Let's scout around a bit," Aubrey suggested. She had worn tennis shoes with Levi's and a T-shirt, and after such a long drive was ready to get out and explore. "The soil is too sandy for Caine to have driven off the road, so the bodies can't be very far away."

"It's been two years. I doubt Lucky can catch any scents, but let's give him a try before we resort to conjuring up Indians."

"That's fine with me," Aubrey agreed, but she handed Jesse Lucky's leash to hold and wandered around on her own. The sand sparkled exactly as it had in her dream, but there were no trails through the wind-sculpted dunes. She closed her eyes and tried to recall how the scene had looked from above when the Indian had carried her aloft, but envisioned no more than a golden haze.

She glanced back toward the highway, and was relieved

to find she had not wandered far. Jesse and Lucky were off to her right, and feeling safe, she closed her eyes. "Come to me, Indian," she begged. "Show me where they are." She had the ridiculous notion she ought to offer a bribe of some sort, but was positive spirits would have no need of Earthly treasures.

A divining rod was a tool for locating water, but she had never heard of anyone using a similar device to discover bodies. She stood still while a warm breeze caressed her face and strove to hush such distracting thoughts. If the Ferrells' bodies were closeby, surely they would be calling out to her just as they had heard Marlene's heartbreaking wail in their garage.

"Call to me," she whispered. "Tell me where you are."

As she waited, the noise from passing traffic blurred to a dull hum but no ghostly voices interrupted her inner silence. Frustrated by her lack of success, she trudged through the sand to where Jesse stood gazing out across the dunes. Lucky was sniffing the ground in lazy circles, but clearly had not caught a scent.

"We should have brought a bloodhound," Aubrey complained. "I drew a blank. Can you sense anything?"

Jesse dropped his arm around Aubrey's shoulders and gave her a quick hug. "Not yet. I didn't realize what a vast area this would be. Let's walk parallel to the highway, and keep moving in. If we don't come across a scrap of fabric, or any other clue today, we can go back to Barstow, buy toothbrushes, and spend the night in a motel. The sand looks as though it's always drifting here, and maybe what we don't find today, we'll be able to discover tomorrow."

"A metal detector might not be a bad thing to have," Aubrey suggested.

"Come on, let's see what we can sense on our own. Let's go in separate directions, and then meet in the center before we walk a new area."

Aubrey believed their task a thousand times more difficult than finding a needle in a haystack, but she was not
ready to give up without making a determined try. "Fine."
She turned away, and started back the way she had come.
Moving slowly, she held her arms away from her sides and
hoped the Ferrells' restless spirits would guide her to their
graves.

The sun was high overhead, and she was getting thirsty,
but she pushed herself up and over the first dune in her
path, and on to the next. She wondered how much Pete
Ferrell had weighed, and how far Caine and Gilroy could
possibly have carried him. Surely there had been a limit to
their endurance, but late at night, they could have stopped
anywhere along the highway to dispose of the grim evidence of their crime.

She stood still for a moment before turning back, but
the only sensations to reach her were the waves of heat
radiating off the sand. Thinking perhaps she and Jesse had
made a mistake in separating, she paused to wipe her
sunglasses on the hem of her T-shirt before turning back.
But as she donned them and looked up, she was shocked
to find Harlan Caine no more than three paces behind
her. He was holding an automatic pistol that fit easily in
his hand, but it appeared enormous to her. She lifted her
gaze to his, but there was no fear in his eyes, only an
expression of fierce loathing.

"Gilroy played a nasty trick on us both," Caine murmured softly. "Only he gave you a map and a head start
before calling me." He moved toward her over the sand.
"I do believe he expected an old-fashioned showdown
where you'd kill me, but that's just not going to happen.
The sands here have probably swallowed bodies by the
score, and a couple more won't make a bump on the
horizon."

He gestured with his weapon. "Now you're going to go

back the way you came, but stop just below the crest of the second dune. Yell to Jesse that you've found something, but don't even hint at what.''

"You'll never get away with this," Aubrey warned in a desperate attempt to stall for time.

Caine laughed at her threat. "My dear, I mastered getting away with murder years ago. Getting rid of you two won't even pose a challenge."

"Wait a minute. If Gilroy telephoned us both, what makes you think he didn't call the police, as well?" Aubrey placed her hands on her hips, planted her feet firmly in the sand, and shouted for Jesse in her mind. If he were listening as closely for the Ferrells' cries as she had been, she felt certain he would hear her and come running.

Caine took another step closer. "Gilroy would never telephone the police. Now I realize this has to be a disappointing way for your afternoon to end, but it's inevitable. Now start moving, or I'm going to cause you some excruciating pain."

He raised the pistol as though he meant to strike her a bruising blow, but Aubrey stood her ground. She again screamed for Jesse in her mind, and began to smile. "You are a lying coward, and this is the last day you'll ever walk the Earth free."

Thinking Aubrey must have a reason for such an outrageous display of courage, Harlan Caine quickly glanced over his shoulder, but the dune at his back blocked his view. Positive no rescue could possibly be imminent, he simply changed his plan and took careful aim. "Good-bye, Ms. Glenn. Do give the Ferrells my regards."

Aubrey saw him slowly begin to squeeze the trigger, but a wild war whoop rang in her mind, and her smile didn't waver.

Chapter XX

Snarling and howling, Lucky lunged over the top of the sand dune a fraction of a second ahead of Jesse. The German shepherd leapt for Harlan Caine's arm, sending his first shot wild, then Jesse tackled the horrified man before he could get off a second round. Aubrey dodged out of the way as the men fought for control of the gun. With Lucky snapping at Harlan's wrists and pantlegs, the developer was at a terrible disadvantage, and Jesse soon wrenched the weapon from his hands.

Jesse tossed the pistol aside and then slammed his fist into Harlan's face. "You son-of-a-bitch. You're going to welcome the gas chamber by the time I finish with you."

Aubrey took hold of Lucky's leash to draw him out of Jesse's way, then grabbed the pistol. She had never even touched a gun, but held on to it tightly. She was confident Jesse was the better man, but should Harlan somehow gain the upper hand, she would see his advantage did not last long enough for him to enjoy it.

Desperate to break free, Harlan fought back hard, but

Jesse's strength had been honed on a lifetime of hard work, and he used every muscle to its full advantage. He had never lost a fistfight in years of scrapping behind honky-tonk bars, and each punch he threw was brutal. He repeatedly yanked Harlan to his feet for the sheer joy of knocking him right back down, and when the developer was too dizzy to stand, Jesse drew a razor-sharp knife from his boot.

Standing over Harlan, he spoke clearly so he could not possibly be misunderstood. "Pete Ferrell was my cousin, and I loved Marlene and the boys. Now I would just as soon gut you right here and leave you screaming your head off while you bleed to death in the sand, but I owe my relatives a Christian burial. I'll give you a single chance to tell us where you left their bodies. If they're not there, I'm going to cut you to ribbons."

Aubrey prayed Jesse's ghastly threat had been made solely for effect, but when Harlan Caine tried to scramble away with a slip-sliding sideways crawl, it was plain he believed every word. The breeze had picked up, and the air was filling with fine grit, but she knew the men could still see her clearly.

She leveled the pistol at Harlan. "He'll never tell us anything, Jesse. Let me shoot him now. I'll start with his knees."

Jesse's rage was barely under control, but he knew Aubrey to be far too sweet and gentle a woman to actually fire at the man. Liking her spirit, he greeted her ruse with a savage grin. "Yeah. I like that. It won't equal the pain he caused the Ferrells, but it will at least be a start."

Aubrey was careful to stay out of Harlan's reach as she aimed for his crotch. "Then again, there are other places where a man's even more vulnerable."

"No!" Harlan screamed, and he covered himself with his hands. Blood was streaming down his face from a broken nose and deep cut above his right eye. "You've got the wrong man. Gilroy's to blame. Not me. I just told him to rough up Pete, to discourage him from talking to other investors. Next thing I knew, the Ferrells were all dead and Gilroy was begging me to help him hide their bodies.

"He was acting crazy and I didn't dare refuse. It was dark and I was so afraid we were going to get caught, I sure as hell didn't stick around to plant markers."

Jesse leaned close and drew the tip of his knife across Harlan's cheek. With just a slight increase in pressure, he would draw blood, and he was ready to do it. "You're forgetting that we've met Gilroy, and he's just a big, dumb jerk who's probably not had an original thought his whole life. No jury is ever going to believe he was the brains of your outfit."

Buffeted by a sudden gust of wind, Jesse felt the sand shifting beneath his feet. Not wanting to risk staying out in what could quickly become a blinding sandstorm, he took the pistol from Aubrey, then slid his knife back into his boot. "Come on, we're going back to my truck to call the Highway Patrol on my radio. If you're real lucky, you'll have found the bodies before they arrive. If not, then they'll have to take you away in a body bag." He nodded in the direction of the highway. "Get moving."

Hurting badly, Harlan had a difficult time just getting to his feet. Walking through the sand was torture. After a few wobbling paces, he stumbled and fell to his knees, but Jesse dragged him upright and shoved him along. They had not strayed far from the highway, but made slow progress back to the truck.

"Where's your car?" Aubrey asked the battered developer.

Harlan's eyes were nearly swollen shut, and sore and stiff, he had to turn his whole body to glance up and down the road, but clearly he did not like what he saw. "I walked," he mumbled.

"Like hell," Jesse laughed. "I'll bet you drove out here with Rachel McClure and the instant she saw the sand flying she took off, which is exactly what you deserve." He reached inside the Chevy, and using his CB radio, requested the Highway Patrol's assistance. "You have five minutes, maybe ten before they arrive. Now where are the bodies?"

Harlan spit out a mouthful of blood, then sent a pleading glance toward a gleaming tractor-trailer rig coming their way. For a split-second, Jesse thought Harlan might throw himself in front of it, and he grabbed his arm to pull him around behind the Chevy. "I want you back here away from the traffic. There will be no easy way out for you."

Harlan responded with a rasping laugh. "You've no witness who'll testify, and no evidence. Do you really think I'd commit suicide just for spite?"

"You're forgetting something, Mr. Caine," Aubrey quickly reminded him. "You threatened my life, and had Jesse and Lucky not come to my rescue, I've no doubt that you would have shot me. A charge of attempted murder will keep you behind bars long enough for us to discover the Ferrells' remains and tie you to their deaths."

Leaning against the truck, Harlan settled down into a tough slouch. "I followed you out here merely to counter Gilroy's lies. I just waved the gun to frighten you. I'd never have shot you, and I have every intention of charging both of you with assault. As for that vicious dog of yours, I'll see he's put down."

Aubrey was astonished by Harlan Caine's gall. "Is there another big truck coming?" she asked Jesse. "I'll be happy to help you toss this vermin under its wheels."

His bravado fading, Harlan pressed himself back against

the Chevy's fender. "You wouldn't dare," he whispered shakily.

"Hell, I'd scrape your carcass off the road and do it twice," Jesse assured him. The wind kicked up again and the cars and trucks passing by were traveling at increased speeds to get past the Devil's Playground before the flying grit ground off most of their paint. Jesse reached for the door handle. "Aubrey, you and Lucky get in the truck. There's no reason for all of us to stand out here in the wind."

Aubrey welcomed Jesse's suggestion, but Harlan was regarding them both with a bitter loathing that prompted her to issue one last threat as she moved by him. "We lied to you, Caine. I am psychic, and now that we have the general location where the Ferrells are buried, I'll be able to pinpoint the grave within hours. Criminals always believe themselves to be clever, but that doesn't mean they're smart. I'll bet you shot Pete and Marlene with the same gun Jesse's holding, and—"

Suddenly erupting in a furious cursing fit, Harlan shoved Aubrey into Jesse, and before he could catch her, she tripped over Lucky's leash and fell hard. With Jesse distracted picking up Aubrey, Harlan raced around the Chevy to the driver's side. When he found it locked, he released a frustrated shriek, but at that instant Rachel McClure pulled up in his Seville on the opposite side of the highway and honked the horn.

The wind was really blowing now, dampening the piercing wail of approaching sirens. The swirling sand turned the sun a dusty orange and blurred Harlan's vision, but with Jesse rounding the truck, he did not pause to look for oncoming traffic before stumbling out onto the highway. He made it across the first lane safely, but not the second.

Aubrey clamped her hands over her ears to shut out the

sickening thump, but it echoed in her mind. Accompanied
by the wrenching squeal of brakes, the horrible accident
gained momentum as car after car swung wide to avoid
the crumpled body lying in the road. With the burgeoning
sandstorm obscuring everyone's vision, near-misses were
frequent, but the Highway Patrol arrived on the scene and
slowed traffic before another tragedy occurred.

Unable to offer the authorities more than basic background information, Jesse helped Aubrey into his truck,
tucked Harlan's pistol behind his seat for safekeeping, and
then held her close. Fascinated by the flashing lights on
the patrol cars, Lucky sat up and rested his paws on the
dashboard to watch. Aubrey searched Jesse's expression,
but saw only the same sorrow mirrored there that shadowed
her own.

"Oh, my God," she moaned. "If any man ever deserved
to die horribly it was Harlan Caine, but I didn't mean to
scare him into running out onto the highway."

Jesse slid his hands to her shoulders. "Listen to me. He
went wild when you mentioned the gun, which has to mean
you were right about it. If Rachel hadn't shown up on the
wrong side of the highway, he wouldn't have dashed out
into the traffic. It was plain he expected to see her when
we marched him out here to the truck. She must have
been parked nearby. Maybe she heard the shot he fired,
got scared, and drove off.

"Something must have prompted her to come back. You
asked if I believed in fate. I think Harlan created his own
disastrous death, and today it finally caught up with him.
We'll have to give the Highway Patrol a statement, but as
soon as the wind dies down, I hope you'll feel up to making
another try at finding the graves. Let's stay together this
time, and maybe we'll have better luck."

Hearing what sounded like his name, Lucky turned
toward Jesse. Aubrey reached out to hug the dog. "I didn't

have time to place an ad, but checked the *Times* for lost dogs. People were missing poodles and collies, even a Chihuahua, but no one was looking for a young German shepherd."

Jesse spoke her name in a tender sigh. "Aubrey, Lucky saved your life today. He was meant to be your dog. I knew that when we were in Sedona, and I didn't intend to keep him long."

That Jesse had already planned to come see her before she had called him thrilled Aubrey clear through. Unable to observe the grisly scene on the highway, she glanced out at the sands swirling above the Devil's Playground, doubted the storm would last long, and had a sudden inspiration. "I can call Cecile Blanchard and ask her to look after Guinevere and Lucifer so that we can stay here. Let's come back tonight after dark. With the stars to guide us, I think we'll have more success."

In so many ways, Jesse believed they already had, but he agreed. They had to leave statements down at the Highway Patrol headquarters, where they learned a hysterical Rachel McClure had been taken to the hospital, but not charged with any crime. They spent the rest of the day and early evening snuggled in each other's arms in a comfortable motel room in Barstow. Then when the wind died down, they gathered their courage and returned to the desert site.

"I think they must have pulled off the road just past the sign for the Devil's Playground," Jesse said. "We covered part of the area where they might have buried the Ferrells today. Maybe we were close when Caine found you."

"No. I don't believe so." Aubrey climbed out of the truck and kept a firm grip on Lucky's leash. They'd studied the Highway Patrol's maps of the Devil's Playground and found the area to be nearly forty miles in length, but less than twenty miles of the narrow width bordered the road.

Oddly shaped, it resembled a glove, with a long index finger extending toward the west.

"The desert dreams were right," she told Jesse, "and the Indian pointed west. Let's go that way, until we feel or hear something compelling."

Had someone told Jesse a month ago that he would soon be pressing the limits of his perceptions into the psychic realm, he would have howled with laughter. Tonight, Aubrey's suggestion struck him as a wise course to follow. "Let's give ourselves plenty of time."

"Yes. I doubt spirits wear watches." Aubrey laced her fingers in his, and they began moving slowly across the wind-rippled sand. There was very little traffic on the highway that night, providing only a faint hum in the distance. She timed her breathing to her steps, and because Marlene was the one they had heard in the Ferrells' garage, she sent her a silent call. It made sense to her that a mother's love would be strong even after death, and she prayed that she and Jesse possessed sufficient psychic ability to hear Marlene's cries a second time.

Hand in hand Aubrey and Jesse walked slowly, aimlessly, while at the same time they strained for even a faint sign they were on the right path. Simply enjoying the exercise, Lucky trotted along beside them. The day had been warm, and stored heat still radiated from the sand, but when Aubrey felt a sudden chill, she tightened her grip on Jesse's hand. He stopped with her, and not daring to speak, she inhaled deeply and her whole body flooded with tingling anticipation.

A tremendous sorrow had filled them at the Ferrells' home, but here in the desert sands, the mood surrounding them became one of tranquil beauty. There was no change in the light, no shimmering sparkle, but Aubrey felt the same blissful calm experienced in a Zen garden. The Indian did not appear in her mind, but she knew this was precisely the spot where he had stopped to scoop up a handful of sand. She knew it without needing proof, as readily as she knew her own name.

"I think this is the place," Jesse whispered softly. "But it isn't sad as I had thought it would be. They must be at peace, at last. I guess there really is a heaven, and they're already there."

They had brought a single wooden stake topped with a red streamer, and Jesse knelt to bury it in the sand. "The authorities will investigate tomorrow, but I don't want to be here. Do you?" He rose and brushed the sand from his hands.

"No. Let's just get up early in the morning and go home."

Jesse draped his arm around Aubrey's shoulders as they made their way back to the truck. Lucky had enjoyed the trek across the sand, and as they drove back into Barstow he leaned out the window, eager to sample the scents floating on the evening breeze. Along with toothbrushes, they had bought a water bowl and dog food, so Lucky was quickly settled for the night.

Aubrey found it impossible to sleep, however, and Jesse knew she did not feel up to making love any more than he did. He had never simply held a woman in his arms, but with her, it felt right. "If we found them," he murmured, "you know what's going to happen to us, don't you?"

Aubrey sighed and pressed her shoulders against his chest. "Yes, exactly what I feared. We'll be asked to appear on all the talk shows and despondent families will deluge us with heartbreaking pleas to find their missing loved ones. The requests began coming in when the photograph of us first appeared in the newspaper. I just don't think I could do this again and again though, Jesse. And yet, we've barely glimpsed what we might be able to do, and it would be cowardly not to pursue it."

"We?" Jesse chuckled. "I won't argue with you. Whatever mystical power we have works best when we're together."

Aubrey covered a wide yawn. She didn't want to be Jesse's business partner, but did not feel up to suggesting a deeper emotional tie. "Let's just go to sleep. Tomorrow has to be a better day."

Jesse smoothed her hair away from her cheek, then leaned close to kiss her goodnight. This had easily been the strangest few weeks of his life, but he would not have traded them for any prize. One thing at a time, he cautioned himself, but Aubrey had been asleep a long while before he finally quieted the noisy memories that too often disturbed his rest.

Jesse spoke with Detective Heffley soon after he and Aubrey arrived home on Wednesday, but gained little satisfaction from her assurance John Gilroy was known to have crossed the border into Mexico, where he would surely stay. Jesse made a brief report of Harlan Caine's death and told the detective to contact the authorities in San Bernadino County, where he had left the developer's pistol for ballistic's testing. It was a strained conversation at best, but all Jesse felt he owed her.

It was Aubrey who answered the critical call that afternoon. Four bodies had been found buried beneath the stake Jesse had driven into the ground at the Devil's Playground, and there was enough left of the charred remains for the county coroner to identify them as Peter and Marlene Farrell and their twin sons. Every word of the grim report stung, and her eyes filled with tears as she hung up the telephone and relayed the message to Jesse.

"They'll need more time to be positive the bullets that

killed Pete and Marlene came from Harlan's pistol, but it's the right caliber, and I've no doubt it was the murder weapon. Your aunt will surely need your help planning the funeral. I'm sorry it ended this way, but at least it's over and Edith will finally have the peace you wanted to give her."

"That's what we all want, isn't it—the peace to greet each new day with joy instead of dread?"

Aubrey had spoken of that very goal in many of her seminars. "Yes. That's the ideal. Perhaps you can arrange for the service to be on Sunday, then all the Ferrells' friends should be able to attend."

Aubrey's mood was as downcast as his own, but she had not known his relatives, and Jesse was afraid to ask why their deaths had affected her so profoundly. "Don't you want to come?"

"No, not if it will lead to a media circus. Pete and Marlene deserve better than that."

"The family generally uses a private entrance at a funeral, and you needn't be seen if you don't want to be." Reminded of how reluctant she had been to help in the beginning, Jesse chose not to push the issue. "Think about it. You've plenty of time to decide. I better get on over to Edith's. She knew what was coming all along, but that doesn't mean this news won't hit her hard."

"Do you want me to come with you?"

"No. I think you need to pull back. Just lie out by the pool, answer your fan mail, and think up some inspiring thoughts for Saturday's seminar." Jesse gave her a quick kiss on the forehead, then stepped away. "Maybe I ought to just stay at my aunt's for the next few days. That way she won't be grieving all alone."

Aubrey swallowed a sickening wave of panic and forced herself to make the gracious response. "That would be very thoughtful of you. Please give me a call if there's anything more I can do.''

"Sure. You have my aunt's number if you need me.''

"Yes. I do.'' But Aubrey knew she wouldn't call while Edith needed him so desperately—and she dared not admit that she did, too.

On Saturday morning, Aubrey wore Levi's, a baggy gray sweatshirt, a colorful scarf wrapped around her head, and dark glasses to confuse the reporters waiting to interview her before her seminar. Fortunately, Gardner had summoned security guards to keep the unruly group well away from the door, and she wasn't recognized. As soon as she had slipped into the conference room, she removed the sunglasses, pulled off the sweatshirt to reveal a blue silk shirt, and tossed the scarf aside.

She fluffed out her curls as she walked over to the table where Shelley and Gardner were huddled together. She had spoken with each of them on the telephone and already answered every question they had. One look at the way their eyes shone when they glanced at each other answered her own.

"This is only the fourth seminar in this series, but I'm going to announce it will conclude today, and send out refunds for the last two dates. This last week has been difficult in the extreme, and I need to get away. I'll cover your salaries though. There's no reason for you to be penalized just because I can't continue.''

Trisha had hoped to arrive early, and apologized as she joined them. "I'm sorry. I meant to be the first to arrive, but just as I was leaving the house Eric called to confirm our plans for tonight and I didn't want to be rude.''

Gardner checked his watch, but discovered Trisha wasn't late at all, and refrained from delivering a lecture on the value of being punctual. "If you're still seeing him, why don't the four of us go out some time? I went to hear Rifficus Rose last night with Shelley,and I'll bet you'd like them, too."

"My God," Trisha gasped. "You went to the Old Towne Pub?"

Obviously offended, Gardner straightened up. "Yeah, I did, and I had a real good time."

"We're going to take Annie camping next week," Shelley added shyly.

Pleased for the quiet couple, Aubrey waited until her assistants had caught up on each other's news before telling Trisha she was ending the seminars for the time being. "I'll need a few days to decide what I want to do about the others we have coming up, but I'll let you know in plenty of time to cancel, or reschedule them."

Trisha's dark eyes widened in astonishment. "But you've gotten such incredibly good publicity from the Ferrell case. This is no time to retire, even if it's only temporarily."

The room was filling, and Aubrey backed away to greet the day's participants. "My mind's made up, Trish. Now let's just concentrate on giving today's session the enthusiasm it deserves." Her warning glance stilled Trisha's complaints, but she had to counter them all again at the close of the day.

"Does Jesse know what you're doing?" Trisha asked pointedly.

"I'll tell him after the funeral tomorrow."

"Eric and I will be there," Trisha promised. "We didn't know the Ferrells, but we know Jesse and want to attend."

"So do we," Gardner added. He had his equipment all packed, and left the room with Shelley.

Aubrey donned the sweatshirt and covered her hair. "I doubt any reporters had the stamina to last the day, but just in case, I want to be ready to fool them."

Trisha had on a short yellow dress, and certain she looked her best, opened the door and peeked out. "It's safe to leave. There's no one here."

"Thank God." As they walked to the parking garage, Aubrey only listened with one ear to Trisha's insistent demands that she ride the current wave of publicity. "Get the refunds ready, and I'll sign the checks before I leave town."

"Where are you going?"

"I haven't decided yet. Maybe Australia."

"Isn't it winter there now?"

"Probably, but I can always learn how to ski." Aubrey laid her notebook on the back seat and got into her car. She had been so depressed all week, she didn't really know how she had gotten through the day's seminar without breaking down. She thought she would have plenty of time to cry when she got home, but when she pulled into her driveway, she saw Jesse's Chevy parked across the street. He had been playing with Lucky in the backyard, and met her at the gate.

"Did you go to your seminar dressed like that?" he asked incredulously.

Aubrey glanced down at her sweatshirt and shrugged, but pulled off her scarf. "It's a disguise. It worked, too. I got by the reporters this morning without having to answer any questions." She looked up at him and wondered why he was taller than she had remembered, and even more handsome. Her chest ached with longing, but she just fiddled with her scarf rather than hug him.

"My editor wants me to write a book about our involvement in the Ferrell case. I told her that was the very last thing I'd ever do."

"Really?" Jesse feared he must be to blame for the sadness in her eyes, and reached out to take her hand. "Come sit with me awhile. I've been trying to mediate a dispute between Guinevere and Lucky, but the two are just ignoring each other."

"I'm hoping they'll eventually make friends, while Lucifer's taken up residence in the house." Aubrey followed Jesse to the glass table, then quickly pulled off the baggy sweatshirt before sitting down. "The book would surely be another bestseller, but it just doesn't seem right."

"Why not? The ballistic report's in. Harlan Caine's pistol was the murder weapon. You could make it a fascinating story, and at the same time, downplay the psychic angle so that you'd not be plagued with more cowboys looking for lost relatives."

Jesse flashed a charming grin, but Aubrey knew she couldn't risk another broken heart, and that was all he was going to leave her. She looked away, and Guinevere came out from under the bougainvillaea to nestle at her feet while Lucky remained close to Jesse. She and Jesse were as great a mismatch as the two dogs, she realized, and the thought didn't make her feel any better.

Jesse had been teasing, but after studying Aubrey's woebegone expression, he knew his joke had fallen flat. He got up and moved his chair closer. "I wanted to talk to you before the funeral. What I mean is, I thought it would be better to talk to you before we all ended up in tears, and no matter how upbeat the memorial service is, I'm afraid that's what will happen."

Aubrey was already on the verge of tears, but at least at the memorial, she would have an excuse. "Is there something you need? I told you I'd be happy to help."

Jesse took both her hands in his. "Yeah. There's something I need. You." Aubrey drew back slightly, and he increased the pressure on her hands to draw her close. "Just listen to me a minute. The first time we slept together, you told me we were too different to have anything that would last, but every man and woman are different. Maybe that's the way it's supposed to be.

"I think you could be real happy working in Sedona and you can fly out of Phoenix to anywhere you want to hold a seminar. I know you have two more scheduled in Pasadena, but—"

"No. I cancelled them." Aubrey wasn't sure where Jesse was heading, but relocating to Sedona and being with him struck her as two entirely different things. She couldn't beg for the love he wouldn't willing give. "I need to get away for a while," she murmured.

Jesse remembered how enthusiastic her presentation had been at the first seminar he had attended. When he contrasted that memory with her dejected pose now, he was overwhelmed with guilt. Earlier in the week she had nearly gotten shot, then she'd seen Harlan Caine hit crossing the highway. They had found the Ferrells, but had had little reason to celebrate. Then he had left her to brood alone all week.

"I should have stayed here with you," he apologized.

"Your aunt needed you."

"True, but I needed you, and while you're too damn stubborn to admit it, I think you needed me, too."

"I am not stubborn!"

That was the most life Jesse had seen from her, and he relaxed into a smile. "I'm trying to ask you to marry me, Aubrey. If you want to get away so badly, why don't we make it a honeymoon? Australia sure seems a little far, but maybe it would give us an excuse to take off a month or two. What do you say?"

Aubrey stared at him. Maybe he didn't love her, but if they married, he would certainly have the time to learn. Then again, what if he didn't, and ended up resenting her, or God forbid, just being indifferent? "Isn't love important to you?" she asked.

Jesse swallowed hard. He hadn't kept a count of how many women had said they loved him, but he had never spoken the word himself. He had always thought that if love created the mess his family had been, then he didn't want any part of it. But Aubrey wasn't like any woman he had ever known. He leaned over and kissed her.

"I don't know much about love," he confided, "but I know I love you. If you'd just give me a chance, I'm sure I could make you happy."

Aubrey reached out to frame his face tenderly between her hands. "I love you so much, but what if we learn how to read each other's minds, and don't like what we see?"

Jesse swore under his breath. "There's nothing but good in you so I'm not worried. But if you ever decide you don't like me, then I'll just grow my hair long, dye it black, buy a pinto stallion, and convince you I'm the man of your dreams."

Aubrey laughed for the first time in a week, and pulled him into her arms. She could see the love in his eyes and feel it in his touch. If he loved her as much as she loved him, then the adventure had just begun and the future was theirs to create. "Oh, Jesse," she swore, "you already are."

NOTE TO READERS

Although they are not real, some characters linger in an author's memory, and Aubrey and Jesse were such a charming pair that it's difficult for me to tell them good-bye. It is so easy to envision them having an exciting life together that I hope you'll also keep them alive in your imagination. If you were moved as well as entertained by their book, please share your thoughts with me. You may write to me in care of Zebra Books, 850 Third Avenue, New York, New York 10022. Please include a SASE for a newsletter.

WATCH FOR THESE ZEBRA REGENCIES

LADY STEPHANIE   (0-8217-5341-X, $4.50)
by Jeanne Savery
Lady Stephanie Morris has only one true love: the family estate she
has managed ever since her mother died. But then Lord Anthony Rider
arrives on her estate, claiming he has plans for both the land and the
woman. Stephanie soon realizes she's fallen in love with a man whose
sensual caresses will plunge her into a world of peril and intrigue . . . a
man as dangerous as he is irresistible.

BRIGHTON BEAUTY   (0-8217-5340-1, $4.50)
by Marilyn Clay
Chelsea Grant, pretty and poor, naively takes school friend Alayna
Marchmont's place and spends a month in the country. The devastating
man had sailed from Honduras to claim his promised bride, Miss
Marchmont. An affair of the heart may lead to disaster . . . unless a
resourceful Brighton beauty finds a way to stop a masquerade and
keep a lord's love.

LORD DIABLO'S DEMISE   (0-8217-5338-X, $4.50)
by Meg-Lynn Roberts
The sinfully handsome Lord Harry Glendower was a gambler and the
black sheep of his family. About to be forced into a marriage of convenience, the devilish fellow engineered his own demise, never having
dreamed that faking his death would lead him to the heavenly refuge
of spirited heiress Gwyn Morgan, the daughter of a physician.

A PERILOUS ATTRACTION   (0-8217-5339-8, $4.50)
by Dawn Aldridge Poore
Alissa Morgan is stunned when a frantic passenger thrusts her baby
into Alissa's arms and flees, having heard rumors that a notorious
highwayman posed a threat to their coach. Handsome stranger Hugh
Sebastian secretly possesses the treasured necklace the highwayman
seeks and volunteers to pose as Alissa's husband to save her reputation.
With a lost baby and missing necklace in their care, the couple embarks
on a journey into peril—and passion.

---

*Available wherever paperbacks are sold, or order direct from the
Publisher. Send cover price plus 50¢ per copy for mailing and
handling to Penguin USA, P.O. Box 999, c/o Dept. 17109,
Bergenfield, NJ 07621. Residents of New York and Tennessee must
include sales tax. DO NOT SEND CASH.*